D1623973

THEM
BONES

THEM BONES

Carolyn Haines

BANTAM BOOKS
New York   Toronto   London
Sydney   Auckland

ISBN 0-7394-0733-3

Bantam Books are published by Bantam Books, a division of Random
House, Inc. Its trademark, consisting of the words "Bantam Books"
and the portrayal of a rooster, is Registered in U.S. Patent and
Trademark Office and in other countries. Marca Registrada. Bantam
Books, 1540 Broadway, New York, New York 10036.

For my childhood friend, Debby Porter Pruett. We survived the seventies—and the eighties. Get on your fancy high heels, girl, 'cause the new millennium belongs to us.

Writing is solitary work, but the members of the Deep South Writers Salon made it less lonely. I thank them for their reading and editing skills and their friendship and support. Thank you, Jan Zimlich, Susan Tanner, Renee Paul, Stephanie Chisholm, and Rebecca Barrett.

Thanks are also due to Neil Sheffield, who showed me the Delta from his unique perspective and also kept me straight on several important issues, not the least of which are the properties of bird shot and the many variations of the blues.

Once again, Marian Young proved the incalculable worth of a good agent.

And a delighted thanks to Stephanie Kip and Kate Miciak at Bantam Books. They promised it would be fun and they didn't fib.

1

Women in my family have a penchant for madness and mysterious "womb" disorders. It's never been clear to me whether one is the result of the other, or if both maladies are a curse upon the Delaney women for acts of desperation, usually associated with a man more deeply involved with either a bottle or a gun than a female.

But it was melancholy, not madness, that was on my mind as I stared at the empty driveway through the rain-pelted kitchen windows of Dahlia House. A misty veil had settled over the old plantation, shrouding the bare trunks of the leafless sycamore trees. This will be my last Thanksgiving on the fine, old estate. The tradition of Dahlia House is drawing to a close—I am the last of the Delaneys, a thirty-three-year-old, unwed, unemployed failure.

"Sarah Booth Delaney, get your skinny white ass away from that window, moonin' around like your great-aunt Elizabeth—and you know what happened to her."

Perhaps it *is* madness, because since my return to Zinnia, Mississippi, the voice of my great-great-grandmother's nanny, Jitty, has become clear as a bell. I turned to confront her and blinked at the bell-bottoms and shiny polyester blouse that are part of her latest fashion trend—retro seventies. Though Jitty died in 1904 at a ripe old age, she has evoked some ghostly privilege and returned in her prime. In other words, hip-huggers look better on her than they would on me. It is only one of the things about her that annoy me.

"Leave me alone," I warned her as I went back to the stout oak table that had been in the Delaney family since Dahlia House was built in 1860. It, along with all of the other furnishings, will go on the auction block the week after Thanksgiving.

"You better quit this mopin' and find us a plan," Jitty said, taking a seat at the table, staring disapprovingly at the mess I had made. "In here in this cold kitchen making fruitcakes when the wolf is at the door. Where we supposed to go when they put us out of here? We're gone be living under the bridge, goin' through the *trash* of all your society friends for a bite to eat. You don't get busy, we're gone be in real trouble."

The cutting board glimmered with the jewels of chopped red and green cherries. I eyeballed the bottle of Jack Daniel's sitting on the table beside them. With sticky fingers I tipped the bottle into the fruitcake batter, and then lifted it to my lips.

"Don't tell me you taking after your great-uncle Lyle Crabtree." She glared at me through another fashion affectation, rose-tinted granny glasses. "Whiskey won't cure what ails you."

There was no point arguing with Jitty. I'd tried that, and I'd tried ignoring her. Nothing worked. I picked up the cutting board and dumped the bright cherries into the batter. "We always bake fruitcakes the week of Thanksgiving," I reminded her. "My life has been sacrificed on the altar of tradition, and I see no reason to quit now."

"In a week's time, *we'll* be homeless." Jitty pushed back her chair and stood, hands flat on the table for emphasis. "It's the responsibility of the Delaney family to provide for me. When you snatched my mama from the soil of Africa, you took on an obligation that can't never be shirked. You belong to *me*."

"I didn't snatch anyone from anywhere." This was old ground, and Jitty loved it. I was thoroughly sick of it.

"The sins of the father," she mumbled darkly.

My hands covered in the cherry-bejeweled batter, I picked up a knife and contemplated its sharp edge.

Jitty snorted. "No matter how I devil you, you can't hurt me with a knife. I'm already dead."

It was a well-taken point, but I wasn't defeated. I turned the blade to my chest. "What would happen to you if something happened to me?" I asked.

Her black currant eyes flickered. I finally had her. I was the last of the Delaneys. If I died, she'd have no one left to haunt.

Jitty sniffed. "Could be that I go wherever you go, for *eternity*." She jangled her annoying silver bangles. "Best thing for you to do is marry that banker man, have some kids, and pass me on to the next generation. It's tradition." She gave me a dark look. "Never been a Delaney woman couldn't catch her a man if she put her mind to it." Her bony finger pointed me up and down. "Look at yourself. You could be a knockout with that Delaney bone structure and your mama's figure, but you a mess, girl. Wearing your dead aunt's muumuu, no makeup and no foundation garments. And after all that time LouLane spent after your mama died, tryin' to teach you how to dress and behave. Wasted. Just wasted. No man wants a woman acts like a bag lady. You act like you've given up on yourself, like you can't tighten the rope on Harold Erkwell." She leaned closer. "Like maybe you're afraid to try."

Anger prevented a reply. The idea that Jitty would so willingly sacrifice me for financial security was infuriating. Especially to Harold Erkwell! But then, according to Jitty, sacrifice of the female was as much a Delaney tradition as tortured female organs.

"You're really pushing me. I—"

The solemn tones of the front doorbell caught me in mid-threat.

"It's one of your friends, one of the rich ones," Jitty said, fading slowly into the drab afternoon light. "What we need is a butler." Her voice echoed eerily in the kitchen. "Your grandma knew the value of a butler. That woman had class, which went a long way toward offsetting her female troubles. If she'd had more children than just your father, me *and* Dahlia House wouldn't be in this condition." She was gone.

Wiping my hands on a cloth, I went to the front door. I had no intention of opening it, but I was curious.

I heard my visitor beating against the old oak. She had tiny little fists, I deduced by the rat-a-tat sound.

"Sarah Booth Delaney, open up right this minute. I know you're in there." Staccato yipping punctuated the demand.

I closed my eyes. Tinkie Bellcase Richmond, one of Zinnia's most prominent "ladies," was at my door. She was accompanied by her six-ounce, pain-in-the-ass dog, Chablis. The mutt was so delicate that "if she fell off the sofa, she might break her legs." In Tinkie's book, that was a good quality. Tinkie's own moment of crowning glory was when the local doctor found her anemic and gave her prescription vitamins, an indicator that she was the type of woman who required high maintenance and special attention. I leaned against the door and hoped she'd go away.

"Sarah Booth, you can't hide from me." She pounded harder while the dust mop yapped at her feet.

I had no choice but to open the door. Avery Bellcase, Tinkie's father, was on the board of directors of the Bank of Zinnia. He might, at that very moment, be reviewing my last, desperate loan application. I didn't need Tinkie running home to tell him I'd been rude to her. At my level of society, being poverty-stricken was far more desirable than being rude.

I opened the door a crack. "Hi, Tinkie." The sun caught the salon highlights of Tinkie's perfect hairdo. "Hi, Chablis," I said to the dog, who was also glitzed.

"Are you going to ask us in?" Tinkie asked, disapproval on her perfectly made-up face.

"I've had the flu. I don't think you should expose yourself to my germs. I've been terribly sick." It was the only excuse that would explain my muumuu and bedraggled appearance, and appeal to Tinkie's view that illness was a sign of femininity.

Tinkie waved aside my concerns. "Madame Tomeeka just told me that a dark man from the past is coming back to Zinnia." She pushed through the door. "What am I going to do?"

Her face was bright with excitement. Obviously this dark man from the past was more exciting than her husband Oscar. A mummy would be more interesting than Oscar. But Oscar had wealth and power, two things in short supply at Dahlia House.

"I need a glass of sherry and a place to sit down." Tinkie fanned her face with her hand, though it was forty degrees in the open doorway and colder inside the house. I'd taken to heating only the kitchen and bath to save on the power bill.

"Tinkie," I said sweetly. "This isn't the time. I'm sick."

She looked at me, and for a moment her blue eyes registered confusion. "You need to go to the makeup counter at Dillard's and see if they can't find some base that will perk up your color. Maybe you should dye your hair." She lifted a limp strand. "Something auburn." One side of her mouth curled as she noticed a clot of fruitcake batter on my shoulder.

"I'm out of sherry," I informed her, hoping the lack of libations would move her back into the yard.

She walked into the parlor. The room was almost dark, what with the heavy curtains and the grim and rainy day. "If Oscar finds out, there'll be a killing." When she turned to face me, there were tears in her eyes. "You're the only woman I know who isn't driven by dark desires and erratic hormones. Tell me what to do about Ham!"

Tinkie was not referring to the staple of the Southern diet, and she was not going to go away. "I'll make us some coffee," I said on a sigh.

In the kitchen, I put the silver creamer and sugar bowl on the tray just as the coffeepot quit perking and Jitty decided to make another appearance.

"She'd pay good money for that ball of fur," Jitty said, nodding. "Cha-blis," she whispered. "What kind of person names a dog after a man in a book who dresses like a woman. Cha-blis."

"Go away," I said, knowing Jitty would ignore me. I admired the elegant design of the silver. It had been in the family for over a hundred years. Soon it would belong to someone else.

Jitty jangled her bracelets in my ear. "Tonight, when little Cha-blis goes out to take a whizz, you snatch her up and bring her home. Let a day or two pass, and you can reunite Cha-blis with her mistress and collect a reward."

"Get thee behind me, Satan." Jitty was fond of quoting the Bible when it served her purposes. I was proud of my rejoinder.

"What you think she'd pay for that dog? Maybe five hundred? Maybe a thousand? Especially if she got a ransom note saying the dog would be hurt."

I poured the coffee into Mother's bone china cups and lifted the tray. Using my hip, I pushed open the kitchen door and went through the dining room to the parlor. At one time, it had been my favorite room. It was where Mother played the piano and Father read the newspaper in front of the fire, where the Christmas tree was decorated and the presents stacked. But that was a lifetime ago. Now the room seemed sad and cold. Steam rose from the coffee cups as I set the tray on the table.

"Who were you talking to?" Tinkie asked. Chablis sat on the horsehair sofa, ears perked at the kitchen door.

"Myself. Bad habit."

"You know your great-aunt Elizabeth went off to Whitfield. And your aunt LouLane was such a dear, but all of those cats. How many was it, thirty-five cats? Now, she was your father's aunt, wasn't she? Folks thought she was a little strange, but everyone in town was hoping she'd be able to exert some proper influence over you. Not that your mother wasn't wonderful, she was just . . . different." She looked around the undusted room. "What was it your mother used to say? 'Give a damn!' Like a battle cry."

"Who's Ham?" I asked to distract her. My gaze wandered to Chablis. The dog would fit in my pocket.

"I shouldn't tell you about him," she said, biting her lip.

"Okay," I shrugged. I drank half my coffee, fast. It was cold in the parlor and I had fruitcakes to bake.

"He's been away for quite some time." She pressed her mouth shut, then sucked her bottom lip. It popped out of her mouth and I could imagine what effect that might have on the mysterious Ham. Tinkie wasn't a power brain, but she fully understood the cause and effect of winsome.

"Ah, a man from your past." I said it lightheartedly. Tinkie's fresh tears were unexpected. Also unexpected was the feel of tiny paws on my bare, chill-bumped legs. I picked the dog up and put her in my lap, glad of the tiny heat she generated.

"I hadn't thought of Ham in years," Tinkie confessed. "But Madame Tomeeka said he's coming back to Zinnia. I can't bear to face him, to admit that I married Oscar. That's what he said I'd do, and I did. But it was only because Hamilton disappeared. He was just . . ." she shrugged her thin shoulders, "gone."

So, Tinkie had dallied with love and married security. Hell, it was tradition for women of our class. Tinkie and I had gone through school together. We'd attended Miss Nancy's cotillion and etiquette classes, had learned to smoke Virginia Slims cigarettes under the bleachers at the high school football game where we'd also practiced kissing. In essence, our entire lives were common knowledge. So who the hell was Ham?

"It might be helpful if you told me about him," I

suggested, snuggling Chablis closer to me. The little dog really was quite warm.

The bone china cup rattled in its saucer. "I know I won't shock you, Sarah Booth," Tinkie said, doing that thing with her lip again. "Of all the Zinnia ladies, you're the most experi—sophisticated."

She meant that I, alone, had defied the societal dictates of the Delta Daddy's Girls. True enough, I had gone to Ole Miss. But there I had forsaken the tradition of university, and the tight-knit sorority structure that was an important part of matchmaking. I had made my friends outside the accepted order and defined myself as a rebel, a woman with dangerous tendencies—and probably some dread womb disorder that was affecting my brain.

"Spill it," I said.

"Hamilton is one of the Garretts." She lifted her chin as she spoke, and it reminded me why I'd bothered to be friends with Tinkie. Underneath all of her craziness, she had a spine.

"The Garretts of Knob Hill?" I hadn't thought of them in years.

"Yes," she answered, chin leading.

"Tinkie," I whispered. The Garretts were notorious for all of the Faulknerian vices—drinking, killing, barn-burning, insanity, morbidity, raging jealousies, incest, and other dangerous passions. They were no different from any other family in our circle, but they had been caught out. "I thought the last of the Garretts had moved to Europe." Paris was the choice of dissolute Southerners.

"He did." Her trembling hand placed the delicate china on the coffee table. "He came back, on occasion." She looked at her knees. "They still own Knob Hill, you know."

I didn't know diddly. The Garretts were more local legend than reality. And here Tinkie had been carrying on with the heir apparent of Southern scandal.

"And now he's coming home again." Tinkie's voice was beginning to grow louder. Chablis snuggled deeper into my chest. "And I've gone and married Oscar! What am I going to tell him?"

"Just keep your mouth shut, Tinkie."

"I never thought Hamilton would return to Zinnia," she whispered. More crystal tears slid down her carefully made-up cheeks.

"Are you certain he's coming home? Have you heard from him?"

"Madame Tomeeka said so. It's bound to happen."

Tinkie wasn't looking, so I rolled my eyes. Madame Tomeeka was a long story, and one I knew too well. "I wouldn't get my knickers in a twist until Hamilton walked down Main Street," I said, relieved that Tinkie's real problem was an addiction to psychic predictions.

"You don't believe in Madame Tomeeka, do you?" she asked.

I knew Tomeeka, or Tammy Odom as she'd been known in school. "I'm a little skeptical about all this special ability," I conceded, as mildly as I could.

"She's always right." Tinkie's color had returned and her breathing was back to normal.

"And well she may be, but my advice is not to worry about Hamilton until he appears. Don't borrow trouble," I said. "She said a dark man. She didn't name names."

Tinkie stood up and reached for her dog. "I feel much better, Sarah Booth. How about meeting me at The Club for lunch? We've all missed you."

A flash of the old days nearly knocked me back to the sofa. There had been a time when I'd driven my convertible and lunched at The Club with the girls. All of us Daddy's Girls had eyed the tennis pro and giggled about our futures. But that was nearly two decades past, and I hadn't paid dues in a year.

"Lunch sounds divine, but maybe another day."

She eyed me up and down. "Find yourself a color consultant. Honey, I hate to be critical of a creative person, but you look like shit."

"Thanks, Tinkie," I said, showing her out the door.

Chablis looked over her shoulder and barked once, an invitation if ever I heard one.

2

"Even if he bites, don't let him go," Jitty said as she hovered in the doorway. "Little dog like that couldn't bite much. Ugly little teeth will hardly get through the fat."

Easy for her to say; she was staying home where the fruitcakes baked in the warm, dry kitchen. Dressed in my warmest jeans and flannel, I closed the front door and stepped into the night. The afternoon rain had turned into a slow drizzle, a perfect atmosphere for a woman of Delaney blood. I snugged my dark hair more firmly under my fedora. It was a night more given to dallying with men than dognapping. Turning up the collar of my leather jacket, I thought of a crackling fire, the fizz of champagne, Spanish guitars spicing the background, and the golden skin of Roberto. With Delaney women, the past was usually a far better place for romantic adventures than the future.

The reality was Roberto was gone, and Chablis was waiting.

The repo man hadn't yet found the Mercedes Roadster in the copse of willow trees, so I removed the camouflage tarp and headed for Hilltop.

To an outsider, Zinnia appeared to be a typical Delta town. A cluster of shops lined Main Street, where the square building of the Bank of Zinnia anchored the town to the flat topsoil. I passed Millie's Café, the Clotheshorse, the hardware store, the old Zinnia Drugstore, the post office, a dime store, and a few scattered beauty salons, insurance offices, and the like. I drove through the heart of Zinnia, cruising through the single green light like a phantom. At the Sweetheart Café, I stopped and got a plain hamburger.

Flat and unimpressive to the visitor, Zinnia is my personal history. My life is etched in this town. I have walked, skipped, cycled, and driven the sidewalks and roads so often that they are pathways in my brain that lead to the memories that define me. Where will I go when Dahlia House is sold?

This was not the proper time for fear or reflection. In less than three minutes, Zinnia was an image in the rearview mirror. Hilltop was only a few miles away.

Tinkie's driveway curved up to the house, where lights blazed from all of the downstairs windows and the upstairs bedroom. The Richmonds are childless. It is just Tinkie, Oscar, and Chablis. I parked on a road that leads back to the river and scurried toward the house. When I was thirty yards away, I eased into the azalea bushes and waited.

At ten, the front door opened and Chablis tiptoed out into the grass. The door closed on Tinkie's wind-chime laughter. None of the earlier distress was in her voice, and I was once again amazed at the artfulness of a desperate woman. A scene in seventh grade math class came back to me, and I knew exactly the moment Tinkie had crystallized, the first time her wiles worked on a man other than her father. The math teacher didn't have a chance. Tinkie's big blue eyes shimmered with tears, and that pouty little lip popped out, followed by a laugh of self-deprecation. She passed.

All of the Daddy's Girls knew the techniques of manipulation, had, in fact, been trained at Daddy's knee. I was the exception. My mother believed in reasoning and logical discussion. My lessons in female skills came later in life from Aunt LouLane, after my parents were dead.

Still, all of us girls, the daughters of privilege and breeding, had been taught that the hardships in life could be avoided by a simple formula that added up to Machiavellian manipulation. Sex appeal was the easiest tool of all to use, but there were many, many others.

But I wasn't lurking in Tinkie's bushes to philosophize on Tinkie's skills. Chablis had pranced just beyond the drive, done her business, and was headed back to the house. I whistled softly to her. At first she hesitated, and I considered running forward and snatching her. She was in the light from the windows, and if Tinkie opened the front door, I'd be caught red-handed.

I whistled again and tossed a niblet of the hamburger. In less than twenty seconds, Chablis was stuffed into the warmth of my jacket, munching the bun and burger.

The deed was done. I had committed theft. Chablis snuggled against my black heart as I ran through the night.

I took the back roads home. With the dog asleep in my jacket, I didn't bother covering the car. Not even a repo man would be out on such a cold and bitter night. I hurried around the house, still not really believing that I'd stooped to stealing Tinkie Bellcase Richmond's pet dog.

"I'll pamper you to pieces," I promised Chablis as I

crept up the back steps. My timing was perfect. The fruitcakes were ready to come out of the oven. I wondered if any other Delaney woman had combined theft and baking. I suppose not. Multitasking is the obsession of my generation.

I was totally unprepared when the man stepped out of the bridal wreath beside the steps. His hand shot out and grabbed my arm. "I've been waiting here for nearly an hour," he said.

Only the fear of setting Chablis to barking kept me from screaming. I stifled the scream and spoke calmly. "Well, Harold, I didn't realize you'd taken to skulking around my yard." I shook free of his grip. I had to get inside and unload the dog before Chablis made her presence known. Harold worked side by side with Tinkie's father at the Bank of Zinnia, and he would easily recognize the dog.

"Where have you been?" he asked.

"I have to go . . . to the ladies' room." It was a statement no gentleman could question. Bathroom functions were never, ever up for discussion. I told him to wait in the kitchen for me as I rushed upstairs and put Chablis in my bedroom. Jitty, of course, was absent. It had been her idea to steal the dog, and she wasn't even around to help.

There was no time for recriminations. Harold Erkwell and the other fruitcakes waited for me in the kitchen. Perhaps it would be easier to give up tradition and let Dahlia House go.

I hurried back down, glad, at least, to step into the warmth of the room. I didn't want to get my hopes up, but perhaps Harold had come with good news—that the bank had approved my loan application. One look at his face told me I was a fool.

"You look flushed, Sarah Booth," he said from the

shadows beside the sink. His was the soft, cultured voice of a man who never had to speak loudly to be heard. "Can I dare to hope that you're anxious to see me?"

There was a courtliness to Harold that barely covered his true nature—bottom-feeder. But, a bottom-feeder with bucks. Fine judgments from a dog thief. He stepped forward, and I took in his suit, impeccably cut, and his salt-and-pepper hair, trimmed to perfection. He cut a handsome figure.

I cut to the chase. "I have a headache, Harold." It wasn't a lie. My pounding head echoed my pounding heart. I was a novice at criminal behavior, and the episode had produced both a rush of anxiety and the most peculiar tingle of exhilaration.

"The bank is going to reject your loan application."

The news wasn't unexpected, but the loan had been my last hope. Even though I'd taken Chablis, the whole dognapping business was a finger in the dike, at best. I turned to the oven and began to remove the fruitcakes.

"I could," he stepped to the table, "put in a good word for you. Perhaps."

Very slowly I closed the oven door. "That would be very kind of you, Harold." I turned to face him. On certain levels and at certain times, conversation is still an art form. For decades, it has been the only weapon a woman is allowed. Though I'd disdained many of the talents Aunt LouLane tried to teach me, I'd proven an adept student at verbal strategies. Between a woman and a man there is a definite balance that must be maintained, a pretense of mutual respect.

"The board will discuss your loan in the morning."

His eyes were ice blue. Their clarity was tempered a bit by speculation, but the acuity had not suffered. He watched me carefully.

"Anything you say in my behalf would be greatly appreciated," I responded. Oh, the dance. No harem woman had ever performed with more nuances.

"It's a long shot," he said slowly, his pupils narrowing as he watched the effect of his words on me.

"I've always heard you were the master of such things," I answered, scoring another good one.

Harold's pupils shrank to pinpoints. "I don't know why I want you, Sarah Booth, but I do."

He had crossed the line. Directness was not part of the exchange. I could have told him that his desire sprang from his need for challenge, something that Harold had seen so seldom that it intrigued him. He was not accustomed to being denied.

"Once Dahlia House is sold, I'll leave Zinnia," I said, taking another tack.

"If I told the board that we were . . . involved, they might look more favorably on your loan. It would seem there was some . . . backing behind you."

No doubt. Harold had come to collect his payment up front, or behind, or any way he could get it. He was not a stupid man. "You can *tell* them whatever you think best," I pointed out.

"I couldn't lie to the board of directors. It would be unethical."

The things he wanted to do to me weren't exactly in the Ten Commandments, but that wasn't stopping him. My only option was to play for more time. "If the board's decision could be delayed," I suggested. "I need more time to think."

"You've been thinking for months now."

"What's another week?" I asked breathlessly, which wasn't artifice. "These things aren't to be taken lightly. It is the fulfillment of a woman's role, Harold. I want to be certain I can put my whole . . . self into it."

"You'll have an answer for me by Thanksgiving?" he asked.

"An answer for both of us," I replied, borrowing the bottom lip thing from Tinkie. I'd already stolen her dog; what the hell was a mannerism.

"Sarah Booth," he said urgently, stepping forward, his gaze fastened on my wet lip. I did it again with such force that it popped out of my mouth with an audible sound. He started toward me with a gasp.

I reached behind me, grabbed a hot fruitcake, and thrust it into his hands. "Take this and think of me," I said.

He juggled the cake.

I covered my face. "I can't bear this torment," I whispered. "I have to lie down." I'd suddenly remembered that I'd left my favorite Italian heels beside the bed, and if Chablis was a normal dog, my last pair of good shoes was in danger of complete destruction.

"I'll see you at Thanksgiving," Harold said, still shifting the cake from hand to hand.

I fled the kitchen, leaving Harold to show himself out. As I mounted the stairs, I heard a distinct sound of disapproval.

"Shut up," I warned Jitty. I was in no mood for her evaluation of the scene in the kitchen.

"He's not that bad," she said, following me up the stairs. "It's not like he was asking to marry you. He just wants a little female companionship. Maybe once a week. Twice at the most. Sitting behind a desk all day countin' his money, that's all he could hold up to."

"Jitty," I spat, "enough!"

I opened the bedroom door to find Chablis perched in the middle of my pillow. Or what was left of it. A single feather floated to the floor.

Jitty looked around the corner of the door. "I say cut

off one of the dog's ears and send it with the first ransom note. That way Tinkie'll know you mean business."

I checked the note one last time. I'd cut the lettering from the local newspaper and used latex gloves and a hot-glue gun. It was amazing; all the tools of terrorism could be found in the local hardware store.

"If you ever want to see your dog alive again, you'll need $5,000." I enclosed a snippet of Chablis's sun-glitzed hair so Tinkie would know I had the goods.

Five thousand was a lot of money, but Tinkie had it to burn, and it was the smallest amount I could put toward the debt I owed at the bank. Five grand would buy me more time to figure out a legitimate way to save Dahlia House. One that didn't involve my healthy, at least for the moment, female organs.

Addressing the envelope was a problem, but I found enough letters in advertisements and finally cut them out and pasted them on. While Chablis dined on Swanson chunky white chicken meat, I dropped the note in the mailbox in the middle of town. Tinkie would have it in her hands by eleven. I consoled myself with the fact that at least she would know Chablis was alive.

There was no time to rest on my laurels. The next communication had to be prepared. If Tinkie had any resistance to paying, the second note would catapult her into cooperation.

3

"You keep jumpin' up and down on that hunk o' plastic without the proper foundation garments, your breasts gone hang to your navel."

I ignored Jitty and followed the video instructor as she executed the steps of the tango on the aerobic bench. I watched her breasts intently. They were large, and yet they didn't jiggle or bounce, and her sports bra was far skimpier than mine. Of course she didn't sweat, either. And not a hair straggled out of place. Perhaps genetic engineering was older than anyone knew.

"What you want to build muscles for? Women are delicate. They don't need those ugly bulges. Men supposed to have the bulges." Jitty laughed naughtily.

Flopping to the floor to add a two-pound leg weight, I glanced at her. She was reclining on the horsehide sofa beside Chablis. The dog watched me with an intensity that bordered on love. We had bonded. My attention went back to Jitty, who was wearing turquoise velveteen hot pants and a white satin blouse. I had to admit she didn't look bad for a double-decagenarian.

Slightly behind the instructor, I scrambled to my hands and knees and started with the doggie hydrant leg lifts. Recognizing body language, Chablis began to bark.

"You'd achieve the same results if you'd just show Harold a good time," Jitty said grumpily. "And you'd save Dahlia House to boot. Why you want to grunt and sweat all over the floor when it don't get you nothin'? I swear, your great-aunt Elizabeth was sensible compared to you."

"I'm getting strong so I can move out of this house," I said, tired and hot and wanting to needle her. Chablis suddenly started an excited bark.

"Uh-oh." Jitty pointed to the door. "Company, and you'd better hide the dog."

I scooped up Chablis and made a dash up the stairs just as the doorbell rang. I'd barely cleared the landing before the pounding began. Tiny little fists once again. Tinkie Bellcase Richmond was back on my porch. Was it possible that she'd figured out I had Chablis?

On the way down the stairs, I steeled my nerves and checked my watch. It was eleven-twenty. Tinkie had gotten the note.

Tinkie's state of panic was so high that she failed to notice my outfit or even my sweat as she sailed through the door, wailing. "They've kidnapped Chablis."

Guilt was my gut reaction, but I overcame it and substituted fake concern. "Oh, my goodness, sit down," I said, ushering her to the overstuffed wing chair that had been my grandmother's favorite. I put her feet up on the ottoman and handed her a cardboard fan from O'Keefe's Funeral Home. The room was cold as a tomb, but Tinkie's face was bright pink. Tears had stained her silk jacket, and for a moment I was sincerely sorry for what I'd done.

"Oscar is insisting that we won't pay the ransom. He says he's going to call the police."

My emotions were getting a better workout than anything my body had attained from the video. Remorse was bulldozed by fear. I'd taken care with the note, but the police, even in Zinnia, were a lot smarter than they used to be.

"What note? Tell me from the beginning," I prompted. I caught sight of Jitty sitting at the top of the stairs. She held her finger to her lip to warn me. Like I was stupid enough to tell Tinkie that the ghost who'd masterminded the doggie abduction was watching us?

"Chablis went out last night to eliminate, and she disappeared. I was heartsick all night, but Oscar assured me she'd just found a little doggie friend and that she'd be home today." Tinkie's face collapsed, mouth widening and cheekbones scrunching into her brow. A sob issued forth. "Someone cruel and evil and mean has stolen my baby. And they want money."

I cleared my throat. "How much?"

Tinkie gasped, "Five thousand."

I swallowed, trying hard to hang on to my nerve. "That's not such a large amount."

It was the wrong thing to say. Tinkie wailed again. "Oscar says he won't pay that for a dog!"

Once when I was playing in the woods by the river I stepped into what we called quicksand. The sensation of sinking, of going slowly deeper and deeper into muck, was one of the most terrifying experiences I'd ever had. Well, déjà vu! Only this time I was going down in my own little private cesspool of black despair. Oscar, who'd never had an original thought in his life, was going to be a tight-ass about five grand! He blew that on a round of golf with his buddies.

"Oscar won't pay?" I croaked.

" 'Not one red cent,' he says." Tinkie turned her swollen face to me. "He says he won't be blackmailed, and besides, he hates Chablis. He was delighted that she's gone. You've got to help me."

It was karma. I deserved this. Every second of it. I'd hidden my financial troubles from the Daddy's Girls and almost everyone else in Zinnia. Now, Tinkie had come to me for a loan. Pride goeth before a fall—and I was busted. "Tinkie, I don't have a penny to my name."

"I don't want money," Tinkie said, eyes widening.

"What then?"

"I have my own money. I'm not completely stupid; I knew better than to put myself at the mercy of a man, so I've been socking away money in my own private account. Money isn't an issue." She reached out and touched my knee. "I want you to make the delivery. When they send me the instructions, I want you to take the money and rescue poor little Chablis. You're so brave, Sarah Booth, going all these years without marrying, living out here in this big old house all alone, hoarding your independence and all. You can do this. I'd just have a heart attack and die right on the spot."

Karma was a tricky beast. Somewhere along the line I'd earned a break. "Of course I'll do it, Tinkie," I said, reaching over and gently patting her knee.

"There's a special hell for hypocrites." This time it was my mother's voice badgering me, but she wasn't a ghost and she wasn't talking from the grave. This was all in my head. Surely, I'd doomed myself to the hottest regions of Hades by stealing a friend's dog and then playing the brave and daring rescuer. But what the hell? Five grand was five grand, and Chablis and Tinkie wouldn't be permanently damaged by my little scheme.

I slipped into my faded jeans and black leather jacket and got my car keys. I'd already sent the second note, setting the drop place and dictating the terms, which didn't make a hill of beans since I was playing both roles in this little drama.

"Be good," I murmured into the cute little tufts of hair on Chablis's head. I was going to miss the damn dog. I hadn't realized how lonesome I was in that big, old house until I had little Chablis to keep me company. I would suffer when she was gone. It was a kind of justice.

I hurried out of the house and drove to Tinkie's to get the loot. She met me at the end of the drive, money in a paper sack, per the instructions I'd written.

"Don't let them hurt her." Tinkie blinked back tears.

Guilt made me twitch, but I took the money. "I won't let anything happen to Chablis," I promised.

In a moment, I was riding free in the night. I drove back to Dahlia House, dropped the money, and picked up the dog.

All the way back to Hilltop I cuddled Chablis in my jacket and felt the pain of the coming good-bye. I hadn't expected the fur-ball to win my heart in two nights. Maybe Aunt LouLane and her cats and I had more in common than I wanted to admit.

My headlights picked up Tinkie's car—she was waiting at the Sweetheart Café just as I'd instructed. Well, she was actually pacing beside her car. When she recognized the Roadster, her face lit up with enough kilowatts to send a power surge through Zinnia. She ran toward me, and when she didn't see the dog, her face fell—until I pulled Chablis out of my jacket.

"My precious."

I never had a chance to say good-bye. Chablis was

swept into her arms, and I was left with the cold cash and an empty place in my heart.

"Thank you, Sarah Booth. Thank you," she said, leaning down to the car window. "I've never known anyone as brave as you. You brought my darling little baby home."

Shame is a peculiar emotion. I blinked back tears, which Tinkie took for compassion. So she had married for money and security and she frittered away her days in idle spending and gossip. She still thought the best of me when I deserved it the least. If the money had been in the car, I would have been tempted to give it back.

"I've gotta go," I said, revving the engine.

"Wait a minute," Tinkie said, kissing Chablis's head. The dog looked at me, longingly, I swear, and I felt another, deeper gouge in my already wounded chest region.

"Tinkie, I—"

"I was thinking, while I was waiting for you to bring my baby home, maybe you could help me out with something else."

I was all out of playing the role of friend and helper. In truth, I didn't have enough money to save Dahlia House, but I had enough to get across the country and try to find a life. "I don't think I'll be in Zinnia much longer."

"Just listen," Tinkie said, drumming her Red Passion nails on my car door as she cuddled Chablis to her bosom. "You're the perfect person to do this. I wouldn't confide in anyone else, but you're smart and trustworthy."

As my soul writhed, Tinkie continued.

"I never really knew what was at the bottom of Hamilton's family troubles. There were so many rumors, so much gossip." Her brow furrowed. "I want to know the truth."

The Garrett tragedies had happened shortly after my parents' deaths. I'd had other things on my mind. "I vaguely remember," I said. The Garrett family had been accused of the usual list of Southern crimes that involved everything that could be done to a relative, but most especially matricide.

"I want to hire you to find out the truth."

Tinkie's declaration caught me by surprise. "Me?"

"You're perfect. You understand the code of our set. Whatever you find out, you'll keep it a secret. And you seem to have a knack for solving things." She kissed the dog. "You got Chablis home safe and sound."

"What good is knowing about Hamilton's past going to do you?" I asked. "You're married." It didn't make a lot of sense.

"I want to know." Tinkie took a deep breath. "We all accepted the gossip and never thought to find out the truth. Well, I want the facts. If Hamilton comes home, I want to be able to look him in the face and know that I made the right decision or the wrong one. I'm tired of living my life based on perceptions and gossip."

"Tinkie?" I started to reach out and feel her forehead. Perceptions and gossip were the parameters of her life—of all the Daddy's Girls', except mine. My parameters were a lot uglier—theft and cheating for cash.

"I mean it, Sarah Booth. This business with Oscar not wanting to pay for Chablis. That's the final straw. I love this dog. And if Oscar really loved me, he would have given me the money. I'm only thirty-three. If I made a mistake by turning away from Hamilton, maybe it's not too late to rectify it. But if he did all of those things . . ." Her eyes rolled.

She had a point, about Hamilton and about Oscar.

Men of our class were used to laying down the law and letting the women live with the consequences. This was an interesting consequence.

"You want me to find out his family secrets?" This didn't sound too hard. There were plenty to pick from in every family.

"Exactly." Tinkie reached into the pocket of her suede jacket and brought out a slip of paper. She pushed it into my hands.

I glanced down at a check made out for ten thousand dollars.

"I'll cover all expenses, and you get another ten if you find out the truth."

Tinkie had paid cash for Chablis, and now she was forking over another ten grand for information I could get by visiting a few town mavens. "I'll get some answers for you," I promised.

"The truth, Sarah Booth. And hurry. I want to know before Hamilton gets here for Christmas. Madame Tomeeka didn't say exactly when he'd be home, but I'm sure it'll be for the holidays."

4

A small town is a hard place to be different. It's also a good place, because you know everyone else who's different. That's how I knew Cecily Dee Falcon, the society columnist for *The Zinnia Dispatch*.

Though I'd not slept well, guilt being worse than a thousand needles in a soft bed, I was up early and dressed for success in wool slacks and a silk blouse. The newspaper was my third stop of the morning; the first had been the bank to deposit Tinkie's check, cleverly written on her mother's account. Once the moola was stashed, I strolled the two blocks to see Cece. On the way I picked up some coffee and two Danishes from the bakery. Cece loved her sweets.

The newspaper office was small, cluttered, dirty, and a hive of activity. No one paid me much mind as I negotiated between the desks. Cece's office was in the back, the only private office. The details of local society do's were more closely guarded than Washington, D.C., political affairs.

I knocked and entered, holding out the coffee and treat as a peace offering.

"Sarah Booth," she squealed as she stood up and rushed toward me. After air kisses on each cheek, she grabbed the pastry bag with an elegant hand adorned with bronzed two-inch nails. She peeked inside. "Cream cheese, my favorite."

The deliberate effort of memory for small detail is a social grace that will take a person far.

Already biting into the Danish, she bumped the door closed with her narrow hip and went back to her desk. "What brings you to the paper?"

The question was casual, but her eyes were not. She'd heard that Dahlia House was in trouble and though she was my friend, she was also a columnist. "I need your help," I said.

"Are you organizing a fund-raiser?"

Now that wasn't a bad idea. I'd reserve it for the future in case my job for Tinkie didn't pan out. "No, actually, it's the past I'm interested in. Discreetly interested."

"Do tell, dahling." She reluctantly deposited the pastry on a napkin, licked her fingers, and found a pen.

"As you no doubt know, Dahlia House is in . . . financial disrepair." This was not news to her, but I had her attention. The fall of the House of Delaney would make headlines in the Delta. "I've decided to write a book to raise some cash." Authors were her weakness.

"What kind of book?"

"Oh, fiction." I shrugged a shoulder. "But I need a good, juicy scandal. I was thinking about the double murder of the goat man over in Natchez."

"No, dahling, that's been done!" Cece pinched off a bit of Danish and popped it into her mouth. She had strong white teeth.

"What about the Crawford love triangle?" I suggested. "She *was* sleeping with both of the brothers."

"Passé." Cece waved her hand.

"I need something really meaty. Something that will titillate the readers." I paused and furrowed my brow.

"What about the Nelsons?" she suggested. "Your daddy heard that case before—"

"No legal thrillers," I said quickly. "Too much competition in this state."

"Hummm," she said, her face brightening. "Think Greek."

My first reaction was disappointment. The last thing I wanted to discuss was a stupid sorority thing. She saw my face.

"Something e-lec-tri-fying," she hinted.

I had a vision of curling irons and singed hair, not the direction I wanted to go at all. "I thought you were going to help me," I grumbled.

"Tragedy," she said.

"Tragic is good," I agreed.

"The Greeks were the masters of tragedy, and every author from Shakespeare on has borrowed the great themes from them."

Cece had been magna cum laude at Ole Miss, with a double major in literature and journalism.

"Definitely something Greek," I agreed, wanting to tap my foot with impatience.

"Although great tragedy is based on fact, the type of page-turner you're talking about might rest more solidly on conjecture," she said, nodding. "Supposition."

This was the alley I wanted to explore. "Such as?"

"Do you remember the Garretts?"

Oh, baited trap, spring shut! "From up around the prison?" I asked, all puzzlement. *My* minor at Ole Miss was drama.

"Big, big house called Knob Hill. Landed, wealthy, and hot-blooded. Mr. Garrett was killed in a dove field. A hunting accident." There was a hint of speculation in her tone.

"Wasn't there a son about our age?" I pressed.

"Hamilton Garrett number five." Cece pushed the Danish away, hands going unconsciously to her hips. "He's a bit older, but I remember him clearly." Her pupils dilated. "It was the Christmas parade, 1979, just after Mr. Garrett was tragically killed. Hamilton drove his father's white Cadillac convertible, and Treena Lassiter was the homecoming queen. The whole parade, with the band and floats and Santa Claus, was coming down Main Street. Treena was in his car, waving. I was watching her, thinking how wonderful it must be to be the one picked to wear a white winter gown with a tiara, and wave and smile. Then I looked at him. Hamilton the Fifth. He was gorgeous." She smiled. "That's when I realized I was not a normal boy." She shifted her bra to maximize her cleavage and accentuate the fine bones that angled out from her throat. "Hamilton went away shortly after that."

I'd accepted Cecil as Cecily for so long that I sometimes forgot about the trip to Sweden and the drain on the Falcon inheritance for medical bills. Cece made a good-looking woman, and she was the best society editor Zinnia had ever seen. She lived and breathed *peau de soie* and Belgian lace, Gucci heels and Versace designs. She brought a touch of the exotic to Zinnia, and the readers of the local paper had grown to love her.

The sex change business had worked against her when she'd applied at *The Commercial Appeal*. They didn't come right out and say so, but they didn't hire her. Nor in Atlanta, or anywhere else. Her talent was overshadowed by her medical history. That's how she'd ended up back in Zinnia. Home is where they have to accept you.

"So Hamilton was your first pulse," I said, figuring in my head. I was thirteen at the time. If Hamilton was old enough to drive, he was fifteen or sixteen. Whatever image I might have had of him on the day of that Christmas parade, it had been blotted out by the death of my parents. They had died in November, a car wreck with a drunk on their way home from Memphis. My world had been destroyed, and it was no wonder I had little recollection of Christmas parades or handsome boys.

"Hamilton was one fine hunk of man."

In deference to the wistfulness in Cece's voice, I phrased my next statement with delicacy. "I remember Hamilton's departure was rather . . . hush-hush."

"He was loaded on a plane and sent to Europe before they could even get his mother in the ground. Sylvia, the sister, had to be institutionalized." She licked a crumb from her bottom lip. "One finds those facts deeply interesting." Cece was over her wistful moment and was in full-blown hypergossip mode.

"I never knew he had a sister." I honestly had never heard Sylvia's name spoken.

"She played Electra to his Orestes."

In contrast to Cece, who'd left college with her brain jammed with facts and ideas, my education was experiential—I had acquired intensive knowledge of moments, men, and mistakes I didn't want to repeat. "Electra?" I asked, wondering if she might have been a Delta Chi sister.

"Revenge is the motif," Cece said. "Rumor has it that Hamilton the Fifth murdered his mother at the behest of his sister."

"No kidding," I answered. This was finally sounding

more Southern than Greek. "Why would he kill his mother?"

"Revenge!" Cece leaned forward. "Hamilton's father, Hamilton the Fourth, was *murdered* in that dove field. It was a gruesome shooting. It was ruled an accidental death, but the gossip around town was that Hamilton the Fourth was actually murdered by his wife, Veronica Hampton Garrett. Somehow the daughter, Sylvia, discovered the plot and enlisted Hamilton the Fifth in the revenge. Supposedly, Sylvia and her mother never got along."

This was a dark tragedy, if there was a scrap of truth in it. The problem with Cece and the Daddy's Girls was that fiction was as good as fact—even better if it made the story move along. "And so now, Sylvia is in a nuthouse and Hamilton is exiled to Europe." It wasn't hard to see which sibling got the best end of that bloody stick. Women always got screwed, even in revenge.

"A private institution. Glen Oaks, over at Friars Point near the river. My understanding is that she committed herself, but there's something fishy there." Cece lifted eyebrows perfectly feathered with gel. "Most folks think she was responsible for her mother's death, but she was never charged. Surely your father talked—" Cece put a hand over her mouth as she realized that by the time the Garretts became the source of gossip, I was an orphan.

"It's okay," I said, then pressed on. "But why was Hamilton the Fourth killed in the first place?"

"Because Mrs. Hamilton the Fourth, Veronica Hampton Garrett, had a lover. She wanted to be free of her husband."

I took a sip of the cold coffee. This was exactly the end to which my affairs were headed—one big sordid mess. And because I was a Delaney, there would be some womb malfunction thrown in. "Who was her lover?"

It was a logical question, but one that put a look of concentration on Cece's pretty face. "No one has been able to find that out. Sylvia won't discuss it, won't discuss anything, from what I hear. Hamilton dropped off the face of the earth. And Veronica is dead."

"Exactly how dead?"

"Very. Car crash, 1980, just a few months after her husband was shot."

"No charges were ever filed against Hamilton or Sylvia?"

Cece gave me a look that showed pity for my chronic stupidity. "There was no evidence. Just a lot of gossip and innuendo."

"A murder and no evidence?" That was a neat trick.

"Veronica and one of the Garrett oaks became intimately acquainted. I was a kid, but I remember the talk. She was hamburger. Her whole body went through the windshield. There was no question that the service would be closed coffin."

Cece's imagery was as vivid as her writing. "Then it was an accident?"

"Only if one discounts the fact that her brake line had been cut."

Cece had a real knack for taking a simple story and twisting it around in so many curves that you were worn out by the time you got to the end. It was how she made all of those weddings fun to read.

"There had to be physical evidence of foul play, then."

"There *should* have been. Rumor had it that the sheriff covered up the whole nasty business. The Garretts were the most prominent family, you know." She picked up the Danish and took a big bite. "You get the verdict you can afford to buy." She licked a crumb off her lip. "A good story just whets one's appetite. What's the title of the book?" she asked.

"I'm not sure yet." I'd almost forgotten the ruse.

"A little birdie told me an interesting thing about you," she said, daintily putting the last morsel of pastry into her mouth. "I hear you like danger and darkness and doggies in distress." She pushed a sheet of paper toward me.

I glanced at the headline. DARING DELANEY RESCUES BOW-WOW. I didn't have to read any further. Tinkie's need to gossip outweighed her common sense. I had assumed that the ransom of Chablis was going to be our secret.

"Were you afraid? Did you see the dognappers? Tinkie was just raving about you." Cece was leaning so far across the desk I could see the false lashes she'd added to her own.

"It was nothing," I said, making for the door. I didn't want public credit in a case where I deserved public blame.

"Can I put it in my column that you're writing a book?" she asked.

"Wait until I have a title," I said, knowing that day would never come. "Thanks, Cece, you've given me a lot of ideas."

"What about Kincaid's luncheon? She said she sent you an invitation and it's going to be *the* charity event of the season."

It was, at five hundred a plate plus bidding on the outfits modeled by the Zinnia Blossoms, a clutch of anorexic twenty-somethings who wanted to be Daddy's Girls but grew up in the wrong generation.

"I think I'd better work on my book."

"Kincaid dated Hamilton," Cece said, flicking a bit of frosting from beneath a fingernail.

I wasn't a math whiz, but Kincaid was my age. That made her thirteen when Hamilton split. Tinkie might be obsessed by him, yet she never said she dated him. Kincaid had a reputation for being fast, but surely she wasn't dating anyone at thirteen.

Cece read the doubt on my face. "Kincaid spent a summer in Europe, dahling. I can't believe you've forgotten that scandal. She was forcibly brought home and pushed into marriage with Chas Maxwell. It was said that she'd fallen completely under Hamilton the Fifth's spell. Some even said she was bewitched."

I wasn't buying into all of these dark Garrett powers, but Kincaid had come home from Europe a different girl. I always thought it was marriage—that she'd given up the aspects of herself that made working in tandem with a dolt unacceptable. Self-mutilation was considered part of the price of security for women in my set. "Kincaid became a wife."

Cece arched one finely penciled brow. "I think it was sexual obsession. There are certain men who possess those powers." She picked up pastry crumbs with the tip of her index finger and transferred them to her mouth. "Men who can pleasure a woman to the point where she wants nothing more in life than their touch."

"What have you been reading?" I asked.

"You didn't spend time with her. I did. I wrote up the wedding, remember?"

Cece had me there. I'd put in an appearance at the church, but in the back row, and with my mind on making an escape before all of the lovely young matrons could aim their pity at me for failing to have caught a husband. Kincaid had been pale, and thin. And rather lifeless, as I recalled.

"She was a zombie," Cece said. "Her mother planned that wedding and ramrodded her through it. I mentioned Hamilton's name, once, and she flushed as if a fever had run through her. She was eaten up with wanting him."

The luncheon was sounding more and more intriguing. I had ten grand in the bank and another five under my mattress. I could afford a place at Kincaid's table. Especially for a chance to talk to her. "What did Kincaid say about Hamilton?"

Cece smiled, a tight little smile that told me she'd assaulted that wall more than once. "Not a word. Not a single syllable. Mention Hamilton's name now and this blank wall drops over her face."

The luncheon was looking expensive again. Maybe I could run Kincaid down in the grocery store. "Does anyone know where he is?"

Cece shrugged a shoulder, a maneuver that showed off her collarbone and the tricolored gold necklace that shimmered in the light. "He travels. One hears that he gambles."

"The Garrett estate, is it still intact?"

"Intact and with the addition of some European holdings. Extensive holdings."

"Will Hamilton ever come home again?"

Cece laughed out loud. "One can never tell, but that's a question for Madame Tomeeka."

"I'll be sure and ask her next time I see her." Which would be in pretty short order. I dropped my coffee cup in the trash, noticing again the ornate mirror that reflected several small statuettes. Cece had taken a number of journalism awards. I wondered if she still dreamed of working on a major daily.

"What about Dahlia House?" she asked, the spider

finally vibrating her web. "I heard rumors that you were putting it up for sale."

"Not this week." I fluttered a hand in the air, hoping to indicate that I was having a creative flash. "My muse is muttering and I need to get to my typewriter."

"I *will* get the galleys on this book before anyone else?" she asked.

"Absolutely," I promised, beating a trail out into the Zinnia sunshine. It was the day before Thanksgiving, and I had a turkey to buy.

5

There are only two grocery stores in Zinnia, the older Piggly Wiggly and the newer Winn Dixie. Winn Dixie has the more modern selections, but I know the aisles of The Pig by heart. I know Wanda, Peggy, and Lucy, the checkout girls, and Arlene, who runs the bakery/deli. Even though The Pig is too close to the Bank of Zinnia for comfort, I decided that tradition demanded that I get my bird from the place where Delaneys had bought turkeys for the past twenty years.

I kept a sharp eye out for Harold. I was certain he'd heard of my large deposit by now. He'd want to know where I'd gotten ten grand. I hadn't yet come up with a lie that satisfied me completely. As I pushed my cart along the worn tile, I tried to think of what to tell Harold. It would be hard not to be smug. I picked up two cans of green beans and ran through the recipe for the casserole. I also needed sweet potatoes, brown sugar, and marshmallows. The items in my cart were disgustingly delicious. No tofu or romaine lettuce for Thanksgiving.

The mountain of fresh cranberries in the middle of the produce stopped me cold, poleaxed by a memory of my mother placing a leaded crystal dish on the table. The contents were ruby red and dancing with candle-light. It was the last touch of the holiday meal, the signal that we could unfold our napkins and eat. I saw clearly the expression of delight on my father's face, the glint of the Delaney silver in the candles.

The memory was so real that it left me breathless. I made myself remember that those times were long ago. Tradition can mimic the past, but it can't make it real. I picked up a bag and felt the light, firm berries.

"I hear you're the one who rescued my wife's dog."

I'd been looking for Harold, not Oscar Richmond. I clutched the cranberries as if they were rosary beads as I turned to face him. "Hey, Oscar," I said wittily.

"I'll give you five thousand dollars if you make that yipping fleabag disappear permanently."

I hadn't realized Oscar was capable of making a joke. "Ha, ha." I laughed. "Tinkie wouldn't find that amusing."

"It's not a joke." Well, that explained it. He picked up the canned green beans from my cart. "Couple of these in a sack, snatch the dog, head for the Tibbeyama River. It wouldn't take long."

"You aren't kidding!" Chablis deserved a better father.

"I hate that animal." He glared at me. "Tinkie said you're working for her mother."

It had occurred to me that the powers at the bank would know that a check on Mrs. Bellcase's account had been written, but I hadn't expected a frontal assault from Oscar. "Yes," I said.

"What are you doing for Mother Bellcase?"

"You'll have to get the details from her." Heaven

knew what Tinkie might have told him. "I'll be by the bank after Thanksgiving to take care of some of my outstanding debts," I said, maneuvering the cart to make an escape.

"Ten grand is just a drop in the bucket on what you owe," Oscar said. He sighed. "It'll keep the wolf from the door for a month or two, but you're going to need a lot more money if you intend to try to keep Dahlia House."

It was true. Even if I got the other ten thousand from Tinkie, that wouldn't effect a real rescue, only a little time.

"Consider selling the property, Sarah Booth." Oscar returned the green beans to my cart. "You don't need that big old house. You could get along just fine in an apartment. We've got a buyer interested in your property, someone who doesn't care about the condition of the house. They're more interested in the land."

I dropped the mutilated cranberries into my cart and gripped the handle. "If they don't want Dahlia House, why do they want the property? No one in his right mind wants to farm."

"They're thinking it's a perfect location for a shopping center. And I agree. Zinnia has to grow or die, and as much as I hate it, the trend is toward shopping centers. The bank is even thinking about putting in a branch."

For a blazing second, I saw Dahlia House razed and a strip mall erected on the spot. I thought the vision would leave me permanently blinded. Oscar mistook my stunned silence for interest.

"I wasn't supposed to tell you about this, but you should know. You can make a good profit, settle your debts, and start over. I heard through the grapevine that you were writing a book. Not my idea of a career plan, but, hey, you've never been the type of girl who did things the easy way. You Delaneys always climbed the mountain when it would have been easier to drive up the road."

Oscar's gossip connection was enviable, but I couldn't stand in the produce aisle with him another minute. "I have to go."

"The reason I'm telling you this is because I think you ought to keep the money you just deposited. Don't pay off any of your debts. We can structure the sale of Dahlia House so that the buyer assumes the indebtedness."

In his own sick way, he was trying to do me a favor. "Thanks, Oscar. I'll think about it."

I hurried toward the section where the turkeys awaited their Thanksgiving fate. I had lost my zeal for cooking, but the requirements of the holiday kept me moving forward. I'd been worried before, but now I was beyond that. The bank had an interested buyer. That would eliminate any leniency I might have hoped for.

I looked at the cold, plastic-coated bodies of the dead turkeys, but I saw Dahlia House crumbling under the blades of heavy equipment. I saw the long line of Delaneys standing beneath the leafless branches of the sycamores as they watched their family home leveled. They did not condemn me. They had lived through war and Reconstruction. They had lost and gained, loved and died. But I was the last. Dahlia House was my heritage, and I would not lose it while I had breath in my body.

I dropped a twenty-pound turkey in the cart, my act of defiance. "I will never go hungry again," I vowed, aware too late that Arlene in the bakery was watching me with pity.

·　　·　　·

I left the turkey on the drain board of the sink with Jitty mumbling incantations about salmonella and Ebola. I ignored her. Ever since the Delaneys had bought frozen turkeys, we'd thawed them on the drain board. I didn't have five days to bring the dead bird gently to room temperature.

"Twenty pounds! You gone be eatin' turkey for the next six months." Jitty gave the bird a dirty look and flipped her dangly earrings. "Martha Stewart says—"

"Martha Stewart be damned," I answered. Jitty adored Martha Stewart. She watched every show, bemoaning the fact that I hadn't made a wreath for the door from the scuppernong vines at my very fingertips in the arbor behind the house. She pointed out that I was blind to the decorating variables of magnolia leaves. I had no imagination for making use of the syca-more balls or pyracantha berries or dried hydrangeas that could be spray-painted to great effect—I was deco-ratively challenged.

I left Jitty giving a holiday rundown of all of Martha Stewart's turkey-day decor and drove straight to the small, barely paved road that marked the transition from white neighborhood to black.

Although modern times had caught up even with Zinnia, there was still a cultural distinctiveness to the Grove. I crossed the railroad tracks that served as the unofficial line of demarcation. Many of the tarpaper shanties of my mother's youth had been replaced with brick homes. There was city plumbing and streetlights, just like the white residential sections. The difference came from the fact that in these yards, children played. Several of the older homes with porches contained chairs. People were sitting in those chairs, talking. They paused and watched my progress along the street, think-ing another white woman with more money than brains was going to Tammy Odom's, aka Madame Tomeeka's. I wondered again what Tammy's neighbors actually thought of her. Did they frequent her for advice on love and money?

I pulled into the bare yard and parked under the big oak that sheltered the small wooden house. I also wondered what Tammy did with all the money she took in from the Daddy's Girls, and the younger set of white girls who didn't fully understand that there was no point worrying about the future—their fates had been sealed at birth.

Tammy's yard was empty of cars. Good. I wouldn't have to wait. I went up the steps and knocked on the screen door. The day was balmy and I could hear a radio in the back of the house crooning Johnny Mathis.

In a moment Tammy appeared in my line of vision. She held her hands up like a surgeon. It was too dark to see what was on them, but I knew I'd interrupted her cooking.

"Got a minute?" I asked.

"Come on in." She disappeared and I went through the shotgun house to the kitchen in the back. She was mixing up cornbread for her dressing.

"Expecting your whole family?" I asked. She had a daughter, Claire, seventeen and a true beauty, who no longer lived in Zinnia.

"Maybe." She pulled a hot black skillet from the oven and poured the cornbread batter into it. There was the sizzling sound and smell of batter hitting bacon grease. She shoved the skillet back in the oven for the cornbread to bake.

"How is Claire?" Tammy had sent her daughter to Mound Bayou to have her baby. There was trouble between them, but I could only guess why. Teenage pregnancy was epidemic in Zinnia. As Tammy knew, it was a hard row to hoe.

"Fine. Had a little girl." Tammy's face gave away nothing.

"What did she name her?"

"Dahlia," she said, and there was the first hint of a smile. "Claire remembers the time she spent with you, Sarah."

"I remember it, too," I said, smiling back.

"You didn't come to ask about Claire," she said, picking up a knife and chopping onions and celery with such speed that her hands seemed a blur.

"No, I need your help."

Tammy's hands never stopped. "You don't believe I can see the future. You're not here for a reading."

"Tinkie Richmond believes."

"Uh-huh," she said, scraping the chopped vegetables into a skillet on the stovetop. She picked up a bell pepper.

"You told her someone from her past was returning. Someone dark."

"I remember what I said." Tammy never slowed her chopping.

"Tinkie has a way of . . . interpreting things to her satisfaction. I want to get this straight."

"Go on, ask what it is you want."

"Do you know if Hamilton Garrett plans to return to Sunflower County?"

Tammy's hands faltered. The knife nicked the end of her finger and blood shot onto the cutting board. I made a grab for a towel, but she turned away from me and went to the sink. She stuck the wound under the running water, creating a pink cascade along the white porcelain.

"I can't believe I'm so clumsy," she said, blotting the

wound with a clean dish towel. She rifled through a drawer and produced a Band-Aid.

I could see only her profile, but it was enough. "What's your connection to Hamilton Garrett?" I asked as she bandaged her finger.

Tammy's dark eyes held a warning when she did turn to face me. "I told Tinkie Bellcase what I saw in the cards. A dark man returns. I didn't say anything about Hamilton Garrett." She dared me to take it further.

"Tinkie assumes it's Hamilton."

"She assumes plenty. I could make you a list. Not everything revolves around Tinkie Bellcase and her silly fantasies. A dark man doesn't necessarily mean tall, dark, and handsome. Dark can mean bad, evil." She put more pressure on the cut finger.

I hadn't realized that Tammy truly disliked Tinkie. Tammy's bitterness toward the Daddy's Girls was understandable, but Tinkie was no worse than the others. "She's hired me to find out the truth about the Garrett family."

My words stopped Tammy cold. "That's a job you'd be better off without."

"I need the money. If I don't do this, I'll lose Dahlia House next week."

Financial troubles were something Tammy knew about. She also knew desperation. I remember when she got pregnant. She was a few years older than me, a fine athlete and a smart girl with real scholarship potential. Claire had put an end to all of that.

Tammy picked up the knife. She stared at it a moment before she started chopping again. "I can't help you, Sarah."

"Tinkie aside, do you remember anything about the Garretts?"

"They had a nasty habit of dying unexpectedly."

"Other than that?"

She dumped the peppers into the frying pan and turned it on. In a moment there was the teasing smell of sautéing onions and garlic. "That family has suffered," she said. "They were cursed."

I was never certain how much Tammy believed of what she told the people who came to her, but there was no doubt that she believed some of it. "The entire family? Like a genetic thing?" I tried not to sound flip.

"All of them, yes. In the blood. Cursed with power and reckless abandon. The combination never brings anything but pain. And especially Hamilton. He had the mark of the curse on his hand," she said. She lifted her face to the ceiling, and I wondered if she was praying. "I saw it there, and I knew that he couldn't escape it."

"What kind of mark?" She was making me feel creepy, but only just the tiniest bit. Healthy skepticism is also a Delaney trait—and this from a woman who lives with a ghost.

"The star of Saturn and the girdle of Venus, a thumb firm and mounded, like his mother's. He bore the mark of great sexual power."

I felt the hair along my neck begin to stand. But of course, Cece and Madame Tomeeka were thick as thieves. They would each exacerbate the other's theories. I rolled my eyes at my own gullible subconscious. I was as bad as the rest of them.

"My dance card is a little boring. Is this sexual powerhouse headed back to Zinnia?" I asked.

Tammy looked at me long and hard. "If he does come back, you don't want to dance with him. Tragedy follows his footsteps."

"Then he is coming home." I was shocked. I'd actually thought the whole "Hamilton returns" thing was something Tammy had fabricated to drain Tinkie's pockets.

Tammy's dark eyes were empty of all emotion. "It's the holidays. Folks like to be at home." She shrugged. "Even Garretts."

I decided to probe the past. "I heard Hamilton cut the brake line to his mother's car. Do you think he's capable of that?"

"You want me to tell you a secret?" she said, staring at me with those dead eyes that made my skeptical Delaney hide do a little goose dance. The kitchen was suddenly too hot, and the cooking onion and garlic were overpowering. I needed to step outside into the fresh air and clear my head.

Tammy leaned across the table and lifted my hand in hers. "I don't need my cards to see your future, Sarah. Stay away from Hamilton Garrett, his affairs, and all of his associates. You want to save your home, but you risk your very soul. Let the dead lie buried."

6

"Mrs. Kepler! Mrs. Kepler! Please open the door." I stood outside the library in the falling dusk and stared through the glass at the older woman who primly stacked the books. It was nearly five o'clock, and the library was officially closed. Mrs. Kepler had never broken a rule in her entire life. But I wasn't about to slink quietly into the approaching night.

My turkey was soaking in a sink of hot water—a definite salmonella no-no, according to Jitty. The pumpkin pie was cooling on the porch, and all was ready for the feast. I had been up to my elbows in giblets when it occurred to me that the library would have all the back issues of *The Zinnia Dispatch*.

"Mrs. Kepler, please! It's an emergency!" I pounded louder. I could see that I was getting under her skin. Her face was pinking up and she turned her shoulder to me. "Let me in!" I pounded until I thought the bones in my fists would shatter.

She put her books down on the counter and came

toward the door, her face the proper reflection of disdain, annoyance, and a pinch of sadness.

"Sarah Booth, whatever are you trying to do?" she asked as she opened the door a crack. "This conduct is unacceptable."

"I need to look at the back issues of the *Dispatch*." I tried to hustle past her but she was having none of that. She was old, but she wasn't about to be bullied.

"It's Wednesday; the library always closes at noon on Wednesday. And it's a holiday to boot. If I weren't so far behind I wouldn't be up here working late. And I don't need interruptions." She reached out a hand and felt my forehead. "Your mother would be appalled by your behavior. Are you ill?"

"Sick with desperation," I said. There was no other way. I was going to have to throw myself on her mercy. "Please, I need to find out something tonight."

"Come back Friday," she said gently. "I was just finishing up, and I want to go home."

"Please, Mrs. Kepler," I begged. "Please, this is very important. It won't take longer than half an hour."

"Why, Sarah Booth," she said, frowning. "Rules are rules. You know that. Though Elizabeth Marie was a little unorthodox, your aunt LouLane knew the importance of orderly conduct."

"I know if you don't let me see those newspapers, I'll do something desperate."

"Sarah!" Her hand went to her throat. "What are you saying?"

I'd actually meant something like push her aside, but she mistook my meaning. I drew my hand across my throat and grimaced. "It's life or death. Mine," I whispered.

It was the whisper that did it. She stepped aside. "You can look until I'm ready to leave."

"Thank you, thank you," I said, jumping from foot to foot. Before she could change her mind I was back in the reference section pulling out the bound editions of the paper from 1979.

I knew Hamilton the Fourth was killed during dove season, which would begin around September, so I started there. It would be front page, so that made the search easier. I had the story in record time.

Hamilton the Fourth was found dead in a cornfield owned by Delo Wiley on October 23, 1979, during the second dove season. Mr. Wiley had gone out to the field to search for him when he hadn't come in with the other hunters at dusk.

The death had been ruled accidental by Coroner Fel Harper. No autopsy had been performed; no charges filed. The newspaper account was not graphic, but it was clear that Hamilton the Fourth had been shot in the throat at close range. I read the account and came to two possible conclusions—murder or suicide. Sheriff Pasco Walters ruled accidental death.

In the code of the Southern gentleman, hunting accidents are a noble way to die. No need to assign guilt to your hunting partners if they blast you to kingdom come. No need to pursue suicide if the family is wealthy enough to buy silence.

But it was a little beyond the pale that one of Sunflower County's most prominent men could have been murdered, and deputies, coroners, family members, and friends had all conspired to brush it under the rug.

Unless, of course, it was Hamilton the Fifth who pulled the trigger. That would cast a whole 'nother light on matters. Cece was right. Money could buy a verdict, or kill an investigation.

Fel Harper was still the county coroner. He was also

not likely to tell the truth to me if he'd been involved in a cover-up.

I flipped forward through the newspapers, fighting the morbid compulsion to seek out the stories about my parents' deaths. This was not about me or my past. I had a job to do.

I scanned through January and found the story in the February 10 issue. The death of Veronica Hampton Garrett was also front page with photos—what was left of an expensive sports car and an old society picture of her. She looked like a movie star, with her hair piled up with glittering combs and a diamond necklace around her throat. Blond and beautiful.

I examined the car again. It looked as if it had been placed in a compactor and squeezed. No one could have survived that crash. And the tree didn't look too healthy, either.

I read the story, which said Veronica Garrett had been traveling the Knob Hill Road toward home at a high rate of speed when she lost control of the car and struck a tree.

The accident wasn't discovered for several hours. Hamilton the Fifth had found his mother's body when he passed by on his way home from a date. He called an ambulance, but his mother was dead.

The verdict you can afford—Cece's words again.

"Sarah Booth! We have to be going." Mrs. Kepler had her purse on her arm and was waiting at the door.

I closed the files and put them away. Damn! I hadn't really found anything, and I'd bruised my perfectly good fists on the library door. And then it struck me. I had discovered something. Two violent deaths had been passed off as accidents. Two prominent people, in the same family, died brutally within a four-month span, and both were ruled accidental.

Someone in the sheriff's office wasn't doing a very good job.

After a long and restless night, I was determined to put the case aside and have Thanksgiving. I dressed festive—newest black jeans and elegant russet velour blouse. The dining room table gleamed with silver and candles. I'd set two place settings, though I didn't know if Jitty would eat with me. I wasn't certain she ate at all. Mostly she mumbled and complained. But this was a holiday, and she was as close to family as I was going to get.

The turkey was a golden masterpiece, and I hauled it into the dining room as the pièce de résistance of the meal. The sweet potato casserole steamed, along with the green beans and dressing. Everything was perfect as I lifted my glass of wine.

"To the future. It looks as if we may actually have one." I was pumped about my discovery at the library and about evading Harold for the holiday meal.

"You start foolin' around like some gender-busted Sam Spade, you gone get your butt caught in a crack." Jitty had taken her place at the table, but she didn't seem overly impressed with the spread.

"Jitty, I can do this. Besides, it's sort of exciting."

"Yeah, that man from Austin was exciting, too. What was it the prison psychologist said about him? Sociopath with paranoid tendencies? When you start usin' the word 'exciting,' I start thinkin' this is not a good thing."

The bad thing about family is that they remember every little mistake, and they feel free to throw it in your face. "This is different. This is a job, not a man."

"It's a job about a man—potentially a man who

killed his mama. I don't like this Hamilton Garrett. No, ma'am, he sounds a lot like Mr. Texas."

"His name was Felix," I mumbled. "Felix Manson." Jitty's hearing was acute and selective. Death had given her the equivalent of bat ears. She heard exactly what she wanted.

"And that didn't give you a clue, did it?" she asked.

"It wasn't his real name, anyway."

"Uh-huh," she said, puckering her lips in the way I hated. "He picked the name Manson. That tells me a lot. If you had half a brain, it would tell you plenty, too. But you were too busy being *excited* by him to notice something like that."

It was time to move on. Jitty was ruining my meal with her memory. Felix Manson *had* been a mistake, but I wasn't about to give her the satisfaction of agreeing with her.

"I have to do something to earn some money fast, and this opportunity has presented itself. Now eat your dinner and quit finding fault with everything I do."

"Uh-oh, company's coming." She vanished before I could say another word.

The doorbell chimed and I peeped out the window, shocked to see a young black woman holding an infant. Jitty's relatives? I wasn't aware that she'd had children.

It wasn't until I opened the door that I recognized Tammy's daughter and the infant named after my home.

"Claire!" I swung the door wide and opened my arms.

She stepped into them with a smile. "Miss Sarah," she said, ducking her head in the old, shy way. "This is Dahlia," she said, holding out the infant.

Babies are not of particular interest to me, but I took Dahlia and was surprised to see her smile. "Come in,

Claire. I was just having some dinner. Come eat with me."

"Mama already fed us," she said, grinning, "but it's Thanksgiving. I can make room for a little more."

A person with a lot of relatives can eat eight or ten times on big holidays. Although most people serve the traditional foods, there are subtle variations that make sampling one of the joys of life.

Claire stopped at the table, noting the place settings for two. "Are you expecting someone?" she asked.

"I had a hunch someone might stop by." I waved her into the other chair, handed off the baby, and began to fill her plate.

We chatted about the baby and her schoolwork, which she assured me wasn't suffering. I watched her closely. She was too thin. The baby had cost her deeply, though it was clear to see she loved the child. I didn't ask about Dahlia's father. If there was anything to tell, Claire would get around to it.

"I guess you're wondering why I came," she finally said, pushing her empty plate away.

"You don't need a reason to visit me," I answered.

"I've got one." She modestly lifted her shirt to feed the baby, who'd begun to fret. "It's Mama. She's worried about you." Claire's soft brown eyes held mine. "She thinks you're in some kind of danger. She had a dream."

"What kind of dream?" I meant to say something about her dream being ridiculous, but curiosity won out. I wanted to know.

Claire shifted the baby slightly. "She said you were doing dangerous things." Claire took a breath. "Miss Sarah, you've always liked to have adventures, but whatever you're doing now has got Mama really upset." She took another breath. "I've already worried her sick."

"I'll talk with her," I promised.

"What are you up to?"

"Nothing dangerous, I swear." She drilled me with those big eyes. "I'm looking into an old scandal. Something that happened twenty years ago. None of it matters now, except to the woman who's paying me. And I need the money. But it isn't dangerous. Everyone who was involved is either dead or has moved away."

"Some buried things stink bad when they're dug up," she said.

"It's not like I intend to publish it in the newspaper. This is for a private client." I liked the sound of that.

"You're determined, aren't you?" There was resignation in her voice.

"I need the money, Claire. If I don't earn some cash, I'll lose Dahlia House."

She looked around her, perhaps remembering the months she lived with me when Tammy was having her own personal problems.

"This place has belonged to your family since it was built. Over a hundred years."

"That's right." I was pleased that she'd troubled to remember some of the stories I'd told her.

Her smile was gentle and suddenly wise for a seventeen-year-old. "Mama thinks I'm a victim of her past," she said softly. "She doesn't want to see you become a casualty of yours."

"We're all victims of our past," I said. It was a hard way to look at things, but it was true. History, genetics, environment—not much room left for the old free-will principle.

"Don't let this big old house be the death of you, Miss Sarah."

"Did your mother tell you to say that?" I smiled so that she'd know I wasn't angry.

"No, not exactly." She pulled the blanket tighter around little Dahlia and shook her head. "She told me to leave you alone. She said if I talked to you it would only make you more stubborn." Her lips hinted at a smile as she watched for my reaction. "I came because I wanted to see you, and I wanted you to see Dahlia. Mama is part of it, but I wanted to see for myself."

"And are you reassured?" I cut the pumpkin pie and slid a piece onto a crested Delaney saucer.

"No, I'm not reassured. I'm more worried. This man you're investigating, Hamilton Garrett. You should talk to Mama again. She hasn't told you everything she knows."

"Tammy never tells everything she knows." I placed the pie in front of Claire. "Pumpkin pie is the best possible nutrient base for breast milk. Eat up."

I caught her by surprise and was rewarded by her full laugh. Claire had always been a delight, and I could see that she was growing into a beautiful woman.

She lifted the fork, and even with a baby in her arms she was graceful. Still smiling, she said, "So along with becoming a detective you've founded the Zinnia La Leche Organization. You're a busy woman."

"I try." I was glad the topic had been shifted from dark and dire. Even babies were preferable.

"Miss Sarah, do you know who my father is?"

The question was as effective as a mule kick. Tammy had never told me diddly about the father of her child. And she obviously hadn't told Claire, which, I suddenly realized, was what this holiday visit was really about.

"Tammy keeps her own secrets," I said. Telling the truth was easy when it fit my purposes. "She never said."

"Can you find out for me?"

I definitely didn't want Claire Odom as a client, not when it meant poking into Tammy's past. "I can't do that, Claire. I've already got one client, and I'm just beginning. I'm not sure I'm going to be good at this."

"You could do it as part of what you're already working on," she said, focusing on the baby that now slept in her arms. "For Dahlia, so she can know who her people are."

"Part of what I'm working on?" I didn't like the sound of that.

"I believe Hamilton Garrett is my father." Claire looked up at me. "I think that's why Mama is so upset. I think that's why she's dreaming of white sheets and blood."

7

Claire and Dahlia were gone before I recovered enough from the shock of her revelation to truly analyze what she'd said. There was no doubt that somewhere in the Odom line Africans and Caucasians had made the two-backed beast. Claire was exquisite, and exotic. But so was Tammy.

What was almost as interesting as Claire's heritage was my own density and callousness. I'd hardly given Claire's father a thought. Tammy had never been linked to any man. She was a girl, like many others I knew, who bore a daughter and who had no connection to the man who contributed a few million sperm to the process. Why hadn't I wondered more about this?

I knew the answer; I had assumed that even if she told me the name, I wouldn't know him.

So who was the father of her child?

Hamilton Garrett the Fifth didn't seem like the right answer, because he'd been spirited away to Europe. That didn't make a liaison between Tammy and Hamilton impossible—Hamilton could have made a return sweep through Sunflower County. But how would Tammy have met him? It was all a bit far-fetched.

For the first time, it occurred to me how alone Tammy must have been, a high school student, pregnant, knowing that her entire life had changed because of the child growing in her belly. She'd lived with her elderly grandmother, a responsibility rather than a protector.

Before the baby, Tammy was the best basketball forward the Zinnia Panthers fielded. She had hoped for a scholarship and even a chance to play on the Olympic team. It was her only possible ticket out of Zinnia, and she lost it with Claire. She had accepted that loss with a stoicism that, with brilliant hindsight, now amazed me.

I thought about paying Tammy another visit, but it was only a passing fancy. If she intended to reveal the past to anyone, it would be Claire, not me and my client, Tinkie.

But who was the father?

In light of Claire's supposition, I had to wonder two things: Had Tammy heard something specific from Hamilton regarding his return to Sunflower County; and were Tammy's predictions for Tinkie motivated by fact or some form of devilment?

The Daddy's Girls were not kind to those outside their clique. Tammy's pregnancy, when it became obvious, had been the source of several comments and jokes, but it had not even rippled the surface of the world where the Daddy's Girls lived. Some of the girls had been catty and cruel, but Tinkie had not been active in that number. Still, obliviousness can be a form of torture to those who live in exile.

"Your hands already look like a scrubwoman's. Soakin' 'em in that hot water's only making 'em worse."

Jitty had slipped into the kitchen. "I don't suppose you're offering to help?" I asked.

"Stay clear of the past, Sarah Booth. There's nothing you can do to change it."

"I was just thinking how the past shifts. It's one way when you're there, and completely different when you remember it."

"Thinkin' is a dangerous thing for women in your family. It leads to those deep, down, and dirty blue funks, and you know where those can take a woman." Jitty walked to the kitchen window and looked out into the clear afternoon. Beyond the sycamore trees was a stand of cedars that marked the Delaney cemetery.

I didn't want to think about my dead relatives, so I asked her, "Who do you think is the father of Claire's child?" Jitty knew as much as I did. Maybe more.

"Someone handsome. Claire is a looker."

That was true, but nonspecific.

"I can't remember ever seeing Tammy talk to a boy." As far as I knew, she'd gone home to tend her grandmother every day after school. The truth was, Tammy could have been carrying on with Brad Pitt and I wouldn't have had a clue. Our friendship was a daytime thing. Her evenings, I had assumed, were spent with Granny.

"The way I see it, don't matter who Claire's father is. That's not your concern. What Tinkie wants to know is about his white family. She's not interested in the colored branch, if there is one."

"Only because she doesn't know it exists," I pointed out.

"Why complicate a simple job?" Jitty nodded slowly as agreement lit my eyes. "No need to tell Tinkie everything you dig up. I think you should make a trip to Knob Hill."

"The house is empty."

"You could interview the help. Surely they had folks workin' for them. Gardeners, maids, mammies. Folks with that kind of money gone have *somebody* to do the daily chores."

It was a good idea, but I hated to give Jitty the credit. She was already too bossy. I checked my watch. It was after three, a good time for a visit. The tryptamines from the turkey would be kicking in and folks might be more receptive to a probing visit from a stranger.

"I think I'll take a drive." I picked up my keys and sauntered to the door.

"Don't go out that door!"

Jitty wanted her pound of flesh—to make me admit I was taking her suggestion. I jerked open the door, intent on evading her. Harold Erkwell blocked my escape.

"Sarah Booth," he said, his voice smooth and refined. "I was wondering if you might join me for a bit of fresh air. I thought we'd go for a drive."

Harold. I had an appointment with him. I suddenly remembered an old story about a man named Daniel Webster. It did not have a happy ending.

The reprieve from my financial woes was utterly temporary. I couldn't afford to alienate Harold completely. An intelligent woman knows that the management of the male is an art, but damn, manipulation was so time-consuming, and I had important things to do.

"That sounds lovely," I said, smiling. As Aunt Lou-Lane said, "A girl can catch more flies with sugar than vinegar," and once they're caught you can smash them flat with ease.

Harold offered his arm and I pulled the door closed after me, ignoring Jitty's smirk.

He opened the door of his Lexus and seated me. I had to admire his impeccable manners. I had gone to college with girls who disdained manners. What fools they were. Manners are the cocoon that softens the journey from youth to maturity. Many a bad moment can be soothed with the balm of courtesy. I could appreciate Harold for his gracious behavior, if nothing else.

I didn't question where he wished to take me. It's better to give men the illusion of control. There is nothing more exciting to a man with power than a Pliant Woman, a PW. There is nothing worse than a Willful Woman, or WW.

During the time when women could not own property or vote, men amassed the bulk of their power. Though women, especially in the South, did the organization and day-to-day running of the large tracts of land and plantation houses, the men owned them.

In the Old South of bone corsets and come-hither glances, femininity was taken to a pinnacle that has never been achieved before or since. The softness, the pliability, the art of flirtation and pleasuring, were taught with a vigor that would make a marine think twice. Babes in arms were initiated into the illusionary cult of helpless PW.

And beneath the guise of the PW beat the heart of the WW. This was the woman who ruled, yet made her spouse believe that he held the reins of power.

As a result of all of this pliant femininity, that highest form of manners—chivalry—was born. The Southern male yang to the feminine yin.

Harold was a superior specimen of the old school, and it was the one thing about him that I truly admired. There is something mesmerizing about velvet-lined power, whether it comes from a steel magnolia or a Southern gentleman.

"How was your holiday dinner?" he asked as he

drove between the bone-bleached trunks of the syca-mores.

"Delicious." He was still sore that I had chosen not to eat with him. Declining an invitation is WW, not PW. Men ask, women accept—with a gasp of pleasure or at least a smile.

He turned left out of the drive, toward open country and away from Zinnia. Harold owned one of Zinnia's large, old houses in town, where he frequently entertained in great style. I was a little disappointed we were headed in the opposite direction because I enjoyed visiting his home. Harold had exquisite taste. His library was a treasure trove, and the walls of his home were hung with the work of the masters and an interesting assortment of new artists that Harold championed and supported. Because of his single status and his tasteful selection of furnishings, there had been talk of his sexual persuasion. But that was simply the talk of disgruntled women, or their mothers. Harold was considered quite a catch, and when they didn't land him, they turned nasty.

We drove through the countryside in an afternoon of slanting sun and brown fields littered with the bolls of cotton that the mechanical pickers had missed. That tattered look the fields had reminded me of the great wealth and great poverty that was the Mississippi Delta. A land of extremes, in almost every way.

"Sarah Booth, you said you'd have an answer for me," Harold said.

I tried once again to pinpoint my objection to Harold. He was handsome, rich, and powerful, and he always treated me with graciousness. It could be worse. Yet I couldn't bring myself to yield to him. And it certainly wasn't because I was too moral to trade my physical favors for his financial ones. Every relationship is one form of bartering or another. This was an honest, forthright deal.

"Why do you want me, Harold?" Perhaps if I understood, I would be better able to accept him.

"I don't know," he answered, glancing at me with some puzzlement. "You're an attractive woman, but there are plenty of good-looking women, and I normally prefer blondes."

I gave him a sideways glance. "And your point is?"

"You're attractive, Sarah Booth, but there are women who are beautiful and not so difficult. Tell me something. Have you ever had a successful relationship with a man?"

His question startled me before it made me mad. What exactly was the definition of successful? "Are you asking me why I'm not married?" I parried.

"In part. Let's start with that."

"It's too much work." That was the one answer guaranteed to fry him.

"So your idea of a successful relationship is short-term, with no work involved?"

I didn't like the way he was handling all of this, but so far he was simply restating what I'd said. Or almost what I'd said. "Pretty much," I answered. "Where is this headed, Harold?"

He turned the car down a dirt lane and pulled over beside Opal Lake. The water caught the slanting rays of sunlight and sparkled like the semiprecious stone for which it was named. It had been a long time since I'd been to Opal Lake, the place where teenagers went parking. But I wasn't a teenager and it was still broad daylight.

"I have a proposal for you," he said. "A formal one."

I wondered if he had a contract in the breast pocket of his coat. Basically, I knew the terms—I would be

Harold's mistress and he would help me refinance Dahlia House. From a cold, practical standpoint, it was a good deal for both of us.

"I can't sleep with you as some kind of business proposition," I said, not meeting his gaze. This was hard for me. Harold was the ace in the hole, the thing I could fall back on. And I was cutting myself free of him. "I just can't do it, Harold. In the long run, I'd feel so bad about it that it would be worse than losing Dahlia House."

"Would it be so bad to sleep with me?" he asked.

"No." That was an honest answer. "It would be so bad to do it because you're blackmailing me." Aha! That was the nub of my resistance. Coercion didn't sit well with me. I looked up into his smile. His happiness concerned me. "What?"

"That's what attracts me, the defiance, the refusal to be coerced. I find that extremely exciting."

And indeed he did. I could tell by the flush of color on his cheeks and the increase in his respiration. The solitude of Opal Lake struck me anew. It would be a long time before the teenagers came out to park.

"You'd find it very annoying after a short while," I said, edging back against the padded leather door of the car. Behind me the automatic lock clicked as Harold pressed the button on his control panel. His smile widened.

"Oh, I doubt that." His right arm moved to the top of my seat and I realized he wore leather gloves. Leather is appropriate for a man like Harold, but the gloves bothered me.

"Harold, you would find me very, very unamusing. Trust me." I was now finding myself very, very concerned. My major at Ole Miss had been psychology, and my fascination had been aberrant behavior. It was not over the top to find control freaks who eventually sought the ultimate level of power—life or death.

The fingers of his right hand flexed in the leather gloves, a slow *cre-ee-ea-k* of material not a foot from my head.

"Sarah Booth, I have to admit, you fascinate me. But there are things about you that worry me."

"I'm sure," I said, giving him a jolly grin. "More than you can count. I'm just not worth the trouble."

"Who is it that you're always talking to?"

His question threw me off balance. "Talking to?" I realized that it had to be Jitty, but when had he been listening? I remembered him standing in the bridal wreath. Was it possible that he'd actually been stalking me? Some detective I was turning out to be. I had a madman in my yard and didn't even notice.

"Every time I come up to the door, I hear you chattering away. And from your tone of voice, I know you think someone is answering you."

His hand inched closer to my throat. I could not push back against the door any harder.

"Who are you talking to?"

"Myself?"

He smiled. "All of the Delaneys are buried at Dahlia House, aren't they?"

I swallowed. Mention of burial and cemeteries did not seem like a good thing. I nodded slowly. "Most of the big old plantations have their own cemeteries."

"Which one of your dead relatives are you talking to?"

Jitty wasn't actually a relative, but she was family. "Someone who is very close to me." I tried to sound sad.

"Don't you think it a little odd for a thirty-three-year-old woman to be talking to dead folks? You've cut yourself off from the girls you grew up with."

Right. I didn't have money to indulge in The Club, or the tennis matches, or the charity events. "Things have changed for me, Harold. My life is different."

"You don't have the money to keep up with them."

He'd hit the nail on the head. "That's one way of looking at it. Another is that I'm not like them." Even as I said it, I realized it was true. They had married and settled, they had accepted a way of life from which I had slipped away.

"You could go back. You were born and bred for it."

"Could I?" I was asking myself as much as him.

His hand slipped over and grasped my shoulder so suddenly that I gasped. His left hand moved toward me in a fist. Suddenly the glove opened and in the middle of his palm was a small velvet box.

"Take it," he said.

My hand trembled as I reached for it. Without being told, I snapped open the lid and gazed down at the diamond. It was at least four carats, but not ostentatious. Incredible. I had never seen a jewel so beautiful. "It's lovely," I said.

"Marry me, Sarah Booth. I thought I wanted a casual relationship, but now I realize that I must have you as my wife. I want you to have my children, to be a part of my future."

I held the ring in my right hand and looked into his eyes. They were the lightest blue I'd ever seen. It was impossible to tell what emotion lay hidden behind them. Conquest, love, something else.

"I can't," I said, handing it back.

"Can't or won't?" He didn't sound upset.

"I know it's going to sound crazy, but I haven't married because I haven't fallen in love." Even to me it sounded ridiculous. One thing that Daddy's Girls knew from birth was that love was a fickle consort—security was the basis of a lasting relationship. "I'll marry when I meet the right person."

Harold's smile widened again. "I knew you'd say that." He turned the key in the ignition and the Lexus purred into life. "It's the perfect answer, Sarah Booth. It only makes me more determined."

Great. That was exactly what I'd intended. "Harold, I don't think this is a situation where determination can make a difference."

He turned the car around and drove slowly back to the road. I was relieved to be on blacktop where there were other cars passing.

"Is there someone else?" he asked.

"No." That was honest.

"Good, because if there was, I might be driven to desperation." He reached across the seat and put his hand over mine, squeezing it lightly. "I look at this as a challenge. You'll marry me, Sarah Booth, and sooner than you think."

8

Knob Hill was an impressive sight, especially silhouetted against the magnificence of a clear Delta sunset. Behind the three-story plantation, the sky burned fiery pink, deepening into coral, mauve, and, near the horizon, a purple of intense richness. Spreading out on either side of the house were the cotton fields, a deep burnt umber in the dying light.

The detail of the house was lost in shadows as I drove along the curving drive that climbed to the top of the hill and ended at the front door. But I could see more than enough.

Dahlia House was beautiful; Knob Hill was the Hollywood version of Southern architecture. The porch fronted the entire first story, a sweep of gray boards that looked, in the waning afternoon light, as if they'd been freshly painted. The columns that supported the second-floor balcony were stout and white. Knob Hill was in excellent repair for a ghost house.

I was surprised when I found the gates open. I'd anticipated driving by for a look, and then proceeding on to the tiny community of Bunker to find the people who had once staffed the great house.

Since the gates were open, I decided to detour for a closer look at the place where Hamilton Garrett had spent his formative years. I couldn't help but wonder how Europe had compared to this kingdom. For all of the culture and glamour of the great Continental cities, it would not have been an easy trade for me.

I got out of the car, more to stretch my legs than with any purpose in mind. Curiosity led me up the steps to peer in the front windows. Eight feet in height, the windows had been designed to open from floor level to allow the Delta breezes to blow through the house during the hot summers.

Through the lacy patterns of the sheers, I could make out a few details of the interior, but the gauzy panels and approaching darkness made it hard to see inside clearly.

I moved along the front porch, satisfying my nosiness without pretense. I was snooping. But then that was what I was getting paid to do. I rather liked this job. I moved back to the glass panes on either side of the front door, surprised to see a suitcase beside the stairs. It should have alerted me, but instead my gaze went directly to a unique sculpture at the foot of the staircase. In clear and frosted glass, the woman stood against a stiff wind, her hair blowing and her hand attached to a tree trunk laced with vines. The statue caught the fading light, and her glass skin glowed pink. I was transfixed by the sight of her, until a motion halfway up the stairs caught my eye. In contrast to the statue, the man standing on the curving sweep of stairs seemed made of metal. Where she was filled by and reflected the light, he seemed to drink it in. He stepped slowly down the stairs, his gaze pinning me. Unable to look away, I felt as if an electric current bonded us. He began to move faster.

I heard his feet pounding toward me. The front door flew open and I turned, my body already shifting toward the edge of the porch. I could jump to the ground without injury. It was only three or four feet. Escape was the only sensible action.

I made it three steps before I felt his hand on my shoulder. The fingers were savage, gripping hard through muscle and clamping on bone. The pain made me stagger, and I went down on one knee, finally looking up to see the devil that gripped me in his talons.

The face that stared down at me was wild with fury. Dark hair curled around a face contorted with anger. Green eyes burned with fevered emotion and his grip tightened, forcing me to cry out as my body curled into itself and away from the pain.

"What are you doing here?" he asked. "Who sent you?"

He must have realized that his grip precluded any verbal response because he relaxed most of the pressure, retaining only enough to lift me to my feet.

My first impulse was to knee him in the groin as hard as I could. I probably wouldn't get away, but it would provide a slight payback. But then, revenge wasn't worth feeling his strong fingers clench around my neck. I settled for slapping his hand away from my shoulder. "You're hurting me!"

"Once again, who are you?" he asked, releasing me.

There was a hint of accent, something not definable. I took a breath and looked up at him. Rage had been replaced by caution. The change in his features was remarkable. The man who stood before me was handsome. Tinkie's phrase, "a dark man," slipped into my mind. There was no better description, physical or emotional. Blood suffused his olive complexion, and the generous lips of his mouth were straight with challenge. He was not a man to tamper with. I knew that instantly, even as I became fully aware of his broad chest, the large hands clenched at his side, the leanness of hip and thigh that spoke of physical strength.

There was impatience in green eyes that also held a warning. He was a dangerous man, and I had better have the right answers to his questions. The thrill was delicious.

"My name is Sarah Booth Delaney, of Dahlia House. And who are you?" Tit for tat. A powerful man is much like a horse—never show them fear.

"Why are you trespassing on my property?"

I had enough sense to hear the operative pronoun in his question. So this was Hamilton Garrett the Fifth. In the flesh. I had to come up with a story, and fast.

"I had hoped to find you or someone from your staff at home," I said. "Cece Dee Falcon asked me to do a story on the Christmas season parties for this area. Since you've returned home, the newspaper wanted to know if you're planning on having a fête here at Knob Hill?"

It was weak, but it was better than nothing. And Cece would stand behind me if I offered her some tidbit of gossip.

Hamilton's left eyebrow lifted. "Knob Hill has been closed for nineteen years. Why would you think we'd have a party this holiday?"

"My thought was it wouldn't hurt to ask." I smiled and wished that I'd had a little more experience playing weak and helpless. He would have recognized that as a lie, too, but he would have been honor bound to respond to it. That was assuming that a potential murderer was still adhering to the Code of the South.

"Delaney," he mused, never taking his gaze off me. "I know who you are."

"Of course you do," I said. "I remember the 1979 Christmas parade when you drove Queen Treena in your daddy's white Caddy convertible." Now this was firmer ground. We were trading pedigrees. The crisis was over, though my body still trembled at the thought of his touch.

"My last Christmas in Sunflower County," he said, and there was a coldness in his voice that made me wish I'd picked another memory. Hamilton stepped back from me. "There will be no parties at Knob Hill. Please don't bother us again."

"Are you home for good?"

His features hardened. "My comings and goings are no one's business. Particularly not a newspaper gossip columnist. Take my advice: Stay off my property, or the consequences will be dire." He stepped back and away and reentered the house. The door slammed with a good, solid thunk.

Walking back to the car, I was aware that my shoulder throbbed. Once the car door was locked, I stretched the neck of my blouse down and saw the clear marks of his fingers. The bruises would be colorful.

Cruising down the gracious curve of the drive, I kept glancing in the rearview mirror. Knob Hill stood like a mammoth black fortress against the silvery night sky. Even as I stared at it, a single light blinked on in a third-floor window. I found my teeth chattering and I turned on the car heater. The falling night had stolen the day's warmth.

And Hamilton Garrett had stolen mine. My fingers were icy as I gripped the wheel and turned right toward Bunker. I still intended to find the people who'd once worked for the Garretts.

I shared one thing with Harold Erkwell—a grim determination that only grew stronger with resistance. Now I was vested in the truth of what had happened nearly two decades ago. Hamilton Garrett had touched my life and left his mark—embedded in my flesh.

Bunker was a four-way stop that featured a gas station/convenience store, a video rental that sold livestock feed, and cotton fields that seemed to stretch forever. The store was open and the owner told me Amos Henry, the Knob Hill groundskeeper, lived on a small farm two miles to the west.

As I cruised toward the Mississippi River, I found myself replaying the images of Hamilton, the dark master of Knob Hill. He was a man a woman wouldn't forget, and I understood Tinkie's fascination with him. But he was also a hard man, one who demanded satisfaction. I hoped, for Claire's sake, that he was not her father.

At the juncture of county road 33, I saw my turnoff. The Henry farm, from what I could see by the car's headlights, was neat as a pin. The small farmhouse had a welcome glow, and I found myself eager to step into the warmth the house promised.

My knock was answered by a woman who could have been fifty or seventy. "Can I help you?" she asked.

I identified myself, honestly this time, and explained that I was looking for information on the Garrett family. She didn't ask why I wanted the facts, and I didn't tell her.

"You'll need to talk to Amos," she said, pushing the screen door open for me to enter.

The house was warm and filled with the smell of good cooking.

"We're having some leftovers for supper," she said. "If you don't mind eating in the kitchen . . ."

I certainly didn't. I followed her and took the place she indicated as she filled a plate at the stove and put it down in front of me. Turkey, dressing, ham, sweet potatoes—all the traditional foods. But each just different enough from my own cooking to make them interesting.

An older man sat to my right, and he nodded and smiled but continued eating. It struck me that his priorities were right, and as soon as Mrs. Henry took a seat, we all gave the food our primary attention. We made small talk about the weather, the coming year, farming, and the price of cotton.

"Wonderful," I said when my plate was empty.

"She wants to know about the Garretts," Mrs. Henry said. "She's from Dahlia House. One of the Delaneys over at Zinnia."

"I knew your father," Henry said. I thought there was a hint of sadness in his eyes as he looked at me. "He was a good man. A fair man. He wasn't afraid of helping others."

"He was like that," I agreed.

"You got some problem with the Garretts?" He sipped at the cup of coffee his wife placed before him. She put another cup in front of me, along with cream and sugar and a large slab of pumpkin pie topped with real whipped cream. My favorite.

"No." I thought about my shoulder and realized it was a lie. "I just met Hamilton for the first time today. He's rather . . . forceful. I'm gathering information for someone else."

"Private investigator?" His brow furrowed.

I hadn't thought of calling myself that. I didn't have a license or anything else. But the term described the job

Tinkie had hired me to do. "Yes," I said. "In a manner of speaking."

"The Garretts had plenty of heartbreak. Maybe it would be better if you let sleeping dogs lie."

There was an undertone in his voice that I couldn't decipher. "My client has a reason for wanting to know. She wants to protect her . . . interests. This is a personal matter."

He seemed to think about that. Mrs. Henry picked up her coffee. "I'm going to watch some television." She left the room.

Amos Henry was still staring directly at the wall when he began to talk. "After fifty years working for the Garretts, I was fired this morning. Thanksgiving Day," he said. He leaned back in his chair. "I cleaned out the fall garden Wednesday, and I was sitting on the porch early this morning. I'd just gone over to make sure I'd locked the toolshed good and tight. Young Hamilton pulled up. He left the car running and walked up on the porch. I thought for a minute that I was having a daydream, seeing him like that. He had grown into a man, but I recognized him. I stood up kind of slow, like I was in a daze, and then I smiled. I remember because that smile just kept stretching and stretching and it hurt my face, but I couldn't stop it because I was so glad to see him. It's hard to work at a place where nobody lives. It's hard to make the flowers grow when nobody sees them or takes pleasure in their beauty.

"I started toward him grinning like an old coonhound and sticking out my hand to shake his. I said, 'You're home. I can't believe you've finally come *home*.'

"And he said, not even looking at my hand, 'Yes, I'm home. Your services aren't required any longer.' And he reached into his coat and pulled out a piece of paper. He put it in my hand and turned around and went back to the car. He drove off."

Amos Henry reached into the pocket of his shirt and pulled out a piece of paper. He carefully unfolded it and handed it to me.

It was a check, and when I glanced at the figure, I took a deep breath. It was for twenty thousand dollars. The signature at the bottom was bold, a scrawl of black letters.

"Mr. Henry, had you been receiving a paycheck for your work at Knob Hill?"

"Every month I got my check, regular as could be."

"This is severance pay?" I handed the check back to him. Hamilton Garrett was forceful, ruthless, and generous.

"That's what some folks might call it." He dropped the check on the table. "I've never been fired from a job. I went there fifty years, working each day when nobody would have known whether I did or not. And I get fired, just like that." He shook his head.

"Did Hamilton ever marry?" I was thinking about Tinkie. This was a fact she'd want.

He shook his head. "As far as I know, neither of those children ever married. Or ever will, I dare say, after what all went on. Until today, I never talked to the boy after he left here. Ever since Mr. Guy and his wife died, I took my orders from Mr. Wade up at the real estate office."

"Guy?" I hadn't heard his nickname before.

"It was what we called him. Too many Hamiltons in that family. There was a time when Mr. Guy was alive, and his father and little Hamilton. You'd think with all that money they could have found a book with some baby names in it."

It was his first smile, and I responded in kind. I liked Amos Henry. He had a lot of dignity.

"Tell me about Mr. Guy and Mrs. Veronica," I said, forking another bite of pie. I was having an excellent time. Being a private investigator was great work. "Were they happy?"

Amos looked at the kitchen wall for a long while. I could tell he was replaying old memories, things he'd thought about before. "Being married is not always a cause for happiness," he said. "Sometimes money complicates things, whether you don't have enough or you have too much. Mrs. Veronica needed money. Mr. Guy had it. It was a situation where the power never changed hands. That can cause a lot of grief between two people."

It was his way of telling me there was trouble in the marriage. Guy lorded money over his wife, or else his wife was so greedy that she could never get enough.

"There was talk Mrs. Garrett might have had a boyfriend." There was no way to sugarcoat this. "Was it true?"

"She was a looker. And she liked for men to look. Any man. It caused more problems with the daughter, Miss Sylvia. Even when she was little, that girl would crawl up under my bushes. She could hold herself still for hours, just waiting, watching her mother. She was always watching. It made me uncomfortable, to be honest. She was a beautiful thing, but she never laughed or played. She just watched. Like she was an old, old woman trapped in that little girl, and she was watching for something she knew had to happen."

He paused for a moment as if he were deciding what else to tell. "Mrs. Garrett sent her away to school up in Tennessee when she was nine. I do believe that child scared her mother."

I filed the information about Sylvia away. She sounded like a strange duck, but my focus was Hamilton the Fifth. "Was there a particular man hanging around, someone who visited Mrs. Garrett a lot?"

"No one special that I saw. Of course, Mrs. Garrett wasn't a fool, either. There were lots of men, and she loved it. She lived for the attention. It wasn't taking anything away from Mr. Guy. She couldn't help it any more than he could help having all that money. Her looks were her power. She had a way about her, when she'd sit out in the sun and run that little butterfly comb through her hair. It was one of her favorite things, that comb. Some kind of special design. She told me once, but I forgot. She said it made her feel magical, and she would draw that comb through her hair and make a man want her in a way that made everything else just fly right out of his mind."

I swallowed, wondering if Amos Henry had felt the lasso of her attraction. Everything around me spoke of a man who took deliberate, practical actions in his life. But every man has a weakness, and for many it's a particular woman.

"So there was a conflict between the parents—his money and her looks."

Amos thought about this for a time before he answered. "There was arguments. I worked outside, tending the yard, but I heard them fighting. They were two folks so different. Mr. Guy was an inside kind of man. He had his work and his investments, and he wasn't the kind to play tennis or swim. Mrs. Veronica, now, she loved the sunshine." He smiled. "She'd lay out by the pool and just soak up the sun. She'd laugh whenever anyone tried to tell her that it would make her old and wrinkled. She just said she didn't intend to grow old. She said that women like her weren't created to last long, they were meant to burn hot and fast and go out with a bang."

Mrs. Garrett's big bang was a tree trunk. And she had lived to fulfill her own words. Suicide flashed in the back of my retinas in big red letters. It was another angle to check.

"Mr. Guy didn't enjoy the outdoors, but he was a bird hunter?" I probed.

Amos snorted. "Not hardly."

"He died when he was hunting. I read the story in the newspaper."

Amos gave me a look like he thought I should be blond. "Mr. Guy wasn't no hunter."

"Are you certain?"

"One summer a big fat moccasin slithered up by the pool. Mrs. Veronica was screaming and yelling, and Hamilton was just a little fella, he was standing big-eyed about a foot from the snake, frozen, like. That ole snake was coiled up, big around as my arm. I called Mr. Guy and he comes running out with a gun. He just hands it over to me and tells me to shoot the snake. His son there, and that snake ready to leap out and bite the boy, and Mr. Guy hands the gun to me. No man who can use a gun would do that."

Amos Henry had convinced me. So what was Guy Garrett doing in a dove field if he wasn't hunting? The possibilities were endless—and they all spelled murder.

9

I had to pass by Knob Hill on my way home. There was no evidence of the house, no lights, or at least none that could be seen from the road. The idea of Hamilton, alone and brooding in that big old house, was chilling. Not even my great-aunt Elizabeth, who wore her petticoat and nothing else to church, had been so far gone into madness that she chose to sit in the dark on a cold November night.

The case—and I had begun to think of it as "my case"—had taken on a different twist. Hamilton had not attended Sunflower County High. Unless he had gone to Memphis or one of the bigger Mississippi cities, he'd graduated from Dorsett Military Academy, the place where all Delta males of blue blood and bad disposition completed secondary education.

And Sylvia? Henry Amos had left me with a vivid image of a young girl, an obsessive child who spent her life in the shadows, watching. I gave a little shudder at the thought of a primary-school stalker. Sylvia had been sent to Tennessee, probably Bethany Academy.

So Veronica had had an open playing field during the day, when hubby was working and the staff could be deployed in other directions.

I had plenty of questions to ask Mr. Henry, but in the proper time. Good manners dictated that a visit should last no longer than two hours. I had stretched my stay, and my stomach, to the maximum.

Feeling satisfied with what I'd achieved, I cleared the Zinnia town limits and decided on the spur of the moment to stop at Millie's for a diet Dr Pepper. I was wired from the excitement of the day, and it also occurred to me that if Millie's was open, business would be slow. Other than Martha Sue Riley at the Glitz and Glamour, Millie was one of the best sources of gossip. She'd know plenty about the Garretts, and whether her gossip was true or not, it would lead me to new possibilities.

The café was open, and Millie was sitting at the counter reading a tabloid newspaper. I could see her in the window as I drove by, so I pulled into a parking space and hurried inside. The night was turning downright cold. By morning, there would be a blanket of frost on the ground.

"How's it shaking, Sarah Booth?" Millie asked as I walked in. Millie would never have spoken to any of the other Daddy's Girls in such an informal manner. But then the others ate at The Club, not at a diner. Even as a teenager I'd loved the thick white coffee cups and the egg-and-bacon sandwiches Millie made while holding conversations with three or four patrons at the counter.

"I'm full as a tick but thirsty." I gave my order as I took a seat beside her and read the headlines of her tabloid. Roseanne was pregnant by an alien. "I wasn't certain you'd be open."

"I cooked, I ate, I washed the dishes, and then I discovered I was bored. It's slow, but a few folks have come in." She lit a cigarette. "Most of them thirsty."

Millie is older than I am, a single mother whose children are grown, married, and producing offspring of their own. There are no womb disorders in the Roberts family. I could understand that opening the café was preferable to staying home alone.

She put the fizzing soda in front of me and reclaimed her seat. I saw that she was reading a story about a sighting of Princess Di at Graceland. The photo that accompanied the story showed a ghostly figure that resembled the late Princess of Wales—and about ten million other slender blond women—peering through the musical gates of Graceland.

"Do you think she's really dead?" Millie asked, pointing at Di.

I hadn't thought about it as up for debate. "I guess."

"Some folks think she and Dodi only wanted to live their lives in peace. They think she's living on an island off the coast of Greece."

It was one way of interpreting the facts. "Sounds like a nice ending to an unpleasant life," I said. I'd seen the handwriting on the wall in that marriage when Di had to do the virgin check and Charles didn't.

"The way I've got it figured is that Charles and the queen went along with it because that way they'd get Diana out of their hair. I mean, she's dead; she can't keep upstaging Charles. And all she ever really wanted was to be loved. So she gets that and peace."

It was a pretty neat bundle, I had to admit. "I hope you're right."

"Me, too," she said, but her voice had lost its conviction. Millie enjoyed creating fantasies, but that didn't mean she was stupid enough to believe them.

"Speaking of tragic families, I saw lights on at Knob

Hill tonight." In the commerce of gossip, you have to learn to trade. I'd just plopped the Hope diamond of red-hot news on the table. Millie's face lit up like she was standing at a Tiffany's counter.

"Lights? On Thanksgiving night?" Then the wheels turned. "What were you doing at Knob Hill?"

"Driving by," I said, waving a hand to dismiss my errand as insignificant. "That house has been closed for nearly twenty years, as best I can remember."

Millie nodded. "Hamilton the Fifth has been home a few times, or that's what I've been told. He hasn't put in an appearance in Zinnia." Her voice had taken on a careful edge.

I nodded and sipped my drink. The fizz was very comforting. Without a qualm, I stole a line from Cece. "His whole life has been like a Greek tragedy."

Millie shot me a strange look but picked up her cigarette. "Yeah, it would make a great miniseries on television. If anyone ever really got to the bottom of it."

Pay dirt. "You mean you don't think it happened like—"

"Guy Garrett wasn't a hunter. He couldn't hurt a fly." She got up and went behind the counter. She picked up a stack of menus and tapped them into a neat pile, laid them down, and began to wrap flatware in paper napkins. She kept her back to me.

I put a few things together fast—Millie's hungry look as I mentioned Knob Hill, her careful tone, and her use of Hamilton Garrett the Fourth's nickname.

"I was a kid when all of that happened." I kept it casual. "How awful for Hamilton the Fifth to lose his father and then his mother. I wonder if he liked Europe."

"He didn't have much of a choice." Millie put the flatware aside and turned to pick up her cigarette, which was mostly a big, long ash. She thumped it and put it out. "There wasn't anybody on the Garrett side of the family left to take him. And his mama's people *wouldn't* take him."

"Why not?"

She stared at me as if she could discern the true reason for my curiosity. "Tragedy has a way of marking a person," she said slowly. "Folks don't want it in their homes. There was enough money for Hamilton to go somewhere far away, to finish growing up in a place where he wasn't viewed as a victim or a murderer. He made the smart choice."

"Murderer? I don't remember anything about that."

I saw the truth strike Millie. "You had other things on your mind then, Sarah Booth. I don't suppose you would remember anybody else's troubles." Her voice had softened. "Anyway, it was never an official murder. No charges were filed, but they spread the gossip. That's how things are done in Zinnia. Nothing official, just trial by innuendo. Drove his poor sister into an asylum. That little girl never had a chance with a mother like that, always more interested in her looks and her collectibles than anything else." She gave a sharp little snort of disgust. "If anyone deserved to die, it was Veronica Garrett. And if anyone wanted her dead, it was me." She lit another cigarette and as the flame met the tip, she stared directly into my eyes with a look that actually chilled me. "Veronica murdered Guy as sure as I'm standing here. She deserved exactly what she got. I just wish I believed she got it."

Apparently Millie had a theme going with women who'd cheated death. First Di and now Veronica. But the anger in her eyes made me sit up straight on the bar stool. After two decades, she still hated Veronica Garrett with a dangerous passion. "Did Hamilton have something to do with his mother's wreck?"

Millie swallowed, her mouth moving funny as she worked to reign in her emotions. "Hamilton was a child."

That wasn't an answer. "Is it possible Hamilton thought his mother . . . that he might have taken revenge on Veronica? There's still a lot of talk that he cut the brake line on her car."

She swallowed again. "Sarah Booth, I'm not feeling well. I know you'll understand if I close up and go on home."

Oh, I understood. "Can I get you something?"

She gave a half snort. "A chance to change the past. Can you manage that?"

"What would you change?" I asked slowly.

"I'd be born in the rich class of folks," she answered. "With a different last name, I could make all the same decisions and still have a different outcome."

My psychology degree from Ole Miss had been an indulgence. I had no desire to spend my time listening to the sordid problems of people who'd screwed up their lives and wanted an audience to whine to. I studied psychology because it was easy, interesting, and, like many of the other students, I hoped to find the answers to my own problems without having to reveal my particular soul-squalor to anyone else.

I had found no answers, but I had learned a great many fascinating things about the human animal. One of the questions I'd pondered in class was the ability of a human to commit an act she personally considered a horror. For example, the woman who abhors violence, yet kills without hesitation to protect her child. In any other circumstances, the woman might be incapable of self-defense. But when it comes to her child, she can blast brains over the wall and never bat an eye.

The underlying thesis of the class had been that each and every person is capable of anything, given the right circumstances. I knew this to be true. In the past week, I'd done things I would never have thought myself capable of doing. Put in the right situation, I could probably kill.

As I drove through the night, top down on the Roadster so that my ears ached with cold and my eyes watered, I put my new view of Millie on top of how I'd always considered her: kind, generous, a mother whose entire life had been devoted to her children. This night, I'd glimpsed Millie the woman, who loved a man out of her reach. And hated the woman who'd owned him.

Was Millie capable of cutting Veronica's brake lines? She had motive and opportunity. Millie's brother was Zinnia's prime auto mechanic. He worked on everyone's vehicles, especially the expensive automobiles of the rich and famous. I made a mental note to stop by Billie's Garage and see if I could finagle a look at his records.

As I pulled up at Dahlia House, I regretted that I hadn't left a light burning. It was almost more than I could abide, walking into that dark house alone. It occurred to me that even the company of Harold Erkwell would be preferable to my singular thoughts on this depressing night.

It had been a long day. An eventful day. I hadn't forgotten Harold's proposal, I'd just shoved it to the back of my mind. Now, as I started up the back steps, I saw the small jewel box. My first reaction was disbelief that Harold had left a four-carat diamond on the back steps. My next thought was that he was in the bushes.

But when I picked up the velvet jewel case, he didn't magically spring out at me.

I flipped open the lid and even in the pale wash of moonlight, the diamond glittered with a promise of ease and security and beauty. The sheer size of it symbolized hearth fires and the relaxing strains of Mozart, the smell of hot food prepared by another's hands. That diamond burned with the expectation of shared conversation over dinner, the safety of someone solid and warm beside me in bed.

Then the Delaney womb kicked in. I was stunned by the remembered feel of little Dahlia in my arms and the simultaneous clamp of pressure in my nether regions. Reproduce! Reproduce! The Delaney womb pulsed the order.

And I resisted, remembering that all of those wonderful things I'd just imagined came attached to Harold Erkwell, a man I did not love. I grasped the rail beside the steps and steadied myself. My legs trembled as raw animal instinct warred with hard-won intelligence. I snapped the lid shut on the box with such force that it sounded like a gunshot. The best thing would be to hurl the thing into the bushes, and I swung my arm back—

"Don't be the jackass I think you're about to become." Jitty put a feathery ghost touch on my arm, and it was enough to halt me. "That ring is worth a lot of dough. All you have to do is accept it. You don't have to marry him. Just accept the ring, say you're engaged, then break it off. Legally, the ring belongs to you. Push comes to shove, we can cash that sucker in and have enough money to keep Dahlia House afloat for a little longer."

I began to drop my arm, and Jitty's gold tooth sparkled in the moonlight as her smile widened. "That's it, girl, use your brain."

Easy for her to say; her womb wasn't sending out mating calls. "Thanks for the plan," I said sarcastically, because I was frightened by my own reactions. I'd been tempted. Tempted! It showed how weak I was becoming. "I've already rolled over Tinkie by stealing her dog, now I should lead Harold on so I can pawn his engagement ring."

Jitty's eyes narrowed. "Don't be getting' all high-and-mighty on me. You could have vetoed the plan with Cha-blis."

It was true. I could have and I hadn't. I still had the five thousand cash tucked under my mattress.

"Let me see that ring again," Jitty said.

I went inside, turning on the kitchen light. The house was cold as a tomb. I turned on the oven, opened the door, and backed up to it while I snapped open the jewel case and gave Jitty a good look at the ring.

"That's a hunk o'diamond," she agreed. "I thought Harold only wanted a playmate for the sheets."

"So did I. Obviously, he's aiming for a more enduring relationship."

"Sort of complicates things, doesn't it?"

There was a hint of sympathy in Jitty's voice, and it was nearly my undoing. My life would become so much easier if I accepted Harold. Maybe I could grow to love him. Or hell, what did that matter? Most all of the Daddy's Girls had married for a list of reasons, and love wasn't even close to the top. They had all secured their lives, while I floated around in the ocean of financial woes like a pathetic single plank. Would I have turned out differently had my mother not died, had I not been influenced by an aunt who taught me to dance the Virginia reel when I felt blue and that math for girls was satanic?

"Don't go there, girl," Jitty said softly. "One thing

about being a spook, aside from the cool thing about passing through walls, is that we see the past a lot differently from you mortals. Dancing and math didn't ruin you, and they won't save you. You were who you were before LouLane put her stamp on you. You came out of the womb a Delaney. No help for it, not in the past and not in the future."

"If you mean to comfort me, you're doing a terrible job." But she had pulled me out of the ditch of the past. "What am I going to do about Harold?"

"Keep the ring. Delay. You have to admit, he's sort of growing on you."

"Like a fungus," I answered. "He looks better than he did, because my options look so much worse. That's hardly a recommendation for matrimony."

The backs of my legs were hot. Really hot. My jeans had gotten superheated and now whenever they touched my skin, they burned me. I danced away from the stove. Jitty rolled her eyes.

"Harold won't push you too hard. Not at first. Later, it'll be fish or cut bait. Right now, you holdin' all the cards. Keep the ring. Don't wear it. Don't even mention it. That'll drive him wild."

It was good advice, but in my heart of hearts, I was feeling low-down about my conduct. Twisting fate was the motto of a Daddy's Girl, but it had always been hard for me. Even now, when I had no other option, I didn't like it.

"I'm going to soak in a hot tub," I said, flexing the shoulder that bore the shadowy pain of Hamilton the Fifth's grip.

"Put some of those salts in the water. Aromatherapy. Hell, your great-great-grandmother Alice knew about all of that back before the War Between the States. Nothing is new; it's all recycles." Her eyebrows lifted.

"If you're desperate, there's that hooch down in the cellar."

I'd forgotten about the moonshine. The trouble with hooch was that it could be really good, or it could contain lead and other poisons that could cause blindness or insanity. Lots of bootleggers ran the stuff through old car radiators or fermented it with cow manure. Of course, Sunflower County boasted some of the finest 'shine makers in the world, the producers of pure, clean, sippin' whiskey. If the bottle was in the Dahlia House cellar, it followed that it was good stuff.

I picked up the flashlight and trotted down the steps. This was one of those days when a little drink was necessary. In the kitchen, I poured a glass. It was clear as spring water and when I took a sip, I felt it running down my throat like liquid fire. It hit bottom with a satisfying roar. Take that, you womb, I said to myself as I topped off the glass and headed up the stairs to the big old bathtub that I intended to fill with enough hot water to swim.

I woke from a troubled sleep to find the sun bright in my bedroom window. It was Friday, November 28. Twenty-six shopping days till Christmas, I thought inanely.

I wanted to burrow back under the pillows, but the fragments of my dreams were like pinpricks. I didn't have full recollection, but the overall atmosphere of the dream had been darker than a bat's butt in hell. It had taken place in the fields beside Knob Hill, the big old creepy house just a black silhouette. I was on the porch, and then Hamilton the Fifth appeared. In the dream he was dressed in a black suit, formal, and his angry green eyes blazed in a mostly monochromatic dreamscape.

Out in the night sky, the red, burning tip of a cigarette wrote the name Veronica in smoke. And then I was in the cotton field, hiding, afraid. A clutch of doves fluttered out of the husk-dry cotton with that terrible whir of wings that sounded like a whispered plea for mercy. And suddenly I was with the doves, one of them. Some of us would die. We knew it and we hung low to the ground for safety.

My tiny bird heart pumped, too full of blood. The huge effort of flying and hugging the brown earth, the panting terror of the boom of the shotgun and the spray of pellets that seemed impossible to avoid made me feel as if my chest would burst. Beside me a dove faltered and fell, mortally wounded. I flew harder, faster, toward consciousness and away from the horror of the dream.

I woke up with my hand on my heart, my forehead sweaty, and the sheets tangled around my legs. It took me a few moments to understand that I was safe in Dahlia House and that the only damage I'd suffered was the dark purple imprint of Hamilton the Fifth's fingers in my shoulder.

Carl Jung considered each person in the dream to be an aspect of the dreamer. According to Jung, I was me, Hamilton the Fifth, *and* the birds. But I hadn't really bought into that theory of dream analysis. I also knew someone who would have her own opinion of what my night terrors meant. After I'd visited the sheriff, the coroner, and Billie Roberts's auto shop, I'd make one more stop, to see Madame Tomeeka. Oh, yeah, and a side trip to Cece to make sure she covered my lie to Hamilton the Fifth, if he bothered to call and check out my story of being a reporter for the *Dispatch.*

10

The house was strangely empty as I pulled on thick socks and long johns under my gown. Dahlia House was bitterly cold. I stopped in the parlor on my way to the kitchen and pushed back the heavy drapes. The land rolled away from the house in a blanket of white frost. Ice crystals in the sycamore branches and in the tall stubble of the cotton fields glittered as if they'd been coated with fairy dust during the night. My love for Dahlia House lodged in my throat, a physical pain. I could not lose this land. I could not.

Harold's engagement ring came to mind, and I felt a lessening of the dreadful anxiety that swamped me. I could marry him, and I would, if I had to. A great bitterness against my ancestors rose up in me. I'd been bred and trained to live in Dahlia House, to manage the land. After my parents and Aunt LouLane died, I'd been told that Dahlia House was in a precarious financial position, but I hadn't grasped the situation. I'd gone on to college as if Prince Charming would ride over the next hill and sweep me into his multiportfolioed arms. I had expected that love and marriage would rescue me—after a successful stage career.

I had *not* learned to yield those parts of me that had made marriage an agreeable deal for my peers. Marriage, I'd learned by watching my friends, was just another job, and one that often cut deeply into a woman's independence and self-esteem. In the world of Daddy's Girls, woman made life comfortable for man by subjugating herself to his every whim, and man brought home the woolly mammoth of blue-chip stocks. Though I didn't like the system, I could not deny that in more cases than not, it worked. Bliss, or even ordinary happiness, was not guaranteed in any marriage. The Daddy's Girls were not blissful, but nor were they hollow-eyed with anxiety over finances. They had fulfilled their expectations.

Catching the male was an entire course of study for Delta girls, and Ole Miss was the preferred hunting ground. My four years there had been wasted. I should have bagged a man, or at the very least a business or engineering or medical degree. Had I really understood that I, Sarah Booth Delaney, could be parted from my home, I would have learned a profession or trade. I would have learned how to make money so that I didn't have to try and take someone else's, whether by theft or marriage.

What I had done was take my drama minor and my independence to New York, where'd I'd spent an interesting decade of failure and frustration, for Broadway took no notice of the last of the Delaneys, no matter how hard I tried.

But that was the past, and I had to work with what I had. Even though Tinkie's assignment was giving me some major anxiety and bad-ass dreams, it was something I had a flair for. I could make this work for me, and for my clients. If I discovered the truth of the Garrett family, I could redeem myself for stealing Tinkie's dog. I could return Harold's ring with a tender rejection. In other words, I could afford to be a lady.

I shuffled into the kitchen and put on coffee. The old percolator spurted and sizzled, and in a moment the robust aroma made the kitchen seem warmer. The view out the window was of the cemetery. There were over a hundred graves there. All Delaneys, their spouses, and their children. My parents were there, and Aunt Lou-Lane. And all fifty-seven of her cats.

There was a place for me. And enough room for my husband and children. The Delaneys had been great planners, and when the cemetery had been laid out, people still had large families so they'd allocated plenty of space.

The coffeepot gave its last gurgle. I poured a cup and raced back upstairs to find some clothes. I pulled on jeans, a sweater, and some hiking boots, and then glanced in the mirror. My dark hair was standing on end. When I brushed it, sparks crackled in the cold air, so I settled for a ponytail. I looked like a young girl, and I thought that might work in my favor. On the way out, I stuffed some hundred-dollar bills from Tinkie's ransom into my pocket.

My first stop was the bakery, where I snagged a cheese Danish and more hot coffee. My second call was Cece. She was submerged in an avalanche of paper, and she accepted the treats with a tight smile. I extracted her promise not to blow my cover, before I told her about the small lie to the heir of Knob Hill.

As soon as the words Hamilton the Fifth were out of my mouth, I realized my own plight was not of the least interest to her. She pushed the papers onto the floor and began patting down her desk in an attempt to locate the telephone. She found it under another stack of papers and waved me out of her office, signaling that I was to close the door.

Well, I thought, walking out of the newspaper building, it served Hamilton the Fifth right that I'd tattled on him. If he hadn't been such a rude bastard, I would have kept my mouth shut. Now, between Millie and Cece, he would be too busy to worry about me.

I decided that Delo Wiley, discoverer of Hamilton the Fourth's corpse, would be my next stop. The way I figured it, the men involved in covering up the murder of Guy Garrett, if there was a murder, all knew each other. The man who appeared to have the least power was Delo, a hardscrabble farmer who leased his cornfields to the dove hunters once he'd harvested his crop. Delo wasn't one of the dove-hunting set. Neither was he an elected official, which was another of the male cliques in Zinnia. He was sort of an outsider, and the most likely to talk, in my evaluation.

He lived to the east of town, and I cruised along the blacktop watching the sun burn away the frost. It was a beautiful day with a deep blue sky and golden light. Delo's house was not far from town. His driveway cut through fields of corn stubble, and when I parked and got out, I heard the sound of an ax. He was in his backyard in a stand of cedars, splitting oak logs.

"Morning, Mr. Wiley," I said as I approached, dodging three holes that looked freshly dug.

He swung the ax into the tree stump he was using as a block, and wiped his forehead on his shirtsleeve.

He was an old man. I hadn't expected this. I'd seen him around town and I remembered him as always busy. But the last time I'd seen him, his hair had been salt-and-pepper and his eyes a clear, no-nonsense brown. Today he was stooped, and his plaid jacket hung on his shoulders. Thick glasses magnified his eyes and made them seem weak. His brown gaze moved up and down me and then dropped to the ground, traveling to the pile of wood that remained to be split.

"What can I do for you, Sarah Booth?" He kept looking at the woodpile.

I was surprised that he knew me, though I shouldn't have been. "I'm writing a book," I said. "A novel. So it's fiction, but I got to thinking back about things that had happened in Sunflower County, and I remembered there was one real interesting story." I waited for him to take the bait.

"Lots of interesting stories around these parts," he said, bending to reach for a log. No bite on my line. I was not deterred.

"I know the whole Hamilton Garrett shooting was an accident, but I was thinking it would make a great book if I made it out to be a murder. You know, fictionalized the events using different names and setting it somewhere other than Sunflower County. Maybe a made-up county like Yoknapatawpha." He gave me a bland look.

"Folks always like to read about murder," he said.

Delo was going to be difficult. He was one of the COR's, Cagey Old Rednecks. Verbal effusiveness would never be one of his sins.

"You were the one who found Mr. Hamilton the Fourth when he was accidentally shot, right?"

"You wouldn't be here if you didn't know that answer."

"Books need realistic detail. I thought I'd get some of the facts from you."

Delo twisted the ax free from the stump. He hefted it high and brought it down on a log. He had surprising strength for a man who looked so old. The log split, and one half of it flew directly at me. I sidestepped just in time, or it would have damaged my knee.

"Sorry about that," he said in a tone that clearly said he wasn't. He bent for another log to split. "Seems to me if you're writing fiction you could just make the whole thing up. What do you care about the facts?"

I had thought of this. "I don't want to accidentally make it sound too much like what really happened and wind up getting sued. That woman who writes about Kay Scarpetta. She got sued by a family who said she put their tragedy in one of her novels." My smile was tight as I recalled Jitty's hell-raising about the issues of *The National Enquirer* I brought home from The Pig. Trash they might be, but they'd paid off. I had the low-down on every celebrity at my fingertips.

Delo brought the ax down on another stump and kindling flew. "It's been my experience with life that few mistakes are innocent."

Now that was a conversation stopper. I picked up the piece of kindling and chunked it onto the pile. Just to let him know I wasn't going to be run off easily, I took a seat on one of the bigger logs. "See, the way I've got it pictured in my head was Mr. Garrett the Fourth had on one of those camouflage vests with all the pockets loaded down with shells. It was a crisp evening, one of those sunsets too pretty to believe. Mr. Garrett was waiting for that last clutch of doves to fly up into that beautiful sky, but he was tired, so he kind of knelt down, and then, unexpectedly, he stood. The other hunters hadn't seen him because he was kneeling, and when he stood he caught the shot in his throat. Is that about right?"

Delo had stopped chopping wood. He was leaning on the ax handle looking at me, and his eyes didn't look weak any longer.

"What is it you really want?" he asked.

"The truth," I said slowly.

"How old are you, Sarah Booth?"

I didn't see where that was any of his concern, but I also didn't see where it would hurt to answer. "Thirty-three."

"Long past the prime age to get a man."

His words were unexpected. They were not wounding, but unsettling. But then I should have anticipated that if I pressed him on his turf, he'd take the fight to mine. Psychology 211.

I decided to up the ante. "If a man was what I wanted, I'd have one. I want something more." I gave the pause three beats. "I want fame, Mr. Wiley. Fame and enough money so that I'll never have to worry again."

Something sparked in his eyes, and I knew we'd finally found our common language.

"It could be dangerous to dig too deeply into the past," he said carefully. "And expensive."

This was a new snag. He was asking for money, but I didn't know how much to offer. Usually, folks around Zinnia were more than willing to talk about somebody else's business for the sheer pleasure of it. Naturally, he would have to be different. But how much to offer?

My first thought was one hundred, but I pulled two bills out of my pocket and folded them down the middle into a long trough. I tapped them against my knee. "How *was* Hamilton the Fourth shot?" I asked.

He took the money, tucking it into his shirt pocket. "Looked to me like he was sittin' on the ground. Lots of possibilities there. It's not a good idea to put inexperienced people out in a field with guns. Anyway, I heard the official sheriff's report ruled it an accident."

"Tell me about that day," I said, hoping his story would clue me in as to other questions to ask.

"It was Isaac Carter who set up the hunt. He called and wanted the Mule Bog field, which is down in the lower acreage and borders the river. It's the best hunting land because there's a lot of natural growth there, but the ground is boggy. It's hard walking."

"How many men?"

He thought a minute. "Maybe eight. It was Carter, Camden Wells, Lyle Bedford, Asa Grant, Myles Lee, Hamilton the Fourth, and a couple of men I didn't know. Investors from out of state, according to Carter."

Delo had just listed the top players for the Buddy Club. They were the movers and shakers of the Delta, the men who controlled the money and who had married the Daddy's Girls of my mother's generation. They were blooded, the inheritors of the earth and all of its bounty. Unlike Harold, who had acquired wealth by his wits and hard work, the Buddy Clubbers were born to it.

It made sense that they were all out together blasting the symbol of peace into tufts of feathers. They were powerful men, and they never tired of showing it by their possessions, their ability to ignore the rules, and their easy laughter.

"I was surprised when Mr. Garrett showed up," Delo continued. Now that the money had loosened his tongue, I didn't have to prod at all. "He'd never hunted with them before. And he didn't look too happy that day." His jaw shifted to the right. "Here's a fact for you. His gun had been fired once. It was right beside him in the field."

"Was it the gun that killed him?"

"No one ever said for sure."

I turned back to the day of the hunt. "The men got there in the morning?"

"It was after lunch. I offered to set them up, but Carter said he knew the field. So they went off together and I stayed up here to tend to my business. I had several other groups in different fields." Before I could ask, he answered. "None close enough to see what happened. And let me say that no matter what Fel Harper or his official coroner's report tell you, Mr. Garrett had been dead awhile before I found him."

"Did anyone call a doctor?"

"What for? He was dead."

One good reason would be that in Mississippi, coroners are elected and can be as dumb as dirt. Fel Harper had never won any IQ contests. Trusting him on the time of death would be asinine, or possibly a deliberate attempt to hide the truth.

"So the other men came in . . ."

"It was getting dark, and I was about to get in the four-wheeler and go round them up when they came in the yard. None of them seemed to have noticed that Mr. Garrett wasn't with them. When I pointed out he was missing, they all shrugged and said they thought he'd come back a long time ago. So I got in the four-wheeler and went out to find him. I called for a while, and when he didn't answer, I began to think that something bad had happened. Sure enough, I was cutting around a stump that had a lot of scrub growth around it and there he was. He was lying on his side, sort of. It was a mess."

"What happened then?"

"I rode back to the house and told the others. Then I called the sheriff and the coroner."

"How did the men react?"

"Carter volunteered to go and tell Mr. Garrett's wife,

and they decided that's what should be done. The rest just milled around until the sheriff came, and then they all went back out to the field in the hearse."

"Did you go?"

Delo's dark eyes narrowed. "I wasn't asked, and I didn't volunteer. It looked to me like a bad day's work had been done. The smartest thing for me was to feed my dogs, collect the money from the other hunters, and stay put at the house."

"You did tell the sheriff, though?"

"Pasco Walters didn't ask me a single question, and I didn't volunteer any information." He picked up his ax. "One thing a girl like you never had to learn was that you don't offer suggestions to your betters." His voice had grown angry. "Now move on. You've gotten everything you paid for."

"If you have any other thoughts on this, I'd like to hear them," I said, standing up.

"I'll give you some advice, Sarah Booth. You ask the wrong question of the right person, and you might find more trouble than you ever dreamed possible."

Fel Harper was a big man and a popular one. Along with pronouncing all the dead folks dead, he fried catfish and grilled steaks for various parties and functions. For as long as I could remember, a political rally wasn't much to speak of unless Fel had his portable cook station there and was serving up the grub. He was a gregarious man who seemed to defy his elected capacity as coroner. For all of his six-foot-five frame and three-hundred-plus weight, he moved quickly as he pulled out a chair for me in the small office at the stockyards, where he worked a day job.

"Sarah Booth Delaney," he said, putting big hands

on my shoulders and holding me at arm's length while he took my measure. "I remember the day you and Roger Crane snuck off from school and rode your bicycles to Leatherberry Creek. Whewee! Your folks were torn up. They thought you'd been kidnapped, or somethin' worse." He laughed loudly.

This wasn't a good memory for me. I had been twelve, and Roger Crane had been three years older. He'd persuaded me to skip school and go swimming with him. It was my first lesson in deception, his, mine, and ours.

I focused on Fel's face. Even though he had to be sixty, his cheeks were smooth as a baby's butt. There wasn't a wrinkle or a sign of beard stubble, and I wondered if somewhere he'd had chemotherapy, because his head was bald and shiny as Mr. Clean's.

"You need me to cook for some 'do' you're planning up at Dahlia House?" he asked as he pressed me down into a chair. "Miz Kincaid has me booked for her charity function. She's doin' up her house in hay bales and gingham to make it look like the country. That's the theme. Fried catfish is the menu, to highlight the fact that Mississippi is the number-one producer of catfish in the nation. You know Miz Kincaid always likes to point out the good things about our great state. She's a charmin' little thing, isn't she?"

"Absolutely," I said.

"Now what's on your mind?"

"History," I answered sweetly.

"An antebellum theme!" he enthused. "I love those Old South parties. I make the best bourbon-soaked ham. Put out some home-baked biscuits and greens, and you got a party."

My stomach growled long and deep. "I'm not planning a party, but I'll keep your menu in mind." I took a breath. "I'm writing a book." This had become the most serviceable lie in the history of whoppers.

"You always were a little peculiar, Sarah Booth. I thought New York had cured you of such foolishness. Book writin' and actin' are career cousins. You know, folks around here thought you'd gone off to have a love child or been put in an institution. No one really believed you'd gone to be an actress. So what kind of book are you writing anyway?"

"A murder mystery," I said, leaning forward and making my eyes as big as possible. "It's about a man who gets murdered in a dove field by his wife's lover." His gaze shifted to the door. "Then just when it looks like the perfect crime has been committed, wham! the wife meets an untimely death—an accident. Something involving an automobile. What do you think?" In the silence that followed I heard a calf bawling.

"I'm not much of a mystery reader," Fel said finally. "Sounds more like something for a made-for-TV movie. Seems I saw something that went that way last year."

"As county coroner, you'd know about every death that occurred here, wouldn't you?" I pressed.

"I don't remember every case that comes along," he said. "Fact is, I try to forget as much as possible."

"You'd remember the Garrett deaths, wouldn't you?"

"Old man Garrett got shot in a dove field. I remember." Fel shifted in his seat.

The calf bawled again, this time with pain. One thing I wouldn't forget was the brutal nature of Fel's surroundings.

"Are you sure Hamilton Garrett the Fourth's death was an accident?"

He leaned back in his chair, ignoring the groaning of the springs. His small eyes assessed me.

"Mr. Garrett was sitting on the ground when he was shot," he said. "He was carrying a Remington pump and it had been fired once, the spent casing still in the chamber. The gun was on the ground beside him, pointing right at him. There were dog tracks all around. Isaac Carter was working a couple of retrievers, and I figured it was those dogs that had been there." He sat forward. "Mr. Garrett wasn't a huntin' man. Pasco Walters and I assessed the situation and figured that Mr. Garrett sat down and rested his gun on a stump. One of the dogs, all excited like dogs get, knocked it. When he reached for it, he wasn't careful. One little touch on the trigger . . . Now that's one way of lookin' at it. The best way."

Best for whom? "Another way would be that someone sneaked up on him, grabbed his gun, and shot him."

His eyes became hard and his mouth tightened. "You tell me which one of those seven men you want to accuse of murder. Especially when the widow is claiming accidental death. Keep in mind that no one wanted a ruling of suicide, which is more likely than murder."

Fel had a point. "What about Mrs. Garrett? Veronica was killed only a few months later."

Fel nodded and his eyes went to the doorway once again. "Car wreck. She was a beautiful woman before she went through the windshield. Awful accident."

"Another accident, right?"

Fel's eyebrows lifted. "That woman died from injuries she got in the wreck. She went through the windshield face-first. That was all I could say; all I ever said."

"Rumor has it that her brake lines were cut."

He gave me a black look. "I'm the coroner, not an auto mechanic." He was across the room fast, his finger pointing out the door and down the hall. "Get out of here. I can't be wastin' my time with foolishness like this."

I let him escort me to the door. "Where can I find Pasco Walters?"

He smiled. "Try Cedar Lawn Cemetery." He slammed the door in my face.

Damn! Cedar Lawn Cemetery. So Pasco Walters, former sheriff of Sunflower County, was dead. There were certainly a lot of dead folks involved in this case. It struck me that perhaps the sheriff was also the victim of foul play.

Unbidden, Hamilton the Fifth's handsome face came back to me and I felt as if Mr. Jack Frost himself had whispered icy kisses along my spine. Was he capable of murder? Of murdering his own mother? It was something I had to find out, and I realized that it wasn't only for Tinkie's money.

11

The Sunflower County Courthouse is centered on a square of land bordered by chestnut trees. A statue of Johnny Reb guards the front entrance, and there is a memorial plaque to the men of our country who died in the War Between the States. I have never passed the statue of the bedraggled and poorly clothed soldier without thinking long and hard about the psychology of war. I always end up angry. My personal theory is that women would refuse to participate in such foolishness. Certainly the Daddy's Girls, who would find the hardships and lack of adequate hygiene enough to put an end to the fighting after the first three hours. It's not that Daddy's Girls don't want their way on global issues, it's just that they prefer less messy tactics.

Inside the courthouse, the smell of old dust is pervasive and comforting. As a child, I came here with my father to attend to tax business or courtroom work. I hid in the nooks and crannies of the old building, spying and eavesdropping on anyone who passed. During some of the more interesting cases, I would sit in the judge's chamber with the door cracked and listen to the trial, judging my father's mood by the power with which his gavel cracked down. Daddy never denied me the freedom to listen to the criminal trials, though Mama did her best to discourage it. She felt exposure to the baser human acts would warp me. Perhaps she was right.

Walking into the rotunda, I realized that I took the operation of the county for granted. I'd never thought to consider where a death certificate might be filed, or where the coroner's reports would be. So I headed down to the sheriff's office, where Coleman Peters currently held office.

Coleman was two years older than me, a boy whose father sharecropped on the Bellcase plantation. I remembered him as a linebacker on the Sunflower High football team, a big boy who did his duty without flinching.

"Why, Sarah Booth Delaney," Coleman said, rising to his feet from behind a desk. "What in the world could we possibly do to help you?"

It is true that up until recent years, people of a certain social status took care of their problems without interference from the law. Cops were hired for the middle class. The highest and lowest rungs of society were basically left to their own devices.

"Coleman Peters," I said, surprising myself at the pleasure I felt in seeing an old friend. "Imagine you as the chief law enforcement officer in this county. I remember when you used to kick butt on the gridiron."

"I'm still kicking butt," he said, grinning wider. "You're not being stalked or anything, are you?"

I considered fabricating a tale to meet his expectations, but then I realized that Harold might get caught in the snare. That would not be a good thing. "I'm writing a book," I answered, watching the interest fade from his eyes. "I need to see some of the old county records."

"What kind of book?"

"Fiction. A murder mystery." I could see that Coleman didn't differentiate between fact and fiction. If it was written down, it was liable to be dangerous. "I'm interested in 1979."

"If it's a murder, the best records may be down in the circuit clerk's. That's where the *trial* notes are."

Score one for Coleman. "Wouldn't the notes from a crime scene be here?" There had never been a trial in this case, but I didn't want to get into that technicality.

"In the back. Things are kind of a mess, but you're welcome to look." He twisted his gun belt. "Me and Carlene are getting a divorce."

"I'm sorry to hear that," I said, surprised at the revelation. It would normally take a dental instrument to extract a detail like this from a man like him. I remembered Carlene as one of the bouncy little cheerleaders. She had a big mouth, a big butt, and big bosoms. She was chronically "cute."

"Is it true you never married?" he asked.

This was not good. This was definitely not good. Coleman was getting personal. "Marriage just isn't the road for me."

"You like men, don'tcha?"

I closed my eyes. "About half the time." Before he could sort through it, I hurried into the back. Things *were* a mess, but I found the jail docket and other records in chronological order, and I started plundering.

Pasco Walters's initial report was neither hard to find nor very informative. The facts, as recorded, matched what Fel and Delo had told me. Tucked in the file was Fel Harper's report, which pronounced the time of death to be 5:10 P.M. on the evening of October twenty-third. I noted that Fel had listed the time of death as the time the body had been found. According to Delo, Guy Garrett had been stiff by then.

There were several black-and-white photographs of the crime scene. One showed a body covered with an old spread, and beside it a tall, lanky lawman who had to be Pasco Walters. I examined his face and remembered him from trips to the courthouse with my father. I had thought him very handsome, and I remembered how he tugged my braids and teased me.

This photo showed none of his humor. He was tense and serious, actually very authoritative looking. I would have voted for him for sheriff.

I read through a few more reports, enjoying the sensation of being alone and privy to the sordid details of the past. I was about to move on to Veronica's file when a shadow fell across my notebook. I turned to confront a tall, slender man in a deputy's uniform.

"You find what you need?" he asked, his face in shadow.

I closed the notebook. "Some of it." He stepped closer and I saw he was staring at me in a way that was deliberately meant to intimidate.

"Looking for anything in particular?" he asked.

"I'm writing a book," I said, feeling the need to rise to my feet. When I was standing, he was still a good six inches taller than I was. He lacked the broad-shouldered physique of Hamilton the Fifth, but he had an edginess that was compelling. He blocked the exit, his hand resting on the butt of his gun like some *High Noon* marshal.

"I heard you're interested in the past," he said.

"Like I said, I'm writing a book." I closed Hamilton's folder, hoping he hadn't seen much. My gut instinct was telling me not to reveal what I was hunting for, and to get out of there as quickly as I could. I would have to come back another time to probe the death of the last Mrs. Hamilton Garrett.

"Folks are touchy about the past," he said quietly. He took a step closer so that the minimal light glinted in his eyes. He looked down at the records I'd been examining. "1979. That would be about the time Hamilton Garrett the Fourth was shot."

I considered calling out for Coleman, but that would show I was frightened. There are certain types of men who take great pleasure in frightening women. I suspected that the deputy blocking my path might be one of them. "Excuse me," I said, starting to brush past him.

His hand found the exact same place where Hamilton Garrett the Fifth had gripped me. He leaned down so that he whispered in my ear. "It might be wise to postpone this little writing project for a while."

I twisted free of him with minimum effort. "Who do you think you are?" It was spoken like a true Daddy's Girl.

"Deputy Gordon Walters. Pasco's son."

His hand was no longer on me but his eyes held me. He had the eyes of a hunter. "Law enforcement seems to run in the family," I said.

His chest moved up and down slowly. "Take a word of warning and stay away from Knob Hill and everyone associated with it," he said. "The only thing you'll find in the past is ghosts."

By the time I pulled up under the big oak tree at Tammy Odom's house, I was armed to the teeth with facts and even more opinions. The "investigation" of Hamilton Garrett the Fourth's death was sloppy. There was no public record of the men who'd allegedly been hunting with Guy Garrett on that day. I had only the list of

Buddy Clubbers that Delo had given me. A bit more digging via a phone call to Cece had turned up that Pasco Walters had died in the Mississippi River in 1980. He'd run his cruiser off the side of a bridge and drowned. I'd stopped by Billie's Garage but found it closed.

As I got out of the car, I saw Tammy sitting in the shadows on the porch. It was late afternoon, and she was rocking slowly.

"Claire said you'd probably be by to see me," she said, rising. "Come on in. I put on coffee about five minutes ago."

"Dahlia is beautiful," I said, following her inside. "And Claire, too. She's a good mother."

"Yes, and smart, too. I miss her."

I wasn't certain what to say. Tammy had forced Claire from her house, had sent her packing to Mound Bayou. "What about school?" I finally asked.

"She's doing good. I think she'll get that scholarship to Ole Miss." Tammy turned and smiled at me. "Times have changed since I was a girl."

They had indeed. And in this instance, for the better. "What about the baby?"

"She can come here, stay with me while Claire gets her degree." Tammy shook her head. "When Claire was born, I was so frightened, I didn't get a chance to enjoy her."

Now seemed as good a time as any to ask. "Tammy, who is Claire's father?"

"Why are you asking now, after seventeen years?" She put cream and sugar on the table. Her movements were casual.

"Claire thinks it might be Hamilton Garrett the Fifth." I watched her face closely, but she gave nothing away. She'd learned to guard her expressions in the game of fortune-telling, and she was a top-notch performer.

"He's home, isn't he?" she asked, eyes suddenly alert. "I knew he'd come back."

I nodded, amazed at the wistfulness in her voice. "I ran into him at Knob Hill. He's a very intense man."

She motioned to a chair at the kitchen table and poured us both coffee. She took her seat before she spoke again. "Did you know that the summer I turned sixteen I worked at Knob Hill, mostly in the kitchen and laundry?" She shook her head. "I hung miles and miles of cotton sheets to dry."

"I had no idea."

"School got out, and you went about your life for the summer. You were taking tennis lessons and planning a trip to Florida. When I was making beds and chopping onions, I thought about you on the beach. I saw you in a red bikini with white laces on the top and bottom. I took the job at Knob Hill because I needed to earn money for clothes."

The fact that I *had* worn a red lace-up bikini on the beach that summer aside, I was stunned. "So Hamilton is the father." As I spoke his name I could almost feel his hand on my shoulder. And I felt something else, too. Disappointment. "He never attempted to help you with child support?"

"He never knew." She reached across the table and touched my hand. Her fingers were dry, and they whispered on my skin. "He isn't Claire's father." She waited until I met her gaze. "Stay away from Knob Hill, Sarah. There are things at work there that you can't possibly stop."

Her words, such an echo of Deputy Walters's, sent a battalion of chill bumps marching up my not-so-staunch spine. "I need the money," I said.

"Money can't buy back your soul."

"If I lose Dahlia House, I'll lose a part of my soul. Maybe the best part." I saw her give up. It was the first emotion I could clearly read on her face. "You worked at Knob Hill the summer before Hamilton Garrett the Fourth was shot. What was it like there?"

Tammy stared down into her coffee cup. "Young Hamilton was sixteen, and I was in love with him." She smiled at whatever she saw in the cup. "I picked up his clothes and did his laundry. He liked lemon meringue pies and he said I made the very best he'd ever tasted. He was nice to me. He'd give me books from the library and talk to me about college."

The tears in her eyes were a surprise. So was her description of the dark master of Knob Hill. "Kind" would not have been the word I chose for Hamilton the Fifth. "What about Sylvia?"

"She was away most of the summer. Mrs. Garrett had sent her to Switzerland because she didn't want her home. No one ever talked about her. It was sad, like there was something wrong with her and they all pretended she didn't exist."

"And Mrs. Garrett?"

"She was a beautiful woman. She'd sit out by the pool and drink gin rickeys in a pewter cup with her name inscribed on it. Then she'd swim laps and get out, all sleek and wet, and drink more. Her friends would come over and they'd laugh together. They had beautiful teeth and dark sunglasses and big hats, and they laughed all summer." She rested her hands on the table. "She had all these fancy bottles, and I hated dusting them. I was afraid I'd break one."

"Did she have a boyfriend?"

Tammy looked up at me. "I couldn't say. There were always men there. All the time."

"And Mr. Garrett, what was he like?"

"He was at work a lot. I'd see him, sometimes, in the upstairs window looking down at his wife. I think no matter what she did, he would always have loved her."

I'd come to the conclusion that if Hamilton the Fourth had been murdered, it was the lover who pulled the trigger. My take on Veronica was that she was too smart to do the deed herself.

"What men were around?" I pressed, thinking maybe a naive young girl wouldn't notice flirtations. I wanted names.

"The husbands of her friends, businessmen, Hamilton's friends, hired help. That was a house full of men."

"Did Mrs. Garrett pay any of them special attention?"

Tammy's eyes darted away. "She wasn't stupid. She wasn't careless in front of the help."

I leaned forward. "Tammy, do you think Veronica Garrett had her husband killed?"

For a split second fear seemed to spark in her eyes. "All that summer I dreamed of doves. I dreamed that I was flying with them. And then the hunters started shooting, and all around me the other doves began to fall to the earth, wounded."

I couldn't believe what she was saying. I tried to speak, but it seemed my throat was frozen, the words blocked. Tammy wasn't looking at me. She was staring into her coffee cup and talking.

"I was afraid to go to sleep at night because I didn't want to have the dream. So I told my granny about it." Tammy nodded. "You know what she said? She said, 'Blood soaketh the earth, and in the proper season the bones will rise.'"

I reached across the table to grab her arm, to stop her from talking. My hand swept the half-filled mug to the floor. The blue cup shattered and the black liquid spread on the yellow linoleum, and for a moment I could only stare at it.

Tammy made no effort to move. She looked at me, waiting. "You've had that dream, haven't you?" she asked. She bent down and picked up a fragment of the cup and held it so that the light from the window struck it. It was a hand-cast mug and on the surface three birds had been etched, the outline of their bodies gathering the blue glaze.

"What does it mean?" I finally asked.

"I don't know," she said. "Just promise me that you'll leave this alone. I'm afraid for you. And for Claire. Is Tinkie Bellcase really worth this risk?"

12

Jitty tapped her fingernail on the crystal decanter that rested on the porch railing. Her long nails were a pale, opalescent pink that matched her frosted lipstick and the paisley pattern of the skintight hip-huggers she wore. "That stuff's gone rot your guts out."

I lifted the glass in a silent toast. Jitty was upset that I was drinking hooch in public. It would be okay in the bedroom, but on the porch a lady only sipped sherry.

"You've been around. You know secrets," I said, aware that my pronunciation had begun to slip a little. I had been drinking, feet propped on the porch rail, for over an hour. I was cold, and too stubborn to go inside. "What do you know about the Garretts? Surely you've heard something."

Jitty traded in her disapproving face for one that held a bit of slyness. "I know you're thinking about Hamilton the Fifth more than you should."

"He's my case," I pointed out, aiming my glass at her for emphasis. "If I don't think about him I won't be able to help Tinkie."

"You can fool other folks, but you can't fool me. I know when that Delaney blood is pumpin' strong. That man's got you stirred up." She grinned. "You thinkin' about how dark and brooding he is, how his fingers dug into you and made you mad and at the same time brought you to life." She nodded. "He's a vital man. His blood's strummin' like a river at flood stage, and it makes you want to jump in and swim."

Instead of denying it, I sipped the moonshine.

"What about Mr. Diamond Man?" Jitty asked cagily.

That was a good question.

Jitty stood up and walked to the edge of the porch. The sycamores closest to the house were bone white in the illumination that reached from the porch like delicate fingers. Beyond them was a rich blackness, a sense of solitude and peace. All around me, as far as my voice could carry, was Dahlia land.

A valiant cricket rubbed his little legs together in an effort to stay warm, and his song was sadly reminiscent of the summers past. I had spent many a sweet June night down by Salem Creek listening to the night-song with a man I fancied and the unspoken birthright of a known future. I would live at Dahlia. I could pursue my dramatic career because Dahlia was always there for me. Like all of the other Daddy's Girls, I would marry a man with financial security. But I would be just a little different. I would also love my husband with a wild abandon that never seemed part of the matrimonial bargain for my friends.

A sudden longing took hold of me, and I couldn't help my thoughts from going to Hamilton Garrett the Fifth. What would it be like to have him sipping moonshine beside me? To feel him move up to stand behind me in the stillness of the Delta night? I shivered.

"You thinkin' crazy," Jitty said without turning to face me. "Next thing I know, you'll be hoppin' in the sack with young master from the big, big house." Her voice grew sharp. "That's your client's interest—the man she's payin' you twenty thousand to check out *for her*. First you steal her dog, and now you're after her man. Hurrump!"

"Thinking and doing are two different things," I said. And they were.

She turned to face me and for the first time she looked old, her voice tired. "You're displayin' the full range of Delaney aberrations. Keep it up and you'll end up at the emergency room with a tilted womb and a frontal lobotomy."

No point denying it. I had a wealthy, successful man wanting to marry me and a handsome, reputed mother-killer on my mind. "I think I'll go inside and type up a report for Tinkie." It would give me something to do, and also help clarify my thoughts. I had only two real leads left—Billie's Garage and a talk with some of the Buddy Clubbers to see what they remembered about the day Guy Garrett was shot. I did not relish confronting powerful old men about a possible murder.

"Sarah Booth, what are you gonna do if you find out Hamilton did kill his mama?" This time Jitty's question was pensive. She wasn't simply needling me. She was worried that at the advanced age of thirty-three I might sustain a serious heartbreak that would steal the last good years I had left.

"I don't know."

"I'm ready for the next generation. Time's passin' by." Her sigh was the sound of the old house settling into the cold night. "I remember when you were born. Your mama was never so happy. And your daddy, he went all over town giving out cigars and buying drinks. Times were good then."

I'd heard the stories. I had been the long-awaited princess. Perhaps I could not settle for a facsimile of love now, because I understood what the real thing felt like. To be truly loved. With that in mind I answered Jitty with honesty.

"I used to daydream about being married. I had it all planned out, how it would be, how I would feel. The trouble is that every man I meet leaves me feeling . . . empty."

"Except Hamilton the Fifth," Jitty interjected.

It was true. Hamilton Garrett the Fifth had made me feel many things. Empty was not one of them. And that frightened me.

"Be careful, Sarah Booth. Emotion and marriage have nothing to do with one another. Your daddy loved your mama, but that was a rare thing."

James Franklin Delaney and Elizabeth Marie Booth had set the Delta on fire with their torrid romance. Heir to the Delaney holding, James Franklin had met Elizabeth Marie at a college dance at Ole Miss. She had been the one signing up volunteers to join the Peace Corps, and had rebuffed his first advances.

In front of his friends, she had pointed out that as a "wealthy planter" he held no interest for her. She intended to go to Borneo and help establish productive farming methods and a 4-H Club.

He had been swept off his feet. A social conscience was born, along with a year-long campaign to get Elizabeth Marie into his bed. "Give a damn" was the slogan Elizabeth lived by, and James set out to prove that he did. He wooed her with roses and dinners and dances. With the zeal of a missionary, she held to her ideals. James could accompany her to the gatherings and protests and political organizations that fired her blood. It was the only place she allowed him to see her.

The only daughter of a banker, my mother had spent her college tuition money on a Volkswagen van and brochures extolling the virtues of giving a damn. Her parents were horrified. Her name was not spoken in her family's Meridian, Mississippi, home, but she made phone calls to and received phone calls from the Kennedy administration.

Her only weakness was blues music, and my father used that to his advantage, proposing to her as they danced to B.B. King's driving electric guitar in The Iron Bedrail, a colored joint in Issaquena, Mississippi. Caught in the pulse of the hot music, she accepted Daddy's proposal. He found a justice of the peace that night, before she could change her mind.

It was only my birth that finally brought my parents to heel. They closed the commune they'd developed at Dahlia House and settled into maturity, of a sort.

"Mother loved Daddy, too," I finally answered. It had not been a one-way street, though it may have started out that way.

"More than life," Jitty answered, and there was grief in the hollow of her voice.

"I wish they were still here."

Jitty came to stand by me and the light filtered through her pink paisley pants, giving the porch a warm tint. "I do, too, Sarah Booth. This old house is empty. You should give Harold's proposal some serious thought. You could go a lot farther and do a lot worse."

"What would Daddy do?" I asked her.

"The most unlikely, wildest thing possible." She smiled. "But your mother would rein him in. Until that night—"

"I know." I interrupted, not wanting to think of the

night they had died. My home held all of my memories, even the tragic ones, and for a moment they seemed overwhelming. "Maybe it would be better if I left. Maybe I should move to California."

Jitty only laughed softly. "Now that's desperation for a Daddy's Girl. Honey, you're not wild enough, tan enough, or blond enough. You go out there and that West Coast wind'll suck the humidity out of you and your lips will crack and fall off."

It was not a pretty picture, and my stint in New York had taught me the hazards of transplantation. Love of my home had brought me back to Dahlia House. Now I wondered if I could live anywhere else. If I left the Delta, would I become a different person? So much of me was this place, these people. My rhythm was joined with that of the Mississippi seasons. To change would shift everything inside of me, as well as outside.

"Jitty?"

When she didn't respond, I looked up to find Harold walking across the lawn toward the porch. I must have smiled, because his serious face showed relief.

"I know I shouldn't press you," he said, hesitating at the steps.

"It's okay." And it was. He was still wearing his banking suit, as if he had no other life to change into. "I'm having a sip of moonshine. Would you like some?" I had been raised with good manners even though I'd been conceived in a commune.

Harold eyed the decanter. Thank goodness I'd poured it from the old bottle or he would have hauled me to the hospital to have my stomach pumped.

"That would be nice," he answered with a hint of a smile.

"It's smooth," I reassured him. "I'll get a glass."

One of my mother's prides was her crystal. Once I

was born, her family had forgiven her "those terrible years of madness" and she'd inherited the Booth family collection of Waterford. I picked up a glass and decided that Harold wouldn't object to drinking it neat.

"Sarah Booth," he said slowly as I poured the liquor and handed it to him, "Avery Bellcase came by my office today."

This was not going to be good news.

"He thinks you're blackmailing Tinkie."

I put my glass on the railing. "Because of the money?"

"Yes. Tinkie won't tell him why she got her mother to write the check. Mrs. Bellcase says she doesn't know."

It was something of a problem, but it was Tinkie's, not mine. "I can't discuss this," I said, wondering if a PI could claim the same privilege as lawyer/client. "Tinkie can tell him if she wants to, but it's her secret."

Harold's smile was something of a surprise. "You have some noble qualities. You protect your friends."

I was protecting my own butt, but it was okay for Harold to put it in the best light. "How long can I go on that money?"

"A month, maybe two. But the avalanche of debt is building."

Harold wouldn't lie about money, even though his interest was vested. He, too, had some noble qualities.

"Gordon Walters came by, too. It's not every day that a deputy sheriff and a bank president ask me about you."

The whiskey caught in my throat and I thought I was going to choke. My nose burned and my eyes watered, but I managed to gasp, "What did Gordon Walters want?"

"It was a very curious conversation." Harold paused.

"He was asking about your financial situation. His implication was that you were doing something illegal. What are you up to, Sarah Booth?"

"Nothing illegal, I can promise you that."

The look he gave me was speculative. "Will you attend a function as my date Sunday evening? A small gathering at my home. It's a business evening, but I'd like to add some pleasure by having you there."

Banking business didn't sound like much fun; on the other hand, Harold put out a magnificent spread. "What's the occasion?"

"An old Sunflower Countian has returned. Did you know Hamilton Garrett the Fifth?"

My mouth went dry. "We've met, briefly."

"He's back in the area, and the Bank of Zinnia would very much like to have his business. It's rumored that he made a large fortune in Europe."

"Doing what?"

Harold lifted an eyebrow. "That's what I intend to ask him. Will you be able to attend?"

I shrugged a shoulder, glad that he wasn't near enough to hear the drumroll of my heart. "I might as well. *Masterpiece Theatre* is a rerun."

Harold studied me carefully. He was not a dull-witted man. "Hamilton and I attended Dorsett Military Academy together."

That was news to me, but he was watching so closely I knew better than to show the slightest interest. "Maybe we should go inside and build a fire." I was freezing, and I needed time to find out everything Harold knew about Hamilton.

Harold stood up, pleased at my unexpected invitation. I was usually shoving him out the door. "That would be lovely," he said. "I'll bring in some wood."

In his fine suit, he walked to the woodpile and began gathering logs. Wood carrying was a man's job. It would never cross Harold's mind that I was capable of it.

In that moment, marriage did not seem impossible.

13

Harold built the fire with the same grace and economy of motion I'd come to expect of him. We settled onto the sofa, drinks in hand, as the blaze caught the dry oak and began to crackle. Though the night was not particularly cold, the warmth of the fire was comforting.

"This is a fine old place," he said, looking into the fire instead of at me. "I've often regretted the loss of my family home. It was nothing like Dahlia House. It was on Birch Lane, a nice old Victorian Gothic with a big yard. I had some pleasant memories there."

His admission caught me by surprise. Harold was not from Sunflower County. He'd grown up in Greenwood, still in the Delta but not part of my world. I knew that his parents were dead, but I knew very little else. His attachment to property that had given "pleasant memories" was unexpected.

"What happened to the house?" I asked. Every Pliant Woman knows that the way to a man's heart is to focus the conversation on him. But this was actually something I wanted to know.

"After my mother died, I sold it. School debts. I

wanted to go to Juilliard." His smile showed amusement at a long-ago dream. "Business school seemed much more practical."

"You've done well." I heard the creak of a floorboard and knew that Jitty, as usual, was eavesdropping. Harold assumed it was simply the sound of an old house standing firm against a north wind.

"There's no sense regretting decisions that are irrevocable," he said. "There are people who spend their entire lives in regret. It's a sad substitute for awareness of the present."

I wondered if his words were directed at me or himself. "You said you went to Dorsett Military Academy. It's difficult to believe you were a discipline problem."

He laughed softly. "I was an inconvenience. But I learned self-reliance at Dorsett. It wasn't a wasted experience."

I had arrived at the tricky patch of road. "You went to school with Hamilton Garrett. Did you know his sister, Sylvia?"

So far, Hamilton's steps had been easy to trace, but Sylvia was elusive, a shadow person.

Harold turned from the fire and looked at me. "Yes, I knew her. Even as a young girl she was striking." He looked at his drink. "We shared an appreciation for art. And music."

Something in his expression made me catch my breath. "I understand she's in Glen Oaks," I said, shaking my head slightly. "What a pity. I believe Hamilton is her only family."

"I thought most people had forgotten she ever existed." He lifted his glass to catch the flames in the intricate pattern of the crystal. "She wanted to be forgotten. It was her stated wish."

"She committed herself voluntarily, didn't she?"

"Her father's death nearly destroyed her. There were problems in the family, but Mr. Garrett's violent end did something to her. Sylvia was always delicate, always so high-strung. I talked to her after her mother's accident. I tried to convince her to seek help outside the institution. She would only say that her life had been one of waiting, first for tragedy and now for the opposite."

This was very dicey. Harold had obviously not forgotten her. "Is she—"

"Insane?"

"Ill?" I supplied in a softer voice.

"Not when I knew her. At least not in the way everyone thought. She had an intensity . . . There was always something between her and her mother. When I knew her she was almost grown, almost ready to have her own life." His voice drifted to a close.

The fire crackled and a log shifted, sending sparks up the old chimney. "I heard she was very beautiful."

He shifted so that he could look directly at me. "She's very different from you, Sarah Booth." His voice grew stronger. "But I didn't come to talk about Delta heritage or intrigue. Or the past." He dropped his gaze to my left hand. "Whatever you decide, the ring is yours to keep."

His change of subject left me momentarily befuddled. I was so deep into my PI mode that I'd forgotten the rules of social conversing. Now it was time for a witty and challenging reply. I fell flat in my mission and mumbled, "That's hardly fair, Harold. It's a very expensive ring."

His light eyes seemed to reflect the restless movement of the fire. "You have some strange ideas," he said. "What is fair in life? Especially in romance?" He lifted my ringless hand and examined it, giving my unmanicured nails a shake of his head. "The diamond would look lovely on you. Your hands, for all that you don't seem to care, are artistic."

By God, the scoundrel had turned the tables. "And I won't keep it unless I wear it as it was intended." I had barely finished speaking when a crash in the kitchen made us both jump.

Harold rose instantly and started toward the sound.

"Wait," I said, reaching out to catch his arm. I knew the culprit, and I knew Harold would find nothing in the kitchen except the stack of fruitcake pans Jitty had sent flying to the floor. "It's the wind. I left the kitchen window cracked."

He swung to face me and before I could react, he stepped forward and caught me in his arms. He did not crush me to him; instead, he brushed a strand of hair from my face. "May I kiss you, Sarah Booth?"

For answer, I lifted my face. His arms around me felt solid, and I was curious. There were things about Harold I was growing to like. Would this be one of them?

His kiss was restrained passion. He was a man who governed his emotions, even his desire. While I was tempted to urge him on, I also checked my impulse. Passion unleashed was a dangerous thing. Some of the Daddy's Girls had confided that they kept their marriage beds free of such troubling emotions. Why swamp a stable and adequate boat in a gale of roaring needs and expectations? Harold was a man who would be safe. Did I truly want to unleash the demon of desire?

Ah, but of course. Just a little.

I kissed him back, closing my eyes and letting the four ounces of moonshine I'd consumed loosen my back and my inhibitions. My response encouraged a bolder kiss. And yet he held back. I was getting ready to up the ante when he broke the kiss gently and stepped away.

"You give me hope," he said. "Shall I send a car for you Sunday?"

He was leaving. I was surprised. "No, I'll drive myself." I wondered if his withdrawal was deliberate. A strategy. Was it possible that I was being outflanked by a banker?

"Wear something daring," he said as he went to the door and let himself out. The front door shut with a solid click.

I was still standing in the center of the room when Jitty came out of the kitchen. She was in such a hurry that she didn't bother with the door, just came right through the wall. "What kind of fool are you? You gone give the ring back if you don't marry him?! I tol' you, the ring is part of the goods. When a man gives an engagement ring to a woman, it's hers if she accepts the engagement. Even if it's only for one night, or a week. Of course, there's some expectation of a good time there. But once she breaks if off, the ring is hers."

She rattled those cheap Mexican bracelets in my face and took another breath. "But no, you gone give the ring back. Miss High-and-Mighty, actin' like we got money to burn."

Jitty was only expressing my thoughts, but I didn't like to hear them. "Fair's fair," I retorted, determined to stand my ground with Jitty if not with Harold.

"I'm surprised that man didn't run screamin' from the room. What woman talks about fair when jewelry is involved?" She shook her head and I realized that something was terribly wrong. Her head was huge, twice as big as I'd ever seen it—and it was covered in an orange net thing with hot-pink and olive green tassels all over it. It looked like some underwater creature had jumped on her head and might be sucking her brain out.

I reached out and pulled the elastic band of the head

cover, but she jerked away. "What is that thing?" I asked.

"It's a curler bonnet," she said, miffed. "If you ever read *Cosmo,* girl, you'd know a few tricks about how to straighten hair."

"That's incredibly ugly, Jitty," I said, snapping the elastic against her forehead. I took another peek under there. "Orange juice cans? Is that what you're using for rollers?"

"What's wrong with that?" she asked. "You put some a' that gel stuff on your hair and then the big juice cans pull it straight. At least that's what the magazine says."

I had a vague memory of such beauty antics. I'd still been in my first decade when the seventies roared into Sunflower County and turned Zinnia upside-down with hip-huggers, long straight hair, love beads, halter tops, sandals, and rich girls who had been trained to barter sex for security suddenly giving it away free to every Tom, Dick, and Harry who could strum a guitar or blow a harmonica.

My mother, who'd had a head full of long, wavy chestnut hair, had read *Cosmopolitan* sitting in the floral chair of the parlor. Mother had already been through her hippie phase, but she was a strong supporter of female independence.

I suppose Jitty had found some of the magazines up in the attic. Or else she remembered that time period. She seemed to have an amazing memory, and an endless amount of time to experiment with fashion. Really bad fashion.

"Wait a minute," she said, narrowing her eyes and beginning to walk around me. "You just hold your horses. I know you're tryin' to divert me. I know your game, Sarah Booth Delaney. You your father's child as sure as the night is dark. I'd get him pinned down in one place and he'd shift around to another subject. That won't work with me anymore."

I rolled my eyes.

"You better figure out a way to keep that ring," she warned.

"Or what?" I asked.

"Or else you gone have to marry that man for real."

It was late Saturday afternoon before I found a pair of shoes that would do for Harold's Sunday soiree. They set me back two hundred dollars, but they were going to be worth every penny. As I glanced at my legs in the full-length mirror of Steppin' Out, I decided not to think about whether I was buying the shoes for Harold or Hamilton. I was still Daddy's Girl enough to know that there was no point spoiling the perfect pair of shoes with too much thinking. The shoes were so striking, I decided a manicure was a necessity.

Although Zinnia is a small town, it's possible to find the latest in fashion at several of the small boutiques. I stopped in at After Nine to look at the winter season's dresses and to do a bit of sleuthing. Martha Wells, the owner, was busy with two customers, so I sauntered around the stylized, faceless mannequins that were draped in black and red sheaths. I was hoping the store would clear and I would have Martha to myself.

Instead, Tinkie came into the shop on a blast of rich perfume and a soft bark. Chablis leaped out of her arms and came straight at me, launching herself at my face. Luckily, I caught the fluff-ball as she licked my nose with amazing dexterity.

"Oh, my lord," Tinkie said, putting a hand on her heart as her eyes filled with tears. "She knows you saved her life, Sarah Booth. She remembers!" She rushed toward me and gave me a real kiss on the cheek.

"Tinkie!" I whispered, but Chablis took that opportunity to give me a dog kiss right in the mouth. Her breath had a hint of expensive leather, and I knew a pair of shoes had bitten the dust. I hoped they were Oscar's. "Tinkie, hush up," I said. "You'll blow my cover." Of course, the dog rescue had already been in *The Zinnia Dispatch* so it was sort of a moot point.

Tinkie hustled me over to the lingerie corner, and my eye drifted to a severely sexy black teddy. Now, that was something that would demand center stage in the bedroom.

"Sarah Booth," she whispered, "have you found out anything?"

In fact, I'd discovered quite a bit, but this wasn't the time or place. What was more important was that I let Tinkie know about the party at Harold's. Except I discovered that I didn't want her there. If she and Hamilton actually had something going on, I didn't want to watch it playing out in front of me. But I'd been paid for the information, and paid handsomely.

"Will you be at Harold's tomorrow night?" I asked.

Her nose wrinkled like a little rabbit's. "Oscar said something, but I just hate those parties where the men discuss business and the women are left to drift around with a glass of wine. I was thinking of developing a minor relapse of anemia. I let my prescription for my vitamins run out, just in case."

I was surprised. Tinkie's description of the parties was accurate, but those were the moments when Daddy's Girls got to preen. I would have thought she'd adore the opportunity.

"You should make it a point to be there," I said, still reluctant to spill the big news.

She picked up on something in my voice. "Why?" she whispered, her eyes big with excitement.

"Hamilton will be there. He's in town." I reached out and grasped her shoulder.

"You've seen him?" she asked.

More than seen, I'd felt his hand on me. But I wasn't being paid to acquire titillating experiences. I was paid for facts. "He's back at Knob Hill. He's doing business with the bank." It was good I had my hand on her because she slumped against the wall. She was not tall, but she was deadweight.

"Madame Tomeeka was right," she moaned. "He's here."

Chablis wriggled free of my arm and began to bark. "Tinkie, you're causing a scene," I whispered. The words were like a slap. She regained her balance and stood straight. Dramatic scenes were never to be wasted in such places as a dress shop with no men around.

"What was he like?" Some of the color came back into her face. "I should have known Oscar was up to something." She looked at me in alarm. "Did Hamilton look poor? Oscar was talking about someone pretending to have money."

I realized that Martha was watching us with open curiosity, and her two customers, women I didn't know, were holding scarves but staring at Tinkie and me.

"I wrote you a report. This isn't the place to discuss it."

"Bring it Sunday night," she said. "I'll be there." She gathered Chablis up in her arms and hurried out of the shop. The small dog barked twice over her shoulder, a parting of affection.

After the scene with Tinkie, there would be no chance of asking nonchalant questions of Martha. I looked over a few alligator bags, and as soon as possible slipped from the shop.

Even Jitty was impressed with the black-beaded dress that hugged my bodice and then changed into chiffon. *Short* swirling chiffon.

"Honey, that skirt hikes any higher, you'll be able to see possible."

"In this dress, anything is possible," I answered her. The shoes were absolutely perfect. The heels were tall, a slender silhouette that widened to a square at the base. Offbeat and perfect for dancing. I checked the backs of my legs in the mirror to make sure the seams of my hose were straight. After all, Harold had said daring.

"What are you up to?" Jitty asked, walking around me three times in a circle like some wicked stepmother about to turn my coach into a pumpkin.

"I'm working," I said. "On several fronts."

"You workin' on messing up your meal ticket. If Tinkie gets a whiff of the fact that you've got the hots for Hamilton, you're gone get fired. And if Harold finds out you've got ulterior motives, he just might take that ring back, along with the marriage invitation."

Jitty had a point. For a split second, I let myself acknowledge the gamble I was taking. Then I caught a glimpse of those damn shoes in the mirror, and I knew that I was holding some awfully good cards. These were shoes that could conquer an entire civilization. What were two mere men?

"I'll give you a full report," I promised Jitty as I palmed my car keys and headed into the Delta night.

14

It was a dazzling November evening, the last of the month, and I turned into Harold's drive with strategies whirling in my head. Although I had resisted much of Aunt LouLane's training in the art of feminine wiles, I did learn one important thing—the aura of desirability is created first in the mind of the woman.

I've seen women working in the cotton fields, their clothes soaked with sweat and hair plastered to their foreheads. But when a good-looking man drove by, they smiled. They were aware of their femininity, of the power of being female, and neither sweat nor dirt nor bare feet could detract from their sexuality. They generated sexy from the inside out, and the men responded.

My mind was on these things as I turned into Harold's long, oak-lined drive. Suddenly a million twinkling white lights dazzled my eyes. My foot jumped onto the brake, and the Roadster hunkered down and held the road as it skidded to a stop.

I was awestruck at what Harold had wrought. Fairy lights followed the graceful limbs of the huge oaks that canopied the drive. The effect was spectacular. I suddenly wanted to forgo the party and all of the attendant intrigues to simply sit beneath the canopy of winter stardust.

But there was work to be done, and I parked at the end of the line of cars and headed to the house.

There is an art to the entrance of a single woman into a party. It is timing and attitude—and dress. I had designed myself for a dramatic entrance, and I intended to see that I got my full due. To that effect I had tucked a few old cherry bombs into my spangled evening bag. I waited for a few stragglers to go inside. As I got on the porch, I lit one of the cherry bombs and threw it into the hydrangeas beside the steps.

Counting the seconds, I rang the doorbell, pushed the door open, and—*kaboom*! Dead hydrangea leaves fluttered behind me like confetti. After a few squawks and shrieks, everyone in the room turned to the door. There was an appreciative intake of breath from the men and a glare from the women, and I knew my strategy was doubly successful. Harold's face showed his sincere appreciation, and Kincaid Maxwell looked pissed.

There was one other reaction I sought, but Hamilton Garrett the Fifth was not in evidence. Disappointment did not begin to describe what I felt.

Harold was immediately at my side, his proprietary hand on my elbow as he steered me into the room. Kincaid was first in line to greet me, and she shifted so that I was cut off.

"Now I understand why you failed in your stage career," Kincaid whispered in the required act of an air kiss. "Dramatic special effects won't ever cover up weak character development."

"Oh, Kincaid," I whispered back, "you look lovely tonight. But how do you get your eyeliner so straight when you don't cast a reflection in the mirror?" Kincaid and I are not bitter enemies, but there is no love lost between us. The breach stems back to our junior play, when I got the lead and she told everyone it was because the drama teacher pitied me since I was an orphan.

She stepped back and away. "Chas!" she called out loudly. "Get Sarah Booth a drink, darling. Some of the good Scotch, since she can't afford it anymore. It'll be such a special treat."

So, my financial woes were common knowledge. All of my hiding out and avoiding my peers had done no good. Well, there was a certain freedom in not having to pretend. "Make it a double, Chas," I said airily, when I felt someone staring at me. It was one of those fully aware sensations. I turned quickly and found myself impaled on Hamilton Garrett the Fifth's direct gaze. He was standing beside a bronze sculpture—a female torso of great sensuality. Beside the work of art, Hamilton was a powerful presence, and I was viscerally reminded of our earlier meeting and the glowing pink woman of glass in his foyer.

His green eyes held me, and I felt my skin chill and then flush warm. I tried to swallow, but my throat was dry. He advanced toward me, one hand brushing the naked hip of the sculpture in a gesture that made me tremble. Harold turned to me, a question in his light blue eyes.

"Miss Delaney," Hamilton said, stepping forward. "I didn't expect to see you here."

Harold cast me a shrewd look. "You two know each other?"

"Miss Delaney came to interview me," Hamilton said in a clear, deliberate voice. "I'm afraid she caught me at a bad time. I treated her rudely, and I want to offer an apology."

I wanted to catch him in a bad place and hurt him. There was no hint of malice on his face or in his tone. Only his eyes gave away the pleasure he was having—at my expense.

"No, it's I who owe you an apology," I said quickly. "I should have called and requested an appointment. It was rude of me to appear on your doorstep."

"What kind of interview were you conducting?" Harold asked, plainly curious about this unexpected turn.

"Didn't you know Miss Delaney works for the *Dispatch*?"

Hamilton was having too good a time, and I was finding it strangely difficult to breathe.

"Sarah Booth?" Harold said.

A convincing lie did not immediately present itself to my mind. "I may have misrepresented myself," I said slowly, making the artless, mischievous face of a female caught in a harmless fabrication. "I thought if I could get a good society scoop, Cece might give me a job." I sobered as I looked at Hamilton, hoping to destroy him with a surfeit of truth. "If you haven't heard already, I'm destitute. If I don't come up with some money, I'm going to lose Dahlia House." For an unguarded second, there was surprise in his eyes.

"So now you know the entire sordid story." I shrugged. The gesture made the chiffon swirls of my skirt shimmer, and I saw Hamilton's eyes flicker down, then back up to mine.

"I admire a person who takes a gamble," he said with his relentless gaze trained on me. "The problem with taking risks is that sometimes you can't afford to lose. My advice to a desperate gambler is to get up from the table."

Hamilton's words, though spoken in the easy tone of

party chatter, were a threat. I knew it, and he knew it.
But I didn't want Harold to catch the undertone. I
smiled and nodded. "I'm certain your words are wise,
Mr. Garrett, but I have a different view. When the only
act left is one of desperation, then you have to put your
whole heart into it." I gave it a slight pause. "An interview with you was a long shot. No damage done."

"Then we both survived your gamble without injury." He picked up my hand. "Perhaps I'll revise my
opinions on gamblers and make a new category for one
with such incredible charm." He bent low over my
hand, his lips brushing my skin, and then excused himself.

Harold watched him go with a frown. "He's very
different now," he said slowly. "Bitter."

"Will you do business with him?" I asked, remembering Tinkie's talk at the dress shop.

"The bank wants his business, but no one is certain
he'll stay in Zinnia. He returned here out of the blue,
and there's every chance he'll disappear again in a matter of weeks."

As Harold took my arm and steered me toward the
dining room, where candles glowed and food that
looked both festive and delicious crowded the long ban-
quet table, I wondered if that last remark was calcu-
lated, or simply an innocent comment.

Harold fed me a curried shrimp, smiling as I licked
my lips. "You didn't tell me about the newspaper job,"
he said.

"I thought if I got a great interview, I might be able
to talk my way into working with Cece." I wanted to
work for the newspaper about as much as I wanted to
have the chicken pox a second time.

"I know the publisher. I could speak to him on your
behalf," Harold said.

"No, don't you dare!" I saw the surprise in his eyes. "I mean, no, thank you. Let me see what I can do on my own."

Harold's smile held a degree of pride. "You are remarkable. You don't want me to use my influence to help you get a job. You want to get it on your own merits. I'd be careful, Sarah Booth, or the other women in your set are going to get very, very angry with you."

He was right. I was betraying my gender and my class. It was not a step to take lightly.

"And Hamilton isn't someone to play with," Harold cautioned.

"Why? Because he's accused of murdering his mother?" I asked, hoping to get Harold's reaction to the charge.

"No, because he *did* kill his mother," Harold answered smoothly.

I was shocked at Harold's blasé attitude, but there was no time to question him further. A cluster of women descended on us and I was trapped at his side.

Harold had claimed me as his hostess, and as such there was little I could do except smile, nod, and reply to the endless banter. At another time, I might have enjoyed the opportunity to shock, engage, or malign. But my mind was on Hamilton, and though I tried to be subtle, my gaze followed him.

He made the circuit of the party, smiling, shaking hands, accepting the women's kisses on his cheek, undressing the pretty ones with a practiced eye. On occasion, he would look my way and I'd feel as if he'd touched someplace private and not very nice.

After half an hour, Hamilton strolled from the dining room and disappeared. It was the way he looked to left and right that made me realize he was up to something. Excusing myself from Harold, Mrs. Carruthers, and Au-

gusta Langford with the excuse that I would check on
the canapés, I slipped into the kitchen and out the back
door. Hamilton had gone out the front, and I eased into
the protection of the camellia bushes that grew beside
the house and made my way toward the front porch.

A cloud of cigarette smoke enveloped his head as he
sat in a wicker chair, alone. He'd had the good sense to
grab his coat, something I hadn't been able to do. Rub-
bing my arms up and down, I waited. When he glanced
at his watch and stood, I knew my instincts were right.
He walked toward the gardens.

I followed, ducking beneath a huge magnolia tree
and stepping carefully to avoid the fallen pods. I slipped
from shadow to shadow, following him, aware that I
was moving deeper into darkness and farther away
from the women's laughter that chimed and rang amid
the hearty conversations of the men.

Harold's big yard was bounded by a yew hedge, and
I pressed myself into the green wall of shrubbery just in
time to hear a man speaking on the other side.

"I know the truth," the man said. Strong emotion
distorted his pronunciation. "I know what Sylvia's been
trying to—"

"Stay away from my sister!" Hamilton warned.

"It's too late for that," the man said, his tone edgy.
"She may be crazy, but she isn't stupid. To think what
she's done to herself. You have to believe—"

"I don't have to believe anything. Sylvia surrendered
to the past a long, long time ago," Hamilton said. "She
has her imagination." I caught the scent of cigarette
smoke.

"Imagination!" The man laughed. "If you have
doubts, why did you come back?"

"My sister left me no choice." Hamilton's voice was
cold. "What's your excuse for being drawn into this?"

"You weren't the only one who lost his father." There was a pause, and when the other man spoke again, some of the anger was gone. "You should sell the estate. Once this is over, clear out."

"Knob Hill is my heritage. Show me your proof."

There was the sound of paper unfolding and rustling. "Your sister had this," the man said with expectation.

"My God," Hamilton whispered, excitement in his voice.

"I thought you'd find it interesting."

"Where—"

At the sound of a female calling, they broke off.

"Hamilton! Hamilton Garrett, you bad boy, are you out here smoking?"

I closed my eyes in disbelief, but it was truly Tinkie. I saw her standing, backlit, on the front porch of Harold's house. She came down the steps and stopped at the edge of light, as if she were afraid to step into the darkness.

"Hamilton, are you out there?"

Before I could move, Hamilton brushed past the hedge and crossed the open space. He went to Tinkie.

"I can't believe you're home," she said softly.

"It's been a long time," he answered, in a voice completely different from the one he'd used only moments before.

I held my breath, praying that neither of them would decide to have a tryst in the garden.

"Are you home for good?" she asked. To her credit, she was keeping her feelings well hidden. This could pass for casual party chatter.

"Tinkie, you're freezing," Hamilton said, taking off his coat and wrapping it around her shoulders. "Let me escort you back inside." With his arm around her, they walked onto the porch and were blocked from sight by the camellia bushes. I couldn't help but wonder if perhaps he bent down to kiss those pouty lips of hers.

I kept very still in the hedges, listening for the other man. When I heard his footsteps echoing emptily on the cold sidewalk, I counted to fifty and then crept out of the hedge. The only evidence of the meeting was a cigarette butt. Marlboro. Clinging to shrubs and shadows, I hurried to the back door.

The warmth of the party hit me like a fist, and I picked up a glass of champagne and drank half of it. The caterers were staring at me, so I slipped through the door into the dining room. Trying to slide along the wall, I was intent on finding Hamilton and Tinkie and avoiding Harold. I finished the champagne and was looking for a place to put the glass when I noticed Hamilton's coat dumped in a corner.

It was a long shot, but I picked it up as any good hostess would do and started toward the bedroom where Harold had put the guests' coats and purses. As soon as I closed the door behind me, I locked it.

The coat was wool and smelled of cigarettes and Hamilton. My hands were shaking as I began to go through it. In the right front pocket I found a page torn from a magazine. I sat down on the bed amid the coats and examined what appeared to be part of a story about a gallery in California that was exhibiting jewelry.

There were photographs of several pieces, all of them created from gold, enamel, and semiprecious stones. The materials were not that expensive, but the craftsmanship was interesting. The article was about the designer René Lalique, a Frenchman. Though I read it twice, there was nothing significant in it. I put it aside and began to search for something else.

A loud pounding on the door made me jump, and I jammed the article back in the pocket and rushed to open the door. Hamilton stood there. He hesitated when he saw me. "Why are you always where no one expects to find you?" he asked.

"I'll tell you," I said, trying to hide my flush, "when you tell me why you've suddenly decided to return to Zinnia."

He stepped toward me so quickly that I almost backed away. Almost.

"I get the impression you're a very curious woman," he said, so softly that it might have been an endearment. His hand reached out and caressed my cheek. "Just remember that prying is a dangerous occupation." He picked up his coat and left, closing the door behind him so softly that the latch barely bumped into place.

15

When I returned to the party, Harold was in the library in the middle of a group of men. I made the rounds of the women in the parlor and dining room, fully aware that the segregation of the sexes foretold a certain stage in the evening. I fortified myself with a quick glass of champagne, replaced the empty with a full one, and circulated, never staying long enough to answer serious questions. I passed through conversations just as Jitty drifted through walls. Hamilton the Fifth absorbed me, though I did the best I could not to show it.

He was a dark force, and no matter how much I tried to deny it, he affected me. As Jitty had so aptly pointed out, this was not a good thing. In a Delaney woman, when the womb overrides the brain, calamity is sure to follow.

I was about to join Tinkie, whose state of inebriation and smile could both be described as plastered, when I felt a hand on my shoulder. My Hamilton bruises tingled dangerously before I turned to find Cece grinning like the Cheshire cat.

"You were alone with Hamilton in the bedroom," she said eagerly. "What's the scoop?"

My, news traveled fast. "He doesn't like desperate gamblers."

"Are you developing a relationship with him?" Cece's smile suddenly looked as false as her eyelashes.

"What do you mean?" I asked.

"Sarah Booth, you're not up to anything, are you?"

"I'm always up to something," I said on a bright note.

"This book you're writing." Her dark eyes seemed to deepen, and I was aware that I was dealing with a dangerously perceptive person. Cece had the intuition and wiles of a woman, but the added dividend of male logic. "You don't have a personal bone to pick, do you?"

It occurred to me that Cece had been goaded into wondering about my book. "Why do you ask?"

"Delo Wiley came by the paper yesterday afternoon."

Her revelation was startling, but I couldn't afford to show it. I was beginning to catch on to the fact that a good PI revealed as little as possible about everything. "I didn't know you worked on Saturday," I parried.

"One normally doesn't."

"And your point is?" I bluffed. Delo wasn't the kind of man who would ordinarily drop by a newspaper office. COR's had little use for newspapers or transsexuals.

"He was checking up on you," Cece said, and I could see the logical part of her mind clicking through options a mile a minute. "He wanted to know if you'd ever written anything before. It makes one wonder about your newfound love of *fiction*." She gave it two beats. "You are writing fiction, aren't you, dahling?"

"Facts are too limiting," I answered carefully.

"That's not a real answer."

"It's as real as it gets, at least tonight." I was tempted to tell her I was a private investigator and give up the whole writing tale. But it had proven to be such a serviceable lie. No one ever wanted to be investigated, but almost everyone wanted to be immortalized in print.

"What are you up to?" Cece asked, but I knew by her singsong tone that it was rhetorical. "Get an interview with Hamilton, a good one, and I'll give you a job." She smiled her hungry smile and turned away.

I was left with the image of a very sleek jungle cat.

Cece headed out the door, and a general exodus followed. The party was over. Several members of the banking board remained clustered in front of the fireplace. When they lit cigars and took up brandy snifters, I knew it was time for my departure, along with the other women. I made sure to slip my typed report to an eager Tinkie at an opportune moment before the crowd thinned.

Harold insisted on walking me to my car. A heavy fog had begun to settle over the Delta, and had turned the familiar night into an eerie landscape. Having arrived fashionably late, I had parked a good distance from the house.

Harold tucked my hand through his arm and guided me down the drive. I must confess that my womb was in a serious state of unrest. I found the solid reassurance of Harold's arm, his simple presence, to be profoundly moving.

At my car he kissed my hand, holding it lightly. "Your entrance was spectacular," he said. "It was everything I expected of you."

I filed that away for further pondering. I was tired and my shoes, though exquisite and worth every penny, had permanently deformed my toes. "Good night, Harold," I said, offering a cheek.

He ignored the cheek and lifted my hand to his lips once more. Instead of the kiss I expected, he sucked my thumb into his mouth. With unexpected expertise, he gave it a delicious tug and a provocative nibble, then slowly released it.

Without another word he left me. Stunned, I watched him disappear into the descending fog that blurred the fairy lights he'd constructed into a soft tunnel of light.

I slept late the next morning, but it was not a restful repose. It seemed that I had two pulses going in my body—one in my thumb and the other more womb-oriented. Awakening, I felt as if I'd been caught between two drumming tribes of warriors.

The first thing to meet my gaze was Jitty, perched on the bed with a black stormcloud surrounding her head.

"Holy DDT," I said, scooting back from her. My vision cleared and I realized she'd given up on the orange juice cans and gone natural. Her Afro was a masterpiece that went against every principle Newton had ever advocated. The dashiki she wore radiated red, yellow, and black with an intensity that hurt my blurry eyes.

I glared at her, then turned my attention to my thumb. It looked normal, so why did it have a heartbeat all its own? I got out of bed and headed for the bathroom when the doorbell chimed. I checked the bedside clock and saw it was nine. Not really late, but too early for visitors. Respectable visitors, at least.

The house was cold, so I hustled into a robe and slippers and made it to the door only to find that whoever had come had also gone. On the front porch was a newspaper, a white box tied with string, and a paper bag from which wafted the aroma of coffee. Delighted, I snatched them up, slipped off the string, and opened the lid of a pastry box whose contents were still warm from the oven. Oh, delight of delights! I rushed back upstairs and crawled under the covers, mouth watering with anticipation.

In New York, when I lived on East Ninety-first Street, half a block from a pastry shop, I'd paid the owner's nephew to deliver hot Danish, coffee, and *The New York Times* at eight o'clock every Sunday morning. It was the height of civilization as far as I was concerned.

Though it was a Monday instead of Sunday, and the paper was the *Dispatch* rather than the *Times*, I was in hog heaven. I turned to Cece's column—after all, it was why she'd made the delivery—and picked up a pastry.

The heir apparent of the Garrett fortune, Hamilton the Fifth, newly returned to his home, made a splash reentering the waters of high society last night at a gala at the home of Harold Erkwell, local banker and art connoisseur.

Hamilton's return to his native soil was a surprise, and one that left the ladies breathless. It did not take Madame Tomeeka's talents to see what was running through the minds of at least a dozen of Zinnia's most prominent blooms. The local dry cleaners will have a booming business this week removing drool stains from the bodices of several expensive gowns.

HG the Fifth is one handsome man, and though his marital status wasn't determined as fact, I did notice that his ring finger was bare, and without even a trace of a tan line.

The hot questions for this week are: What brought Hamilton home and how long will he stay? And does he lack for female companionship? More on this as the story unfolds.

So, Cece was stirring the pot. It would drive Hamilton wild that he couldn't control the mad dog of the press, Cecily Dee Falcon.

"Hot bath," I said, diagnosing exactly what I needed and wondering if Jitty missed such mundane pleasures. I hadn't even considered sharing the pastry with her.

"Cold shower would serve you better," she replied.

"You're jealous," I teased.

"Harold threw you for a loop," she said smugly. "You got a decision to make, girl. And it won't be easy. I tol' you there was more to Mr. Banker than fine art and financial security."

I hate it when Jitty is right, especially about men. "If you're so damned smart about romance, how come you never married?" I asked. I had a second cup of coffee waiting for me; I was content to lounge in bed and chat for a while.

"I don't suppose you ever heard of a small disruption called the War Between the States. Funny how a thing like romance takes a backseat to survival."

We'd started the day on a mutual snarl, and I decided to make the first move in improving things. Something about her posture touched me. "So were you ever in love?" I asked.

I was surprised to see Jitty, normally an in-your-face sort of ghost, turn away from me to gaze out the bedroom window into the crisp December morning. I could tell by the bright sunshine that it was going to be a cold day.

Though I could only see the curve of her cheek, shaded by the huge Afro, I knew that she was sad. "I'm sorry, Jitty. I didn't mean to pry." I actually hadn't meant to upset her.

"It was such a long time ago, you'd think a body would forget."

I knew better than that. There are certain things that a body simply doesn't forget. Not ever. It is a cruel fact of nature that a subspecies that cannot wring out a dishcloth or understand the importance of one-syllable words such as "thank" and "you" can leave indelible marks on corporeal memory. There are certain moments that are branded into flesh, and for me, most all of them involved men.

"Tell me about him," I requested.

She was still staring out the window, but I could see that her smile had rounded her cheek. "He was a man," she said simply, "good in many ways. I fell in love with him when I was sixteen. For a long time we were separated, and then your great-great-grandmother, Miss Alice, discovered that I was in love with him and she arranged to buy him." Jitty chuckled softly. "You know she was something else." At last she turned to look at me. "She gave him to me."

"As in legally?" I was astounded.

"She gave me his papers. I owned him." Jitty shook her head, laughing softly at the memory. "She said that I had the perfect opportunity to make my man responsive to my desires. She said she would check on the progress."

Jitty got up and walked to the window, and I knew she was staring down into the cemetery.

"Did you marry him?"

"I never did," she answered. "There was no need, and then suddenly we were at war. Coker went off with Mr. Karl to the cavalry unit in Nashville. Coker had his own fine horse, and he and Mr. Karl rode with General

Forrest. Now Coker wasn't part of the Confederate Army. He was with Mr. Karl. But he might as well have been a soldier for all it mattered." She came back to stand at the foot of the bed, her hand on the poster. "Neither of them came back. Not Coker and not Mr. Karl. The story Miss Alice and I got was that Coker got hit first and Mr. Karl went back for him. They were both shot."

There was nothing I could say.

She sighed and picked up her story. "That was the first year of the war. And then it was just a matter of days and weeks and months and years before everyone we knew suffered death. We were so busy trying not to starve or be killed by soldiers or deserters or renegades or the Home Guard that we didn't look ahead or behind. When it was finally over, we didn't remember what we'd been like before."

I sipped the hot black coffee and let the horror of the past wash over and through me. I was not immune. In some way I felt as if I, too, had been a part of it. It would be impossible to live in Dahlia House, filled with relics of the past, and not understand the undeniable link to history.

"Grandma Alice remarried," I pointed out.

"She needed a man to organize the labor in the fields. The free Negroes and white trash wouldn't work for her." Jitty spoke without bitterness. "They wouldn't work for me, either. We were women and not worth listening to."

"But the two of you brought Dahlia House back. You saved it."

"And your grandmother had to marry to see that it was safe," she pointed out, and the sadness in her eyes was replaced by fire. "Which isn't a point I intended to make, but it's a dang good one now that I'm here at it."

"I'm well aware of the Delaney ability to sacrifice life, limb, and womb in the name of heritage." And I was, but I wasn't going to follow that particular martyr's path.

"So when are you seeing Harold?" Jitty asked.

"I don't know." I finished the coffee, brushed the crumbs into the box, and flipped back the covers. "But I'm seeing Hamilton this afternoon." I had decided, on the spur of the moment, to pay another visit to Knob Hill. "Cece has offered me a job if I can get an interview. It's a good excuse to talk with Hamilton. He can't deny me, because he knows I'm destitute without the newspaper job. Code of the South."

"How'd you get an appointment with him?" she asked.

"I don't have one, which isn't the issue. The important thing is, what am I going to wear?"

"Just go naked. It'll save a lot of time," Jitty mumbled.

"Too cold to go naked," I answered, popping out of the bed. I felt young and impulsive. "And I don't have the right coat. Naked requires some magnificent fake fur." I reached into the closet. "What about this red sweater dress?" I asked, lifting it from the rack. Even though Jitty wasn't going to be any real help, I wanted to discuss wardrobe with someone.

"Why not just wear a sign that says, 'I'm a sexually frustrated slut'?"

Perhaps the red sweater dress was a little clingy. "The green wool suit? I'm working on a holiday theme."

"You've been so fond of that muumuu, why not show him the real Sarah Booth Delaney?"

"I don't want to scare him off. At least not yet." Jitty's barbed remarks couldn't dampen my spirit. I pulled out a beige suit and pushed it back.

"Try your jeans and a sweater," Jitty said, shaking her head. "You go all dolled up like the Queen of Sheba, he's going to know you're trying to impress him. Go the other way, real casual. That'll keep him guessing."

I looked at her and realized the wisdom in her words. "Sometimes, Jitty, I'm almost glad you're my own personal haint."

"I don't belong to you, and I wouldn't give you advice if I didn't have a stake in the outcome here. I want a baby, and I guess it doesn't matter to me how you get one. Just get one."

"I'll do my best," I said as I headed for the bathroom with my jeans and a dark blue sweater with gold piping tucked under my arm.

I hadn't made it to the door before I heard the second disruption of the morning. Instead of the chime of the bell, someone was trying to beat the front door down.

"Just a dang minute," I called as I dropped my clothes and ran barefoot down the stairs. Jitty was right. We needed a butler. I looked out the peephole and stepped back from the door. Of all the people I expected to see, it wasn't Gordon Walters all dressed up in his deputy's uniform. He had that lean and hungry look that made me think he could beat up a suspect in a jail cell. I cracked the door slightly.

"Yes," I said. "Can I help you?"

"Sarah Booth Delaney, I have some questions to ask you." He didn't sound friendly at all.

"I'm getting dressed, and I have appointments all day. How about tomorrow?" I didn't want to answer any of his stupid questions at any time. I didn't want him in my house. He'd tried to intimidate me in the sheriff's office, and he'd succeeded. But he was on my turf now.

"I'm afraid you'll have to postpone the activities you planned for today."

Now that stopped me short. "And why would that be?" I asked haughtily.

"Delo Wiley was killed yesterday."

16

I sat in the straight-backed chair beside Gordon Walters's desk and resisted the impulse to scratch my head. My hair wasn't dirty, but Gordon had hustled me out of the house without a chance to shower, much less soak in a hot tub. At the moment, I was more concerned about my personal hygiene than about the fact that the moron with the badge considered me a suspect in a killing. Or at least that was the implication, though he hadn't come out and said as much.

"What business did you conduct with Mr. Wiley at ten-hundred hours on the morning of November twenty-eight?" Gordon asked, his eyes foxy and mean.

"We had a lengthy discussion about the weather." I knew I was only prolonging my agony, but I couldn't help myself. I hadn't been offered a phone call, and though I had no intention of calling a lawyer, it did cross my mind to call Harold. The Bank of Zinnia no doubt held the mortgage on everything Gordon Walters owned or ever hoped to own. Gordon was messing with me—and one act of terrorism deserved another.

"Strange that you'd visit an old man you hardly knew to discuss the weather," Gordon said, showing his willingness to play my game.

I checked the time. It was ten o'clock. I'd give Gordon an hour for his fun. I settled back into the chair, crossed my legs man-style, and lifted my chin. "I've been thinking about growing corn at Dahlia House. The fields have been fallow for the last eight years. I think I could get a pretty good crop. Delo grew corn, so I stopped by for a chat."

Gordon picked up a pack of Marlboros and shook out a cigarette. He offered it to me with a grin that some women would have found intriguing. "Are you going to have time to farm while you're writing your book?" Gordon asked.

I considered the cigarette but shook my head. It had been three years since I'd smoked. "Working both activities simultaneously will produce synergy."

"No wonder your eyes are brown," he answered, but there was something new in his expression. Open curiosity. "You're not the average little Delta belle, are you?" he asked.

I chose to ignore the condescending personal question and directed my answer to the real reason I was downtown in the sheriff's office. "Look, I don't know what happened to Mr. Wiley," I said. "I talked to him, but not about anything that would get him killed." I suddenly remembered his warning to me about stepping outside the boundaries of my "class." He had said I was drifting onto dangerous ground. But it had proven more dangerous for him.

"Something wrong?" Gordon asked.

He was rather astute. I suddenly wished the sheriff would walk through the door. "Where's Coleman?" I asked.

"Gone to Jackson to pick up some state funds. He won't be back until tomorrow." Gordon grinned. "I'm in charge."

"Look, Deputy Walters, I'm not involved in this. But I have some ideas. Tell me about the body. How was he killed?"

Gordon stared at me. "You want to see?"

I most certainly did not, but there was a challenge in his question, and I wasn't about to show that I'd never viewed a murder scene. In fact, Gordon hadn't said whether it was murder or not. "Killing" was a rather generic term that meant death but not necessarily murder.

"Sure," I said, "let's go."

He let me ride in the front seat of the patrol car, but he didn't look at me or talk to me as we drove out of town toward the flat, open fields. It gave me a chance to study his profile, and I duly noted the roguish nose that had been broken, the rugged looks that might be considered handsome.

"Was Delo shot?" I asked.

"Very effectively."

"Could it have been suicide?"

"Not unless he pulled the trigger with his toe and then got his boot back on with only a bloody stump for a head."

Now that was an image I didn't want rattling around in my brain, but it bore a shocking resemblance to the death of Hamilton Garrett the Fourth. The graphic details were meant to deter me from asking other questions. "So it was a shotgun?"

"A twelve-gauge." Gordon turned right. "It must have happened about eleven hundred hours yesterday."

Just before Sunday dinner.

"Where were you about that time?" he asked.

"Painting my fingernails." I held out my hands for him to see the Little Red Russet shade. I had indeed been getting ready for Harold's soiree. I started to ask where the shooting had taken place, but we'd turned down Delo's drive, passed the house, and headed out across the cornfield. The patrol car bumped gamely over the rows of brown cornstalks. A clutch of doves flew up to the right, and I watched them line out on the horizon and fly hard and straight.

I remembered the dream I'd had. The one that Tammy had also had. Though it was morning, and bright and cold, the day had taken on the muted tones of the dream.

We bumped over Delo's fields until I spotted an ambulance and several other vehicles up ahead. It had not occurred to me that the body would still be at the scene. The parallel to Hamilton the Fourth's death was unmistakable. No wonder Gordon was smiling that secret little smile. So this was going to be another of those warnings about consequence—as in each action has one. But I couldn't help but wonder why both Gordon and Hamilton the younger seemed so determined to make that point with me. The obvious answer was that Hamilton had killed his mother, and Pasco Walters had covered it up. Gordon's involvement came in protecting his dead father's name. Honor has always been a tyrant of the South. A man's good name is, often, all he owns.

The car stopped, and I got out without being told and walked toward the cluster of men. Fel Harper nodded at me, and I recognized Isaac Carter, who looked out of place in his double-breasted suit and gleaming loafers. He stared at me before he turned a hateful look at Gordon. There was no love lost between the two of them.

There was also another deputy, and two black men

who were trying to put leashes on several hounds that lunged and whimpered at the overgrowth.

"Sarah Booth," Fel said. "I didn't realize you were interested in current murders." He shot Gordon a curious look.

"I'm a woman with a lot of interests," I said, determined not to be upset by whatever they showed me. My great delivery of the line was somewhat offset by the fact that I stumbled in a deep hole and almost fell down. Gordon's hand steadied me. His eyes narrowed at the hole as he helped me to level ground.

The men had gathered at the edge of a twelve-by-twelve-foot patch of thick growth, mostly young trees and weeds that were out of place in the otherwise open field. As I stepped closer, I saw the old stump in the center of the growth. Swinging around, I caught a glint of sunlight on the river in the distance. We were in the Mule Bog field—the same spot where Guy Garrett had been shot and killed.

"Good thing Cooley and James followed the dogs over here," Fel said. "No tellin' how long Delo woulda laid here."

I looked at the black men. Their faces revealed no emotion, but the older one shook his head slowly. "It's an awful thing," he said. "Delo never harmed a soul."

"Delo got any folks?" Fel asked.

The older black man shook his head again. "His sister died last year. There's no one left."

"You ready for me to load him up?" Fel asked Gordon.

"Let the writer have a look," Gordon said.

I was afraid I'd get sick, but I stepped through the men to the edge of the bushes and caught sight of Delo's feet. I kept my focus there for a long time, taking in the laced-up work boots that looked almost new. He was on his stomach, indicating, I supposed, that he'd been shot from behind. The shotgun was beside the body.

I finally let my gaze travel up to the place where his head should have been. Gordon had not exaggerated. I was strangely calm in the face of such harsh destruction.

"That's the murder weapon?" I asked. Why would the killer leave the gun? I bent down to examine it more closely. It was a Remington 870 pump. Something had been removed from the stock.

"We'll test it out for fingerprints," Gordon said. "Ballistics can't do much with a shotgun except confirm it was number eight pellets."

I was more than ready to leave, but I knew that I was not in charge. Whatever purpose was behind Gordon's decision to bring me here, he wasn't finished.

"Did Mr. Wiley say anything to you that might indicate he was worried about someone being after him?" Gordon asked.

"Not to me, but I wasn't friends with Mr. Wiley. I wasn't someone he would confide in."

"Don't you find it odd that you pay a visit to a man and soon after he ends up dead?" Gordon asked.

They were all staring at me, all except for Cooley and James, who had gathered the dogs and headed, wordlessly, back across the field. I started to call out to them to wait for me, but I knew they'd keep walking. They wouldn't even turn around and look, and I didn't blame them.

"I find it odd that you connect my visit with his death." I flipped my limp hair off my shoulder. "I find it odd that you connect talk of corn crops with murder." I turned to address Isaac Carter. "And I find it odd that you're out here, Mr. Carter, but since you are, I've been meaning to stop by and talk with you. When would be a good time?"

Carter didn't say a word.

"I called Mr. Carter here because I was reminded of the death of Mr. Garrett the Fourth," Fel said quickly. "I wanted someone who'd seen the prior accident to take a look at this one. To back up my memory."

"And it's identical, isn't it? Except there's no reason to pretend this one was an accident." I was surprised by the anger I felt. An old man was dead, and no one standing around his corpse really seemed to give a damn. "I'll tell you something Delo told me that should be of interest. He didn't hunt. And neither did Mr. Garrett. Yet both of them are dead in a dove field. That tells me that dove fields in Sunflower County are a mighty dangerous place to be."

I turned to Gordon. "You can take me back or not. I'll walk. But I'm not staying here." I wasn't sick from seeing the body, but I was cold. It was an arctic freeze that went straight through the bone. "I'll call for an appointment," I said to Carter as I started walking across the field, dodging two more holes, one freshly dug and quite deep. Gordon hadn't charged me with anything. He couldn't hold me. I was going home.

"Miss Delaney," Gordon said, catching my elbow. "Get in the car. I'll take you home."

I was too cold to argue. As I started back his way, another clutch of doves flushed out from just at my feet. The flutter of their wings was loud and crisp, and for one terrifying second, I thought I could feel the drumming beat of their hearts.

The sky above me began to spin and I felt my knees buckle as the memory of the dream seemed to drown me. A strong hand gripped me and steadied me, and in another second I had regained my equilibrium.

"Are you okay?" Gordon asked.

"Yes," I said, surprised that I could talk so calmly. "I'm perfectly fine. Just take me home."

We made the drive in silence while I pondered the message Gordon was so clearly giving me: Mind my own business. Delo had talked, and look what happened to him.

It had not escaped me that Delo's murder coincided with Hamilton's unexpected return. But Hamilton was accused of his mother's death, not his father's. How would Delo's death benefit Hamilton? Or, for that matter, Gordon Walters?

Was it realistic to think a man would go to such lengths to protect his family name? There were numerous case studies of aberrant behavior of men and women who did terrible things for just that reason. Gordon had a manic glint in his feral eyes. And he had followed his father's footsteps into law enforcement, a classic sign of the underdeveloped personality.

"Very interesting."

Gordon's tone of voice snapped me out of my reverie, and I looked up to find we were at Dahlia House and Hamilton the Fifth was sitting on my front porch. Hamilton flicked a cigarette butt over the porch rail and rose to his feet as we pulled to a stop.

"Boll weevil!" I said with emotion, feeling a rush of warmth to my face. Of all the times for Hamilton to pay a surprise visit, it would be when I'd just been to a murder scene in a dove field.

"I didn't realize you and Mr. Garrett were friends," Gordon said as he stopped the cruiser at the front door. He opened his door as if he was going to get out.

"Thanks for the lift. Now go away." I got out quickly and walked away from him. I had no idea what

Hamilton was doing at my house, but I didn't want Gordon hanging around eavesdropping.

I started across the lawn. Hamilton, with his long hair gathered back at the nape of his neck, looked very Continental. As I walked up the steps, I suddenly wondered if he'd figured out I'd gone through his coat pockets at Harold's party. Perhaps I'd been too rash in sending Gordon away.

"I need to talk with you," he said.

The skin beneath my right eye began to twitch. I could feel it flutter every time he looked at me. "Delo Wiley was killed yesterday," I said, and remembering the awful scene in the dove field effectively squelched my twitches.

If I had expected a reaction, Hamilton disappointed me. I couldn't tell if he'd already heard the news, or if he simply didn't care. His lack of response provoked me further.

"He was shot on the exact spot your father was killed."

Ah, I saw a narrowing of his eyes, but nothing more. He came toward me across the porch.

"My father's death was ruled accidental."

Perhaps he had spent so many years accepting the facts that he'd drained them of emotion. It still surprised me that he spoke so calmly, especially when I so clearly believed that Guy Garrett had been deliberately shot. And I had assumed that he believed that, too. Believed it and may have acted on it.

"Your father was murdered," I said. "You and I both know this. I suspect a lot of people know it, but no one wants to acknowledge it. Why is that?"

Hamilton's eyes had grown cold. "Sheriff Walters didn't see it that way. He felt it was a hunting accident," he said carefully. "This doesn't really concern you."

"What do *you* believe?" I asked.

"I believe this is a subject best left where it is," he said, coming down the steps so that he stood beside me. "But your interest in it makes me wonder. Why do you care what happened to my father twenty years ago?"

It was a good question. I wished I had a good answer. "I'm writing a book," I said.

"So I've been told," Hamilton replied, and there was something hot in his eyes now. "Did it ever occur to you that I might object to being the vehicle you ride to save your home? Did you ever stop to think of the repercussions your book might have on my family?"

He had me there. I had not thought of those things, because I had no intention of writing a book. But I couldn't very well tell him I was prying into his business because of Tinkie.

"It's a work of fiction," I fumbled.

"Fiction based on my family tragedies," he answered. He leaned closer. "Do you have any idea what it might have been like for me? My family destroyed, me forced to leave my home and everyone I knew. I don't think you can possibly imagine, because if you could, writing a book would be the last thing on your mind."

One look into his eyes and I knew that though he presented himself as a controlled man, there were hot passions boiling beneath the surface. Unfortunately, they were not the kind of passions that ended up with sweaty bodies tangled in sheets.

"I don't want to hurt anyone," I said.

"Then you'll drop this and quit prying into my business?"

I couldn't go that far. "Don't you want to know what really happened to your father?" I countered.

Hamilton's eyes narrowed. "I came to appeal to your conscience. I had hoped to make you understand that my family has suffered enough." He stepped closer to me, so close I could feel his breath as he said softly, "Find another host to bleed."

He'd ambushed me on my own porch. I wasn't responsible for what had happened to his family, or to Delo. I grabbed his hand and halted him. "Did you kill your mother?"

I had hoped to shock him, perhaps even to wound him. I was disappointed. His lips thinned but held the shape of a smile. "I may have misjudged you. Perhaps a tabloid would be a more suitable employer than *The Zinnia Dispatch*." He shook free of me and got in his car.

17

Jitty sat on the closed toilet lid as I slowly sank beneath the hot water in the tub. Instead of being irritated at her for invading my privacy, I was glad she was there. I didn't want to be alone.

"Sarah Booth, get out of that tub."

Neither was I inclined to be bossed. "I'm never getting out," I answered as I surfaced long enough to turn the hot water on with my toe. "I'm staying here for the rest of my life. He thinks I'm slime. He thinks I'm a parasite, a tick, a leech, a maggot feeding on the corpse of his family."

"The best relationships start off with an honest awareness of each other," Jitty said. "He knows the worst about you. It can only go up from here."

I wiped the soapy water out of one eye and looked at her. "Thanks."

"It's true. All isn't lost. Now you just have to figure out a way to make him see the other aspects of your character."

I didn't like it that Jitty had accepted, without a

qualm, that I was a bloodsucking insect. But I was surprised at her willingness to help me where Hamilton was concerned. She had begun to mellow toward him.

"What do you suggest?" I asked, sitting up and turning off the water. "Give me one good plan."

"Hummm. Too bad he doesn't have a dog," she said.

I caught the hint of her smile. I chuckled for the first time since Hamilton's departure, and reached for a towel.

"Seems to me Hamilton would be grateful to you if you discovered who killed his daddy," Jitty pointed out.

"Unless it was his mother, which then provoked him to kill her," I explained as I dried off.

"Climb on out," Jitty ordered.

I shook off a leg and put it on the floor, following with the other. It was noon and I was hungry again.

"You got to come up with a plan," she said. "You're in too deep to back off now. And Hamilton will come 'round once he realizes you're on his side."

"I didn't realize you'd made a study of Pollyannaism," I said sarcastically.

"Seems to me the obvious step is a visit to that fancy sanitarium up at Friars Point," she said as she vanished through the wall, her nose straight up in the air and her Afro shaking with indignity.

I hung up the thick towel and considered my accomplishments for the morning. I'd eaten two thousand empty pastry calories, viewed a bloody corpse, given Gordon Walters food for thought by allowing him to see Hamilton at my home, pissed off the aforementioned Hamilton, and gotten Jitty in a snit. The day was proving to be exceptional.

Jitty did have a point, however. Since Hamilton was never going to speak with me again, it seemed Sylvia was the next best possibility. But could I put any trust in what a crazy woman said? Hah! That was the pot calling the kettle black. I'd just had a fight with a ghost.

I went to my room and pulled on jeans and a red sweater. Something bright. But not even my reflection in the mirror cheered me as I applied some makeup and trudged down to the kitchen. I ate cold chunks of turkey and pumpkin pie and headed out into thin sunshine that was more glare than heat.

I'd get to Friars Point, eventually. But first I was going to Billie's Garage. I knew about as much about mechanicking as I did about sleuthing, but I wasn't going to let that hold me back. I opened the hood of my beloved Roadster and wiggled one of the spark plug wires.

When I turned the ignition, the car sputtered and coughed. The smooth purr of the engine was gone. And though it hurt me to drive it into town in that condition, I headed straight to Billie's Garage, lurching and backfiring.

I couldn't remember if Billie was older or younger than Millie, or if they were actually twins, as their names implied. I pulled into the apron of the garage and got out. A slender man in his mid-fifties came toward me. He didn't look exactly like Millie, but pretty damn close.

"Mornin', Sarah Booth." He eyed the Roadster with great pleasure, even letting his fingers brush the Chinese-red paint of the fender. "Nice car, but it's running a little rough."

"Can you fix it? I've got to take a trip, and it was running fine yesterday." Not a lie. I'd begun to wonder if the weight of all my falsehoods would crush me.

"Pull 'er into the garage," he said, waving me into an empty slot.

I did as he instructed and then went inside to wait

while he examined the car. The waiting room was dirty, with a coffeepot smudged with greasy black fingerprints and a stack of Styrofoam cups that also looked as if one hundred and one dalmatians had shaken their spots all over it. Behind the waiting room was the office. It was a small, airless place, which offered not a single excuse for my presence if Billie caught me. So, of course, I went right in.

In the movies or on television, spies and detectives go exactly to the place where the important documents are kept. Though I'd watched millions of those scenes, I still had no idea how they did that. I took the desk first, pulling open drawers only to discover heaps of screws, tape, paper clips, pens, wadded-up bits of paper, magnets, wires, screwdrivers, and assorted other tools, including a crowbar. There was an old check ledger, but all of the stubs were unused. Billie's accounting system was eerily like mine.

I banged open the old metal filing cabinet and came across a grimy series of manila folders. To my delight, they were organized by name, and all of the names were folks I recognized. The tabs were handwritten, some in a neat, feminine cursive hand and others in a crablike scrawl. Had Millie been here?

The Garrett file was in its proper alphabetical place, and I felt a real thrill of excitement that I'd found it. Pulling it out, I sat down in the creaky, greasy chair and spread it open on the desk.

The stack of yellow paid receipts was impressive. The fact that they ended in 1980 was a blessing, and more to the point, the receipt right on the top of the stack was for Veronica Garrett's little convertible. I inhaled sharply at the date. Feb. 10, 1980. It was the day she died!

The car had been in Billie's shop. I closed my eyes as I

thought of what Millie had said. I'd never really considered her a suspect. Until now.

The bill was for a general checkup on the car, and I saw that Billie had replaced the oil filter, changed the oil, checked the timing belt and found it okay, rotated the tires, and lubed the chassis. He'd replaced a fuse for the horn and given the car a clean bill of health. He'd even noted that it had twenty-four thousand and five miles on it, a 1979 Jaguar XKE. Hunter green with tan leather interior. Veronica had done some serious road-running in the year she'd owned the car. But the Delta was so vast, and with shopping trips to Memphis, parties hither and yon, and two children in boarding school, the miles would add up, I supposed. Or she could have burned all that rubber meeting her lover.

Outside the open door of the office I heard the motor of my car catch and run smooth and easy. My time was up. I closed the file, returned it, and made it into one of the plastic waiting room chairs just as Billie came in the door.

"Loose spark plug wire," he said.

"What do I owe you?" I pulled my checkbook out of my purse.

"Nothing." He tilted his head. "I don't mean to scare you, Sarah Booth, but it looked as if someone wiggled that wire off there deliberately. You had any prowlers out around your house?"

"Only the repo man," I answered with a smile.

"I heard you were having some financial difficulties," he said. "I'm sorry to hear of your troubles."

"That doesn't mean I can't pay for car service," I told him, a little embarrassed that he wasn't charging me out of charity. This was almost more than I could bear after my morning with Hamilton.

"There's no charge, because I simply pushed the plug

back into place." He picked up one of the pink cloths that always hang from the back of a mechanic's pocket. "Go on and have a good day. I hope your luck turns," he said. "I know what it's like to be in a tight spot."

I had a couple of options open to me, but neither of them held any appeal. I could go see Isaac Carter at the Zinnia International Export office. Carter's family owned the cotton gin for Sunflower County, and he had developed himself as the broker for cotton and other goods.

The idea of confronting Carter after our powwow in the cornfield didn't strike me as a lot of fun. So the other possibility was to go to Friars Point. The private mental institution called Glen Oaks was north of Zinnia, up toward Memphis in a small, scenic little river town near the Helena, Arkansas, bridge. I could get there by three with time enough to get back at dark, or just after.

I didn't mind talking with a crazy woman. Most of my family had been crazy women, so it wouldn't be a hardship. What I did mind was the idea of what would happen when Hamilton found out I'd been to see his sister.

He would be pissed.

Too bad.

The Mississippi Delta is extraordinary land. Black topsoil stretches flat into the distance, so vast and so fertile it's hard to recognize it as part of the poorest state in the Union.

As I drove through the winter fields, I saw the efforts hard work had begotten. My land had once looked this way—neat rows, fences up, combines working the land. And it would again. The land demanded it. It was a sin to allow such fecundity to lie fallow.

With that reminder of my heritage, I hardened my resolve to do this thing for Tinkie. Hamilton had made me feel bad about myself, but there was nothing shameful in wanting to know the truth. How else could Tinkie make a decision that would affect the rest of her life? There was nothing wrong with my work as a PI. It was Hamilton's misfortune that events pointed the finger of guilt at him. And if he was innocent of wrongdoing, then surely he would thank me for confirming it for the world. Or at least Zinnia.

I left the flat fields behind me and headed toward the levee that signaled that the Mississippi River wasn't far away. Friars Point was on the river, but protected by the giant levee built after the 1927 flood that struck the Delta with relentless devastation.

I made good time and I was eager to discover if Sylvia Garrett would actually see me. She had no reason to. Then again, I didn't think she had a busload of visitors. Perhaps curiosity and loneliness would work in my favor.

I pulled into a Double Quick, filled the tank, bought a Coke and some peanuts, and got directions to the mental institution. The woman behind the counter was extremely cheerful about Glen Oaks and assured me that everyone in Coahoma County was delighted to have the hundred-bed facility—"for folks who're havin' a little trouble adjustin' to the real world"—in their community.

"Everybody's a little crazy some time," she reassured me.

She was a big, rawboned woman with blond frizz and black roots, but she had the prettiest set of teeth I'd seen outside of Hollywood. Her big gray eyes were nicely set in her head, and there were laugh lines around her mouth and eyes. I liked her, and poured some peanuts in my Coke, prepared to chat. I'd been alone with my thoughts too long, and Ina Welford, as she introduced herself with a firm handshake, was a delight.

"My uncle Tip was half a bubble off," she said, lighting up a cigarette and taking a sip of strong black coffee. "We loved him, but he could be a handful when he decided that the Arkansans were coming across the river and trying to steal our land." She chuckled. "I spent many a night camping on the river standing guard. It was easier to pacify him than it was to fight about it."

I had a terrible longing to have known a family that camped out on the riverbank to accommodate a crazy old man's fantasy. "What happened to your uncle?" I asked.

"Oh, he drowned one night. He saw a log floating down the river and he was sure there was an Arkansas man attached to it, so he jumped in the river and took off after it."

"Couldn't he swim?"

"Like a fish, but it was flood stage and one of the currents got him. Or else another log or some trash in the river bumped him in the head. It was dark, and we weren't ever certain what really happened. We found his body downriver, hung up in the top of a tree. His eyes and mouth were wide open, like he was still searching for something."

"That's terrible."

"Naw, not really. Think how he coulda died in a hospital or locked up somewhere. He loved the river and he died on her. Just hope that you get to die somewhere you love."

There was no arguing with those words. "Thanks for the story," I said, starting out the door.

"Hey, have a good time out at Glen Oaks. Just check your backseat before you leave. The patients sorta come and go. Like this weekend, one escaped and they didn't round her up until Sunday night. I heard she'd gotten over to the Delta and was in the middle of a cornfield in her nightgown."

Tammy believed in sixth senses, and I wasn't about to deny that they existed as goose bumps marched over my arms. "Do you know who it was?"

"Not by name. She's been there awhile. Lollie—she's my cousin by marriage and she works there as a nurse's aide—anyway, Lollie said she was some rich woman who'd been there a long time. Nearly twenty years."

Now I was sure who she was talking about.

"Hey, you look a little pale, are you okay?"

"I'm fine." I drained the Coke and left the bottle on the counter. "Thanks again."

I took the directions Ina had written down and found myself at the mental institution in less than fifteen minutes. Based on this latest information, I wondered if I stood a prayer of getting to see Sylvia Garrett. What was troubling was that she'd made her escape on the very weekend that Delo Wiley had been killed. And Delo had been murdered in the exact same spot her father had died.

18

A wise woman would probably have turned the car around and headed home, but I wasn't about to give up. If I was going to get to see Sylvia, though, I had to come up with a good story, and certainly not anything about a book. I looked down at my wardrobe and considered. I was the right age to be a cousin, so I decided to try that angle.

I walked into the building with a big smile and all the confidence of a Daddy's Girl. I headed to the main desk where I introduced myself as Sarah Booth Mason, a second cousin of Sylvia Garrett.

"You're not on the list of approved visitors," the nurse said, eyeing me suspiciously.

"I'm from New Orleans," I said. "I haven't been in the Delta in years, but while I'm here, I want to visit Cousin Sylvia. I promised my mama I'd be sure and stop by and see her. We all feel so guilty that we don't get up to visit more often. You know how it is, though, with kids and jobs and all." I smiled my Daddy's Girl conspiracy smile to let her know that though I was born into a life of privilege I was no better off than she was.

The nurse nodded knowingly. "My aunt Martha has been ill in Greenwood and I can't seem to make it to see her. She raised me when I was little." She picked up a chart. "It says here that I'm supposed to call the doctor before I let anyone see Miss Garrett."

"Honey, I don't have but ten minutes. I'm on my way to Memphis. I know Cousin Syl had a rough weekend, slippin' out and all. I just want to say hi. What could it hurt? If she doesn't remember me, then there's no harm done. If she does, it might make her feel better."

"She has been something of a problem lately," the nurse said, checking the clock on the wall. "She came back from her little adventure covered from head to toe in mud. She must have made a horrible mess in that big, fancy car when they brought her back." She studied the chart.

"She came back on her own?"

"She did. Got dropped off at the gate. Okay, you can have fifteen minutes. It might help her, poor thing."

I followed the nurse down the corridor wondering how long it would be before I was a "poor thing." That's a classification of unmarried females which negates whether a woman is single by choice or not. A woman could have been the first female to the moon, or have invented the cure for cancer, but if she doesn't marry, she will end up being a "poor thing."

"Does Cousin Syl get many visitors?"

"More than usual lately." She stopped. "Here's her room."

When the nurse pushed open the door, I walked into a lovely suite that could have been part of an English estate. The woman sitting at a delicate antique desk had a sheaf of white-blond hair that hung down below her waist. Rich, luminous hair that seemed to radiate its own light.

"Miss Garrett," the nurse said, her voice holding a degree of respect. "You have a visitor." Sylvia turned to face us.

What I noticed first was that Sylvia Garrett's silver eyes fixed on me and pinned me like a butterfly to a corkboard. She shared her brother's directness, but there the resemblance ended. Her face was completely unlined, her skin opalescent and beautiful, framed by the mass of straight, incredible hair. She was a study in moonlight, a woman of alabaster.

"Cousin Sylvia," I said, recovering and stepping forward. "Do you remember me? Sarah Booth?"

Her smile was sly. "Of course I do, Sarah Booth, come in and sit down."

I looked at the nurse, who nodded. "Just a few minutes," she agreed. "Don't get her upset."

The door closed behind me. "Did Hamilton send you to convince me to behave?" Sylvia asked, motioning me into the room.

"No." Although I was raised not to stare, I couldn't help myself. She was beautiful. Her darker eyebrows and eyelashes contrasted with her delicate, flawless skin.

"People do find me interesting to look at," she said, not at all perturbed by my rudeness.

"I'm sorry," I mumbled and looked down at the floor, which was covered in an expensive hand-woven carpet. On the bedside table was a fresh bouquet of birds-of-paradise, the purple-and-orange blooms exquisite in a globe of blue that seemed to glow with the afternoon light.

She noticed my interest. "The vase was a gift from my father," she said. "At Knob Hill there's a sculpture."

"The pink lady," I said, immediately remembering the fascinating work.

"Yes." She nodded at a collection of breathtaking colored bottles in a glass bookcase and I thought of Tammy. These had to be the bottles she once dusted with such concern. "Beautiful, aren't they." She went to the case and picked one out, fondling it carefully.

For a moment she stared out the window at the manicured grounds. "Do you know how long a day can be here?" she asked. "Some days are like years, and those are the good ones. Others last for decades. But prisons come in all shapes and degrees of luxury. A room, a continent, a dark corner of the mind."

I looked at the shelves of books and music. Someone had tried to make her prison as palatable as possible, but she was right; it was still a prison, even if she'd volunteered to stay.

She seemed to reassess me. "Who are you and what do you want?"

"Information. About the past."

Her hand on the arm of her chair trembled, but her fingers grasped the carved wood. "I've been here nineteen years. Why the sudden interest in the past?"

"I was thirteen when your father was killed."

"And that explains nothing," she answered. "I was seventeen. Away at school. My father's body had already been prepared for burial by the time I was told of his death. My mother had decided everything. Even how she was going to sell Knob Hill and move." She moved to a seat facing me.

Sylvia's anger seemed alive in the room. I wondered what would happen if she were turned loose. "What do you want to know?" she asked, eyes wary and alert.

My time was short, and she didn't seem the type to suffer a fool. "Do you know who killed your father?"

She leaned back in the chair and slowly relaxed her hands. "My version of the truth is somewhat suspect. Haven't you heard? I'm insane."

I couldn't tell if she was mocking herself or me. "I'm willing to take a risk on your version."

She was so still. "I don't know," she said. "I was at school. Mother was careful. Oh, so careful. She had friends, male friends, but they came and went. They danced and laughed and played cards." She leaned forward, a blush on her ivory cheeks. "There was never a hint of such dark passions. It was all so socially acceptable." Her smile turned bitter. "But there was someone. And she knew that I knew. I told her so. And I told her I would find out. I told her that I would never rest until I made her pay for what she'd done. And that was my mistake. I warned her."

She rose from her chair so suddenly that I pressed back in mine. My reaction made her laugh. "You're smart to be afraid of me. There's no telling what I might do." She walked to a desk in the corner of the room and I was taken with the way she moved. She had the grace of a dancer, the body of a woman who worked at keeping fit. And that sheaf of blond hair swung around her hips. She was thirty-six. Nineteen years must have been an eternity. "Ask something else."

"What were you doing at Delo's?"

"Looking for buried treasure. There's half a million buried somewhere in Delo's fields." She faced me and smiled. It was chilling to witness. "Everyone's hunting for it. Haven't you heard?"

"Treasure?" Was this some *Gilligan's Island* fantasy? It was an act of pure insanity to go out to a cornfield on a freezing November night, unless there was a mighty good reason. "Where would Delo get half a million dollars?"

"It wasn't Delo's. It was payoff money. Meant for my father."

I didn't follow. "Your father was in a dove field to get a bribe?"

She gave me a long look of contempt that chilled me to the bone. "My father couldn't be bought. What is it you really want?"

"You know Delo's dead."

One eyebrow lifted. "And you wonder if I might have killed him."

"Did you?"

"The gun they will have found beside the body is mine. A Remington. A gift from my mother when I was twelve. She had my initials engraved on a brass plate. She thought hunting would be good for me. Or maybe she hoped I'd shoot myself." She picked up the bottle she'd held before, lifting it to the light so that it seemed to glow. "I'm allowed a few harmless indulgences here. One of them is collecting. I bought this only last month from an auction in California. Amazing what items come onto the market. People get in financial situations and they're forced to part with valued possessions. Acts of desperation." She came to me and put it in my hand. "Lovely, isn't it?"

"Yes." It was exquisite, but her train of thought shifted faster than the Orient Express. I believed she was crazy.

"Give this to my brother. Tell him that the pits of hell are opening and the bones are crawling from the cold, damp earth. Vengeance is neither swift nor just, but inexorable." Her eyes glittered. "Tell him the waiting is over, for both of us."

•　　•　　•

The drive home was a blur. I played an old Arlo Guthrie tape and sang along, remembering my mother, who knew all the words. Even when the songs began to repeat themselves, I kept driving and singing. The beautiful glass bottle was on the seat beside me, but I didn't look at it. I didn't want to think, because there was no good place my thoughts could go. By the time I turned off the old highway and started down the drive to Dahlia House, night had fallen, and once again I regretted that I had not left a light on. Sylvia Garrett had spooked me.

I was interested in Hamilton. Very interested. In a way that had brought turmoil and grief into my life. I did not want to believe that he had deliberately plotted to kill his mother. But Sylvia had left me with some mighty big doubts where Hamilton the Fifth was concerned. Had he left her institutionalized for nineteen years to take his rap? Or was she the murderess? Of her mother *and* Delo?

If she wasn't at the scene of Delo's murder, then she had been in the vicinity, digging in the mud. After nineteen years, she made a break for freedom on the weekend Delo was shot. The timing was suspicious, to say the least.

I parked beneath the big magnolia tree and quickly pulled the tarp over the car. My first order of business in the morning was going to be to pay a few back notes on the Roadster. I had the cash now, thanks to Tinkie.

The night was cold and I shivered. Dahlia House was a huge square of blackness, and I hoped Jitty was waiting for me in the kitchen.

As I started around to the back with Sylvia's bottle in hand, I saw movement on the front porch. Remembering Hamilton's earlier visit, my impulse was to run inside and lock the door. But it might be Harold, waiting for me. I headed that way.

"Home at last," came the sultry tones of Kincaid Maxwell. "I was beginning to think you'd skipped town and left all your debts for poor old Harold to settle. Interesting bauble. Where did you get it?"

"A, I'm capable of settling my own debts, and B, none of your business," I informed her, overcoming my shock at her visit. Kincaid wouldn't normally waste her social hours on the likes of me. This had to be a business call, and since there were no witnesses to this exchange, I had a feeling that the gloves were going to come off. In a way, it was the best thing that could have happened to me. I'd had a rough day, and there was no one I'd rather dump on than Kincaid.

"Is that why Harold Erkwell sent me a check for your lunch at the charity ball?"

"Probably Harold sent it because he's a gentleman, and a generous one at that," I replied, wanting nothing more than to wring Harold's neck. There was no way he could have anticipated the repercussions of his act, but nonetheless . . .

"They're all generous, until you marry them," Kincaid said.

"That was your mistake, Kincaid. Not mine." A little salt in an open wound is always refreshing.

"That's true, I don't have to come to parties dressed like a slut to get attention," she parried.

I was getting a little tired of the banter. "What do you want? Say it and then leave."

"I hear you're good at finding out things."

If I had not been leaning on the porch railing I would have fallen into the azalea bushes. "What?"

"Don't play dumb with me. My money's as good as Tinkie's."

I wanted to strangle Tinkie more than Harold. "What kind of things do you want found out?" It would be quicker just to listen to her. I pushed open the front door. A week ago I'd been ashamed of the state of Dahlia House. I wouldn't have wanted a Daddy's Girl inside. But I'd changed. "Come on in, Kincaid. I'll pour us a glass of moonshine."

"That sounds divine," she answered, trotting in behind me.

I carefully placed Sylvia's bottle on the sideboard by the decanter. When I snapped on a lamp, the little bottle glowed with life, and I couldn't stop myself from thinking about Hamilton. I now had a reason to see him again.

"Sarah Booth?" Kincaid said, almost at my elbow.

I divided the last of the moonshine. I also lit a fire with some of the wood Harold had carried in for me. In five minutes the room had taken on a pleasant glow.

"This is strictly confidential," Kincaid began.

I wondered if she was stupid or desperate. "What do you want?"

"It's a delicate matter." She stared into the moonshine but failed to continue.

She was obviously getting cold feet. "Man or money?" I asked. There were no matters more delicate for a Daddy's Girl.

"Both," she said and pressed her lips together.

It occurred to me then that she was afraid. Kincaid, who got the tennis pro first, who always had the newest car, who wore the sexiest clothes and then called others sluts.

I would like to say that her situation didn't give me pleasure, but I'd lied enough in the past week. I was having a good time. "Tell me about it," I said smoothly.

"It's Chas. If he finds out about the money—"

I waved her to silence. "From the beginning," I ordered.

"My God, it is such a mess," she whispered and then belted back all of the liquor. She regained a little Kincaid hauteur and met my gaze. "You've got to go out to Delo Wiley's house and find the check I gave him yesterday morning before he was killed. He didn't have time to cash it, being Sunday and all. If Chas gets wind of this, he'll—why, he'll divorce me."

19

It was my turn to knock back the rest of the moonshine, and I steadied myself against the mantel. There was the tinkling sound of Jitty's bracelets, but I knew Kincaid would assume it was a wind chime caught in the blustery north wind. After a deep breath, I excused myself and went down to the cellar to hunt for more whiskey. This night required libations. I also needed a moment to think. Kincaid's revelation had opened the door on a lot of questions, and though she was worried about a missing check, I saw potential for a murder charge. Kincaid, sheltered her entire life, obviously had not thought of this.

Among the jars of jam and syrup, I recognized another of the dark brown bottles Uncle Lyle had preferred for his liquor, saying that too much sunlight took the bite out of good whiskey. I pulled it out, blew the dust off, and headed upstairs.

Kincaid asked no questions; she simply held out her glass. Her hand was trembling. I poured us both a goodly measure and then took a seat. "The most obvious question is, why were you giving Delo money?" I said in a cool, flat voice.

"Tinkie said you could keep a secret."

I considered pointing out to her that if Deputy Gordon Walters discovered a check from her to Delo, the questions would be very public and very ugly. Gordon didn't have an appreciation for the delicate treatment needed by a Daddy's Girl. "If you want me to help, you have to tell me the facts."

"Then you'll sneak in there and get the check? I'm sure it's somewhere in his old shack."

"I haven't committed to any course of action." She was still Kincaid, perfectly willing to risk my neck to solve her problem. "What was the money for?"

Kincaid put her drink down and clasped her hands. She seemed to be struggling with herself. When she spoke, she didn't look at me. "I was renting one of his camps from him."

Kincaid didn't hunt, and she wasn't the rustic type. Roughing it, to her, meant leaving the nanny behind. Which meant she was meeting someone in the cabin for some mattress maneuvers. "I see."

"Delo knew how to keep his mouth shut," she said.

"Did it ever occur to you that a check wasn't exactly a brilliant way to pay Delo?"

She ran her fingers through her hair. "*I* didn't normally pay him. It was an emergency. I got a call Sunday morning and was told that Delo needed the money right then. The, uh, other party couldn't make it, so I had to."

I didn't actually have to know her accomplice's name, but I wanted to. It was a rare luxury to have Kincaid on the ropes. "Who *usually* pays?"

"The man," she said. "You remember that much, at least, don't you?" The sarcasm was back.

"Does this man have a name?"

"Yes," she answered, "I call him Mr. Sat-is-fac-tion."

"I can only hope he was worth it," I pointed out to her. I could see that she still didn't get the big picture. "Chew on this, Kincaid. You were probably the last person, other than the murderer, to see Delo alive. He knew things about you that you'd prefer to keep secret. Now the way I understand law enforcement, they look for someone with means, opportunity, and motive." My brick-by-brick approach to the facts was having an effect. Kincaid had gone deathly pale. "I see you as the number one suspect in Delo's murder."

"This can't be happening," she whispered, and her hand shook so hard I reached over and took the glass from her fingers. No point sloshing out perfectly good whiskey.

"It is happening," I said. I had another little time bomb to drop, but I didn't want her to faint. When she reached for the whiskey and took another sip, I nodded. A little liquid courage. "There's also the possibility that whoever you've been meeting at Delo's set you up for his murder."

The swallow of liquor got caught in her throat and I thought I'd have to use the Heimlich maneuver, but she got her breath and stood up. She began pacing in front of the fire. "He wouldn't do that. He wouldn't," she said, but it was clear she wasn't talking to me.

"Did Delo call and say he wanted the money?" I asked.

"No." She stopped and froze. "No, it was . . . him. And Delo acted a little surprised when I showed up with the check."

Betrayal is hard to watch, even when it's so deserved. I led Kincaid to her chair and eased her back into it. She took the whiskey and drank again.

"Who were you meeting?" I asked.

"This can't be real," she said, and her eyes searched mine for some sign that I was in on the joke.

"Who?" I asked.

"My God," she whispered. "You know Chas is absolutely going to kill me."

"Who?" I asked with a snap.

"Isaac Carter."

I dreamed of fields covered in corn stubble. The stalks had been chopped and broken, and dead leaves and tassels rattled in the wind. I was hiding among the debris, listening to the sounds of the hunters' boots crunching toward me. Their laughter seemed to expand in the early morning sun, golden notes hanging in the wind.

They had come to kill. They would pull the trigger two times, quickly, buckshot scattering in an ever-widening pattern. It was a morning of recreation to them, small deaths that registered only as amusement.

Hidden in the dry husks, I felt the ground seep blood, and I darted into the air.

"There she is! Shoot her!" I was flying hard, but I looked over my shoulder and into the green eyes of Hamilton Garrett the Fifth. He stood among a cluster of men, all with shotguns to their shoulders. I heard the roar of the guns and felt the air around me shudder with the shock of the blasts.

I woke up gasping for air. The sheets were soaked with sweat, and the bedside clock showed two in the morning. I had kicked away the covers, and though I was sweating, I was freezing. I hurried into the bathroom and lit the space heater that had become dear to my heart. In a matter of moments I was holding my nightgown over the heater, catching the hot drafts of air in the folds of the gown.

"Mary Margaret Allen caught her gown on fire and burned to death two years ago doin' that exact same thing. They said she flared like a human torch, runnin' through the house and screamin'." Jitty appeared sitting on the side of the tub.

"It was a tragedy," I agreed. After my dream, I would have been pleasant to Satan if he had stopped to converse. I was not ready to go back to bed.

"You'd sleep better if you got laid. Call Harold. I'll bet he'd be over here before you could hang up the phone." At the mention of Harold, my thumb pulsed wickedly. I captured one last gust of hot air in my gown and ran back to the bed, jumping under the quilts.

"You've been reading too many back issues of *Cosmopolitan*. You're talking mighty trashy," I said, to cover my own confusion.

"I'll rephrase it. You need the release of—now how does that book call it? Sexual climax," she said, grinning. "I read some of your college books."

I had a terrible thought that Jitty would get too comfortable with Sigmund Freud. I could just see them both, in the parlor, deciding what was best for me, and I certainly didn't want to hear about penis envy from her. "Psychology isn't a science, exactly," I reminded her.

"I don't need a book to tell me you need to work off your rough edges." She pointed to the sheet. "More wasted sweat. If you'd applied that to Harold, our future would be secure."

"I'll think on it," I said.

Jitty took a seat on the edge of the mattress, and in the glow from the alarm clock she looked slightly ashy.

"Are you okay?" I asked. I had never seen her so gray and translucent.

"I'm a little tired. You a full time job, Sarah Booth. You enough to wear a ghost to a frazzle."

"Tell me about it," I answered. "Do you think Isaac Carter killed Delo?" I asked her. Since Kincaid left we hadn't actually talked, but I knew she'd been privy to the entire exchange.

"Strange that Isaac Carter keeps turnin' up in that dove field. Ever' time you turn around, he's standing there at the scene of tragedy. Maybe Delo was trying to blackmail him."

"But to kill Delo in the exact same spot as Guy Garrett. That's—"

"Sick? So? Have you considered what type of man would crawl naked between the sheets with Kincaid Maxwell? He's lucky he came out whole. Kincaid likes her meat sliced and portioned."

"Kincaid is pretty," I felt obliged to point out.

"Pretty bitchy. She doesn't strike me as the type to risk her marriage and security for the pleasure of a little thigh rubbin'. Unless she was getting somethin' in return."

"Like what?" I asked, curious about Jitty's train of thought. Kincaid had always made it clear that for her, sex was a form of barter and a means to scale the social ladder. She only screwed the tennis pro for the prestige of saying she had him first—and she got a great deal on tennis lessons.

"Like revenge."

"Against Chas?"

"Who better? He's the kind of man could make a woman's blood run cold. I don't lay claim to bein' no psychiatrist, but I'll bet life with Chas Maxwell has been about as pleasurable as summers on the Sahara."

I hadn't actually thought of Chas as a man. Not ever. He was thin, effete, and prissy. And he was the heir to the Maxwell estate and railroad holdings. He spent a great part of his day in business negotiations with Isaac Carter.

"But Carter's old enough to be Kincaid's father," I pointed out. "In fact, he and her father are friends. They play golf."

"Exactly," Jitty said, raising both eyebrows. Her skin flushed back to its full, rich color. "You got to admire the way Kincaid can pack a double whammy."

Kincaid's visit had given me bad dreams, and the ammunition to enter the glass-and-wood office of Zinnia International Export. I had not looked forward to meeting with Isaac Carter, but now it was necessary.

Kincaid wasn't my client. Not officially. I had accepted three thousand dollars, cash, as a retainer, which I told her I would hold until I made up my mind whether or not I could help her. I wasn't playing hard to get; I truly didn't want to go out to Delo's house and hunt through a dead man's things. Then again, it appeared that Delo's murder was firmly tied into the case I was already working on.

Isaac did not look happy to see me, though he allowed his secretary to send me straight back to his office. He remained seated and waved me into a chair—a faux pas, or else a deliberate move to let me know that he didn't consider me to be on the same social level as he was. I took it as the latter and put an enormous "Bite Me" smile on my face.

"You've left Kincaid in rather a bad position," I said, gratified to see that his calm quickly turned to panic. "If she gets pegged for the Delo Wiley murder, you won't walk away from this clean. I can promise you that."

"What do you want?" he asked, opening his drawer and bringing out a checkbook.

Aha! He thought I'd come to blackmail him. That would be the first thought that jumped into a Buddy Clubber's peanut-sized brain.

"I want to know what happened on the day that Hamilton Garrett the Fourth was killed," I said, glad to see that my change in conversational direction had caused him even more consternation.

"What is it with you, Sarah Booth? Why can't you leave well enough alone?"

I had an answer for him. "Call it a Delaney gift," I said. "We Delaneys have a thing about difficult paths. I suppose a search for truth after twenty years of lies could be considered one of those rock-strewn road-ways."

He narrowed his eyes at me and took a breath. He was still a handsome man, though wattles—even small ones—were not something I found sexually stimulating. Still, there was snap in his gaze and tension in his lips as he returned my perusal.

"Nobility is an expensive habit," he said. "I never figured you for that kind. I always viewed you more as, shall we say, hedonistic and lazy."

"Unlike Kincaid, who is uptight and busy?" I asked. "But she is married, too, which adds a bit more spice to it. Especially for a man who never really had to risk much in business, since it was all handed to him." I didn't mind crossing swords with Isaac. Though he had been an associate of my father's, I'd never heard his name spoken with any great degree of respect.

"You're a disgrace to your family name," he said between clenched teeth.

"We can trade complimentary observations all morning, or we can get this over with," I said. "I'm not leaving until I find out a couple of things. Why was Guy Garrett in the dove field when he wasn't a hunter, and who were the two strangers that you brought to the field with you?"

"And if I tell you these things, you'll keep quiet about Kincaid?"

"You've set your mistress up for a murder rap. I'm a little curious about the reasons behind that, so I can't make any empty promises. But I will agree to destroy the tape recording Kincaid made of you requesting her to pay Delo off."

It seemed that Isaac Carter brought out the very best in me when it came to doing PI work. I had no compunction about lying to him. *Au contraire!* It gave me great pleasure.

"She taped me?"

The tête-à-têtes between Kincaid and Isaac were now history. I had torpedoed their trust factor. Too bad. But I had also thought of a way to save Kincaid's skin, only because I knew she hadn't killed Delo. Kincaid was not passionate enough to pull the trigger twice at a man's head. Besides, if she'd actually decided to kill someone, her husband would have been at the top of her list. Wealthy widowdom is the pinnacle of achievement for a Daddy's Girl.

My plan was to blackmail Isaac into stealing the check back, since he was the one who'd gotten Kincaid into the jam to begin with. Then I could keep the three thousand.

"When you decided to take a Daddy's Girl as your mistress, you should have been prepared for the consequences," I told him. "We're always prepared. Always."

"The men in the field were Arthur Lowry and Aubrey Malone."

The names were not familiar. "Should I know them?"

His look spoke volumes about how I shouldn't presume to know anyone who might be anybody. I had been born a Daddy's Girl, but I was hanging on by my teeth.

"They're businessmen. From Memphis. They had come down to talk with Hamilton the Fourth about some investments. And that's also the reason he was in the dove field. It was a business meeting, and though he wasn't much of a shot, I'd talked him into going along with us. Guy sometimes gave the impression that he wasn't really a man's man."

I lifted my eyebrows for clarification.

"He wasn't gay, he just wasn't . . ."

"He didn't feel the need to express his manhood in stupid, macho ways," I supplied.

"He put people off. His only saving grace was Veronica. Now she was all woman, and that was a good reflection on him."

If I'd had time I would have given him my thoughts on women who "reflected" on their men. But as Jitty would say, I had bigger fish to fry.

"Who shot Hamilton?" I asked.

He started to stand, then didn't. "I don't know." The furrow between his brow spoke of his truthfulness. "I was down by the river with the rest of the boys. I meant to go check on Guy because I knew this wasn't his sport, but I saw him walking off with Lowry and Malone, so I hung back. It was a business meeting, as I said."

"And what was the business?" I remembered Sylvia's remark about a payoff.

He placed a hand on his chest. "Some of us men had come up with a development plan for the county. We wanted to try to push it through the Board of Supervisors before too many questions were asked."

"And Hamilton was part of this?"

"Not exactly." Isaac picked up a pen and tapped it on the desk. "The plan didn't come about. After Hamilton was killed, Pasco felt we should drop it."

"Hamilton was opposed to the plan?" This was tougher than pulling teeth.

"Lowry and Malone were supposed to talk him into it."

"What was the plan?"

"It wasn't exactly a plan. It was more of a zoning thing."

I had always hated business. I knew instinctively that where there was a buck to be made, someone was manipulating the rules. Zoning was a perfect example. I signaled him to continue.

"We had a county-wide zoning plan that would restrict commercial development in certain areas, and change residential to commercial in others."

"All to benefit—"

"Don't be so stupid, Sarah Booth. Who the hell do you think it would benefit?"

"And Hamilton? Where did he fit in?"

"He was president of the county zoning board." Isaac put the pen down and clasped his hands. "And not likely to go along with this idea."

I really had him talking. "So . . ."

"So a lot of the zoning changes were in the black part of town. There were plans for developing a county-wide park with a movie complex, bowling lanes, and eventually to attract a gambling boat on the river. It would have been a great thing for Sunflower County."

"And let me guess, the best location was where most of the black people live." The Grove bordered the Tibbeyama River. For decades, the land had been considered worthless because it flooded and was the breeding ground for mosquitoes and other plague-carrying insects. With the prospect of gambling, it would have been priceless.

"They would have gotten fair market value."

He might have believed it or he might not have. "There is no fair market value for someone's home," I said.

He stood up and leaned on his desk. "You can say that because you've never done without. Not even now, when you think you're impoverished. But the money we intended to offer could have made a big difference to some of those families. They could have relocated, bought more land, built new homes. Don't be so quick to judge. It would have displaced some people but, in the long run, everyone in Sunflower County would have benefited."

It took about five seconds for me to put the rest of it together. "They were going to buy him." The scene in the dove field became clear. The seclusion of the Mule Bog field, the men with their big hunting vests and gear, a perfect place for cash to change hands. "How much?"

"A million dollars."

I swallowed. "And he had agreed to take the money?"

"More or less."

"So what happened?"

"I don't know," he said. "I truly don't."

I wasn't certain I believed him. "Those men, Lowry and Malone, were the last to talk with him?" I wondered if they were businessmen or mobsters. "Did they give him the money?"

"As far as I know." He stood up. "But I don't think they killed him."

I was surprised that Isaac had enough testosterone to set a perfect scapegoat free. "Why not?"

"He wasn't any good to them dead. Besides, the money disappeared." Isaac straightened his shoulders.

"Perhaps he didn't agree, and they killed him and took back the money." This had to be the money Sylvia had made reference to. It crossed my mind that Isaac Carter wasn't above walking off with a cool million, either.

He shook his head. "They didn't have it."

"How can you be so sure?"

"They were as upset as I was. And they were too afraid to complain."

"Then who do you think took it?"

He paced the room. "I always thought it was Veronica. It was a perfect opportunity for her. All of that money right in her hand. Then if she got rid of Hamilton, she'd be a wealthy widow. She told me once that being married to Hamilton was like being chained to a stone wall in a place that no one ever visited. She said she'd never been so lonely, and she wanted a divorce. I figured she saw that a widow was in a much better position, financially, than a divorcée."

"You think she knew about the payoff and had him killed?"

He nodded. "A lot of folks don't think a woman could pull the trigger and shoot a man in the back. I think she could have done it and then gone home and eaten a big supper. Veronica had a healthy appetite, for everything."

I couldn't be certain if he was bragging that he'd sampled Veronica's smorgasbord of delights, or if he was just gossiping. "But someone in the dove field shot him, whatever his or her motives might have been. And you helped cover it up."

"I did what I had to do," he answered. "Hamilton was dead. The way I saw it, no one would benefit by filing a murder charge. Malone and Lowry had come up with the money from a variety of sources, none of which could stand the scrutiny of an investigation."

That was pure Buddy Clubber logic. "And Delo, was he in on it?"

Isaac shook his head. "I was never certain how much Delo knew. But I did get a call from him the Saturday before he was killed, asking for money. He said he knew things he'd never told, and that someone was willing to pay to hear them. That's when he said he wanted cash. Kitty and I were obligated to go to a christening, so I called Kincaid and asked her to take him some money. I told her it was for the use of the cabin."

I was about tired of his way of looking at life. "Before you go home to Kitty tonight, go over to Delo's and get that check Kincaid wrote."

"Gordon Walters is all over that place."

"That's why you need to be very, very careful." I got up to leave. "There's only one problem with your scenario. Veronica was killed and the money was never found."

20

I was exhausted. What had started as a simple probe into historical gossip had turned into a current murder with lots of ugly implications. I had interviewed half a dozen people, and I was no closer to finding the truth than I had been the week before when I wasn't even a PI. The problem was that I'd discovered more than I ever thought possible. My initial take on this job was completely wrong. I'd imagined digging up a few half-truths and rounding it all out with some creative faction. I'd read Truman Capote and his army of imitators. I was clever, imaginative, and equipped with a certain infallible female logic. I could have created a yarn to suit Tinkie's purposes—and maybe even save her some grief on down the road.

Somehow, everything had changed. This was no longer a Tinkie-driven investigation. Guy Garrett had been murdered. Likely Veronica, too. A large sum of money had gone missing—and never been reported. And Delo Wiley was dead.

My mind kept going back to Sylvia. Nineteen years in

Glen Oaks. She had struck me as someone who, if she hadn't been nuts when she went in, was certifiable now. Guilt *could* drive a person mad, I reasoned. But so could living in a mental institution for nearly two decades.

On the spur of the moment I decided to stop in at the bank. I really had to pay some back notes on the Roadster. And I wanted to see Harold. I didn't want anything in particular from him, I just wanted to see how he reacted to me. I realized that it was a trapping of a Daddy's Girl, this need to check my ability to draw a reaction. But I decided to indulge it anyway. My visit with Sylvia and the ensuing dream had left me wary of my desires where Hamilton was concerned. Maybe Jitty was right. Harold was not such a bad option after all.

I walked into the lobby, went to the first available clerk, and stated my intention to bring my car notes up to date. She disappeared into the depths of the bank, and in a few minutes, Oscar Richmond appeared at the window. He grinned. "You looked terrific at Harold's party," he said, nodding. "Nice entrance."

"Thanks." Oscar wasn't given to compliments. He wanted something. "You'll be glad to know I'm bringing my car payments up to date." I pulled a checkbook from my purse.

"Tinkie still hasn't told me what you're doing for Mother Bellcase."

So this was what he wanted. I winked. "Oscar, honey, you know I'm the only one of our set who can keep a secret."

"I'm worried about you, Sarah Booth."

Right, I thought. Worried about Mother Bellcase's money slipping from his grasp. "You're such a big old bear to worry about me," I said, sweeter than prune juice and producing the same effect. "But I'm fine. In fact, when I finish my business here, I'm going to stop in and surprise Harold."

Oscar nodded. "Now that does relieve my mind, Sarah Booth. Harold has a good head on his shoulders. He won't let you get in trouble."

"Exactly my thoughts," I said. I looked at the amount the clerk had written on a slip of paper and nearly staggered. I was four thousand dollars behind on the car. But I wrote out the check like a grown-up, and smiled as I turned it over.

My trip across the lobby drew speculative gazes as I headed for the closed door of Harold's private domain. His secretary announced me, and in a few seconds his door swung open. Harold, in a gray pinstripe suit that made his steel gray hair seem even more distinguished than normal, took my hand in a warm grip.

"What a delightful surprise," he said, ushering me into the room and closing the door behind us. "What are you up to today?" he asked, still holding my hand.

It occurred to me that Harold might be the perfect person to ask about some of the things that were troubling me. "Did you ever hear that a large sum of money went astray when Hamilton Garrett the Fourth was killed?"

Harold lifted his eyebrows. "I wasn't in Zinnia when Mr. Garrett died."

"But since then?" I pressed. "Bank gossip, over coffee with the directors, that kind of thing."

"It's a bad policy for a banker to deal in speculation and gossip," he answered. "Why are you so interested in the Garretts' old affairs?"

He was jealous. "Oh, Harold, don't be stuffy," I said. "I came to you because I knew you'd know. And I knew you'd tell me the truth." Fiddle-dee-dee almost jumped out of my mouth, but I bit it back.

He shrugged. "There were *rumors* about money out at Delo's. Buried treasure, that kind of thing. But it was all foolishness. Some folks still go out there digging, I understand, looking for the lost money." He looked down at the desk. "If a large sum really went missing, someone would have investigated it."

"They hardly investigate murder here in Zinnia. Why should they go after buried treasure?" I pointed out.

"I doubt there's a bit of truth to any of this, Sarah Booth," Harold said in a gentler tone. "The Garretts were a wealthy family who suffered great tragedy. That kind of thing always breeds gossip and tales."

I heard Harold, but I wasn't paying much attention to his excuses. My mind was off and running. If a large sum of money disappeared, where would it have gone? Since Veronica was dead and Sylvia was in the nuthouse, Hamilton the Fifth was the obvious answer. I looked up to find that Harold was watching me. "It *could* have been buried in the fields at Delo's house. Perhaps that's why someone killed Delo. Now that I think about it, there are some strange holes there."

"That's a romantic notion," Harold said, lifting my hand and examining the still-ringless fingers. "It's bad business, whatever happened. Not something I want my future bride to worry about." He pointed to his desk. "Come over here. I want to discuss Dahlia House."

My hackles rose instantly, until he continued.

"I thought we might live at Dahlia House after the wedding," he said as he handed me into a wing chair to the side of his desk. "It is your home, and I know how much you love it. And my house in town will be easy to sell. But I think we should put the land to use, don't you? It seems such a waste for that soil to grow nothing but weeds."

Hearing him talk about Dahlia House as if he cared

about it, not as some valuable piece of real estate, was almost more than I could take. "I didn't realize you were interested in farming," I said.

"I'm interested in making you happy. Farming seems to be required to reach my goal."

Before I could answer there was a tap at the door and Oscar entered.

"It's a good thing you're still here, Sarah Booth. Gordon Walters is outside with a court order for us to turn all of your financial records over to him." Oscar gave me a dirty look. "This means Mother Bellcase's name might come up."

"My records? Why?"

"You're under investigation," Oscar said simply.

"For what?"

"Oh, murder and some other things." Oscar shrugged. "Just keep Mother Bellcase's name out of the press. She's not in good health, and a scandal might finish her off."

I wanted to ask him what he thought a scandal would do to me, but I knew the answer. He didn't care. I looked at Harold. "Can we block this?"

"Not if the court order is legitimate." He came around the desk and put a hand on my·shoulder. "Not to worry, Sarah Booth. This kind of thing happens more than anyone knows. Financial records have become a primary source for law officers to track the comings and goings of wanted felons."

"I'm not a felon," I insisted.

Harold's grip tightened slightly, and he leaned down to whisper in my ear. "Even if you are, it doesn't matter. I'll still marry you."

Great, I thought. Just great.

•   •   •

After I watched Gordon haul off my sordid financial past in a cardboard box, I decided that grease and ketchup were required to elevate my mood. I refused Harold's offer of lunch and went solo to Millie's Café. I was really too depressed to continue my PI work. I just wanted a double-cheese-and-bacon burger, 'tater wedges rolled in Cajun spices, a diet Coke over crushed ice with a straw in it, and a bottle of Heinz ketchup. Millie served only the finest yellow rat cheese, in contrast to that plastic stuff most fast food places used, and she always had Heinz ketchup. If a body is going into a grease-and-ketchup slump, only the real stuff is effective.

I parked on a stool at the counter and waited my turn. It was in the mirror that I caught Millie staring at me. Not directly—she was using a shiny napkin holder to watch my reflection. My PI antenna cranked up, though I was careful not to change my posture or my expression. When Millie turned around to face me, I gave her a friendly wave and my order.

The café was busy, and Millie was on her feet hauling iced tea, hot coffee, and platters of food that smelled so good my mouth was watering. As a crisp mountain of fried onion rings passed by me, I regretted not ordering both wedges and rings. No wonder Millie looked like a thirty-year-old. She crisscrossed the café at least a hundred times. All the while she kept shooting glances my way. I wondered if Billie had somehow discovered my snooping in his garage.

Millie swung down the counter, refilling iced tea glasses, and picked up my order from the window. When she put it down in front of me, she avoided my gaze.

"Have you got a minute?" I asked.

She looked everywhere but at me. "There are a lot of

hungry folks in here . . ." She reached up to the window and picked up two plates loaded with fried chicken, mashed potatoes, and fried okra. I was struck by the thought that almost all brown foods are delicious. If brown was the basic group at the bottom of the food pyramid, I would be a very healthy woman.

"It won't take but a minute. Millie, did you ever work for your brother at the garage?"

I don't know what made her drop the plates, but they tumbled from her hand. They flipped three or four times, the okra and chicken flying but the mashed potatoes hanging on before the plates hit the floor and shattered.

Millie stood there, staring at the mess and then looking at me. I half expected her to be furious. Instead, a large tear rolled out of each eye and tracked down her cheeks. The café had gone silent, and everyone seemed to be staring at us.

"I didn't work for Billie," she said. "Why can't you mind your own business, Sarah Booth? I hear about you asking questions. Well, if you have to know, it was Janice, my baby sister. She worked for Billie that summer."

I didn't know Millie had a sister. So that explained the feminine handwriting on the files. "Let me give you a hand," I said, standing up from the stool and walking behind the counter to help her clean up the mess.

"Sit down and eat your lunch." She grabbed a handful of paper napkins and stood clutching them with white knuckles. "Lon, give me two fried white meats, okra, and mashed with rolls," she called through the window. She turned back to me. "Go eat while it's hot. I'll take care of this."

I picked up the chicken breasts and dropped them in a trashcan. "I don't mind—"

"Go," she said, putting a firm hand on my arm. "Don't make it harder than it is. One thing I don't need is a Daddy's Girl behind my counter."

Millie's words cut deep. I'd never given her reason to treat me in such a way. I nodded and went back to my seat. The noise level in the restaurant began to climb again, a din of cutlery, glassware, laughter, whispers, and general conversation.

I drowned the wedges and the burger in ketchup and began to eat. The food was delicious, but Millie's emotional barrage had taken the pleasure out of the meal. I ate slowly, and watched the townsfolk of Zinnia having their lunch. The front of the restaurant held small tables, and the counter was along the back by the kitchen and the grills. Each table seated four, although people often moved from table to table, talking and catching up. Elections were determined in that café, paternity settled, menus planned, and marriages mended or ended. I eavesdropped. Coleman Peters seemed to be a popular sheriff, based on the gossip, and there was a low buzz about Hamilton returning to town and the tragic deaths of his parents. A few people looked at me or Millie and then away, but no one said anything about our encounter. As far as I knew.

I dipped my last potato wedge in ketchup and swallowed it down, even though the waistband of my jeans had cut off the blood supply to my lower extremities. I didn't need circulation in that direction anyway. I wanted my brain in control. I put money on the counter, stood, gathered my purse, and prepared to leave.

On the way to the door, I felt a tug on my shirt. When I turned around, Clara Beth King held out a hand for me to shake. She was ninety if she was a day, an old scrapper who'd lived through fevers and depressions and who looked at life through a sharply focused lens.

She had been one of my mother's greatest pleasures. When I was a child, Clara Beth, who had never married, often rode over to Dahlia on her big gray stallion named Spartacus. She'd spend the morning talking with Mother and then mount up and ride home, a distance of four or five miles. My mother had greatly admired her.

"Miss King," I said. "You look wonderful."

"I'm feeling spry for a woman of my advanced years. I attribute it to the fact that I never allowed a man to attach himself permanently to me. I see you're following in my footsteps."

"I'm too busy to worry about men," I answered, though I had two of them in the back of my mind.

"I just wanted to tell you that Millie isn't upset with you, honey. Her younger sister disappeared one day when she was working at Billie's shop. Millie and Janice were very close, and no one ever found out what happened to her. Millie keeps it all inside her, but I think you just pried the lid off."

I leaned down so I could talk softer. "Did Janice run away?"

She shook her head and sipped her glass of iced tea. "No one knows. She was tending the shop, and Billie took a client out on a test ride with his car. When he came back, the shop was wide open and she was gone. There's never been a trace of what happened to her. No sign of trouble. She left all her things at Millie's. It was like she picked up her purse and took off."

Miss King sipped her tea, then carefully wiped her mouth on her napkin.

"How old was she?" I asked.

"Eighteen or twenty. A young thing. It was said she was seeing a man from across the river. A married man."

I felt terrible for Millie.

"Janice was on the wild side. Not mean or a trouble-maker, but she was high-spirited. I wouldn't be sur-prised if she's not living it up somewhere."

"Wouldn't she call her family?" I asked.

Miss King gave me a smile that was so sad it hurt. "I never did. I came here sixty-seven years ago with a man I decided to marry against my family's wishes. We never made it to the altar, and I never once called back to Hammond and told anyone where I had moved to, not even when he left me. When I severed the ties with my family and my town, they were slashed. Sometimes, you just have to walk away and never look back."

21

I went back to Dahlia House and threw myself on the sofa. It had been a rotten day. My legs and lower extremities had gone numb from gluttony and tight pants. I unzipped the jeans and put a sofa pillow over my face.

"Hidin' in here won't do a bit of good. Not a bit."

I eased the cushion aside to look up at Jitty. She'd plopped down on the arm of the sofa. Her 'fro was gone, replaced by hair carefully straightened into a pageboy. She wore heavy silver eye shadow, burgundy lipstick, and a halter dress made of a silvery/metallic material. "You look like some kind of hellish, backup-singing astronaut," I told her.

"Bein' ugly to me won't make your troubles go away." She smiled, and I noticed that even the lipstick had little glittery sparkles in it. Where did she find this stuff? There had to be a heavenly outlet store trafficking in ungodly cosmetics.

"I'm goin' to a party tonight. It's disco." She sounded delighted.

"So you're here to rub it in that even a ghost has more of a social life than I do."

She laughed. "You'll have company tonight."

"And who might that be, Disco Duck?" I pulled myself into a sitting position. "Have a good time."

She stood up and walked to the armchair, settling gracefully onto the cushion in her metallic skin of material. I had to admit, the dress looked terrific on her. It reflected every move she made.

"Do you remember back when you were a little girl and your daddy was still a judge on the bench?"

Very clearly. In fact, at times those days seemed more real than the life I was living. I nodded.

"Hamilton the Fourth visited your daddy a few times. Neither of them were hunters. And they shared a love of music, among other things, as I remember."

As she talked I did remember a tall, handsome man coming to visit, and playing the piano while my mother and father listened and drank wine. My parents believed in "quiet" evenings, when I was sent to my room with my supper. It wasn't punishment, simply a way for them to have an adult evening and for me to learn self-reliance. It was only as an adult that I realized they were undoubtedly talking business. Something I shouldn't hear.

I started to ask Jitty about those visits, but when I looked up she was gone. "Jitty?" I said softly.

There was the distant jangle of her bracelets, but I was alone in the house. Perhaps it was evening in ghostville and she had gone on to her party.

I thought about Hamilton Garrett the Fourth and his music, the way the lively piano tunes had drifted up the staircase to my room. The time I was thinking of, it had been hot weather, the windows and doors open throughout the house. I could remember the laughter, and then my mother came up to check on me, and my father and Mr. Garrett talked. It was the summer I was thirteen, the year my parents died, the year Guy Garrett was murdered.

Were his visits about more than a love of music? My father had been a circuit court judge. A lot of people sought advice, or help, from him.

Those tiny thoughts darted through my brain like frightened minnows. I had a lot of loose ends and no conclusions, and I was out of ideas about how to find the truth. I decided to nap off the lunch I'd eaten at Millie's.

I awoke with the slanting rays of late afternoon sun filtering through the parlor windows. At first I was disoriented, waking downstairs in the cold. I roused myself from the sofa and retrieved the mail, flipping through bills and catalogs without much interest. My brain felt fuzzy and my heart unsettled. The quality of light just before dusk on a clear winter day is loaded with poignancy. My mother had called it "the blue hour," when melancholy slips into a room unnoticed and touches everything with a sprinkling of pain.

I saw the heavy, square envelope and flipped it over. My name and address were written in elaborate calligraphy. I recognized it instantly as an invitation and tore it open with some relief—an antidote to my blue yearnings.

It was the last-minute details of the summons to Kincaid's charity do. It outlined in great detail that this year was a theme party with "country" being the operative word. *Costumes required.*

How like Kincaid to demand costumes at the very last minute. She'd probably had hers planned for months, and deliberately saved this little fillip to make everyone else crazy. Perhaps I shouldn't have intervened on her behalf and sent Isaac to retrieve her check.

But even as I steamed over the last-minute rules Kincaid had dictated, I remembered a long-ago party my parents had attended. They had gone as Porter Wagoner and Dolly Parton, reigning royalty of country music during the early seventies. Perhaps I could give Kincaid a run for her money. I seemed to recall a lot of rhinestones and fringe.

The attic was a part of the house I seldom visited. Jitty seemed to love it, going through the stacks of old magazines and the wardrobe trunks that contained crinolines and bustles, whalebone corsets and real silk stockings. The Delaney women had always been sharp dressers. I hustled up the three flights of stairs and pushed open the door that led to the vast attic.

As I stepped into the twilit room, I considered waiting until morning to hunt through the trunks and wardrobes, but time was pressing. The costume would have to be cleaned, possibly altered, all by eleven o'clock tomorrow. It would be better to find it now and get the show on the road.

There were lights in the attic, and I turned them on, but still the room was eerie. The bare overhead bulbs cast strange shadows, and as I looked out the west window, the last pink warmth of the sun disappeared. It was cold and getting colder fast now that the sun was down.

I chose a corner and began opening trunks, pushing aside material that smelled old and yet feminine. I remembered the costume as white, sexy, and crusted in glittering faux diamonds with spangles that ran down each arm. There had even been a blond wig.

I found the outfit in the fifth trunk. Pulling it from the tissue paper, I caught the scent of White Shoulders and for one brief instant, I thought perhaps my mother had come up behind me. I held the heavy dress and inhaled.

The wig was beneath the dress, along with some pointy-toed white boots in tooled leather with rhinestone insets. Hot stuff. I gathered my spoils and headed down to my room to try it all on.

It's difficult to live in the shadow of the past and not compare oneself, and as I stepped into the form-fitting dress that had been made for my mother, I realized that time had led me to a shape that closely duplicated hers. I put the wig on and matched what I saw in the mirror with the past.

Almost, but not quite, Elizabeth Marie Booth Delaney gave me a hesitant smile. My eyes were Delaney, as were my lips, but the shape of my face was Booth. My size was Mother's, and my chestnut hair could have come from either of them. My mother had been close to my age when she'd worn this dress, but she had been married with a child. I wondered if she watched me now, and worried that I would forever be alone.

I cocked half an ear for Jitty, realizing that I missed her company. She'd be able to bring the past into sharper focus.

It was full dark outside, and though it didn't seem possible, my stomach was grumbling about an evening meal. I checked the mirror one last time. The dress zipped in the back, and I reached behind to find the tab, pulling it down slowly, watching the paste jewels catch the bedroom light and glitter as the material fell away. It was a lovely dress, low-cut and sexy.

I felt an electric chill on my back as the dress slipped apart. Looking deep into the mirror, I found that I was staring into the green eyes of Hamilton Garrett the Fifth. He was leaning against the doorway of my bedroom, watching me as I undressed.

I did not freeze. That phrase doesn't begin to convey the breathless second that seemed to stretch for an eternity as I took in his intense gaze, the sensual mouth that hesitated between desire and challenge, the dark hair, unbound and brushing his collar. In that stretched second, I was aware of the breadth of his shoulders and the casual athleticism of his stance, hands hanging at his side. I wanted to turn to confront him, but I honestly couldn't move.

It wasn't until the dress moved that I recovered my faculties. Released by the zipper, the bodice slipped down my unfettered breasts. I caught at the material and held it against me, whirling to confront him.

"What are you doing here?" It was a lame question and not up to my usual abilities, but I was flustered. I attempted to make up in dramatic delivery what it lacked in originality.

"You're a little old for playing dress-up, aren't you?" He stepped into the room. "But then again, I can see the appeal of the game." Even his voice was dark. I felt like a black icicle was moving slowly down the small of my back, deliciously chilling every nerve in my spinal column.

"Get out." I spoke calmly, or as calmly as a half-dressed Dolly Parton can.

"I never thought of you as the kind of woman who dressed in front of a mirror. I like that."

"If you don't leave, I'll call the sheriff," I threatened.

"Coleman Peters is in Jackson, but I'm sure Deputy Walters will come on the run. In fact, that's who I've come to talk to you about." He walked to my bed and took a seat in the chaise lounge beside it. "Take your time getting dressed," he said.

I picked up my jeans and a blouse and stomped off to the bathroom. I slammed the door as hard as I could for good measure. The man had broken into my house, invaded the privacy of my bedroom, and caught a free peep show without bothering to make his presence known. So why was my heart racing with exhilaration? Perhaps I needed to take a moment and go through my old psychology texts. I was sure I could find myself under "foolish women who seek the thrills of dangerous men."

While I was in the bathroom I brushed my hair, applied some lipstick, and pinched color into my pale cheeks. I slipped into the more modest clothes and went to confront the beast.

The sight of him, in my chaise lounge, with my underwear dangling off the back not inches from his head, almost made me reel. Jitty had warned me about leaving my personal items strewn about the room. A woman who did not pick up her "delicates" deserved what she got. I would never hear the end of this.

Hamilton sat up and patted the edge of the bed. "Have a seat," he said, as if he were in his own home instead of mine.

"I didn't think you'd lower yourself to converse with a parasite like me." What a pathetic return.

"You're up to something, and it isn't writing for a newspaper or working on a novel," he said, pleased that he'd ferreted out that information.

"Maybe I'm just nosy," I answered hotly. "Maybe I'm fascinated by your business because I have none of my own."

"You're not in a financial position to indulge being nosy. That's for people who have everything, or those who never intend to have anything. You're playing an angle."

I wish I could say that I was completely focused on his accusations, that I was angry at his intrusion into my home, or that his harsh tone made me realize the potential danger I was in. Those emotions were the melody, but there was also something else happening, a base beat of raw chemistry that was dangerous and exciting. Hamilton was not two feet away. I could reach out and touch him, place my palm along that straight, determined jaw. I was a private investigator, but I was also a woman. And, unfortunately, a woman with a womb that was dictating orders.

"I heard you visited my sister." There was both question and demand in his statement, the stern master grilling his staff for an infraction of his rules.

"What if I did?" I threw the challenge back. The delicate glass bottle Sylvia had given me for him was down in the parlor, safely tucked on the sideboard.

Though he appeared relaxed, I saw the turmoil in his eyes. "My sister isn't well. You can't rely on anything she said. You certainly shouldn't trust her. She could get you in trouble."

"She's very angry. I think it's directed at you." I held my breath, wondering if he'd suspect that his sister had pointed the finger of blame at him.

He didn't take the bait. "Sylvia has always been . . . different. She has the strongest will." He looked at me as if I might have an answer. "Even as a child she made choices and never wavered. My father thought the sun rose and set in her. It only made a bad situation worse."

The softening of his tone caught me off guard. "What was she doing in Delo Wiley's cornfield?" I caught the slightest movement of his foot inside his shoe. He was balling up his toes and releasing them, an unconscious gesture. I watched the polished leather swell slightly, then relax.

"She believes some money is buried there." He

leaned toward me as if he would touch me. "Sarah Booth, whatever she told you, don't listen to her."

"She said the gun used to kill Delo Wiley is hers. I was wondering who else had access to that gun."

"Damn her!" he said, his brow furrowing. He recovered and straightened up. "Tell me the truth. Did you help her leave Glen Oaks?"

I realized I hadn't figured out how she'd gotten from Friars Point to Zinnia. In a nightgown. She didn't have a car. "No. It wasn't me."

Hamilton gave me a speculative look. "Did she say anything about Mother?"

I wasn't a suspect, and he wasn't Jack Webb. I decided to ask him a question. "Why did you leave her there, Hamilton? There were never formal charges filed against her. She could have left at any time—if someone had been willing to take her. Obviously you could have afforded to care for her."

A slap would not have been more shocking to him. His face paled, then flushed. "You seem to have decided to make a career of poking into my family's past. The problem is you dig up only half-truths. I'm sure there's money in this somewhere for you, but it won't come from me. No matter what you think you can unearth."

I was tired of his cavalier attitude toward my reputation. And I was tired of the conflicting impulses I felt. Hamilton Garrett was close enough to touch, and even while he hurled accusations at me, I couldn't help but register the dark stubble of beard, the weariness at the corners of his eyes. I wanted him, and yet he was there to accuse me of all sorts of odious acts. I'd had enough. "So you think I'm a blackmailer, and I think you're a—" The word stuck in my throat.

"Say it," he demanded in a harsh whisper. He sat up straighter and bored into me with that cold green stare.

"Be the one person in this town who'll actually say it to my face."

He leaned forward, and we were only inches apart. I realized how foolish it was of me to have this man in my bedroom, or any room of the house. No one knew he was here. He could kill me, and unless Tinkie came to see if I'd learned anything new, my body might lie around for days. And what would become of Jitty? I didn't want to find out if she really could follow me into eternity.

But as I looked into his eyes and caught the rhythm of his breathing, none of it mattered. Or not as much as it should have.

"Say it, Sarah Booth," he demanded, this time with a roughness to his voice that made my skin flush.

"I can't," I admitted.

"Everyone in this town wants to believe that I killed my mother. It's the perfect bone of gossip, the ideal story to gnaw and chew over a glass of wine or a lunch with friends. I've walked into restaurants and heard conversations grind to a halt. I've heard the whispers as I turned to leave a room. I know what people say, but if you're going to be the one to put all of this in print, then at least be strong enough to say out loud what everyone whispers." He reached across the short distance and caught my hand firmly in his. "Say it!"

I felt my jaw tightening. "Maybe if you'd defend yourself, people would quit talking. You're not above giving an explanation. You left the country, and you left your sister in a mental institution." I tried to remove my hand, but he tightened his grip.

"People want *proof* that I didn't kill my own mother. And I don't have any for them. I gave up a long time ago caring what people said." His voice softened, and his thumb made a slow, circular motion on the back of my hand. "But I do care what you think. Right at this moment, I care a lot. What would it take to convince you, Sarah Booth?"

He brought his other hand up to enfold mine in both of his. "Tell me what you need to believe I'm innocent." He sighed. "Or tell me that you believe I'm a murderer. Say it, and I'll walk out the door."

My brain had fallen silent. Only my heart had something to say, and there was a strange murmuring from behind my navel, something like a Gregorian chant. "I can't say it," I answered.

"Why not?" His gaze held mine and demanded an answer.

"There's no real evidence." I could have lied and said that I didn't think he was capable of murder, but I'd already accepted that everyone is capable of almost anything.

"Would you believe me if I told you I had nothing to do with my mother's death?"

"I don't know," I answered. "I can't say you're innocent, either. There's no proof either way. That's the problem."

I was surprised at his smile. "Who taught you to speak the truth?" he asked. "You've managed to escape the Delta training of your peers."

"My mother was a socialist," I replied and was rewarded with his laugh.

"I always heard the Delaneys were peculiar." He seemed to search my face. "Why did you visit my sister?"

"I need to find out the truth about the past."

"Why? Can't you simply leave it alone? What could it possibly matter to you?"

Desperation was creeping back into his tone, but he held my hand gently, his strong fingers beginning to knead the tender flesh between my thumb and fingers. He moved on to the firm base of my thumb, and his touch became increasingly erotic. My thumb gave one weak pulse in memory of Harold, which I squashed.

I could not tell him about Tinkie. She was my client, and I had an obligation to protect her. I captured his massaging hand with my free one and slowly turned it over. I bent to examine the palm. Tammy had said he was marked with trouble. He held his hand open, fingers slightly curled, like a trusting child. I brushed my fingertips across his palm and was surprised when I felt him tremble. I knew then that swooning was not something Margaret Mitchell had invented for her feckless Southern women. That I had the power to make him tremble was almost my undoing.

I focused on his palm. The base of his thumb was full and developed, and in the center of his palm, an unusual pattern of lines created an M. I could not see the tragedy that Tammy read, but I could feel his tension and pain. "I wish I could read the future here," I said.

"I wish I could change the past," he said.

I suppose that what happened next was inevitable. His hand moved around my head and then drew me gently toward him. My arms went to his shoulders and then slid around his neck. We rose together and stepped into an embrace.

With the first kiss, I was lost. Hamilton practiced no restraint. His kiss was consuming and alive with lust and pleasure and the strong, deep river of passion that is not a place for wading. We dove into that desire and swam straight for the bottom.

Silk is not an easy fabric to tear, but my blouse parted and fell. There was no time for buttons, no time for talk. He pushed me back onto the bed, and as he leaned over me, I remembered Jitty's description of

Hamilton as the "dark master." She had been righter than she knew. In that secret core of myself that I had always guarded, I felt myself yielding to him in a way I had fought against my entire life.

Even as I caught his thick, heavy hair in both of my hands and pulled his face down to me, I realized how extreme my danger was. And I didn't care.

22

I wish I could report that my madness was fleeting, but it wasn't. Lying tangled in the sheets with Hamilton's head cradled on my breast, I thought about the bad choices I'd made in the past. I allowed myself to visualize their faces, and then to bid them good-bye. I forgave myself for being foolish and naive and needy and, sometimes, giving and strong. Though I hadn't honestly known what I was searching for, I accepted that I had found it.

I wasn't projecting a future for me and Hamilton—no fantasies of weddings and growing old together—but for the first time in my life, I was willing to consider that there might be a future with one particular man. Yes, it was hormones and chemistry and my age. Perhaps Harold had softened the ground, and Jitty had certainly prodded me to think about children and a family. It was all of those things, and so much more. Hamilton Garrett the Fifth had touched me in a place that no one had been able to penetrate. My heart and womb recognized him as "the one."

I was not allowing my brain to cast a vote. Not yet.

Hamilton breathed deeply and stirred, shifting so that his breath teased my nipple. Perhaps among my other vices, I was greedy. I whispered my fingertips along the sensitive skin of his waist and hip, and was rewarded with the feel of his eyelashes blinking open against my breast.

His lips began to do the job they were created to perform, dropping kisses as he moved, in tiny, teasing increments, down my body. Yes, I was greedy, and I reveled in my lust.

I was surprised to look out the window and see that the sun was coming up. The hours of the night had passed like moments, and I wondered if the morning light would end the fantasy.

Hamilton was as uninhibited when he was visible as he was in the dark. It was only the need for food that finally made us take notice of our surroundings.

"I'll make some eggs and toast," I offered, not believing that he was actually leaning back against the cherry headboard of my bed. It occurred to me that, though I'd tumbled in the cotton and the soft grass by the river, in the hayloft of the barn, the tack room and the spring house, the old slave quarters that were used as storage, and the front porch swing, I'd never actually made love under the roof of Dahlia House. It was fitting that it should be Hamilton.

"I have to go home," he said, swinging his legs off the bed. And what legs they were. Strong, muscled, a manly amount of dark hair. I decided food wasn't important.

I stood beside him, delighting once again in how my head tucked beneath his chin. "I'm not that bad a cook," I said, not wanting to let him leave. Once he donned his clothes and walked out, I would be left with the repercussions of my actions. This was the part of a new romance that I hated the most. There were other egregious stages, but this was the worst. I had a rush of queasiness as my brain began to demand a hearing on the matter.

Once Hamilton left, the bogeyman of what-if's would begin to climb on my back, and there was one granddaddy bogeyman I didn't want to confront. *What if the man I'd just made love with had killed his mother?*

The ordinary old what-if's—what if he doesn't call, what if he was only pretending, what if he's married— those wouldn't hold a candle to the big one.

He pulled me against his chest and looked down with speculative eyes. "I'll take a shower, okay?"

"Then I'll make some breakfast." It was an excellent compromise.

Wearing sweatpants, socks, and my old flannel shirt, I hurried down to the kitchen and began rummaging around the refrigerator. Over breakfast, I would raise some of the issues I should have asked about last night. I would do it in a chatty way, some morning conversation as we sipped our coffee and smiled at each other. I'd shown the man I trusted him enough to let him in my bed. It was only rational that he might consider putting his touchy pride aside and answering a few questions.

Cracking the eggs into a bowl, I realized that he had never actually stated that he didn't kill his mother. He asked me what I believed. It was a technicality worthy of a lawyer. Once he had a few bites of my famous omelet, he'd tell me anything I wanted to know. I realized that it was borderline lunacy to bask in my culinary skills. Next I'd be wearing flip-flops and polyester. But I couldn't help myself. I wanted to feed the man who'd expended so much energy taking my womb from singing Gregorian chants to crooning "Wonderful Tonight."

I also wanted to ask him about the magazine clipping I'd found in his coat pocket the night of Harold's party, and about his strange conversation with the man behind the hedge. The catch was I didn't want him to know I'd been spying. I put on a pot of coffee and checked to make sure the juice was fresh. As I turned the heat up on the sausage in the pan, I thought I heard the sound of the shower running. I began crumbling Parmesan cheese into the eggs.

Outside it was bright and sunny, a perfect December day. I caught a glimpse of the bumper of Hamilton's car, parked out behind the old barn, that sly devil. I considered pulling a spark plug wire to detain him for a bit longer. That was just my greed and insecurity acting up. Perhaps I'd do a little Christmas shopping instead. For the first time in years, I liked the idea of the approaching season. The knock at the back door almost made me drop the bowl of eggs.

"Sarah Booth!" Tinkie called out. "Are you busy?"

I thought of hiding, but I saw her face at the window, and she saw me. She held Chablis up and waved a little paw at me. "Let us in, it's cold out here."

I opened the door, realizing it wasn't locked. Hamilton's entry, at least, wasn't a mystery. "Tinkie," I said, trying to come up with an excuse to make her leave before she saw Hamilton's car.

"Kincaid has decided—at the very last minute—to make this a costume luncheon," she said, her voice filled with wrath. "That's just like her. Get the drop on everyone with a beautiful costume while we're cutting up paper sacks and trying to be inventive."

I had to laugh. I'd completely forgotten Kincaid's party. But I had not forgotten Hamilton upstairs, and I wanted Tinkie gone. "Wear some overalls and a kerchief," I suggested.

"You think it's funny because you don't care. That coffee sure smells good." She opened the cupboard and got a cup. In a moment she was installed at the kitchen table, eyeing the bowl of eggs. "My Lord, Sarah Booth, how many eggs are you going to eat? Do you know the fat grams? And cheese?" She sniffed. "And sausage? Maybe I wouldn't mind a bite or two. You've got plenty here for both of us, if I do say so myself."

I desperately tried to think of a way to get rid of her. Where was Jitty when I needed her to rattle a chain or moan?

Tinkie eased Chablis to the floor. "She'll be fine," she assured me. "She's perfectly trained."

Perfectly trained for destruction. I could have told her about a pillow and a pair of heels. "What's on your mind?" I drained the sausage and put the eggs on to cook. The sooner I fed her, the sooner she would leave.

"I read your report," she said.

"It's a little early for conclusions," I said, hoping that the evidence of my nocturnal appetites didn't show. I sidled over to the toaster and tried to check my lobes and neck to make sure there were no marks of passion. When I caught a distorted image of Tinkie, slumped at the table, it dawned on me that she might be about to fire me.

She waved her hand at my look of concern. "Something's bothering me."

I slipped into a chair. "What?"

"Why did Hamilton come home now? I mean why now, after all this time? He's been gone for years, and now he's out there in that big old house all alone. Maybe you should back off this case. What with Delo getting killed and Sylvia Garrett's night out from the institution, maybe it would be best if we dropped this whole thing." Her manicured nails twisted the table-cloth into tiny little knots.

"What's really wrong, Tinkie?" I picked up my mug.

"I've been thinking. Maybe I'd rather keep Hamilton as a fantasy. You know, the dangerous man that I dallied with . . . and escaped without injury. I had a talk with Hamilton at Harold's party. He said Oscar was a good man. He made me feel okay about marrying him." She bit down on her lip, but this time it was not a sensual effect, it was to stop her tears. "Maybe it would be better for everyone if you quit asking questions."

I was relieved to see that Tinkie's interest in Hamilton had waned. That somewhat redeemed the fact that I'd just crawled out of bed with him. But something else was going on here. "I can't stop right in the middle of everything."

Tinkie's hand on my arm was so sudden I almost knocked over her coffee. "You have to stop," she said, eyes wide and lashes spiky from unshed tears. "You have to stop this instant, Sarah Booth."

"You don't have to pay me the rest of the money," I said, knowing that I would suffer greatly for that stand on principle. After all, she was backing out of the deal, not me. She really should pay all she promised.

"It isn't the money," she answered. Her nails, changed from Red Passion to Tangerine, dug into my forearm. "It's the fact that you're creating a lot of problems for some people."

"Who?" I asked, suddenly very interested.

"I can't say," she sniffed, and I thought she was going to cry. "Your eggs are burning," she said instead.

I got up and flipped the omelet. Even in grammar school Tinkie could be mulish. I'd never get the information out of her if I tried to force it.

"Okay, Tinkie, if that's the way you want it. I have another client, anyway."

"Who?" she asked, frowning.

"I can't reveal that. But as far as you're concerned, I've retired. If my other case happens to bleed over into this area, I'll stay on the lookout for people I'm pissing off."

"Sarah Booth, you think this is a game. Well, it isn't." She stood up. "Oscar said there was—" She stopped.

"The eggs are ready," I said, pretending I hadn't heard her slip. So it was Oscar, rumbling about me and my business. No surprise. I put a plate in front of her. "My special recipe," I said.

Tinkie caught my hand again. "Sarah Booth, there's talk that Hamilton killed Pasco Walters, too. You know Pasco's car ran off the road in Memphis. He went in the Mississippi River and drowned. They didn't find the body for a week."

"Hamilton was in Europe when Sheriff Walters drowned. Eat while it's hot." Maybe Oscar was afraid of losing Tinkie. He had plenty of money, but most of it, and his position at the bank, had come through his marriage to her. If he'd discovered that she had a yen for Hamilton, he might be trying a flanking maneuver.

Tinkie toyed with her food. "You have to stop asking questions, Sarah Booth." She looked up into my eyes and I saw real fear. "It was wrong of me to start this, and now it has to stop. Delo Wiley is dead. Hamilton is here, right here in Zinnia, and he's a man capable of any deception, any crime."

I knew another side of Hamilton. He was a capable man, on many levels and in many positions. There was a primal force in him that made sex more compelling than chocolate. That didn't make him a triple murderer. Necessarily.

"Tinkie, Oscar has figured out that you gave me ten thousand dollars, and he's trying to spook you into behaving." That was the logical explanation. He was also the biggest gossip in Zinnia—quite an accomplishment, and a fact I delicately didn't point out.

"Oscar wasn't telling me this. He was talking on the phone with someone else."

"He has a videotaped confession, no doubt," I scoffed.

Tinkie scooped Chablis into her arms. Though Tinkie had lost interest in her food, Chablis remembered my Delta-famous sausage omelet and tucked in as well as she could with her underbite. "I've fantasized about Hamilton for so long, dreaming of how he'd come home and realize that he loved me. That we would leave the Delta together and make a new life somewhere, a place where I didn't have to conform to what everyone thought I should be." She closed her eyes. "I'd like to style hair," she said. "Isn't that silly? Me, Tinkie Bellcase Richmond. Four years of college, a banker husband, an estate, and security to last an eternity. But what I'd really like to do is go to cosmetology school and build those incredible hair sculptures that black women wear. I want a hair show in Chicago!"

I was struck dumb. I had a vision of Tinkie in a pink smock erecting a towering mass of gleaming black hair into a pattern like I'd seen on the lamp in Sylvia's nuthouse room. Art deco. That was what it was called.

I went to Tinkie and awkwardly patted her shoulder. I couldn't give her any words of solace. There was no way her husband or her father would ever allow her to pursue her dream. "Maybe you could buy some wigs and practice while Oscar is at work." It was the best I could do.

"It's stupid. Go ahead and say it," she said, finally collecting herself. "It's a stupid fantasy, but Hamilton was part of it. And now I find out that as stupid as my hair design dream is, my crush on Hamilton is even stupider. All of these years, I've pinned my hopes on a freaking murderer!"

"Tinkie," I said gently. "You can't be calling Hamilton a murderer." It wasn't my job to resurrect Hamilton's reputation, but if he was going to hang around Dahlia House, I didn't want folks thinking he was cold-blooded. "There's no proof."

"But there is. Physical evidence."

"What?" I asked, willing to humor her if she'd leave sooner.

"That's what I overheard Oscar talking about. Veronica Garrett's brake lines were cut, and it was Hamilton's knife that cut them."

I stopped her before she could get cranked up. "That's just gossip." I'd heard that cut-brake-line theory from a number of people, but no one had verified it. Technically, Fel hadn't denied it. He'd said he wasn't a mechanic.

She shook her head. "I wish it were. The lines were cut. Oscar was talking with Gordon Walters. He's the one who told Oscar about the brake lines. And about the knife. Hamilton's knife. It was found in the house."

I felt a surge of anger. "Gordon's just stirring trouble." And he was doing a damn good job of it. For whatever reason, he had it in for Hamilton.

"He's not, Sarah Booth. That's what I had to tell you. Gordon confessed that he took part of his father's report out of the records—the part about the cut brake lines. He'd heard you were poking into things and that you were going to write a book. He knew his father had acted improperly by not pursuing the wreck, so he went into the records and pulled that report. Fel wouldn't talk about it because it would incriminate him, too, for covering up a crime. Gordon thought if he could purge the records, you wouldn't be able to find anything. He was protecting his father's name. See, Pasco chose not to pursue Veronica's murder, because he knew who did it."

I swallowed, only partially successful at blocking a few graphic memories of the night before. "As sheriff, he was obligated to file a charge and bring Hamilton to trial. It's ridiculous that he would *choose* to ignore a murder." I fought her facts with everything I had.

She nodded, stroking Chablis's little head. The dog had gone into a cholesterol coma. "Think what you're saying. The Garretts were one of the most respected families in the state. Mr. Garrett was dead; Veronica was dead. Sylvia claimed the knife was hers. Sheriff Walters took the easy way out and did nothing. Sylvia went to Glen Oaks, and Hamilton was exiled to Europe."

My heart was racing, and a cold sweat had begun to trickle down my spine. I felt dizzy and nauseous. I had all the symptoms of betrayal.

"Do you really expect me to believe a sheriff would allow a murderer to go free?"

Before she could answer, Chablis leaped from the table and squeezed her six-ounce self through the kitchen door. There was wild and excited yipping from the stairs.

Hamilton! He was still in the house. Probably listening at the kitchen door.

"Chablis!" Tinkie called, getting up.

"Eat your breakfast," I said, ignoring the fact that

her plate was empty. "I'll get Chablis, the little darling."
I rushed out of the kitchen, closing the door behind me,
and hurried through the house.

As I darted through the parlor, there was the soft
sound of the front door clicking into place. A ray of
morning light caught the exquisite glass bottle that Sylvia had given me for Hamilton. It had been on the sideboard, and now it was sitting in the middle of the dining
table. The sunlight seemed to set the glass on fire. I
didn't have to look. I knew that Hamilton was gone.

Jitty gave me some warning as she jangled her bracelets
behind me. I had taken a seat on the top step, and I was
huddled down in my shirt, trying not to cry. Tinkie was
finally gone, saved from costume hell by my suggestion
of some Daisy Dukes and a bandana crop top that tied
under her breasts.

"Honey chile, where did you learn to pick your men?
I tried to warn you." She took a seat beside me.
"Twenty generations of Delaney women are turnin' in
their graves. I mean rollin' and cuttin' flips. I'll bet if we
looked out the kitchen window, the cemetery would be
quakin' and shakin', headstones about to tumble
down."

"Don't go there, Jitty," I said. "I'm a fool."

"Yeah, and you're hardheaded, too. That's the worst
kind."

I was too heartsick to defend myself. Hamilton had
sneaked up on me and I'd invited him into my bed. A
man, a suspect in the death of his own mother—and a
growing list of others—had broken into my home, and I
had spent twelve hours with him making the most passionate, intimate love I'd ever experienced.

Jitty was staring at me with a cool regard. "Chances

are he won't be back this way again, but he certainly did bring a nice gene pool with him. Were you using protection?" she asked.

If I hadn't been so mortified by my own behavior, I would have tried to hurt her. But as it was, Jitty was my only friend. I couldn't afford to run her off, too.

She took my silence as permission to continue. "I personally favor Harold as the father of your children. Harold strikes me as the kind of man who'd stay around and watch them get big, the kind of man who'd invest wisely and grow portfolios so that the future of Dahlia House would always be safe."

"Hamilton is wealthy," I countered in a monotone. "And you sound like you're reading a Smith-Barney advertisement."

"Hamilton *says* he's wealthy. The man just blew back into town from Europe. Nobody's seen or heard from him in eighteen years. He could be Count Dracula for all we know," Jitty pointed out reasonably. "Harold is a known quantity."

"They're not coffee beans," I said wearily. I was physically sick. My stomach was giving me signs that revenge would soon follow.

"Back when your many-g's-grandma Alice was a single woman, it was up to the relatives and neighbors to find her a man. They did all the investigatin' before they ever introduced her. That's the way it worked back then. Relatives took it on themselves to check out a man, look into his past. Things were simpler then. If somebody of low character came along, they didn't let the young girls near 'em."

"Sort of like Rhett Butler meeting Scarlett at the Wilkes ball, right?" I wasn't buying into Jitty's love affair with the past. It was the past that had me in the mess I was in.

"That was a book, Sarah Booth. Surely you know the difference between books and life."

I stood up. "Yeah, and look what happened to Scarlett." I looked at Jitty for the first time. She was still in the silver skin dress, but her eye makeup was smeared and her pageboy had begun to kink. "You look like you had one helluva night."

"It's a reciprocal thing. You were busy so I grabbed a little fun for myself. You know, Sarah Booth, you need to do the wild thing more often. I really needed that."

I turned and walked down the stairs to the kitchen to put on some more coffee. "If your sexual health is based on what I do, I pity you," I called out. "I'm no good at this, and I think a convent is the only solution."

"Honey, you just rode the one horse. My favorite is just comin' to the post."

When the coffee had perked I took a seat at the table, not caring that the kitchen was freezing. I leaned my head on my hand and tried not to think back to the night before. How had something so wonderful turned into such a nightmare? It was the question of my life.

Jitty drifted through the wall, completely redone in purple hip-hugger jeans and a paisley body shirt of pink and purple. I knew I was in bad shape, because her outfits were beginning to grow on me.

"You don't have time to sit around here mopin'," she said, pacing back and forth in front of the stove.

"The last time I looked, my agenda wasn't exactly full." I sank deeper into self-pity.

"Snap out of it, Sarah Booth. Remember Kincaid's charity do."

I sat up. I had forgotten. My Dolly costume was lying in a heap in my room. There was no time for anything except to get dressed and get there.

"You'll be a knockout," Jitty pronounced with a surety that made me feel marginally better.

"I could simply stay home," I said.

"Yeah, just go on and crawl up under the porch like a kicked dog." Jitty looked at me in disgust. "All your Delaney blood must be in the womb, 'cause you don't seem to have a drop in your spine."

She had thrown down the challenge. I rose from the table. "Okay, I'm going."

"Do me a favor, Sarah Booth," she said.

"Maybe." I was leery of Jitty's requests.

"You left the barn door open and one horse has run out. Don't close the door yet. Another one might run in."

"If that's your euphemistic way of promoting Harold, give it a rest. I'm over men. All of them." My thumb gave a pathetic little gasp of a pulse. I rushed to the table and stuck it in the cup of hot coffee. "Take that!" I cried.

"Girl, you ever heard of that drug called Halcion? Maybe you ought to get you a few tablets."

I chose to ignore Jitty as I took my coffee and headed up the stairs.

Wisteria Hall was not as big as Knob Hill or as old as Dahlia House, but it was a lovely setting for a luncheon. Kincaid had gone the extra mile. Gingham bows had been tied around the huge oaks that lined the drive, and she'd hired a troupe of singing midgets dressed as cowboys to escort us from the driveway around the rose arbors to the old patio. One short cowpoke gave me a wolf whistle as I got out of the car.

True to Fel Harper's gossip, hay bales were scattered about, highlighted with vibrant mums. In the center of the half-acre patio was a swimming pool shaped like a cut emerald. The water sparkled aqua, and promised that summer would indeed return.

"Sarah Booth," Kincaid said, rushing forward in a hand-tailored, leather-and-suede Dale Evans outfit. She air-kissed my cheeks. "Where did you get that costume?" she said loudly, then threw her arms around me and grabbed me in a bear hug. She whispered, "You've got to do something."

"And you're welcome for saving your ass from the fire," I replied calmly, though her grip was amazingly tight for someone who was almost a skeleton. She'd lost another ten pounds.

"That fink Isaac backed out. He didn't get the check."

I felt the eyes of everyone on us. It looked as if Kincaid was giving me the hug of the century. I tried to escape, but she held on and we danced clumsily together for several steps. "Let me go," I ordered in a tone that made her loosen her hold. "Get a grip, Kincaid. This isn't the way a Daddy's Girl behaves."

I stepped out of her arms and looked at her. Her tawny eyes were wild, and her cheeks had that hollowed look of someone who is starving or drinking too much—or both. "Chas wants me to see a psychiatrist. You know he'll use that against me if we divorce." Her eyes brimmed with tears.

Disaster was imminent. When Lesley Gore sang, "It's my party and I'll cry if I want to," it was obvious that she was not a Daddy's Girl. Kincaid simply could not cry in front of her guests. It wasn't done. I gripped her elbow and propelled her toward the house. "Kincaid, dahlin', I have to be sure Fel used the right bourbon in his sauce. Come show me," I said, waving with my other hand to the gathered daughters of the South. I felt needle pricks in my spine and I turned into the gaze of Bitty Sue Holcomb. She was not smiling.

I ignored them and hustled Kincaid into the house. Once I had her inside, I poured her some of the bourbon I found in the liquor cabinet and propped her on the arm of the sofa. "Isaac didn't get the check?" This was a problem.

"He was afraid he'd get caught. And he and Kitty are going to Greece for the entire holiday season. He's leaving me holding the bag," she said bitterly. "If the law finds that check and he's gone, it's going to be all on me."

I hurried into the kitchen, snatched two paper towels, and handed them to her. "If you cry, you'll ruin your makeup."

She sniffed and straightened her spine. There wasn't time to reapply. "I'll give you another three thousand if you'll get the check," she said, then amended. "Five thousand. That's all I have in my secret account."

The environment of a working PI sometimes left a lot to be desired, but the hourly wage was more than adequate. I'd been to Delo's. It wouldn't be that hard to break into the house. But finding a check would be difficult.

"I'll pay you if you just look," Kincaid said.

"On one condition." I had my own Achilles' heel. "I want to know about you and Hamilton."

Kincaid's mouth opened and she drew a soft, whistling breath. "What?"

"You went to Europe just before you married Chas. I want to know about Hamilton." I had hardened my heart, and now I wanted a Kevlar vest. If I knew every dirty, low-down thing about Hamilton, at least my pride wouldn't allow me to mourn for him. He'd done something terrible to Kincaid, and I wanted to know what it was. I remembered the way she looked when she came back from Europe. It was almost as bad as she looked now.

"Why?" The word came out on a gust of air, like she'd been punched.

"Another investigation." My own, perhaps, but it was none of her business.

"Bitty Sue hasn't hired you to look into this, has she?"

I saw terror in Kincaid's eyes. Bitty Sue was the most petite of the Daddy's Girls, and a force to be reckoned with.

"It isn't Bitty Sue," I reassured her.

Kincaid swallowed the glass of bourbon. She was developing a serious drinking problem, along with a potential murder charge.

When she met my gaze there was a steeliness to her that I'd never seen before. Not the hard, mean edge, but a firm resolve. "I went to Europe to see a doctor. Not the medical kind. A brain doctor. I had an eating disorder, and I tried to kill my father."

I took the glass from her hand and sucked out the last drop, then went to pour us both a big one. If Kincaid's background came to light and the check wasn't recovered from Delo's, she would inhale the sweet promise of the afterlife in the gas chamber at Parchman State Penitentiary.

I composed my face before I took our drink back. "How did you try to kill him?" Not why, which didn't really matter now, but how. I prayed it wasn't a gun.

Her grimace told me my prayers were futile. "I shot him with his shotgun."

I sank down beside her on the sofa arm. "Why, for God's sake?" Now I needed to know.

"I was in love with someone. Someone he didn't approve of. He told me if I married this man that he'd disinherit me. He said he wouldn't allow Mother to speak my name. That I would be dead to the family and to the town of Zinnia." As she talked, her voice grew stronger. "I didn't know anything but the Delta. I didn't have the courage to go away, like you did."

Forrest Gump had it wrong. Life is not a box of chocolates; it's a kaleidoscope. In the flip of a wrist, realities are shredded and the world takes on a totally new shape. Never in my wildest dreams had I thought Kincaid would love anyone, much less a man outside her social circle. I would have bet Dahlia House that the only passion she was capable of feeling was acquisitive in nature—the purchase of a designer label or the perfect shade of nail polish.

"Did anyone know you shot your father?"

Kincaid stood up and began to pace. "Mother went into hysterics and called the sheriff. Pasco came and called Doc McAdams. Daddy wasn't hurt bad. It was bird shot, and from a distance, so it was more messy than life-threatening."

"No report was filed?"

"Well, Pasco said he was going to have to write it up, but he said he'd make it accidental, like Daddy said." She stopped her pacing. "You know, Daddy was madder at Mother for calling the sheriff than he was at me for shooting him."

After a week as a PI, I understood that perfectly. Written records, official reports—documentation of that ilk is dangerous. One small mistake could haunt a person for the rest of her life. In Kincaid's case, an incident from her teens could easily prove the foundation for the state to view her as a murderer. She'd shot a man—her father—once. She had a history of solving problems with violence. I could only hope that Pasco had never gotten around to writing the report. Since he was dead, he couldn't mitigate the bald facts of a shooting.

"So what role did Hamilton play?"

"When I was in Europe, they kept me in this place, a hospital, sort of. I couldn't leave or have phone calls or friends. My parents didn't even send me a letter. I was completely alone, and one day I got in the trunk of one of the doctor's cars and escaped."

I schooled my face to hide my amazement. "Where did you go?"

"I didn't know anyone in Switzerland. I'd heard my parents talking about Hamilton and how he was supposedly amassing a fortune in Paris. I went there."

"Without money or anything?"

"I found him in the phone book and called him and he came to get me. He helped me. And I threw myself at him, but he never touched me. He said," her voice broke, but she continued, "that it would be immoral to take advantage of me in the state I was in. And so he kept me in his house and protected me for several weeks, until I cut a deal with my father. I would marry Chas, and I could come home."

"But everyone thought you and Hamilton . . ."

"I made up the story about having a torrid affair with Hamilton because I was so ashamed of where I'd been and what happened. The truth was, Hamilton was very kind, but he frightened me. So intense. He kept turning every conversation back to Sylvia, his sister. Whatever happened in that crazy family of his, he was more messed up than I was."

There was the sound of tiny footsteps coming. Kincaid pointed to a photograph of an old cotton gin on the wall. "Chas says Emerson Glade will be famous one day. I love his use of light."

"I always preferred black-and-white," I stumbled, trying to fall into Kincaid's cover-up.

"Well, I never," Bitty Sue said as she came into the middle of the room and stopped. "Kincaid Maxwell, there are about a hundred people out there looking for you. *Your guests*," she said with great emphasis, "in case you've forgotten that you're the hostess for the biggest charity event of the season."

She looked at me. "I know you," she said slowly. "You're . . ." She wrinkled her little rabbit nose.

"Sarah Booth Delaney," I said, ordering my body not to show my distress. "We went to school together for twelve years, Bitty Sue. You probably don't recognize me because I'm wearing a blond wig and my family is in financial ruin."

My sarcasm was wasted on her. She gave me a sour look. "If you lost your social skills along with your money, that's fine for you, Sarah Booth. But Kincaid has a position to uphold in this community. She is a Maxwell, and this is the charity event of the year. You need to quit dragging her off to look at stupid pictures of cotton." She reached out and grasped Kincaid's hand. "Your guests are looking for you."

Kincaid gave me a look, but I shrugged her on. I'd found out more than I ever anticipated.

23

I endured the rest of the party—including a lengthy speech by Kincaid, which was delivered with the cool, bitchy façade that I now admired. I suffered through the fashion show by the twenty-year-old mannequins, the fried catfish and hush puppies, the speculative glances of all the Daddy's Girls who were afraid my impoverishment would rub off on them, and the singing cowboy midgets who also square-danced.

I waited for my chance to corner Fel Harper. Kincaid's passing remark about Hamilton's fondness for his sister had shaken me. I was tired of playing nice. I wanted answers, and I wanted them now.

When Fel disappeared behind the house to put his portable kitchen back into the trailer, I followed him. He was bent over a vat of hot grease when I tapped him on the back.

"Holy shit," he said, whirling fast for a fat man. "I almost burned myself."

"Guilty conscience?" I accused.

He gave me a dirty look and started throwing tongs and scoops into the trailer.

"Who killed Hamilton Garrett the Fourth?" I demanded.

"You know Mr. Garrett's death was ruled accidental." He scooped a crusty hush puppy from the grease and pretended to examine it.

"He was murdered, and you know it. Delo knew it, and now he's dead." I didn't expect my words to have an effect, but I saw his eyes squinch and he looked past me, as if he expected someone to come up from behind.

His heavy hand on my arm was unexpected, and unpleasant. "Stirrin' up the past is a dangerous business. For you and a lot of other people. Mr. Garrett's dead and buried for twenty years. Digging in his moldy grave won't bring him back to life. Leave it alone, Sarah Booth, before someone else gets hurt."

His words might have scared me, except they weren't spoken as a threat. Tension radiated through him.

"Who are you afraid of, Fel?" I asked. "Is it Gordon Walters?"

He stepped back from me and looked around again. "You go diggin' up old bones, they're liable to stand up and walk," he said. "I'm afraid of ghosts, Sarah Booth. The kind that slip into your house at night and stand by your bed. The kind that press the pillow down over your face with a handsome smile."

My heart clutched. There's no other way to describe that sensation of racing blood and frozen muscle. Fel could not have known about Hamilton's visit to my home. I hung on to that as hard as I could.

Fel looked around again and leaned closer to me. "Delo is dead. He talked to you and then he was shot. I don't think it was coincidental that he was killed in the same spot as Mr. Garrett, and I don't want that to happen to me." He put a skimmer over the big vat of grease and hefted it up. It made a sizzling sound as he poured it back into a container. "Don't come near me again," he said.

I had never made the direct link that I was responsible for Delo's death. *That my visit had precipitated his murder.* I wasn't a threat to anyone. Not me, Sarah Booth Delaney, failed Daddy's Girl, actress, heir, female, and week-long private investigator, not to mention fool for love. The fried fish churned in my stomach at the memory of Delo, chopping his wood and tending to his own business. He was a Cagey Old Redneck who took money for gossiping about the past, but he didn't deserve to have his head blown off.

"What do you know about the knife that was used to cut Veronica's brake lines?" This was familiar ground, but I was hoping Fel would rethink his answer.

"Not a damn thing. If Delo had remembered to forget certain things, he'd still be alive today." He tossed his equipment in the trailer and was getting in his truck when I put a hand on his shoulder.

"Pasco Walters drowned in Memphis. What's the story on that?"

Fel considered for several seconds. "If I tell you, will you stay the hell away from me?"

I nodded.

"Pasco had him a girlfriend up in Memphis. He would go up there on weekends and see her. I think they both liked to do a little drinking. Anyway, he'd been there, and the best we could figure was that he got a late start headed home on Sunday night. Chances were good that he'd been drinkin' hard. He was apparently goin' pretty fast when his truck missed the bridge and went into the river. It had been a spring with a lot of rain and the body didn't float up for about a week. My guess is it got hung on something." He stared at me. "Does that satisfy you?"

"Who was his girlfriend?"

"Who the hell knows?" Fel asked with irritation. "The ladies liked Pasco. He tried to keep that business in Memphis so it wouldn't make his wife and family suffer." He shrugged. "Seems like Pasco had a new woman every few months."

"Was there any sign of foul play in his death?"

The look he gave me was suddenly interested. "With Pasco? Not to my knowledge. Check with the Memphis police. They handled everything, and it all seemed cut and dried. Pasco's blood alcohol was real high, and folks kind of hushed that up to spare the family. That's all I know."

Before I could ask another question, he slammed the truck door and drove away.

The luncheon was still going on—the women writing down silent bids for the various outfits that had been modeled. If I left now, everyone would think it was because I didn't have the money to buy anything. I slipped around the side of the house and made my escape.

I couldn't risk breaking into Delo's until nightfall, so I went home, changed into jeans and my black leather jacket, and went to the courthouse. I checked the cars in the sheriff's parking lot and made sure that Gordon Walters's truck was not there. It was mid-afternoon, and I'd assumed, rightly, that he worked the eleven-to-seven shift. I needed to see some old files and talk with the sheriff.

At the courthouse, I discovered that Coleman had rushed home for an emergency. The deputy behind the counter noted, rather indiscreetly, that Carlene was always calling with fake emergencies so she could get Coleman home for another fight.

I looked first for a record of the shooting of Jameson O'Rourk, Kincaid's father. If Pasco had followed up on his threat to write the report, I couldn't find it anywhere. I felt a measure of relief for Kincaid, and turned my attention to the records of Guy Garrett's murder. I went over the reports again and spent a while examining the photos of the body. The placement of the bodies of Guy Garrett and Delo were similar—deliberately so, I thought. There seemed to be a theme at work. And very possibly the same killer. No one else seemed to see this but me.

I saved the best for last—Veronica. With an ear tuned for Gordon's return, I went through the file thoroughly. There was no report of severed brake lines, but there was evidence of a missing page. The work was deft. It looked as if a razor had been used.

The missing page could have contained only meaningless doodles. Or it could have been Pasco's notations about a severed brake line and a knife. Or—one final scenario came to mind—Gordon could have cut out a meaningless page simply to stimulate the suspicions already whirling around Sylvia and Hamilton. I was fond of the latter explanation for a number of reasons, one being that Gordon was the one saying he'd cut out the page.

I mentally went over my list of murder suspects. The problem was that I had three separate murders, maybe four, if Pasco hadn't died in an accident, and they all seemed connected. In the death of Hamilton the Fourth, I suspected Veronica, her unnamed lover, Isaac Carter and his Memphis associates, Pasco Walters, Fel Harper, Sylvia. And Hamilton. At the thought of him I went hot and cold, but I forced myself to keep thinking.

In Veronica's death, I was looking at Hamilton the Fifth, Sylvia, Pasco, and, to some degree as an accomplice, Fel.

In Delo's death, the prime suspects were Isaac, Hamilton, Sylvia, and, once again, Fel, as an outside possibility. Gordon was a question here, too. Delo might have known something that would dishonor the Walters name, and Gordon might have killed him to keep him quiet.

The motive for Pasco's murder would be that he knew too much. But the more I thought about Fel's recounting of the drowning, the more likely it seemed that Pasco's lifestyle had finally caught up with him.

In all of the murders there were common suspects, and like it or not, they were Hamilton, his sister, and Isaac. They all had motive, means, and opportunity.

I slammed the dusty record book shut and left, heading three blocks across town to City Hall. My chosen career of acting had taught me many things, but it was the dinner conversations orchestrated by my father, the circuit court judge, that had laid my bedrock understanding of civics.

Meetings of the city aldermen and zoning boards are public records, and I asked for the minutes book from 1979. It was going to be a few long, boring hours of reading.

I took the heavy clothbound volume and found a seat in the boardroom. Page by page I began to scan the typewritten records of Zinnia's guiding fathers. I did note that they were all men.

It was March before I came across a reference to a request for a zoning change on land in the northeast part of town. That would roughly comprise the black section, I estimated. The request was filed by Aubrey Malone, real estate developer. He was asking for commercial zoning of residential property and a permit to construct a docking facility on the river. That was exactly as Isaac had told me.

At the thought of Isaac, I checked my watch. It was four-thirty. I had half an hour left to read, and soon after it would be dark. I could swing by Delo's and see about Kincaid's check. Once I had it, I was going to tear it into bits and make Isaac Carter eat them.

That train of thought hit a junction, and I took the left-hand fork. Of all of the suspects, Isaac had a double motive for killing Delo. The past and the present. And knowing how women like to bond after sex, I found it highly possible that Kincaid, in a moment of afterglow, had told Isaac all about her little trip to Psychoworld in Switzerland and how she'd shot her own father. It would make Isaac's planting of the check doubly despicable.

I turned back to the minutes book and read on. On March 14, 1979, a citizen's group appeared before the board to protest the zoning change. The group was led by James Levert and Bessie Mae Odom. The name stopped me dead in my tracks. Bessie Mae Odom was Tammy's old granny. This was a woman who was older than Methuselah when I was a teenager. And yet she read a statement to the board. I scanned the record and could almost hear her rusty old voice talking about her heritage and her home. She spoke my feelings for Dahlia House, for my land and my family. She vowed to cling to her small house on her bit of land until she was dead. No matter what it was zoned or who came by and offered her money to leave Sunflower County.

There was a timid tap on the door and the city clerk peeked in at me. "Time to close," she said.

My eyes were burning and I needed to walk around

and think, so I gave her the book and walked into the twilight of downtown Zinnia.

Up and down Main Street, shops were closing and men and women were bundled in coats and hurrying to their vehicles. The Wal-Mart chain had not found its way to Zinnia, but based on what Oscar Richmond and his ilk were saying, it wouldn't be long before this pattern of small-town life ended.

I drove by the Sweetheart drive-in and treated myself to a real chocolate malt before I headed back toward Delo's. I didn't want to do this. I didn't like the idea of breaking into a dead man's house. But I felt this overwhelming urge to protect Kincaid. I couldn't explain it and didn't want to try. Maybe I simply felt luckier than she was. My parents were dead, but they would never have bartered me into marriage with a weasel like Chas Maxwell.

I drove past the turnoff to Delo's, turned around, and came back, driving past again. I couldn't see the house, and Gordon Walters and an army of deputies might be waiting in ambush at the end of the road. There was no way to tell.

It was a three-quarter-mile hike back to his place, but I pulled the car down an old farm road, parked, and cut across the cornfields. The moon wasn't full, but it cast plenty of light and I had a good sense of direction. I had only a few acres to cross, and I knew I could hit pretty close to Delo's.

My breath plumed out before me and seemed to hang in the cold night air. In the pale moonlight, the cornfield was ragged, and I cautioned myself not to be startled if I flushed a covey of quail or doves from their winter sleep. Clear and cold, the night was also silent, except for the light crunching of frosted husks beneath my feet and the fast, regular sound of my breathing.

I'd been walking for ten minutes when I heard the dogs kick in. I'd forgotten about them, coursing the ground by Delo's body as the two black men tried to pull them back. They were hounds, normally a gregarious breed of dog. I whistled softly to them and was rewarded by lonesome whines. Delo had gone off and left them, and I could only hope someone had remembered to bring them food. I eased up by the pens and held out a hand, rewarded by the warm lapping of tongues.

In the moonlight I could make out their sad eyes. They were not Chablis, but then I wasn't Tinkie. Perhaps a hound or two would give Dahlia House a homier look. I slipped away from them and circled the house. It seemed abandoned. There was no sign of the yellow crime tape I'd seen so often on television, but then the actual murder had taken place outside. Trying not to have a panic attack, I walked to the front door and turned the knob. The door swung open on a hinge that gave only the faintest creak.

It was pitch black inside. Inching forward, I closed the door and held my breath, listening for the sound of someone else. Only silence came back to me.

I don't believe in ghosts, or at least not the amorphous kind that show themselves as wavering banshees out to terrorize little children and play practical jokes on mortals. I believe in Jitty, an extension of my family's past *and* my own personal warrior goddess. Still, I have to admit, I was scared. Jitty was benevolent; she was family. Delo was undoubtedly pissed. If he decided to make an ethereal appearance, it would not be to give me advice on my clothes or love life.

I'd been smart enough to bring a small flashlight, and I clicked it on and held it low to the floor. The odd lighting gave the room a theatrical appearance, and I found that it calmed me. I went for the drawers and the stack of unopened mail that someone had piled carefully on the kitchen table. Then I went into the kitchen shelves and canisters, hoping that there was a general "junk" collection that served as a temporary filing system.

As I sifted through the odds and ends of Delo's life, I wondered if Gordon Walters and the other deputies had been there before me. Surely they'd already searched the obvious places. I was wasting my time and freezing to death in the cold house. Yet I searched on, determined not to let impatience or discomfort rule my success.

The kitchen was small, and I eased around the table where two coffee cups remained. As I turned away my jacket sleeve caught an ashtray and sent it crashing to the floor. It was a heavy piece of glass and didn't break, but a cigarette butt and a book of matches scattered across the old oak boards. I gathered them up and put them back.

The butt brand was Marlboro, and as my freezing fingers clutched at the matchbook, I felt the embossed letters with a sense of wonder. I swung the light to them. *La Tour d'Argent.*

There are no French restaurants in Zinnia. Nor in Sunflower County. The cigarette brand was the same as the butts left behind Harold's yew hedge. This and the matches spoke of one person. Hamilton Garrett the Fifth.

I had not recovered from the surprise of my discovery when I heard the mild creak of the front door. I instantly clicked off the flashlight and was swallowed in blackness. Very slowly the night sky appeared in a bright wedge that grew as the front door eased open. A tall, dark form stood at the threshold.

I stood perfectly still, praying that the intruder would

not be able to see me if I didn't move. My muscles trembled with the strain. With no way to defend myself, I watched the larger silhouette shift, and then there was the glint of starlight on sleek black metal. Slowly the barrel of the shotgun rose to chest level, and then swung to point directly at me.

24

"Don't move."

The voice was male but soft as warm cotton. It was not Hamilton or Gordon. Relief was sweet, but also limited.

"My name is Sarah Booth Delaney," I said, but I didn't move. The intruder was young and black. This was not Chicago or Los Angeles. Chances were, if I didn't know this man, he would know me. The day I saw Delo's body, there had been two black men who'd taken Delo's dogs. The older was James and the younger . . . "Cooley?" I asked.

"Yes, ma'am," he answered, and the barrel of his gun notched down slightly. "Come on outside where I can see you. What are you doin' in Mr. Delo's house?"

He stepped back from the door so I could walk out on the porch. "Looking for something."

"Lot's o' folks say they lost things here in a dead man's house."

Healthy skepticism is a sign of intelligence, and I

stepped forward so that he could get a glimpse of me in the moonlight.

"I'm looking for a check written by Kincaid Maxwell." My eyes had adjusted to the darkness, and I could see his expression, a narrowing of his eyes, which signified wariness.

"Mr. Delo told me that he rented those cabins for money. It seems that money was owed."

"I'm not disputing the debt, but someone else should pay it." I thought about my options. "If the sheriff finds that check, Mrs. Maxwell will be a suspect in Delo's murder. She didn't kill him. If she's investigated, a lot of secrets will come out and a lot of innocent people will be hurt."

He lowered the gun to the floor. "If you're talkin' about her meetin' that old man in the cabin, she shoulda thought of that before she got caught." He gave a soft snort of contempt. "And you're just here to help your friend."

One of the dogs gave a mournful howl. "Kincaid isn't exactly my friend. She's my client."

"Seems to me she ought to be here riskin' her neck."

He was right, but I needed the money, and Kincaid would be even worse at this than me. "She paid me to do this."

He nodded and motioned me out of the house. "So you think it's okay to bust into a dead man's house and rummage through his things to find evidence that might go against your client."

He was not stupid, and he'd mastered the art of sarcasm. "I think it's probably against the law. But the way I'm looking at it is that a bigger injustice would be done if Kincaid were falsely accused."

"What if she did kill him?"

"She didn't. I've given it a lot of thought. There are

two people Kincaid would have killed before she even thought about killing Delo. Her husband and Isaac Carter. Kincaid would have bought Delo off."

Unlike most men, Cooley seemed willing to accept my evaluation as fact. He nodded as if the wisdom of my words were growing on him. "Maybe you killed him," he suggested.

Now this was something I didn't expect. It was possible my actions could be interpreted in that way. "If you believed that, you'd have the gun pointed at me," I noted. I saw a fleeting smile on his face. "Are you looking after his dogs?"

"Me and James. Delo loved those hounds. Nobody's been up to see about them." He shook his head. "Delo never expected they'd outlive him."

"Maybe you should take them home with you," I suggested. If the dogs' fate was left in the hands of the court system, they might be destroyed.

"James and I talked about it, but we wouldn't want to be accused of stealin'."

There was a long and tangled web of innuendo attached to his simple words. "What if I just turned them loose?"

"I live across that field," he said, pointing. "I bet if you open the pens those dogs will find their way to my house."

"Looks to me like they need some exercise," I said as I walked over to the pens and examined the lock. It was little more than a latch used to hold a screen door shut, and I flipped it up and opened the door. The four hounds came out in a wiggling mass. Their tails thumped my legs and their tongues found every inch of exposed skin. As soon as they heard Cooley's clear whistle, they charged in his direction.

"Walk with me," he said softly.

It wasn't exactly on my way home, but I no longer believed I'd find Kincaid's check at Delo's and I had a few questions for Cooley. I jogged over and fell into step with him as the hounds, delighted with their freedom, coursed through the cotton fields in an ecstasy of sniffing and running.

"Did you see anyone visiting Delo? Anyone unusual?"

"Delo didn't have many friends. Only folks ever talked to him were me and James. Until lately." Cooley kept a fast pace over the uneven rows. Up ahead the dogs caught the scent of something and took off baying and yelping.

"'Coon, most likely," he said without breaking stride.

"Who was talking to Delo, lately?" I pressed.

"You were the first to stop by. Then that woman who left the check. The deputy—"

"Gordon Walters?"

"Yeah, him."

"Who else?"

"Mr. Garrett. He was over there Sunday mornin' early."

Hamilton had been there. I'd made a correct deduction. "What did he want?"

"Mr. Delo didn't tell me his business. I just know what I saw."

Up ahead the lights of a house glowed bright. The dogs were still baying at the edge of the woods, and Cooley paused long enough to whistle them up. As he started up the steps, they went under the porch.

"They'll be okay here, right?" I asked.

"They'll be fine."

I hesitated, wondering if he intended for me to go inside with him. When he opened the door and the yellow light spilled out and over me, he waited. "You comin'?"

I hurried inside, glad for the warmth and the cheerfulness of the room. At first I didn't notice the older black man sitting in a big armchair, reading. He looked up at me over his glasses. "Miss Delaney," he said softly. "What brings you here?"

"She was breakin' into Delo's. That's what the dogs were fussin' about."

I had seen James in the cornfield, but I hadn't realized he was so old. His hair was grizzled and there were deep lines in his face. He examined me in a way that let me know he knew me, and that whatever status quo I'd been raised to believe in, he was his own man.

"Would you make us some coffee, Cooley?" he asked politely, but his gaze remained on me.

"Sure." Cooley left us and James waved me into a chair beside his.

"I knew your daddy," he said. "We did some business. And I knew your mama." He chuckled softly, and the seams in his face shifted into new trenches. "They were somethin'." He laughed even deeper. "Your mama was a pretty thing, and she had fire in her eyes. She'd look at folks and say, 'Give a damn.' It made some people real mad."

"I've heard a few stories," I answered.

"Times were troubled back then."

I wondered where this was going, but I could smell the coffee brewing and the warmth of the fire was turning my cold bones to gel. James had a soothing voice, rich and worn.

"When your mama got pregnant with you, that was when your daddy decided to put his law degree to work. He came by here and told me he'd never meant to practice law. He loved that land and wanted to work it. But it was a hard time for big landowners. The weather and the economy had turned against him. He was worried, too, about your mama. She stirred people up. She never believed anyone would hurt her for what she believed. Your daddy knew better, so he practiced a little law, mostly free, and then got elected as a judge."

"Did you know them well?"

He nodded. "I'd say pretty well." He shifted in his chair so he could face me more directly. "I gave your daddy some advice, on occasion, and I'm gonna give you some, too. Stay out of Delo's house. Stay away, Sarah Booth. It's not finished, and you don't want to be in on the end of it."

He wasn't trying to frighten me. "What's going on?"

He shook his head. "Delo Wiley never hurt anybody in his life. He let those rich men hunt his fields when the corn was in, and he took their money. I told him not to let that Maxwell woman use his cabin. But it was easy money, and it tickled him that such high-and-mighty folks acted no better than what they called poor white trash."

Kincaid's reasons for meeting Isaac Carter were too complex to explain. More revenge and power than lust and sex. Perhaps the same was true for most people who cheated on their husbands or wives. I shook my head. "Kincaid didn't kill Delo."

James nodded. "Delo was killed so secrets wouldn't be told."

My heart began to beat faster. "What secrets?"

"You want to come back here tomorrow and find a dead old Negro sitting in his chair?"

"Isaac Carter and his toady Deputy Walters have already been out here to talk to James about the good ol' days," Cooley threw in from the kitchen. "A blind man could read that message."

James ignored the younger man's outburst. "Delo didn't really know anything. He suspected, but he didn't know. When I saw that dead man's grown son over there, I knew it was trouble. And that sister out in the cornfield, digging like a madwoman. She nearly scared Cooley half to death with that long silvery hair and that nightgown blowing in the wind. It's a wonder she didn't freeze to death."

"You saw Sylvia in the cornfield?" I asked.

"She got out of a car about midnight. Then it drove away and she started digging."

I remembered Hamilton's question about his sister's means of conveyance. "What kind of car?" I questioned.

"Big car. Dark color." James looked past me as he thought. "An older-model Lincoln," he said. "It had a big, smooth engine, because when I heard the dogs barking and I got up to check I remember thinking that the car was fine-tuned, in perfect condition. The woman got out of the car, and before she had time to close the door, the car was pulling away."

"They just let her out?" Sylvia had obviously arranged a pickup point, because she made it back to Glen Oaks. Crazy she might be, but she was also smart. Very smart.

"There was a cold wind, and she was walking across that cornfield with her nightgown billowing out behind her. The sight of her made me afraid. After a while, I sent Cooley out to bring her in here before she froze. She saw him coming and ran into the woods. I figured that's why the brother showed up just at dawn. He was looking for his sister."

"How long did Hamilton stay?"

James looked at me long and hard. "I saw him and Delo walk out in the cornfield. Then I went on to church with Cooley. I was gone awhile, visiting, but when I got back he was gone and Delo, I suppose, was dead."

The pictures his words created were as sharp and painful as nails in my flesh. Cooley came into the room bearing a tray with three mugs, three spoons, sugar, and cream. I took mine black and sat back in the chair. "Did you tell the sheriff about this?"

Cooley gave that soft snort of contempt I'd heard before. "We don't tell the law anything. If you were black, you wouldn't talk to anybody in a uniform. For the last twenty years those fools have been comin' out here in the dead of night, diggin' up the corn and the fields. It's gotten worse lately. They're ruinin' Delo's crop, and ours, too. Like we might have buried it. We called the law plenty of times, but you know what was done. Nothing. They're out there looking for that—"

"That's enough, Cooley," James said gently but with a hint of iron. "Miss Delaney doesn't want to hear about such foolishness. I'm sure she'd rather hear about the time her father and I caught that big tabby cat in the river. It almost took the boat down."

I wanted to hear a tale about my father, but I wanted to find out who was digging in the cornfield more. One look at James's face and I knew he wasn't going to tell me anything else. I sat back and drank my coffee and listened.

Jitty hovered around the kitchen table, her normally serene face a knot of concern. I'd been gone all day and most of the night, and the house was freezing. The oven was on broil and the door open, but it seemed as if the liquid in my body had turned to slush. I sighed and shuddered, wrapping my hands around the bowl of soup I'd heated and then decided I didn't want.

"You knew all along he was a suspect." Jitty had a bossy tone in her voice, as if I were a naughty child who'd hurt herself doing something against the rules.

I pushed the soup bowl away, untouched, and sat back in my chair. What she was saying was true. Hamilton the Fifth had always been the prime suspect in his mother's murder. Now, he'd been placed at Delo's murder only hours before the body was found.

"It's just 'cause you dropped your drawers for him," Jitty said, nodding knowingly. "Look at it like this, Sarah Booth, you've slept with worse. And he didn't hurt you. Fact is, you had a good time and you needed it."

"Stop it," I hissed at her. I hated it when she tried to reduce sex to some kind of physical therapy for the lonely. I huddled deeper into the jacket I was too cold to take off.

Jitty leaned stiff-armed on the table in front of me. "Fact is, you don't use it, God'll take it away from you. A woman needs to pop her cork at least twice a month, or all her juices will dry up." At my shocked expression she leaned down closer. "I read about it in one of those magazines. You know it wouldn't hurt you to read some women's magazines. Might remind you about what a body needs."

I sighed. It was pointless to argue with Jitty. In a month she'd be throwing my night of sexual liberation in my face, but at this moment she was determined to take the "modern" approach to the fact that I'd slept with a man who might have killed a slew of people.

Even as I thought it, I got a flash of the night we'd spent together. A man like that couldn't be a killer.

But of course he could, my brain argued. Killers weren't always rot-toothed, hollow-eyed desperados who slapped their kids and kicked their dogs. Parchman

Prison was filled with all sorts of men who'd committed crimes of every description. Some of them were bound to be good-looking, charming, and smart.

Like Hamilton.

I felt Jitty staring at me and I turned to find her, arms akimbo, glaring.

"You sink any deeper, I might as well shovel dirt on top of you," she said.

"I don't want him to be a killer," I finally admitted, shocked at how pitiful I sounded.

"Well, quit wallowing in self-pity and go find who did it."

It was great advice. I'd even thought of it. But *how* was the question.

"Maybe you should get some help," Jitty suggested.

Coleman Peters came to mind. He was the sheriff, and he'd always seemed like a decent sort. Maybe if I explained my suspicions to him, he would help me out. Even as I thought about it, I knew it was stupid. Coleman didn't need to agitate Isaac Carter and the Buddy Clubbers by reopening a murder twenty years old that cast doubt on their business ethics, not to mention multiple murders and massive cover-ups.

"Everyone who might help me is a suspect," I whined.

"Your mama never raised a hand to you, but if she was standin' here she'd slap you right across the face."

Jitty's angry words had the intended effect. I sat up and lifted my chin. She was right. Mother was kind and compassionate and patient—but she couldn't abide whining.

"Use your brain, Sarah Booth. There's someone who was in the Garrett house the summer before Mr. Garrett was killed. Someone who saw things."

"Tammy," I said, half rising. I hadn't forgotten her. I

just hadn't considered that she might have vital information. But she had been there every day. And her grandmother had fought against the zoning change.

"Thanks, Jitty," I said, this time not even caring that she'd gloat and torment me with this for months.

"Get goin'," she said.

I jumped up, pulled my gloves from my pocket, and started the search for my keys. As I shook out the gloves, a piece of paper dropped to the floor. It was a neatly folded square that I picked up and opened. The check was made out to Delo and signed by Kincaid.

I held it a moment in my hands, stunned. Then I realized that Cooley must have tucked it there as he walked me down the rows of dead corn when he'd escorted me to my car. I'd felt his hand on my elbow, fumbling.

"I'll be damned," I said softly. When I looked around for Jitty, she was gone, replaced by a tapping at the kitchen door.

For a split second of foolishness, I thought it might be Hamilton and I sprang to my feet. Sneaking to the window, I peered out. Harold stood on the back steps.

My thumb gave a feeble protest, just before the big monkey of guilt jumped on my back. Little monkey paws all over me. I had not played fair with Harold.

I confronted a hard fact. Though my thumb throbbed for Harold, it was Hamilton who controlled the rest of my body. Murderer he might be, but I'd fallen for him. I didn't intend to pursue the Dark Lord of Knob Hill, but I could no longer even consider Harold as a mate.

And coward that I was, I couldn't face him.

Clutching my keys, I crept out of the kitchen to the front door. Then I ran across the porch, jumped in the car, and drove away.

25

I considered driving around until Harold was gone, and then going up to my room and flinging myself on the bed where I could kick and scream and cry in a fit of fury. When I was four and five, that behavior seemed to make things better. But then I'd had my parents, who waited until the storm passed and then came in to soothe me with touches and a voice of reason. Often that voice was describing punishments and restrictions for my tantrum, but it didn't matter. After the excess of emotion, I needed the reason.

But there would be no one to reason with me once I pitched my fit. The only man who had cared enough to try had just been jettisoned out of my life because I lusted for another.

Before I could sink into the depths of self-hatred and shame, I focused on the clouds building in the night sky. They were huge and gray-black and rumbling with thunder, which added to the excitement and pleasure of driving the Roadster. The car was all mine, for the mo-ment. I had to concentrate on that. Not on being decent or nice or loved or noble—but being solvent. It was the way of the world for bottom-feeders like myself.

I drove to Tammy's house.

Unlike the afternoon when there had been people on the front porches, her neighborhood was now shuttered against the storm. The street seemed eerily abandoned, and I drove slowly, avoiding a trashcan that rolled into the road and a stray dog that scampered, teats almost dragging the ground, through my high beams. I passed a big Town Car bumping out of the Grove in the opposite direction, and caught a glimpse of pale blond hair at the steering wheel. More than likely it was someone who'd been to see Tammy.

Tammy's house looked closed and uninviting, but I could see a light on in the back. I wondered what she was doing. Claire was back in Mound Bayou, living the life of motherhood with her infant daughter. Tammy, like me, was alone.

Instead of knocking at the front, I walked around the house toward the light. It did occur to me that it was foolish behavior. She might mistake me for a robber. The strains of a scratchy Billie Holiday record seeped out of the house. "Lover Man." It wasn't exactly upbeat music. I knocked at the back door.

The kitchen light came on, the door opened a crack, and Tammy's face appeared. She was well schooled in guarding her reactions. She showed nothing as she pushed open the door to let me in.

"Cold night for creeping around houses," she commented as she led the way through a porch and into the kitchen. The smell of fried chicken lingered near the stove, and in another room, Billie Holiday sang good morning to a heartache.

"Are you busy?" I asked. It seemed that we had lost the way of our friendship. There had been a time, a brief time, when we'd been able to smile at each other and reveal our deepest secrets. My life had pulled me in a different direction, as had hers. But it struck me that I hadn't had a friend like her since. Not in college or New York. There had been girls and women I liked and admired, but none like Tammy.

"I was making some clothes for Dahlia," she said, motioning me to follow her into the next room. A sewing machine was set up on a table, and beside it were dainty pieces of material, a bright summer pattern of red and yellow and blue. "Sundresses," she said. "It'll be summer before you know it."

"Tammy, who is Claire's father?" I hadn't meant to ask so bluntly. I hadn't meant to ask at all.

"You can't leave it alone, can you?" she asked.

I shook my head. "I've discovered some things about myself I'd rather not have known. Now I want to know everything."

She walked to the record player, an old turntable of a type I hadn't seen in years, and turned it off. In the silence her voice sounded tired. "We all learn things about ourselves we don't like to accept."

"Please tell me."

"If you'd really wanted to know a long time ago, it might have made a difference. If anybody except my granny had thought to ask, it might have changed my life. She died believing that my pregnancy was her punishment for trying to hold on to her home, for fighting against the land development. I was too afraid to speak the truth."

She went to the table and picked up Dahlia's little dress. "Your daddy gave Granny advice. He helped, and Mr. Garrett was helping, but that was a long time ago." She looked up at me. "I wanted things to be different for Claire, and they are. She fell in love with a boy, and together they made a baby. At least it was joyful. It didn't happen that way for me."

"How did it happen?" I was afraid to hear, and I realized that perhaps, all along, it was fear that squelched my curiosity.

"Remember I told you I worked at Knob Hill that summer, before Mr. Guy was killed?"

I nodded.

"I worked in the house with Lolly and Missy, and I worked in the gardens with Mr. Henry. Late at night when everyone was asleep, Hamilton would get me in the pool and teach me to swim. I was terrified of that beautiful aqua water. During the day when I was carrying laundry or cleaning vegetables at the kitchen sink, I'd watch Mrs. Garrett swim, all sleek and wet like some animal with a special talent. I wanted to feel the water sliding over my body. I wanted to wear a bikini and climb out of that pool with the water running down me and puddling at my painted toes. But I was afraid of it, like it would grab hold of me and pull me down to the drain."

She put the dress down and her hand idly stroked the material.

"Hamilton taught me how to swim, and late at night I'd get in the pool in my underwear and swim for a long time, practicing all the strokes he taught me. I got where I could swim real good, without breaking the water or making a sound. Clean, just the way he showed me."

I held still. To move would have stopped her.

"That was the summer I started dreaming. At first it was small things. I'd dream of fresh strawberries with sugar and cream, and that's what Missy would fix for dessert. Or I'd see a pattern, and suddenly Mrs. Garrett would be putting up new wallpaper that looked exactly like I dreamed. It was fun. I told Missy and Lolly, and they laughed, but I could tell it also bothered them. Then I started dreaming about the doves."

She realized she was still stroking Dahlia's dress and she stopped. She tucked her hand in the pocket of her slacks and sighed. "Remember, you asked to hear this, Sarah Booth."

I didn't say anything. I couldn't. She walked past me and into the kitchen. As she started a pot of coffee, she picked up her story.

"The dreams got worse and worse, until I would go to the kitchen all tense and hollow-eyed because I couldn't sleep. That's when I started swimming more. It seemed to relax me and help me sleep. I was out there swimming one night when I heard voices. Mr. Guy was gone, and Mrs. Garrett had been in Memphis shopping for a few days. The house had been quiet, and I didn't even know she'd come home. But she was home, and she was in her bedroom over the pool. A man was up there with her, and they were talking about—"

She broke off and turned to face me.

"They were talking about killing Mr. Garrett, weren't they?"

She nodded. "They planned it just the way it happened."

"Who was it?"

"I can't say," she whispered, and as she reached for the sugar bowl her hand trembled so that I got up and took it from her.

"All of these years I've ached to tell, and now I can't," she said. "I can't say his name."

"Why not?" I asked. "Are you afraid he'll hurt you?"

"He can't. Not any more than he already has," she answered softly. "He's dead. But his blood lives on. It's the son I'm afraid of."

She didn't have to say the man's name. There were

plenty of dead folks in Sunflower County, but I knew who it was. Pasco Walters. I suppose I'd known for a long time that he'd figure into this. And Gordon Walters was certainly a man who could wield the power of the law in his favor.

"I know who he is," I said. "You don't have to say."

She looked at me. "He comes to me in dreams, and I know that means I'm going to die. That's why I sent Claire to my cousin's in Mound Bayou. I didn't want her here, in danger. I didn't want her killed by her half-brother."

I had been standing, the sugar bowl in my hand. I carefully put it on the table and pulled out a chair for her and one for me. When we were both sitting, I reached across the table and took her hand.

"Pasco Walters was Claire's father?"

She nodded slowly. "He must have seen me in the pool. I slipped out and ran into the house. I thought for a long time that I'd gotten away. But it was after Mrs. Garrett died that he was waiting for me after school. He ordered me into the patrol car when I was walking home. And he drove me out to Knob Hill. Nobody was there. They'd all scattered. It was just him and me, and he asked me if I could swim. I knew that he knew. I knew he was going to kill me, too. But he made me take off my clothes and get in the pool and show him all the strokes that Hamilton had taught me. And then he raped me. And he told me that he would do it again and again if I ever opened my mouth. And I never told anybody. Nobody ever asked, except Granny's friend, Mr. Levert."

"I'm sorry, Tammy," I said. "I'm so sorry."

"Mr. Levert knew something was wrong, but he didn't press. He knew I wasn't the kind of girl who'd throw away her future like that. He knew I was afraid.

He and Granny were up at City Hall all the time, fighting against the development, and I was so afraid for them, too."

Her body was trembling, and I held her hand like it was a lifeline. When the first tears rolled down her cheeks, I got up and went to her and held her in my arms while she cried.

"I'm sorry," I told her, smoothing her hair as I held her. "I'm sorry."

"It was bound to come out. Mr. Levert was over here this evening, asking questions about the past. His friend was killed out in that cornfield, too."

"Delo Wiley?"

She sniffed and nodded. "Delo sold him that land when nobody else would. They were neighbors."

"James Levert?" I finally made the connection. "The old man who fought the land development with your granny?"

"Do you know Mr. James?"

"I do," I said, remembering the Town Hall minutes.

"He's a good man. A troubled man."

"Tammy, I need to go," I said, rising. "Are you going to be okay?"

She nodded. "I needed to tell someone. I'm glad it was you."

"I wish I'd asked earlier. And I'm sorry for digging all of this up. I really thought it would be a few rumors and Tinkie would be satisfied."

"It was bound to come up. Bones don't rest easy when the truth is buried with them."

She seemed to be getting a grip on her emotions, and I felt a pressing need to act. I wasn't sure how, but I needed to do something. I gave Tammy a hug and started toward the door when I remembered the big Town Car.

"Tammy, did someone leave here just before I arrived?"

That slightly stubborn look came over her face. "I don't talk about my clients."

I wanted to shake her. "This is important."

She must have sensed my desperation.

"It was Millie," she said. "She comes by late, after she closes the café."

I started to ask Tammy something else, but the door had already closed behind me. I heard the lock shoot into place. I didn't need Tammy's confirmation, though. I knew where I had to go. I was suddenly certain that Millie had been the person who helped Sylvia get out of Glen Oaks. It made a crazy kind of sense. The nurse had mentioned a big car, as had James and Cooley. A Lincoln, specifically. And Millie had been deeply in love with Hamilton the Fourth. Sylvia would be her last connection with him, possibly her last chance to avenge his death.

It was time for a serious talk with Millie.

26

The low rumbling of thunder could be heard in the distance as I parked in front of Millie's house. The big Lincoln wasn't there, so I figured she probably wasn't home. The night was damp and cold and I knocked until my knuckles felt battered and abused.

The question I kept asking myself was, why would Millie leave Sylvia, in her nightgown, in Delo Wiley's field? The next logical question was, what, exactly, was Millie's connection to Sylvia? Was she a friend, or a co-conspirator in murder? Or worse?

It occurred to me again that Millie could have slashed Veronica's brake lines at the garage and then planted the knife on the Garrett siblings. Her motivation in helping Sylvia escape might have been to set Sylvia up, once again, as the scapegoat. This time for Delo's murder.

I left Millie's house with reluctance and headed to the only person in town who might be able to help me.

Cece Dee Falcon lived in a charming Victorian on Longpull Street. It was named after a type of cotton, not an incline. I turned into her drive, glad to see lights on in the living room. As I climbed the brick steps, I could hear the droning sound of a television. Cece answered my first knock with an expectant smile on her face. It vanished as soon as she saw me.

"What are you doing here?" she asked, not opening the door any wider.

"I need to see you. Actually, I need to see some back issues of the newspaper. I know Mrs. Kepler won't open the library for me. I'm hoping you'll let me in the paper."

"I'd love to, dahling, but one has to consider other plans." She looked out into the night.

"Cece, this is serious." I took notice of her dress, a slinky number that did justice to her slim hips and exquisite throat. She was expecting someone, very probably a romantic interest.

"Any other day, I'd be glad to help you with your book research, Sarah Booth, but not tonight."

"It isn't book research," I said, finally and at long last tired of the lie. "It's a murder investigation."

She smiled. "I always thought you were good at spinning a yarn. That's why you'll be such a good writer. So what murder are you bird-dogging?"

"Veronica Garrett's."

She raised one feathered eyebrow. "There was plenty of *talk* that Veronica Garrett had been murdered, but there was no evidence. Of course, in a book—let's discuss this tomorrow."

"I need to see the newspapers." I could be very stubborn. "I'll stay here until you let me."

"You can't do this," she whispered urgently. "You can't camp out on my doorstep."

"I can and I will. Or give me the key to the newspaper office. I only want to look at some back issues."

She hesitated. "You'll go away?"

"I'll leave the key in your mailbox when I'm finished."

"Just a minute." She closed the door and returned in a moment with a key on a ribbon. "Don't you dare turn on a computer or try to get in my office."

"Scout's honor," I said, wondering if Cece would remember that I'd been thrown out of the Girl Scouts because of my predilection for cherry bombs and bonfires.

She handed the key through the door, and then watched as I hurried out into the night that had just begun to drizzle with a cold, miserable rain.

The beauty of a small town is that nothing is more than five minutes away. I was at the *Dispatch* in a flash. To avoid prying eyes, I parked in the back, only to discover that the key worked the front door. Pressed against the damp wall, I sneaked to the front and entered. Skirting desks and chairs and stacks of books and printed matter, I navigated the dark office by the flashes of lightning that popped outside the window. The bound volumes were in the very back of the building, in a room with no windows. I could afford to turn on the lights.

The records from 1978 back had been put on microfiche, but the ones I needed were still in print. The pages felt thin and flimsy, an old smell of dust and ink rising from them as I scanned again the story of Hamilton the Fourth's death. It was as I remembered—presented as a tragic hunting accident.

I moved on to February 10, 1980, and Veronica's car wreck. I read the story carefully, three times. There was no mention or even hint of foul play. Car meets tree— end of story. All very tidy.

I examined Pasco Walters's statements, knowing that

he'd been Veronica's lover and that he'd helped plan her husband's death—if he hadn't been the triggerman.

Pasco's quotes were carefully drawn. He called the wreck a tragedy, and pointed out how much the community would miss the good works of Mrs. Garrett. There had been nothing personal, no hint of grief or sorrow.

It was possible that the relationship had not survived the murder of Guy Garrett. Once Veronica had what she wanted—freedom and money—she might have found the handsome sheriff an encumbrance.

I read the funeral arrangements, a tasteful affair of a memorial service held in the Garrett family cemetery. Veronica was laid to rest beside her husband. The reporter gave a little too much detail about the flowers, but the choice of hymns was startling. "Swing Low, Sweet Chariot" seemed a bad choice for a wreck victim.

I started to flip over to see if an additional reference had been made in the days after the wreck, but a photo on the bottom of the page caught my eye. Millie Roberts stood with her arm around a striking blonde. They were both smiling happily. The story was a brief report on a nineteen-year-old girl, Janice Wells, who'd vanished without a trace. It was only three paragraphs long and gave the basic facts. Janice had disappeared from Billie's Garage around lunchtime. No one had seen her leave and she'd taken only her purse. Since she had no car, it was assumed she was on foot.

Millie had offered a three-thousand-dollar reward—probably her life's savings—for information leading to her sister's whereabouts. The sheriff's office had basically labeled her a runaway.

In the photograph, I studied the features that marked the women as sisters. Janice was obviously the younger by a few years, but she had the same easy smile and curious look in her eyes as her older sister.

I looked at the way Janice had slung her arm so casually over her sister's shoulder, and I knew that Janice had not run away with a man. I was no Madame Tomeeka. I didn't have a vision, or read the past or future in a deck of cards or a palm. I simply looked at the love between the two sisters and I knew that Janice had met a tragic fate. If she were alive, she'd have put her sister's mind at rest.

I shuffled through the rest of the month, but there was no follow-up on Veronica's wreck or Janice's disappearance. Both stories evaporated; one deliberately buried, and the other simply ignored because Janice was a girl who didn't matter in the social structure of the town.

No wonder Millie had been snappy at me. If a Daddy's Girl had disappeared, every man and dog in the county would have been put on the trail and would probably still be looking.

I closed the files, restacked them neatly, and headed back through the dark office. I had found no new facts, only a bitter taste of sadness. When I passed the plate glass windows, I caught a glimpse of a sheriff's patrol car gliding like a shark through the turbulent night. I thought I recognized Gordon Walters's profile, his roguishly dented nose undoubtedly the result of a fight. Without the broken bridge, he would look remarkably like Claire. The answer had been there all along.

The car moved slowly down the street. Gordon played a role in this, an important one. The sharks were out and feeding. I would have to be very careful.

· · ·

Dahlia House held tremendous appeal for me at that moment, but where I needed to go was Friars Point. It was probably true what Hamilton had said, that his sister was indeed insane. The glass bottle she'd given me for her brother obviously meant something to him, though he'd left it at Dahlia House. I wanted to know what. I made a squealing U-turn in the newspaper parking lot.

I was traveling fast when a dark figure stepped out from behind a garbage Dumpster. I registered that it was a large male as I slammed on the brakes. The drizzling rain had dampened the asphalt just enough to loosen the grease and grit. I felt the car begin to spin and I forgot everything except controlling the slide. It took fifty yards of fierce struggle, but I fought the car back under control. When I finally had it stopped, my hands refused to let go of the steering wheel so I sat there, shaking, too tired and, at the same time, too pumped with adrenaline to move.

At the tap on the passenger window, I looked up to find Hamilton staring in at me. He opened the door before I thought to lock it, and climbed in.

"You almost made me kill myself," I said, furious at him for pulling such a stunt. "Is that how you sent your mother into a tree?"

His face darkened, but when he spoke his voice had a tightly controlled formality. "You've pried into my business, and now you're in over your head. Gordon Walters is looking for you, and he has a warrant for your arrest for the murder of Delo Wiley. My suggestion is that you go to Memphis, check into a nice hotel, and stay there for a few days until this is over." The dim glow from the dash cast a strange light on his face, making his eyes seem to glitter.

I wondered if there was a hint of satisfaction in his

tone. "I suppose *you* would think that running away is the best answer." For all of the many things I dislike about the training of a Daddy's Girl, the emphasis on pride and dignity is unbeatable. Hamilton had used me. He had slept with me and won me over, and then run out without an explanation or even a good-bye. He had gutted me, and I was angry. And hurt. And wanting to hurt him back.

"Sarah Booth, you've been a thorn and a nuisance since you agreed to investigate my past for Tinkie. Gordon isn't in the mood to put up with you."

A strange calm settled over me. "How long have you known I was working for Tinkie?"

"I made it a point to find out what you were really up to after your visit to Knob Hill."

So he had known when he slept with me. I nodded, accepting the fact that he was the dark master—of manipulation, gratification, and expectation—all of the *-tions* that lead a woman to vulnerability and pain. I stiffened my spine and gave him a cool smile.

"Well, we both expended a lot of energy, but I don't think either of us got much information." I would never let him know that for one night I believed in him, in his innocence and his place in my world.

Even in the dim illumination from the car's panel, I could see the flush on his face. "What, exactly, did Sylvia say when she gave you the glass bottle?"

"First, you tell me what significance the bottle has."

He considered a moment, as if he might not answer. "My mother collected glass and jewelry by a particular artist. René Lalique. That bottle and several other pieces disappeared the day of the wreck. Sylvia has been advertising in art magazines, looking for my mother's things. Once that bottle came on the market, she knew that the murderer finally felt safe enough to begin selling off the pieces. Sylvia got a response to one of her ads and she called me to come home, to help her set the trap."

I finally understood the magazine article in his coat pocket, his sudden return to Sunflower County. "Sylvia isn't crazy, then. She's just—"

"Obsessed by revenge. Some people would call it insane to focus your life on revenge, to cloister yourself from any pleasure so that you'd never be tempted to forget the unforgivable. Maybe she's crazy; I can't say. I do know she's smart and patient and determined. Sylvia knew, eventually, those valuable pieces would be sold. And so she's waited, all of these years." He looked at me, and I felt a rush of sorrow. What a waste. Hamilton in exile, his sister in Glen Oaks.

"What did Sylvia say?" he insisted.

"She said that time had run out, for both of you."

Hamilton pushed open the door and and began to lever himself out of the car. I grabbed his arm and restrained him. I could feel his forearm beneath the layers of his jacket. He halted his exit and turned to look at me. The memory of his mouth moving over my skin was as intense as if it were happening that second. And yet I felt a great distance between us. As if Hamilton had stepped backward into a void.

"If you don't let the past go, it'll destroy you," I said, repeating the things that Tammy and Jitty and Tinkie had tried to make me understand. "Please, Hamilton . . ." Memories of the night we'd shared seemed to fill the car. "Come back to Dahlia House with me."

"Aren't you afraid I'll get up in the middle of the night and murder you?" he asked in that arrogant tone that implied he was capable of anything.

"You wouldn't kill me. There's no profit in it."

My cynicism made him laugh, and once again I felt the surge of raw desire. There was something wounded and fierce in him that I could not help but respond to. I had found in Hamilton an opponent worthy of my own passions, and I did not want to let him go.

His hands moved from my shoulders to my collarbones, inching slowly lower. I made no effort to touch him; I waited. His hands slipped inside my coat, finally sliding over my breasts. His breathing had become short and fast, like mine. And yet we could not look away from each other.

"Sarah Booth—" His fingers brushed back up and stopped on my shoulders. "I've tried not to care for you or about what happens to you. I've tried to frighten you away, but none of it has worked. Now I'm asking you. Will you go someplace safe and stay there? Go to the Peabody in Memphis. I have a room. Wait for me there."

"I can't walk out of this now," I answered. "I won't."

He opened the door and was out in the night before I could stop him. To my surprise, he dropped down beside the car. It took me a moment to register what he'd done. By the time I got out and ran around to check the tire that he'd slashed, he'd disappeared between the rain-drenched buildings of downtown Zinnia.

27

I had no option—I started walking toward Cece's house. Before I made it a block, the sky opened. In thirty seconds, I was soaked. My leather jacket grew heavy and made disturbing sounds as I slogged forward. The cold water did nothing to cool my temper. I had great plans for Hamilton Garrett the Fifth, and all of them involved pain and suffering.

A set of high beams bounced off the plate glass window of Steppin' Out, and I took a chance that it wasn't Gordon Walters out patrolling for me. I put on a smile, stuck out a thumb, and stood, hair plastered against my skull. In the weird reflection of the big glass window I looked like a bad cartoon character. To my amazement, the car slowed.

It was a big Caddy, and as the passenger window slid down, a cacophony of barking greeted me.

"Chablis!" I cried, recognizing the big bark of the little dog.

"Is this some new weight-loss regimen?" Tinkie

asked as she leaned toward me. "You look like something out of a John Carpenter movie."

"I had car trouble," I said, surprised that Tinkie knew anything about horror films. I was learning there were many sides to Tinkie Bellcase Richmond.

"Hop in." She unlocked the door. "I told you to buy American. Those foreign cars aren't reliable."

I was too cold to argue the politics of the car industry, so I slid into the car, turned a heater vent directly on me, and eased back in the leather seats. We made a quick detour by Cece's house to drop the key in her mailbox.

"I was headed to your house to tell you about Sylvia," Tinkie said, her foot pressing the gas pedal to the floor. The Caddy purred through the night, gobbling the asphalt while it surrounded me with leather and luxury. There was something to be said for American products.

"What about Sylvia?" My teeth had almost stopped chattering, but it would be a long time before my heart recovered from Hamilton's betrayal.

"She's gone."

"She's gone from Glen Oaks?" I was hoping I'd heard wrong. But I hadn't, and I also remembered that Millie was not at home.

Lightning forked in the sky, and a peal of thunder seemed to split the heavens. With a sound like a fist slamming the hood of the car, the rain came down in a wall. I picked up a trembling Chablis and cuddled her in my arms.

"I love storms," Tinkie said. "I just love the wild energy. Oscar hates them. He's afraid. He's gone to the hunting camp over on the river to talk business and shoot a few ducks. You know, I'd like to hear of one goddamn deal they did without having to kill some animal as part of the ritual." She chattered on as she flew over the wet road in an easterly direction.

"Turn around," I suddenly demanded.

"Excuse me," she said. "You can add a 'please' onto that request."

"Please turn around. Quick," I said. "We have to go to Tam—Madame Tomeeka's."

Tinkie's huff evaporated. "Well, why didn't you say so," she said, mollified. "No wonder you're acting so pushy. I know what it's like to need a reading." She shot a look at me. "I didn't think you believed in Madame Tomeeka."

I cuddled Chablis up to my face and kept my silence, willing Tinkie to hurry. I didn't have to tell her my real reason.

Chances were good that someone else was destined to die before the night was over.

There was an old beat-up truck at Tammy's, and I silently cursed our luck. The prospect of waiting didn't bother Tinkie at all. With Chablis snuggled in her shirt, she ran across the yard and dashed up to the front door, flinging raindrops from her face with a giggle.

Tammy met us, and I had the distinct feeling she was going to turn us away, until James Levert stepped up behind her.

"Let them in," he said gently and then faded back into the darkness of the house. Tammy unlatched the screen and indicated that we were to follow her.

We bypassed the living room and the room where she'd been sewing little Dahlia's dresses, and ended up in the kitchen. Coffee was brewing, as if she'd anticipated our visit. I settled into the chair she indicated. The shotgun leaning against the china cupboard in the corner was not obvious, but it was handy. I looked up to find James Levert staring at me.

"It's a bad night," he said in that soft, well-spoken voice. "Lucky you young ladies decided to come in out of it, though this isn't the best place to be."

I nodded at the gun. "Is there something I should know?"

"Tammy's been helping to lay a trap. The problem is, if it don't snap shut tight then there might be trouble."

The gun was within easy reach, and he was sitting so that he could clearly see the back and front doors in the narrow house.

"Tammy," I said. I needed to speak with her alone.

She ignored me, pouring the coffee into the cups.

"Tammy, Sylvia Garrett has disappeared from Glen Oaks," I said softly. The stream of black coffee wavered, spilling out of one cup, but she didn't stop pouring. When she'd filled all the cups, she began to place them, two by two, on the table. She put mine in front of me.

"You need a towel," she said, disappearing through a doorway and returning with a cheerful red-and-yellow-striped bundle that she handed to me.

"Tammy, I need a word with you," I said, standing. I held the towel to my chest.

"It was bound to come to this eventually," she said, and her face fell into lines of weariness. "Sylvia shut away in Glen Oaks, those men digging in the cornfields, thinking that Mr. James or Delo had that money. All of these years they've kept looking, kept accusing. They couldn't accept that the money was actually gone. But Grandma told them that ground soaked in blood yields a strange harvest. I tried to keep you out of it, Sarah Booth."

I glanced at Tinkie just as Chablis popped out of her jacket and gave a friendly bark.

Tinkie didn't have a clue, but I had begun to develop a theory, and it involved James Levert. "Why did Guy Garrett, a man who didn't hunt, choose a dove field as a place to transact business?" I asked him.

His old eyes lingered on me, and he nodded almost imperceptibly. "I was supposed to meet Mr. Garrett in that dove field. He was going to give me the money, which we would use to fight the development of the Grove. It was a slick plan. We'd use their own money to defeat them."

It was a dangerous plan, but I had a new appreciation for the kind of man Guy Garrett must have been.

"Your father was in on it," James said. His eyes behind his glasses were sharply focused. "He and Mr. Garrett didn't like the way the developers were trying to cheat folks out of their land. It was dirty and underhanded. Mr. Garrett, he came up with this idea where he'd take their million-dollar payoff and pretend he was going to vote for the rezoning. But he was giving the money to us, so we could hire lawyers and fight the rezoning. Then Mr. Garrett was going to pretend he'd never received the money. There were no witnesses, except the men who paid him off. They really couldn't complain, at least not to the law."

I remembered my recent talk with Jitty, the way she'd reminded me of Guy Garrett visiting our home. He had come to talk about thwarting the development plan. I glanced at Tinkie and saw the honest confusion on her face. There wasn't time to explain this right now.

I refocused on James Levert. "After Mr. Garrett's death, the development was dropped. Why?"

"That's something I never understood," James admitted. "They could have pushed it through. We didn't have the resources to fight it after your father died and Mr. Garrett was killed. But the whole thing was dropped."

Even Chablis was watching James with fascination. "When you went to meet Mr. Garrett and get the money, he was dead."

James nodded slowly. By his expression I could tell he was remembering the clear October day and the way Hamilton Garrett was lying in the corn stubble. "And the money was gone," he said. "There wasn't a soul in sight, so I headed straight for the woods. I went and told Delo, but he said it would be best to wait until someone else discovered the body."

James didn't have to say why. Delo would have been the perfect scapegoat. He would have gone to Parchman, and no questions would ever have been asked.

"So, who got the money?" I asked.

"That's a question that's floated around for twenty years," James said. "I think it was the reason that the development plan fell apart." He allowed himself a tight smile. "They all suspected each other. Mr. Isaac, the two Memphis men, the rest of the investors, every one of them thought the other had killed Mr. Garrett and made off with the money. Then it got started that Delo had it hidden, and they watched him all the time. That's how they knew you were out there talking to him. They thought the money was in the cornfield, so they'd go out there on nights with a full moon and dig. As far as I know, no one ever found the money, but everyone still believes it's around here somewhere." He sighed. "Now Miss Sylvia's gone and made it worse, making up more tales about hidden money, running around like a crazy woman in the night."

The idea of all of that money lying around some-

where must have driven the men who'd hatched the
plan wild, but I didn't believe any of them had killed
Hamilton the Fourth. "I'm pretty certain that Pasco
Walters killed Guy Garrett," I said into the silent room.
I looked at Tammy, hoping to reassure her that I
wouldn't reveal her secret. Pasco's actions deserved cen-
sure, but it wasn't my place to act as judge and jury.

Only Tinkie seemed surprised. "The sheriff? I always
thought he was nice."

"Pasco and Veronica were lovers," I explained.
"They killed Guy to get him out of the way, and so
Veronica could inherit his money."

"The Garretts had been married twenty years. They
had two children!" Tinkie said, looking from one to
another of us. "Twenty years, and he didn't have a clue
who she really was."

"I think he knew who she was, but I think he loved
her anyway," I said, understanding exactly how that
could happen to a person with an average-to-high IQ.

"Who killed Veronica?" Tinkie asked, watching me.

"It could have been Pasco," I said. "I'm not certain."

"Was Pasco murdered or was it just my lucky day?"
Tammy asked with an edge to her voice.

"I don't know that, either." I had some questions of
my own. "Mr. Levert, are you certain Mr. Garrett had
that money?"

"He had it. The plan was that he would take his
position by that old stump once he got the money from
Mr. Carter and his associates. The stump was close to
the fringe of trees, and I was hiding in the woods. Once
Mr. Guy had the money, I was supposed to run over to
him, take the money, and disappear back in the trees.
The money was supposed to vanish. Mr. Garrett would
say he never got it. It would look like some of the developers were double-crossing each other."

Before anyone could say anything, Chablis leaped from Tinkie's arms with a ferocious growl. Tinkie made a grab for her, and it was the only thing that saved her life.

The shotgun blast came through the window and over her bent head. Within seconds Tinkie, James, Tammy, and I dove under the table.

"Is that what you've been waiting for?" I asked James.

"It's what I've been afraid of," he said. "Folks who've killed once don't think twice about doing it again."

I would have liked a better explanation, but there wasn't time. I aimed for the kitchen door and went rolling and tumbling out onto the back porch and into the rain.

I don't know what I expected to see, but it wasn't the big Lincoln. The car reversed out of the driveway, tires whining. It was Millie's car, and the driver was a blond woman.

It was a habit of all Daddy's Girls—the assumption that no one would dare take their vehicle—and as I ran through the dark and mud toward Tinkie's car, I knew the keys would be in the ignition. I slid into the driver's seat and felt something wet and hairy scoot by my leg. Chablis popped up on the front seat beside me with a chipper little bark.

I started the car and took off, mud spinning from the wheels in two long jets. The Lincoln was out of sight, but as I made the corner, I saw the red taillights as it sped toward the highway.

As I drove I tried to untangle how Millie had become so caught up in such violence. I'd figured her as a suspect in Veronica's death. Not really a cold-blooded, drive-by killer, but more as one woman who decided to get even with the woman who killed her love.

I halfway expected her to go to the café, but she kept straight through town, headed south. Watching the car ahead of me, I realized Millie was drawing farther and farther away. Once she cleared town, she'd put the pedal down. I floored the accelerator in the Caddy and found that I was hitting a hundred and ten on the wet, slick road. A fine drizzle continued to fall, and on either side of me the black night swallowed the flat outreach of the Delta soil.

I kept doing my best to dodge thoughts of Hamilton, but it wasn't easy. I no longer believed he was a murderer, but I wasn't sure that mattered in the long run. I wanted a life where I fell in love with a man, then fell in bed with him, or vice versa, but also where he called me and asked me to dinner and where we could sit on the porch and sip moonshine and laugh. Murderer or not, Hamilton would never fit that bill. The very intensity that drew me to him was the reason that he was not suited to the role of suitor.

Lost in the dense blackness of the night and my thoughts, I wasn't certain where we were when I saw the brake lights flare on the car in front of me. I hung back, hoping that Millie wouldn't know I was following her. To my surprise, the car turned left. I cruised forward.

We were at Delo Wiley's place.

It made sense. Delo's was where it all started. There was probably no better place to finish it. But how exactly I intended to finish it was something I hadn't thought through. Maybe I could just keep an eye on Millie and call the sheriff.

The Lincoln bypassed Delo's house and bumped over the corn rows, headed out to the Mule Bog field. I parked the Caddy on the side of the road. In the darkness I'd have a better chance on foot.

As I got out, I realized that I couldn't leave Chablis on the front seat. Anything could happen.

"This isn't the time for bonding," I warned as I picked her up and stuffed her into my damp jacket. She was already wet, so it didn't seem to matter. We began to cut across the field.

A Daddy's Girl's imagination is often her worst enemy. As I slipped through the foggy fields, I imagined Sylvia Garrett carousing in her nightgown. She was out of the mental institution, again, and I could only hope she hadn't decided to come back to Delo's and do her rage-filled corn dance. My poor, battered heart couldn't take a vision like that.

28

Delo's house was pitch black, a term I now had a new appreciation for. I'd stumbled over the corn rows and finally made it to the front porch. Pushing open the creaking door, my nerve almost failed me. Only thoughts of Millie bouncing over the cornfield in her Town Car with her loaded shotgun made me move forward. All I had to do was get to a telephone. 9-1-1. 9-1-1. I droned the mantra as I forced my reluctant body to move forward.

One thing was for certain: As soon as the hardware store opened in the morning I'd have a flashlight that fit in my pocket. I'd make another stop at Johnny's Pawn-O-Rama and pick up a cell phone and, though I could hardly believe it, a gun. Creeping into Delo's house, I wished for the protection of even a can of Mace.

I eased into the living room and headed toward the table where I knew a lamp had been. It was risky to turn on a light, but I could stumble around that house for a long time without finding the phone. I wanted to dial, report, and run back into the safety of the foggy fields.

Or maybe even over to Cooley's house where I could crawl under the porch with the hounds.

I found the lamp and snapped the switch. Nothing happened. I tried again, a tiny click in the thick silence of the dark house. Nothing. Goose bumps danced as I wondered if it was the power company or someone with very different motives who'd shut off the electricity. Chablis's tiny head popped out of my jacket and she gave a low, warning growl.

There was no choice. I'd have to find the phone in the dark. Moving carefully I began to search with my hands. I took tiny little baby steps, shuffling forward, doing my best not to stumble over a piece of furniture, not to make noise.

I'd made it halfway around the room when my feet connected with soft resistance. I shuffled a little, surprised to feel the barrier quiver. Squatting, I began to examine it. As soon as my fingers touched it, it began to jerk and writhe. The movement was so unexpected that I almost shouted as I fell backward.

"Polyester!" I cursed.

Chablis leaped out of my jacket and began to snap and growl. The thing on the floor stopped moving and made angry, demanding noises.

Touching it, I identified ankles bound by a rope, then thighs. Working my way up I found breasts—an awkward moment—then long hair and a gag.

"I don't know who you are, but I'm going to take the gag out and when I do, you'd better stay quiet," I warned. "There's a woman out there with a gun, and she seems in the mood to use it."

I unfastened the gag.

"Well, if it isn't Cousin Sarah Booth," the cultured voice of Sylvia Garrett said softly. "You'd better get out of here before he comes back and gets you, too."

"Sylvia?" I rocked back on my heels.

"If you aren't leaving, you might untie my hands," she whispered. "I don't know where he is, but he can't be far."

Another moan came from somewhere in the room. The hair on my neck honestly stood on end. Chablis moved away in the darkness and began to growl.

"It's Millie," Sylvia said as she shook her hands free of the rope I'd untied.

It couldn't be Millie; she was out in the car with the shotgun. The moan came again, and I crawled over the floor until I bumped into another female form and this one was crying.

"It's okay," I said as I worked.

She shook her head, making it hard for me to undo the knot. As soon as the gag was loose, she took a deep breath. "We're not safe. He's around here somewhere."

"My safety wasn't your top concern earlier," Sylvia said, and she sounded perfectly sane and very pissed-off. "You tricked me into coming back here with you. You said Hamilton was here."

"I had to do what I did," Millie said. "I didn't have a choice." Her voice broke. "They said they'd tell me about Janice. I knew all along that they'd done something to her, but I hoped I could find her." Her voice disintegrated in grief. "He showed up at my house, and I thought I'd have a heart attack right on the spot. He said if I'd get Sylvia from Glen Oaks, he'd tell me where Janice was. I'm sorry, Sylvia. Since you got me to bring you out here the time before, I didn't realize it was a trap." Millie's sobs were harsh and raspy. "He said Janice was happy, that she'd found a good man and settled down. He said she had three children, two girls and a boy."

Sylvia's voice was low and tight with anger. "You

thought he'd tell the truth? What a luxury to be naive at fifty. I was seventeen when I learned the ugly reality about the people I'd been taught to trust."

Sylvia Garrett might not be insane, but she was consumed with bitterness. I crawled past Millie and headed toward where I thought the phone might be. I had followed the exchange pretty well, except for one thing. I slowed my crawling and asked Millie, "Who told you to get Sylvia?"

"That would be me." The unexpected male voice was accompanied by the beam of a flashlight, which caught me directly in the eyes. I was blinded, and I threw up my hands to block the light.

"Who the hell are you?" I asked, fighting that terrifying fear that came with the knowledge that he'd been sitting in Delo's chair listening to us the entire time.

"Well, if it isn't Sarah Booth Delaney. The last time I saw you, you were a little girl in pigtails running around the courthouse with your daddy. So glad you dropped by."

I thought I had lost my mind, but I recognized Pasco Walters's voice. He'd deliberately triggered the perfect memory for me to identify him. He was alive, and not ten feet from where I sat on the floor. I heard a chair creak and the sound of footsteps as the flashlight rose up and came closer.

"You couldn't mind your own business, could you?" he said, but there was no anger in his voice, only mild bemusement. "Your folks were always hard to deal with. Strange people, I'd say, always interfering in things that didn't concern them."

I wanted to say that I thought he was dead, but even though shock had impaired my ability for witty repartee, I managed to bite that back. I was actually too busy to talk. My brain had finally manipulated the pieces of the puzzle into a picture. Pasco had killed Guy Garrett and most likely Veronica. He'd also stolen Veronica's Lalique collection, and after all this time, he'd begun to sell off the pieces.

Another thought came to me: When I'd been hiding in the hedge, eavesdropping on Hamilton, the other man had said he'd lost his father, too. Gordon Walters was the other man. He and Hamilton had some kind of hellish alliance.

"You're mighty quiet for such a nosy woman," Pasco said.

"It isn't every day I get to talk with a zombie," I answered. In all of my psychology classes, there had been no mention of tactics for talking to someone risen from the dead.

"Let me tell you," Pasco said on a soft laugh, "the afterlife has been wonderful. The last nineteen years have been the best anyone could ever wish for."

I wanted to see his face in the light. I shifted, and I heard the hammer of a gun click. The flashlight beam swung back over me. "I wouldn't make any sudden moves," he cautioned.

"What are you going to do with us?" Sylvia asked in her cool, controlled voice. She sounded so much like Hamilton, so unwilling to show fear or any other emotion considered weak. My heart dropped to my knees.

Pasco seemed to be making up his mind. "You, I'm keeping, so your brother stays in line. I don't think I could get rid of the last two Garretts without drawing suspicion." There was a pause. "The others . . ." He let the sentence fade, and since I couldn't see his face I had no idea what that might mean. My womb was strangely silent, but my gut was telling me this was not good. "I think they probably know too much," he finally added with a nice touch of fake regret in his voice.

He was going to kill us, and I had to give him credit, it was a perfect setup. By keeping Sylvia alive, he could control Hamilton. His sister's safety was his Achilles' heel. And even if Sylvia swore on a stack of Bibles that she'd been abducted by Pasco Walters, everyone would think she was just a little crazier than they originally thought. She'd be back in Glen Oaks in five seconds, this time by court decree.

"You got the money, didn't you?" I asked. "You took it off Mr. Garrett after you killed him."

"God, it was a beautiful sight," he answered, his tone boastful. I didn't need a light to feel his ego swell and fill the room. "I opened that briefcase and saw all of those fresh hundred-dollar bills, and I knew my life had changed forever."

My Daddy's Girl training kicked in and I recognized an opportunity. "What a brilliant plan," I said. "You got the money and a brand-new life without anyone even thinking to look for you. It's pure genius."

Pasco chuckled. "It was a perfect plan. Absolutely perfect. I walked out of one life and into another. For nineteen years I've lived like a king. But a million dollars will only stretch so far. We had to sell some of the baubles, and just when things were looking grim, we heard that Delo had buried another sack of money. The old bastard had pulled a fast one on us. That's when we decided to pay him a visit and get the rest."

So Pasco had run out of cash and begun to sell off the jewelry. It was the first misstep that he'd made. The second was in coming back for more money. Beside me, Millie gave a ragged sob, and it seemed my brain jolted forward. If Millie was on the floor . . . "Who was driving Millie's car?"

As if to answer my question, a feminine voice came

from my right. "Since we're all gathered here, I think it's time for some light. I flipped the breaker back on."

There was a scrabbling sound on the floor beside me, and the lights came on in a blinding flood just as Sylvia gained her feet and prepared to launch herself at the woman who stood in the doorway of Delo's kitchen holding a shotgun.

"You goddamn bitch," Sylvia said, and she dropped to a crouch. "For nineteen years I've dreamed of this day. I'll kill you with my bare hands."

Veronica Garrett's laughter was as cool as rippling water. "You always were overly dramatic, Sylvia. I detested that about you, always playing for the center of attention." She aimed the shotgun at her daughter. "You're not in a position to do much of anything."

"I knew you weren't dead." Sylvia was panting. "I knew it. I told them you weren't dead and they thought I was crazy. When I demanded to see your body, they thought I was morbid and insane. But I knew it wasn't you. What poor son-of-a-bitch died to give you a new life?"

Millie let out a wail. I put a hand on her shoulder and tried to comfort her, but there was nothing that could blunt the force of her pain. She had finally learned the truth of what had happened to her sister.

I had to do something, but I didn't know what. Sylvia was liable to charge into the muzzle of the gun, but I felt as if a wizard had cast a spell on me—I was mesmerized by Veronica.

The woman who stood before me was well over fifty, but she looked no older than thirty-five. Her face was unlined, and her moon-glow blond hair, so like her daughter's, cascaded down to her shoulders in a thick, luxurious fall. She wore a black pantsuit cut sleek and stylish, and on the shoulder was an exquisite hummingbird pin. Lalique. My gaze returned to her face. It seemed impossible that she was old enough to be Hamilton's mother.

She stood in the kitchen door, and Pasco, who showed his age, sat by the dining room table. They had us caught between them.

"Janice . . ." Millie sobbed. "She was just a kid, just a happy kid."

"The girl's death was a lucky accident," Veronica said, her gaze shifting to Millie. "I didn't mean to hit her. But she was going to die, and I realized it would give me a new life if everyone thought I died in the wreck."

I hadn't felt actual bone-aching horror until that moment. When I realized that Veronica and Pasco had put an injured woman in Veronica's Jaguar and then aimed it at a tree with enough speed to send the young woman's body through the windshield, I knew with certainty that cold-blooded murder was something of a habit for them. There was also the small matter of the dead body in Pasco's casket.

Even as I accepted the danger of our situation, I couldn't help but be impressed by Pasco and Veronica's criminal cleverness. Fel Harper wouldn't dare question Pasco's finding that Veronica had died in the wreck. So there had been no autopsy. No attempt to make certain that the disfigured body was actually Veronica Garrett. It was a masterful plan.

"The entire thing about the severed brake lines, that was just something you made up," I said, looking at Pasco. "As sheriff, you could make up anything. You used it to frame Hamilton and Sylvia, to throw suspicion on them." His smile told me I'd pieced it together properly. "And the gun that killed Delo? That was Sylvia's. It was a setup, too."

Veronica answered. "Hamilton should learn to lock up better. He always took it for granted that things would go his way. No effort on his part. He was born the heir. I would have had to beg crumbs from him for the rest of my life."

"You won't get away with this," Sylvia said, her eyes sparkling with high-voltage hatred. "All of these years, I've waited to find you. I've watched the magazines. I didn't care that people thought I was insane. I knew you'd taken your precious Lalique. Even when you were supposed to be dead, you were too greedy to leave it behind. It must have broken your heart to have to leave 'The Pink Lady' in Knob Hill. Father gave her to me, but you always wanted her."

"I'm certain your brother will see fit to ship her to me," Veronica said, unperturbed by Sylvia's anger. "You're going back to Glen Oaks, this time as a convicted murderess. Once Hamilton realizes that at any moment someone can walk into that institution and visit you in your sleep, he'll give me anything I want. And he'll keep his mouth shut."

That didn't sound like the Hamilton I knew, but I wasn't going to risk giving any advice.

Pasco shifted in his chair, and I knew he was growing tired of show-and-tell. "So where is the rest of the money?" he demanded.

"You got the million—" I started.

Sylvia interrupted me. "Delo buried it. You thought you were so smart, but you weren't. You walked off and left half a million in cash in a dove field." She laughed at him.

Pasco rose slowly. My gaze shifted to Veronica. Of the two, she was the more deadly. She hated her daughter.

"Where is it?" Pasco asked too softly.

"I'll die before I tell you," Sylvia taunted.

And she would, because there was no money. Isaac Carter had said a million, and though he might not recognize a moral if it bit him, he was a man who was accurate with monetary amounts. This "forgotten" half million was the bait Sylvia had used to set her trap—and she had snared all of us.

Once the pieces of Lalique began to appear in magazines, Sylvia had cast her web. She'd started the rumors about the "forgotten" money. She'd brought Hamilton back from Europe. She'd plotted her first escape from Glen Oaks and the eerie visit to the cornfield—all to draw Pasco and Veronica out of hiding. And she had succeeded masterfully. Except the bad guys now had the guns, and they were pointed right at us.

"Sylvia doesn't know where it is," I said quickly. "I do. If you promise to let me go, I'll tell you where it is."

"You'll tell us without any promises," Pasco said, reaching into his pocket for a cigarette. He lit one and handed it to Veronica and lit another for himself. He held the pack out. "Want a smoke, ladies? It's traditional."

"I'll take one," I said quickly. I'd read that hostages who developed a bond with their captors stood a better chance of surviving. Pasco lit another cigarette and brought it to me.

"Where's the money?" His eyes had gone cold.

"I'll have to show you," I said.

"If you're playing games, Sarah Booth, I'll shoot you in your knees and make you crawl back here. If you doubt it, think about Delo. He wouldn't tell me where the money was."

Maybe my plan wasn't such a good one. Then again, I didn't have an alternative. "I wouldn't mess around with you, Pasco. I'll show you. Delo told me where it was." This was a better lie even than the book business. And it was the only way I could see to get Pasco and the gun out of the house.

"That stupid old man," Veronica said. "He said he didn't know. He didn't believe we'd kill him. Now we've wasted all this time."

Pasco stood up. "Let's go," he ordered, motioning the gun at me.

I rose slowly. "You have to promise me that you won't kill me," I said. "You don't have to give me any money, just promise you'll let me go."

I saw Millie's disbelief turn to revulsion at my betrayal. I also caught a glimpse of Chablis, her nose sticking out from under the ruffle of the sofa.

"Where's the money?" Pasco asked. He didn't have a high tolerance for negotiating.

"Promise?"

"Oh, for God's sake, promise her," Veronica said.

"Sure, we'll get the money and then we'll let you go."

Pasco didn't even bother to make it sound sincere. But it was all I was going to get. I'd delayed as long as I dared. My only real hope was that Tinkie, Tammy, and James would somehow figure out where I'd gone and send help. "It's in the dog pen," I said. "Delo told me. Mr. Garrett had given him one of the hounds, so he buried the money in the pen. He said it was blood money and that it would only bring bad luck." It made just enough sense that Pasco bought it.

"I'll get a shovel," he said. He stepped across the room and grabbed my shoulder, his fingers digging into the tendon. "You're coming with me."

"I'll watch them," Veronica said, and I was chilled by the way she looked at her daughter. Sylvia wasn't long for this world, if Veronica had her way.

Pasco pushed me out into the night, and Chablis

darted out in front of me and disappeared. The rain had stopped, but the fog was so thick I couldn't see anything. I wasn't familiar with the property and neither was Pasco. We stumbled around looking for the toolshed, and then finally made our way to the dog pen.

Pasco thrust the shovel in my hand as he swung the flashlight beam over the ground. "You dig."

"It'll take me forever," I said. "It's buried pretty deep."

"Dig. We've got all night."

I didn't like the sound of that, but Pasco had the loaded weapon. As I started to dig, I realized I'd chosen a pretty good location for a rescue—if the cavalry had been called.

I began to turn the earth in small, shallow shovelfuls. Soon enough Pasco would tire of my pace and be forced to dig himself.

"Dig faster," he directed with a sharpness that let me know I was getting on his last nerve.

I pretended to comply. The sound of barking, muffled and distorted, drifted through the fog. I thought of Chablis. It was a bitter irony that I had gotten into this mess by stealing her. Now I would see the end of it—at least the end of my role in it—still worrying about that damn piece of fluff.

The barking seemed louder, and even Pasco shifted so that he could crane his neck around the door of the pen and take a look. He saw nothing more than I— dense fog. I heard the click of the hammer on his pistol, and I knew his patience was almost gone. It would be only a matter of moments before he killed me.

A deep, morbid howl seemed to come out of the night not ten feet away. Pasco grunted, edging out a little farther to check around the pen. A low, throaty howl came from behind the toolshed. It was a long, hungry sound.

"Keep digging," Pasco said as he stepped away from me. His back was to me as he looked into the darkness. I eased the shovel into clobbering position, and got ready to make my move.

Out of the fog a giant, hairy rat scuttled toward Pasco's feet. The vermin grabbed hold of his leg and locked on to his calf. Pasco let out a yelp and began to dance. He pointed the gun down, but couldn't shoot for fear of hitting his own foot.

"Chablis!" I cried at the same instant that I rushed out of the pen and brought the shovel down on Pasco Walters's head. The clang of metal on skull was totally satisfying.

Pasco stumbled, then slowly turned toward me. He brought the gun up and aimed at my chest. I'd hit him hard enough to fell an ox, but he was still standing. He drew back his leg and kicked, and Chablis went flying into the fog.

"You stupid bitch," he said, and his words were mushy, as if he were drunk.

I tried to think of a prayer, but terror blotted everything out of my mind.

Chablis gave one ferocious bark, and then a large body seemed to emerge from the night itself. It was lean and rangy, and it came at Pasco with such force that it struck his shoulder and sent him sprawling backward into the dirt. The gun flew out of his hand.

Before he could regain his feet, I rushed forward and brought the shovel down on his head again. His body went limp, but I hit him again for good measure. Trembling, I stood over him until I felt the cold nose and wet tongue of one of Delo's hounds nuzzle my hand.

"Revenge is sweet," I said to the dog. I got Pasco's

flashlight and went in the direction Chablis had been flung. I found her little body near the side of the dog pen.

"Chablis," I said, overcome with grief. She had been such a delicate thing. Jumping off the sofa could have broken her front legs. Pasco had punted her like a soccer ball. She simply wasn't tough enough to survive a man like him.

I bent to pick her up. I wouldn't leave her in the mud and the cold night. As I lifted her into my arms, I felt her tremble. Then she gave a low growl and before I could stop her, she snapped her under-bitten little jaws shut on my chin and began to tear into me.

"Chablis," I said, as well as I could with a six-ounce biting fury hanging from my chin. "Chablis, it's me, Sarah Booth."

At last my voice penetrated her anger and she opened her jaws. I groped at my chin. I didn't feel a gaping wound, but it hurt like hell. "Good girl," I said, kissing her hairy, pugnacious little face. A bitten chin was a small price to pay for my life.

I found Pasco's pistol and started toward the house.

In the distance, the mournful wail of a siren was headed my way. Out in the fog the hounds began to howl. To my surprise, Chablis, snug in my arms, joined in with them.

29

Because my experience with guns was limited to water pistols, and because my knees had begun to feel liquidy and unreliable, I waited for the cavalry.

Sheriff Coleman Peters got out of the car first, with Hamilton rising out of the passenger side. His eyes moved up and down me, and I felt a surge of warmth. Tinkie and Tammy got out of the backseat.

Gordon Walters rode alone in the second patrol car.

Hamilton started toward me, but Tinkie beat him to the punch.

"My darling," she cried as she lifted Chablis from my arms. "Sarah Booth, are you okay?"

"Sylvia and Millie are in there," I said. "And—" I dreaded saying it, but worse than the shock of my telling would be seeing her alive. "And Veronica. She isn't dead, Hamilton."

"I know," he answered, and then he put his hand on my shoulder. "Sylvia never believed she was dead. And I've suspected for a long, long time."

"Veronica has your sister and Millie." I knew I

sounded pitiful, like a whipped dog. This wasn't a fitting conclusion for the fact that I had single-handedly—
well, with the help of the dogs—brained Pasco Walters.
I bucked up and gave a tight smile. "Pasco Walters is by
the dog pen. He won't be giving anyone any trouble for
a while." I was rewarded by Gordon's hand lifting his
service revolver out of the holster.

"Good ol' Daddy. I knew he was too mean to die,"
Gordon said as he checked his clip.

For all of my bravado, I wanted to fling myself
against Hamilton's chest. It wasn't a Daddy's Girl maneuver; it was a simple human need. I wanted to rest for
a moment against someone who seemed capable of taking the reins. But Hamilton only rubbed my arms and
then moved toward the house with Coleman.

"Take the back door," Coleman directed him.

Tinkie and Tammy huddled behind the patrol car.
"Oscar is just going to die when I tell him about this,"
Tinkie said. "So when you were telling me about a dark,
dangerous man from the past, you weren't really talking
about Hamilton. It was Pasco all along."

"I was afraid it was Pasco. In my dreams, I'd seen
him in the dove field with a shotgun. I feared that he
was still alive," Tammy said. "Millie let it slip that Sylvia was laying a trap for them. She got Delo to play
along, never dreaming that he might be hurt."

Gordon started toward the dog pen. "I'll take care of
my father."

I started after Gordon. Pasco was my trophy.

"Mrs. Garrett," Coleman called out into the night.
"We've got you surrounded. Pasco is in custody, so
you'd better come out."

The house was dark and silent as I slipped into the
fog and followed Gordon. He looked back over his
shoulder at me. "You know, you're a real pain in the

ass," he said. "Hamilton and I figured you'd get blown to bits before the night was over, but there wasn't a damn thing we could do to stop you from poking your nose in it."

"Thanks," I said. It was something of a compliment.

He went to his father's inert form and stood over it. He nudged him with a boot. Pasco's eyes blinked open.

"Hello, Daddy," Gordon said, before he bent down and snapped on the cuffs. He pulled Pasco to his feet, and I followed them back to the house.

Headlights cut a dim halo in the fog as another car approached. I wondered if it was going to be old home week at Delo's house. I wasn't even surprised when I recognized Harold's Lexus, the headlights aimed directly at the front door of the house. He left the lights on and got out of the car. My thumb gave a weak tingle, and I waited for him to come to me. I was simply too tired to move.

"Stay back," Coleman ordered Harold. The sheriff stepped to the front door. Just as he was about to kick it in, the door slowly opened. Then Millie and Sylvia ran out onto the porch and fled into the yard.

"Sylvia!" Harold cried. He rushed past me and caught her in his arms. "Sylvia," he said again, crushing her to his chest. Tinkie, Chablis sleeping in her arms, and Tammy surrounded Millie and pulled her back to the safety of the patrol car.

I was left alone, standing in the yard, holding a pistol that I wasn't even certain I could use. The man who'd offered me marriage was consoling another woman. Somehow, I wasn't surprised.

Hamilton had obviously made his way through the back door and into the house. "We're coming out," he called from the dark interior. "She's unarmed."

As Coleman stepped back from the door, Hamilton and his mother came out into the high beams of the car lights. Hamilton held the shotgun loosely in his hand.

Veronica looked like the star of a B-movie. She drew herself up, threw back her shoulders, and stared all of us down.

"She's all yours," Hamilton said to Coleman, brushing past his mother and joining Harold and his sister. "Thanks for coming, Harold. For the past twenty years, you were the only person in this town that Sylvia ever mentioned with any degree of affection. I figured if it came down to it, she might listen to you."

"When you said Sylvia was in danger, I realized how much I cared," Harold said. "I'm just glad it's all over."

The three of them got in Harold's Lexus and drove away without another word.

I watched as Coleman cuffed Veronica and put her in the patrol car. Gordon put Pasco in the other car. Tinkie and Tammy had settled Millie in the backseat of the Cadillac. It seemed I was the only one who didn't know where to go or what to do.

When Coleman approached me, I tried for a smile, but I knew I looked pretty undone.

"I ought to give you a lecture about putting yourself in a dangerous spot," he said, "but instead—" He pulled me into a bear hug. "Good work, Sarah Booth. You're the only woman I know who can stir shit and not get it all over you."

"Thanks, Coleman," I said, feeling a tremendous urge to cry. Of course, I didn't. Over at the Caddy I could hear the excited babble of Tinkie and Tammy trying to comfort Millie.

"Would you give me a ride home?" I asked the sheriff.

"Sure thing. Let me drop off the prisoner. Then how about we have that cup of coffee?"

I had no reason to hurry home. Jitty would be there whenever I finally made it back. Harold was busy with Sylvia, and Hamilton had left without saying good-bye. "That would be nice," I said, because I simply didn't want to confront the fact that in my finest hour as a PI, I'd lost both of the men I cared about.

"Tell me the part again where you whacked Pasco with the shovel," Jitty said, her feet propped on the porch railing. She wore white go-go boots, white hip-hugger shorts with a wide patent leather belt, and a lime green polyester blouse. Though it was thirty degrees on the porch, she was impervious to the cold.

I sipped my glass of moonshine and told her again. I knew she was only trying to keep my mind off my heartbreak, and I appreciated her efforts. It was not her general nature, and it couldn't last for long.

The first rim of the morning sun crept over the horizon, and I felt a sense of accomplishment that I'd made it through the night without tears.

"This is the first day of the rest of your life, Sarah Booth," Jitty said.

I looked at her. "That's the stupidest thing I ever heard. I don't have a life. I have responsibility and obligations—no life."

"I'll tell you the stupidest thing I ever heard. A girl rides two horses and gets dumped by both. Quit wallowing in self-pity, get your lasso out, and go find another horse."

Ah, the real Jitty had returned. I dropped my feet to the floor and stood. It was time to go inside and figure out what to do next. Sleep would have been the obvious choice, but I wasn't sleepy even though I was bonetired. I suppose it was the six cups of coffee I drank with

Coleman as he gave me a blow-by-blow of his disinte-
grating marriage. Misery did love company, and besides, it had kept my mind off Hamilton.

Somewhere in my subconscious, I saw the rightness
of Harold and Sylvia. He'd been in love with her since
she visited Hamilton at Dorsett Military Academy. I
remembered the way he'd spoken of her. He'd also
pointed out that she was not like me.

Perhaps not in the obvious physical ways, but I think
what made him want me was that I was actually a great
deal like Sylvia. We shared a directness, a lack of facade,
that appealed to him. Though we had both been raised
in the realm of the Daddy's Girls, neither of us had
become one.

"Look, Sarah Booth," Jitty said, that grating, reason-
able tone in her voice. "It ain't over till the fat lady
sings."

"If you quote one more cliché, I'm going to . . ." I
couldn't think of a threat dire enough.

"You never really wanted Harold, though I still con-
tend he was the man to pin your future on. My point is,
you can't whine now that he's gone."

"You're mistaken," I said, pacing the porch. "I can
whine as much as I want to. I don't even have Chablis,"
I pointed out. Once Tinkie had her back in her arms, I
simply couldn't demand that she give her to me.

"Take a look at yourself in the mirror, Sarah Booth.
You aren't exactly a froufrou dog kind of woman. I'm
sure James will give you one of those hounds. And that
little dust mop bit your chin. Don't forget about that.
Looks like some kind of nearsighted vampire got hold
of you."

"It'll heal," I said. "The point isn't that I can get a
dog, the point is that I can't get the dog I want."

"Oh, I see," Jitty said, jangling those damn bracelets on her wrist. "You still want Hamilton."

"You're damn right." I did want him. And this time I wasn't taking orders from my womb.

"I sort of like it with just the two of us here," Jitty said.

"Good for you." I was reduced to true childishness.

"Course, all is not lost."

I walked around so I could face her. The morning sun bathed her face in golden light, and slowly she began to smile. "There's always a chance that you're carrying the Garrett heir, as well as the last of the Delaneys."

My hands went to my stomach. It was true. I'd slept with Hamilton without protection. Although I had the most demanding womb in the universe, I didn't pay a lot of attention to its cycles.

"I'm not pregnant," I said, determined that it was true. Jitty might want a Delaney heir to haunt, but I didn't want a baby if I didn't have the father of that child in my bed every night.

"Well, you should be—but I suppose he's not ready for that, either," she said as she began to fade in the strengthening morning light.

I heard the sound of the car approaching as soon as she was gone. Hamilton's Mercedes pulled into the driveway, and he got out of the car and walked up on the porch. He was a handsome man.

"I came to apologize," he said. "Billie is putting a new tire on your car. I'd hoped to keep you out of trouble, but in the end I think it's a good thing you were there. Pasco would have killed Sylvia, and probably Millie, too. He admitted to killing a vagrant in Memphis and putting him in the river. Another body-double."

It was so much easier to talk about the case than

anything else, so I found a question. "The half million Pasco was looking for—Sylvia made that up, didn't she?"

Hamilton shifted so that his weight was on the porch railing. "Yes. Pasco and Mother had it all to begin with. Sylvia started rumors, and Tammy, James, and Delo reluctantly went along with her. All along Sylvia believed that Mother was alive. The Lalique hair combs were missing from the body. Mother never went anywhere without them. When I found the wreck, the body was so disfigured I couldn't tell it wasn't Mother. And Sylvia wasn't allowed to view the body."

He walked to the railing and looked out over the beautiful fields. "I didn't believe her. I didn't want to believe. It was easier to let her go her own headstrong way. But she was right, damn it. Right for twenty long years. She knew that greed would eventually bring Pasco and Mother out of hiding. They couldn't resist coming back for more." There was grim satisfaction on his face as he turned to me.

My anger was inexplicable. "You've both wasted the last twenty years waiting for revenge. Your sister's life has been spent in an institution."

My raw emotion made him pull back. "There are some things worth waiting for, Sarah Booth. If you don't understand that now, you will before you die."

"Revenge isn't one of them," I answered bitterly. It seemed no matter what the topic, Hamilton and I were doomed to argue—unless we were in bed.

"My life hasn't been wasted." He spoke with patience.

I wondered why he felt compelled to respond to my anger. "What about Sylvia?" I countered, determined to fight.

"She made her own choices. Perhaps now, she'll be

strong enough to make some different ones. I never realized how Harold felt about her, but I think she's found an anchor."

I knew only too well how stable and giving Harold could be. "I think he's loved her a long time," I said.

"He told me he also loved you."

I finally looked up, shocked by Harold's candor. "He only thinks that because I remind him of your sister."

Hamilton moved so swiftly that I had no time to back away. His hands caught my shoulders. "You aren't a thing like Sylvia," he said. "If you were, I'd have to be worried about myself."

I lifted my face to meet his kiss. His lips were demanding, and I rose to the occasion. I wanted nothing more than his arms around me, his lips on mine. Well, maybe a bit more. I had been so certain that I'd lost him, and now he was here, with me, on Dahlia House's porch.

I was about to take his hand and lead him into the house when he stepped back from me.

"I came to tell you good-bye," he said, and he kept his hands on my shoulders to steady me. "I have to go back to Europe. I left my life there on hold."

Ah, his life in Europe. He'd said he hadn't wasted the last nineteen years. He was probably married. Probably had five kids, a mansion, a country estate, and a wife who looked like Gwyneth Paltrow, thin, blond, and intelligent.

I had one option—I could beg him to stay. But somehow, I knew the words would never leave my lips.

"Will you ever come back to Zinnia?" I asked.

Instead of answering, he said, "Sylvia is moving into Knob Hill. Be a friend to her, Sarah Booth. She's going to need a lot of friends."

I nodded.

"I will come back. I'm just not sure when. We never had the money people thought we did, and it's depleted our resources to keep Knob Hill up. But I knew one day Sylvia would want to go home. We have a lot of good memories there, along with the bad."

I felt a strange thud in my womb and I wondered if it might be the dividing cells of a little Garrett already at work.

Hamilton took a card from his pocket and handed it to me. "This is my home number. If you need anything, call me."

So I was going to be allowed emergency calls. No long-distance chitchat, no letters, no promises of meetings in the future. He really had come to say good-bye.

I took the card. "I'm in the book," I said.

"I've never met a woman like you, Sarah Booth. I'm going to miss you." He bent to kiss me again, but this time his lips only brushed over my cheek.

"I'll miss you, too," I said, holding tight to the card to prevent myself from grabbing on to him.

"Good luck in your new PI business." He stepped back. "Be careful."

"You, too."

He smiled and headed down the steps. Back straight, stride long, he walked to his car, got in, and drove away.

I stood on the porch, clutching his card, and knew the meaning of heartbreak. I felt Jitty behind me, and I turned to her. "He's gone. Back to Europe."

"He'll be back," Jitty said matter-of-factly. "Once a man tastes a Delaney woman, he can't leave it alone. It's in the blood."

A cool, ticklish sensation brushed over my arm, and I realized that Jitty had touched me. "Let's make some breakfast," I said, suddenly hungry.

As we walked in the door, the telephone began to ring. I picked it up and smiled at the verve in Cece's voice.

"Sarah Booth Delaney, you get yourself down to the newspaper office right this minute. I want all the details—all of them. Coleman Peters is calling you a hero. Tinkie Bellcase Richmond is saying you solved the mystery of the Garrett murders, and that she's putting you on a retainer for all future investigations that she might need. Kincaid Maxwell is claiming—off the record, of course—that you saved her good name from a scandal which she won't even begin to talk about. You must come right down here and give me an interview. I hear you're going to be the hottest detective this side of the Mississippi."

Given our geographic location, Cece was hedging her bets. But it struck me that Hamilton, too, had referred to my "new PI business," and with a certain degree of pride. I looked over the telephone at Jitty. "Should I?"

"You'd be a fool not to," she whispered, and then she smiled. "You'll have more clients than you can shake a stick at."

"I'll be there at ten," I said to Cece.

"Don't forget the Danish, dahling," Cece ordered. "One gets hungry in the pursuit of a good story."

I hung up the phone and turned to face Jitty. "Two weeks ago we were afraid we'd lose Dahlia House, I was unemployed, and I had given up on men and sanity."

"Honey, you're doin' fine in three out of four," Jitty said, jangling her bracelets as she led the way to the kitchen for breakfast.

About the Author

A native of Mississippi, Carolyn Haines first explored the Delta as a photojournalist working on a series of stories about the Mississippi State Prison at Parchman. She is the author of *Summer of the Redeemers* and *Touched.*

A Conversation with Carolyn Haines,
author of *Them Bones*

In response to a request from newspaper columnist Cece Dee Falcon, author Carolyn Haines agreed to answer some questions about her work, her characters, and the future of Zinnia, Mississippi. Although Cece wanted to conduct the interview, Jitty insisted on doing it. Since the weather was nice in Mississippi, Carolyn and Jitty met on the front porch of Dahlia House for a chat.

JITTY: *Before this interview actually gets started, I want to make one thing perfectly clear. I'm not responsible for all of Sarah Booth's actions. That girl is so hardheaded, if she drowned, they'd have to search for her upstream. The way you write the book, sometimes it seems that I ought to have some influence with her. But I don't. Nobody can influence a Delaney. Keep that in mind when you're writin' about us. Now that we're clear on that point, we can get going.*

CAROLYN: Exactly what kind of questions do you have in mind?

JITTY: Well, as the author, I thought maybe you could tell me, and everyone else, a little about the future. I mean Sarah Booth has lost her man and gotten an opportunity to start her own investigation service. There's the chance she may carry the heir to Dahlia House. What does the future hold for us?

CAROLYN: I see, you just want me to blurt out what's going to happen next. As a mystery writer, I have to point out that's against the rules.

JITTY: Don't be cute with me, girl. I'm nearly a hundred and fifty years old. I'd say that's considerably your elder, though you aren't gettin' no shorter in the tooth. Didn't your mama teach you not to sass your elders?

CAROLYN: My mother had no idea I'd spend my time consorting with folks like you and Sarah Booth. My parents thought I'd be something respectable, like a journalist.

JITTY: Are you mockin' me?

CAROLYN: Well, maybe just a little. To be honest, I've never been interviewed by a character. Let me ask you one question that's been nagging at me. When you first walked onto the pages of my book, you were wearing this god-awful seventies outfit. Why the seventies? Bad clothes. Bad music. Why?

JITTY: Havin' lived through a number of decades, I got some historical perspective that you youngsters don't have. Sarah Booth was right on the verge of losin' everything she ever cared about, including *our* home. You picked up on the fact that Sarah Booth isn't exactly smooth when it comes to handlin' her men. It was up to me to do somethin', and I figured that if she couldn't catch her a man outright, then maybe she could at least get us an heir. The seventies were a time when women declared their sexual liberation. I thought I could give Sarah Booth a little nudge toward gettin' the baby we both need.

CAROLYN: Ah, I see. So it was just an empty threat when you said you'd follow Sarah Booth to eternity if she didn't produce an heir for you to haunt?

JITTY: I don't know for certain. But neither one of us wants to risk it. Hush up now, I'm supposed to be askin' the questions here.

CAROLYN: Sorry. It's just that I have a few questions of my own.

JITTY: So I see, but the publisher didn't give you this space to conduct an interview. They gave it to me. And I'm doin' the askin'. You get to be in charge the whole time you're writin'. This is my fifteen minutes, and you better back off.

CAROLYN: My goodness, I'll try to stay in line.

JITTY: See that you do. Maybe you'd like a drink. Ghosts don't have much truck with liquor, but Sarah Booth likes a mint julep ever' now and then. Here you go, now sit back in that rocker and let's talk. I've got a few more important questions. Sarah Booth let Hamilton slip back to Paris. He was a fine specimen, but he's gone. Could you put in a good word for Harold? I mean, he's solid and stable, and for a while there, he was burnin' for Sarah Booth. As the author, couldn't you reignite that fire?

CAROLYN: Harold's kind of busy. What about Sylvia Garrett? Should I just kill her off?

JITTY: Girl, you got a sassy streak a mile wide in you. I didn't ask you to kill anybody off. Couldn't they just have a fallin' out? How hard is that for you to write?

CAROLYN: I don't know, Jitty. Sarah Booth already dumped Harold once. I've gotten kind of fond of him.

Maybe I don't want to put him in the line of fire for that kind of abuse again.

JITTY: What? Did I hear you right? Last time I looked, Harold was a man! Abuse won't hurt him one little bit.

CAROLYN: You're sounding a little sexist, Jitty. Maybe I'll put in some sensitivity training classes for you.

JITTY: You remindin' me a whole lot of Sarah Booth. Both of you stubborn and full of the devil. But forget about men, let's move on. Is Sarah Booth really goin' to become a private investigator?

CAROLYN: She certainly has the talent. And I will tell you that in the next book she has a new client. I'm just a little worried, though. If she becomes successful as an investigator, you know what that means. She'll have to make a choice, family or career.

JITTY: Oh, no. Don't be asking' her to choose between savin' Dahlia House or catchin' her a man. Don't do that!

CAROLYN: But this is reality, Jitty. Women today have to juggle and choose. Just because Sarah Booth is a fictional character, I don't think it's good if she's the perfect detective *and* the perfect wife and mother.

JITTY: Girl, I was countin' on you to help me talk some sense into Sarah Booth. She can do whatever she sets her mind to, and at the top of that list should be findin' her a good man and a bundle of joy. I don't think I like the influence you're havin' on her. I can see it's goin' to be up to me to put the emphasis where it belongs—on the family.

CAROLYN: I'm not certain I like that look on your face. Jitty, what are you thinking?

JITTY: You got your secrets, I got mine. Just remember. I been around a long, long time. You're gonna have to wake up early to get one over on me.

CAROLYN: I have to wake up early to get my writing done. And while we're pointing out flaws, what about those nights you woke me up? You thought that was amusing, to slip into my dreams and make me get up and write?

JITTY: It's my job. Where would you be without me?

CAROLYN: A lot better rested, I'm sure. Do you have any more questions?

JITTY: I got a piece of advice—stop askin' the questions. You're like one of Oprah's bad guests. You get to goin' and all you want to talk about is yourself.

CAROLYN: Jitty, dusk is approaching. Forgive me if I say I'm not inclined to hang out on the porch of Dahlia House after dark with a ghost. If you want to know something else, you'd better ask.

JITTY: You write a lot of other things. Are you goin' to be able to give me the attention I deserve?

CAROLYN: Absolutely. It goes without saying, Jitty, that you're not easily ignored. All of you, Sarah Booth, Harold, Hamilton, Tinkie, Tomeeka, Millie—you all demand your due.

JITTY: That's good to know. Just a few more questions. Were you a Daddy's Girl?

CAROLYN: Only in the sense that I was an only daughter. I grew up in the pine barrens of Mississippi, way down in the southeast corner in a small town called Lucedale. There weren't any plantations around those parts, mostly small farms and paper company land. But I've known a few Daddy's Girls. It's an interesting culture, and one that's fading away. Like everywhere else, Mississippi is changing.

JITTY: What's your fascination with the Delta?

CAROLYN: Now, that's a good question. The Mississippi Delta is this huge triangle of land bordered on the west by the Mississippi River and a line of hills on the east. They say the topsoil is eight feet deep. Back in your day, it was the part of Mississippi with working plantations, and it's where the blues was born. The story goes that the cotton fields were so vast that the slaves would call out to one another, passing the messages or songs from one to another across the fields. That's how the call-back, or repeated lines, came to be so much a part of the blues.

JITTY: The blues is some mighty powerful music. My man, Coker, now he could sing. I sure miss him sometimes. Hey, maybe you could write me a new man.

CAROLYN: Maybe if I found a man for you, you'd leave Sarah Booth alone.

JITTY: I'm not shirkin' my responsibilities for any reason. I can manage career *and* a personal life. But let's get back on track. What's Sarah Booth going to get into next?

CAROLYN: I'm not Madame Tomeeka, and I can't predict the future, but since I've started writing the next book, I can give you a hint. A famous literary figure is murdered, and Sarah Booth is hired to find his killer.

JITTY: Don't be putting my girl in danger.

CAROLYN: She *is* a private investigator, Jitty.

JITTY: Is Harold in this book?

CAROLYN: Indeed he is. And Tinkie, Tomeeka, Cece, Chablis, and the other residents of Zinnia. Of course there'll be a few new characters. Do you think Sarah Booth would like to meet an artist from Nicaragua? He's a very charming man.

JITTY: He's not the killer, is he?

CAROLYN: I haven't finished the book yet. I'm waiting on Sarah Booth to solve the mystery.

JITTY: She already has a problem with men, don't go gettin' her involved with a killer. And one who's not even from Mississippi! I don't think this is a good idea. What would I do if Sarah Booth decided to move off to Nicaragua followin' some man? Just give her another shot at Harold.

CAROLYN: We'll see.

JITTY: Come on, you can tell me. Who's the killer?

CAROLYN: You'll have to wait, Jitty, like the rest of us.

JITTY: Well, don't think I'm goin' to be easy to manage. I know what Sarah Booth needs, and it looks like I'm gonna have to struggle against both of you to get it for her. But I have a plan.

CAROLYN: Uh-oh. What kind of plan?

JITTY: Let's just say that I've been studyin' up on some of that psychology Sarah Booth thinks so much of. I'm determined to be a better influence on her this time. I'm gonna be a role model she can be proud of. Maybe I can even get my own television show—*Jitty Knows Best*.

CAROLYN: Why does the sound of that frighten me?

JITTY: Good, solid family values. That's what Sarah Booth needs. It's been good talkin' with you, Miss Author, but I'd better get back to business. You keep on writin', girl, and I'll be seein' you in your dreams.